To: Craig

Shadows II, Skulls II & Spooks II

To Joann's great
son.

Donald Render
Jr. December 7, 2000

This is an historical, autobiographical work of informed fiction, and any resemblance to persons living or dead is purely coincidental.

To order additional copies, please contact us.
BookSurge, LLC
www.booksurge.com
1-866-308-6235
orders@booksurge.com

DONALD JAY DENTON

SHADOWS II, SKULLS II & SPOOKS II

Shadows can do harm.
Shadow Governments deny.

2006

Shadows II, Skulls II & Spooks II

PREFACE

This time around, the story must be dedicated to the first team of illusionary, nonexistent Shadows that worked covertly for a Shadow Government. The Black Chamber unit of this secret operation could make believers out of those who did not believe in ghosts, goblins, or shadows that go bump in the night. The Black Chamber unit within the Shadow Government was established by executive orders in 1955, and was terminated by executive orders in 1975. This never-heard-of operation successfully functioned during the cold war period with complete anonymity, and no congressional oversight. The fact was, Congress appreciated the desirability of having no-see, no-hear, no-smell or touch shadows that provided deadly bumps in the night. These visitant spooks were often referred to as the Pooka Brigade, and no one within our government wanted to know that invisible, phantom Pookas were really U.S. citizens.

The Black Chamber unit was funded with off-budget financing from the private business sector, to protect the mineral, agricultural, petroleum, and economic political interests of the U.S. of A. around the world. The first group of Immolators have now ended their term of service, with nine being discharged and seven playing pinochle with the angel Azrael. So the time has arrived for a new group of sixteen to be selected and trained to terminate souls for the common good of "one Nation under God."

By today's standards for politically correct subterfuge and skullduggery, this shadow government operation would be totally illegal. But thank God, it remained a deeply buried secret within the Library of Congress until exposed in 2003, while the never-happened, nonexistent workings of the Shadow Government have long ago vaporized into a fictitious labyrinth of historical facts. But the record only clarifies what those in literature throughout history have previously stated,

"There are more things in heaven and earth, Horatio. Than are dreamt of in your philosophy."

"Out, out, brief candle! Life's but a walking shadow, a poor player, that struts and frets his hour upon the stage, and then is heard not more."

"Is man no more than this? As flies to wanton boys, are we to the Gods. They kill us for their sport."

The story of the new group of sixteen young people selected for the Black Chamber will speak for itself. These new phantom Pookas will be considered the tools of the trade, performing their services quietly and efficiently when disposing of many of humanity's disgusting and painful hemorrhoids from the "nasty now and now" into the "sweet bye and bye." These new transition and displacement specialist will prove their worth by stopping the nationalization of U.S. business interest around the world and silencing loud-mouth revolutionaries with T-shirt promotions.

The author's only comment is, "no comment," except to thank his wife, family, and a reappearing friend for the encouragement to prevail and write this second part of an historically relevant novel.

Donald Jay Denton

CHAPTER I
Cultivating Batch Two of Walking Shadows!

The end of one adventure had the beginning starting all over again. As someone once said, "There is always a black spot in our sunshine, and it is often a shadow of ourselves." So again, upon the ending of one adventurous tale, this person started the beginning of another strange adventure. The concern was: is it still me, him, or the he of the person I see in the mirror? Or is it only a clear reflection back into my mind's eye as a shadow of who may be — the me, myself, or the I that may be the real me, if ever put to the test?

A dual-life covert existence of nonexistence can test one's soul when participating in a life of intrigue, subterfuge, skullduggery, innuendo and pretext. So, could the real me be the person behind the mirror as shown by a reflection, or might it be the person on this side of the mirror — a real me?

The "Scaramouch" existence is a lonely and dangerous one, and frequently provides a reality check on life's learning experiences. One quickly learns that there are secrets within secrets, truth within lies, and that life as with fame can be fleeting. Most certainly so when one has a covert life with no allowable fame or recognition, even when successfully struggling to prevail and survive at the game — particularly within a dual life existence of having alternating realities that may or may not have ever happened, so to speak!

Yet this time around, being the shepherd and not part of the flock had new responsibilities of serious consequence. Now I had become responsible for those who would walk through the valley of the shadow of death, and would be deciding who might live and who might die. The hope, therefore, was that they — like myself — would come out of the other end of the valley alive. There was a time when another sixteen young people believed they were invincible, and thought they were the meanest and deadliest S.O.B.s in the valley.

But as the past would have it, the Grim Reaper interfered with the crossing of seven young Immolators. So the past was as self-evident as a cancelled check for the previous young Pookas now out to pasture or dead, while the new invisible, nonexistent specters are given only a promissory note as to their future once we have them trained. Then they will be blindly indoctrinated with "all that is needed for evil to triumph is for good men to do nothing." One could only hope that the future score would not be similar to the prologue past of Lions seven, Pookas twenty-one; but the claimed excess numbers were collateral necessities of being in the wrong place at the wrong time.

The newly selected chosen would be young naive bodies, but there would be a quality assassin hidden somewhere inside them. Our team's job would be to find, train and develop it, and have its skills and talents available for service to God and country. This time around, the era of training replacements had changed philosophically into creating "apparent suicides" and "apparent accidents," which were now politically more acceptable for public relations purposes than assassinations. So the intent would be to create "fog" for these new recruits, who would soon be displacing souls accidentally for the common good of "One Nation under God."

This meant that the basic rule for sniper Immolators — that distance creates safety — was now secondary. The training had to concentrate on the visitants getting up close and personal with their assigned targets. Therefore, the priority was to develop efficient and effective training for covert defenestration as an alternative method for the conversion of souls from the "nasty now and now" into "the sweet bye and bye." Let it be understood that this responsibility can cut to the quick, and quickly get to the terminal core of things when mistakes are made.

The nasty and determined Grim Reaper had already walked by my window several times, and once he even knocked on my life's door. The fact is, a miss by the Grim Reaper sobers one up to reality, then that reality moment helps one quickly learn to appreciate the gifts of yesterday, and the benefits of today. Someone else may have said it best: "Yesterday is a cancelled check, today is the only cash one has, and tomorrow is a promissory note." So as for the tomorrows, in the very near future it would be up to me to start making many difficult decisions — not of triage, where one decides who has the best chance to live, but of "duage," where one decides who gets a chance to risk their life, or to live another day.

The time had now arrived, and the new show on the world stage began again. The phone call confirming the time and place of the first-stage reorganization meeting for the second Black Chamber unit was received yesterday. The meeting should have been scheduled much sooner, not two months away, in early May. This lag was just too much of a dormant period for my thinking process, wondering what hemorrhoids of humanity our group would be transitioning into the great beyond, since at the time this person did not desire to be thinking much about subterfuge, covert intrigue, and skullduggery around the world.

I was hoping to have a calm, relaxing and enjoyable Saint Patrick's Day and Easter, with a clear and uncluttered mind. But no question about it, my vivid imagination would be hyperventilating all over the place between now and then, particularly as to how and where the new recruits being placed under my wing would be used in maintaining the "balance of power" and the "world order" of things — those secret covert actions as they relate to our country's best political, social, and self-serving economic interests in the world. The irritating issue was that I was already having annoying thoughts and concerns about how many of the selected new recruits might end up playing pinochle with the angel Azrael too soon. After all, it was way too soon for 45 percent of our original group who vanished into the great beyond.

What a confusing time for this new group of naive young men! They had all recently graduated from high school, and would soon be making their transitory trip into manhood. Having been selected, they were in for the big shock and surprise of learning that they would soon become nonexistent persons. And all this shock and confusion was only because they joined the military. These young kids would be participating in the real problems of the world while dealing with unbelievable problems on their own home front. They would be confused as to where our country's priorities lie and where the resources were being focused to ensure the survival of our freedoms and democracy. My curiosity was killing me; I wanted to know just how many recruits the powers that be had pre-screened and selected for my perusal. My curiosity begged me to wonder who this assortment of individuals were, that I must screen down to the final sixteen members and then induct into the Pooka Brigade, and where — at that point — I would again be starting a new era in this life on another Memorial Day. Then our training staff would have to indoctrinate these kids with total dedication and blind obedience to duty, God, honor and country. Once this was accomplished, we would train them to be successful stalking cats, while also teaching them to survive as scurrying mice of prey.

The hope was that the naive young people we would be choosing as rabbits had developed a strong intestinal fortitude, for they would all soon be putting their lives on the line by killing for the common good of humanity. It was hoped that they had had the benefit of inspirational mentors along the way, to provide them with mental, emotional and moral balance. These factors were self-evident in my own covert and dual adventurous lifestyle during the previous ten years. One cannot describe or explain the experience of being the stalking cat that has completed its mission to suddenly being forced to experience the excitement and adrenalin rush of surviving and prevailing as the scurrying mouse of prey. These experiences make one find meaning in what was once meaningless, because the history of one's life flashes before one's eyes. At that moment, one suddenly appreciates certain people of meaning and influence in one's life.

Thank God for those normal, publicly unrecognized, everyday people who had meaning in my life. I did not really appreciate or understand them during my self-centered youth. Suddenly, their philosophical mentoring, badgering and discipline was appreciated by this once rebellious teenager and naive soul. The hope now was that I might be able to successfully pass on this knowledge to others, along with my own learned experiences. Then, hopefully, these young people would have a better than fifty-five/forty-five chance of surviving their tours of duty.

Several key people had an unknowing magical influence on my life; they taught me to always prevail over situations, not to simply survive the circumstances. The first person to have this positive effect on my life was my Grandfather Jay. He was a hard-working, struggling farmer who went to his Methodist church every Wednesday night, Sunday morning and Sunday night, and never said a mean or bad word about anyone. Grandpa Jay gave me two great pieces of philosophical advice. At the time, I thought they were just humorous remarks directed at me after I had done something stupid, and I didn't really get the point of his remarks until I started dealing with the Grim Reaper. Of the two most memorable statements Grandpa Jay made to me, one was: "One day, you will be learning about the human body in school. The teacher will be explaining to you that your body is made up of approximately 90 percent water and only 10 percent matter. At some point during your life, you alone must decide whether you are going to be a person or a puddle."

The other great statement was: "All successful farmers know that one cannot fertilize the field by farting through the fence."

How true, how true, most certainly true; particularly in any successful professional or business venture. This was not all the good common sense Grandpa Jay taught me over the years. He once made it clear, after an unfortunate circumstance of not defending myself against some bullies while in grade school, that this made me appear to be a sissy and a coward. I was a farmboy who had to go to a school located in a small backwater coal-mining town, and this was not a pleasant experience. I was the new kid in this oversized, four-classroom dump filled with coal miners' kids, and the worst part was being one of the few outsider farmboys at the school. Needless to say, I was scared to death each school day. They took my lunch, de-pants me, and laughed with joy as they tossed me to the ground. These tough coal miner's kids waited for me daily, so I quickly learned to stay my distance until the school bell rang. I waited until they all had entered the school and then, when the coast was clear, I nervously entered and went to Mrs. Stuck's classroom a couple of minutes late. At the end of the school day, I was the first to leave the school, and got out of the area before they had an opportunity to kick my butt again.

Now, Mrs. Stuck had to do her duty and contact my grandparents about my problem of always being tardy. Needless to say, my grandparents were slightly perturbed by my actions. They believed in the "spare the rod or spoil the child" principle, but this time they quietly asked me to explain myself before deciding on discipline. This was a lucky break for me. Grandpa listened to my story, and then he took the situation seriously, with a degree of personal offense. He immediately grabbed my hand and walked me down toward the barn. I thought he was going to whip my butt. Instead, he got a piece of rope, tied it to a hundred-pound bag of cattle feed, and hung it from a barn rafter. He told me to watch him carefully while he walked casually toward the bag, then wham! He hit the bag with all his might and said, "That is what you will do to the first coal miner's kid who gets close to you. You do not say a word or show any aggression until it is too late for his nose. Now, we have the rest of the day, all day Saturday, and all day Sunday to prepare you to be on time for Mrs. Stuck's class on Monday."

Grandpa had me put on a work glove, walk up to the bag, and hit it solidly over and over for three days in a row. I was tired and worn out, but the repetition created a routine and habitual reaction that I never forgot. Grandpa lectured that it was normal to be afraid, but with manhood came the act of overcoming fear and destroying its cause. He assured me that once they knew I would fight back and would hurt them — win or lose — only then would they decide to leave me alone. As usual, Grandpa Jay was right. I was never late for school again, and thereafter took my time walking home. No question about it, growing up is a hard thing to do.

The next valuable advisor in my youth was Dad Lewis, the adult Masonic advisor to our DeMolay Chapter. The sad part here (in hindsight) is that, like my relationship with Gary the Chef, I never knew Dad Lewis's real name. He was just another person taken for granted in my self-centered youth, and he died before I could ever thank him. I was a Master Counselor, and Dad Lewis taught me the responsibility of leadership. He said that irresponsibility was when one takes responsibility for other people's irresponsibility. Dad Lewis taught me to always take charge and always prevail. He often said, "Don't be afraid to make tough decisions and, as a leader, to lead or get out of the way." Regarding the chairing of a committee, Dad Lewis said clearly, "Never let a committee be a committee. You direct and assign; for if you do not take control, they will always operate in agreement toward the lowest common denominator." Now, his leadership training proved invaluable time and time again, and will certainly be applicable to all the upcoming events related to our group. Our little covert group of nonexistent people doing nonexistent things that were in faraway places that most people never heard of or even thought about.

The distinction of being the first person involved with changing my comfortable little world goes to good old Sergeant Turner. The Sarge was the nicest, biggest, blackest, toughest and meanest sergeant I ever met. He taught me to be a top-quality sniper. I really learned to appreciate this guy after he busted my ass and tossed me to the ground like a ton of bricks.

Never again would I let my ego come out of my then-nasty mouth, because this sergeant put me in my place and taught me humility. Also, for the first time in my life I learned what it meant to never hit a man in the jaw who chews tobacco. The Sarge's training proved to me that survival is achieved only by prevailing over a situation, and he taught me how to deal with the unanticipated changes in one's life circumstances.

Sergeant Turner's training provided the ability to appreciate staying alive as the scurrying mouse of prey. This staying alive occurred only after first succeeding as the stalking cat terminating its prey. The good sergeant and I had a special relationship from the time he and the others on the team toasted me at my assumed wake. The other team members had reported my presumed demise after a mission, and they got a real shock when I walked into the barracks alive. At that point, Sergeant Turner made his memorable remark, "Man, boy you did not plan on staying dead too long." Our relationship is why the good sergeant is going to be part of this new training team. He'll make sure the new Immolators improve their odds for a long, healthy and successful life, with marriage, children and careers.

Yet one of the strangest mentors was Gary the Chef. The man should have died a thousand times, and I never knew his real name while he was the liaison leader for our very secret, nonexistent group. Gary disappeared off my radar of friendship after our small group's final separation and discharge meeting last year, and it is quite doubtful that we will ever meet again. Gary and I once had a very memorable experience in common, which neither of us will ever forget, and we will definitely remember each other fondly until we die. Gary the Chef was my hero of heroes. The man always had a sense of humor and a positive, can-do attitude, even after surviving four years in

Auschwitz, where he was selected for one line at stage left and the rest of his family members were directed to stage right for their final act.

When the Russian Army threatened the German's tranquility at Auschwitz, he was quickly transferred to Mauthausen. The Germans' intent with this hasty transfer was to try and preserve some of their healthier zooids, who were still capable of working. Gary spent nearly seven months there before being rescued and freed on May 5, 1945 – the fifth month, on the fifth day, at five minutes to five as shown on the prison camp's clock. Therefore, Gary gave me the inspiration and the will to never give up; to always remain steadfast and keep the mind visualizing myself in my dreams for my tomorrows. Gary's constant dream while in Auschwitz and Mauthausen, even though he had never been outside of Europe, was that he would someday be sunning himself on a Florida beach – even if it was snowing. A strange fantasy for hope, yes, but one dreamed to ignore the horrors of the concentration camps. As for our relationship, Gary's one defining statement made it clear what the object for all our missions was about. "Your job is to scare the hell out of those people we want to impress, and then turn their brains to jelly."

As they say, time flies when you're having fun. The time had arrived for me to depart for the May meeting in Washington, D.C., at the Willard Hotel. It would be nice to see old committee members for the last time. At this meeting they would be turning over the reins of power to the new committee members, and then would clarify to them what their responsibilities were between the nonexistent parties of interest. I guessed this would make me the common denominator intermediary to maintain stability, plus assure secrecy and order between the powers from above and the nonexistent persons below everyone else's field of vision. Oh, well, I would just see what came and take things one step at a time. But for the time being, while on my way to Washington, D.C., I had to tolerate a two-hour layover in Pittsburgh with Agony Airlines. To kill time, I indulged myself with one of the world's best shoe shines, provided at this airport.

Finally arriving in Washington, D.C. was a relief, and it was a real pleasure to enter the lobby of the Willard Hotel. Standing there before me were Captain Dan, Colonel Cole, and Colonel Knapp, who were soon to be the now-departing committee of power. They immediately approached to welcome me, and told me to check into my room and meet them in the lobby in thirty minutes. I checked into my room, unpacked, freshened up, and called the wife to tell her I had arrived safely at the insurance conference. Following orders as directed, this foot soldier promptly reported to my leaders in the hotel lobby. They then escorted me to a private meeting room not far from the lobby. The room was already adequately stocked with food and drinks. The conference table had place settings and seating for eleven people, and a speaker's podium was standing at one end of the table. With all the formality at this upper-crust hotel, Robert's Rules of Order were definitely going to come into play, yet I was beginning to feel a little uncomfortable and out of place in the ritzy political environment.

Colonel Knapp and Colonel Cole must have noticed the subtle signs of my apprehension and uneasiness when walking over to me. Knapp said, "Relax, Benton. We are having a piano moved into the room for your use, so we can have some relaxing entertainment and drinks during our breaks, and after a hard day's work with the new committee members. During the rest of today and tomorrow morning, you will be meeting only with us. The new members will not be attending any meetings until they arrive tomorrow afternoon."

Colonel Cole then spoke up. "Our private discussions will be directed to the issues of what was right with the Chamber's operations, what was wrong with the group's operations, and what corrections and changes need to be made for a more efficient and effective program. You should also tell us, during our private meeting, what changes you would like to make, how you would like to operate your part of the program, and why!"

Knapp said, "The object is to make a presentation to the new committee members: that this is the way it is, that this is the way it will be, and that this is the way that was proven to be effective and efficient for successful operations."

At this point Captain Dan came across the room, handed me a thick packet, and stated, "The material in this packet is for you to review and analyze. We will discuss this confidential information tomorrow morning. The packet contains forty-seven brief dossiers for all of the new potential candidates. As for the balance of the afternoon, let's have a social drink or two. Make sure the piano gets delivered to the room so that you can tickle the ivories and discuss old times without getting too serious. We will then take a break so you can gather your thoughts, and will meet back here for dinner at nineteen-thirty hours. After dinner you can give us your ideas, opinions, and thoughts as to current events and Chamber operations, as you perceive them to be."

We went to the bar to get something to drink. With drinks in hand, we went to the food table for a couple of snacks, and settled ourselves in the comfortable chairs at the side of the room. There we enjoyed an hour or so of idle and meaningless conversation. We talked about our original start-up meeting at Mount Fuji and the uniqueness of the original group, but no comments or references were made about the bad times. We avoided those negative events and issues that tended to haunt all our memories. Once we ended our little social gathering, I went to the room to make a quick perusal of the dossiers and to review my notes about issues that needed to be presented at the meeting.

The dossiers were quite interesting, and they followed the usual rules of confidentiality. They disclosed in detail only the quality of training, physical abilities, and a thorough analysis of the candidates' psychological profiles. Suddenly, I was hit with a few moments of déjà vu while reading the reports. There were thoughts about the strict and trying training provided by Sergeant Turner, and all of those mental and physical testing sessions with Doctor Colonel Frankenstein (more formally known at Fort Leonard Wood as Doctor Sattler). One could only imagine what these forty-seven kids have gone through just to reach this point, but the worst was yet to come for the final sixteen candidates that our training staff would select.

I noticed something that made me a little uncomfortable. With new techniques and technologies, the methods and awareness of terminations had changed radically over the past several years. The world of covert skullduggery and subterfuge now required more refined skills, and more developed talents, as to creating illusions and out-of-sight moments. This meant we would need more diversification and integration within our secret structure. I noticed there were no Arabs, no Croatian Ustasa-types, not one Hispanic person, and no blacks or women. This was bad, very bad, to have all these white Anglo-Saxons who would stand out like sore thumbs in the rest of the world. Let's face it, the rest of the world would become their assigned theater of operations and terminations, and it would be quite hard not to notice a white Wasp in the Congo, along the Nile, deep in Bolivia, or as a skeleton in someone's closet.

Oh, well. I had a good night's sleep, and the wake-up call was on time. I was totally prepared for the day's meetings with the retiring powers-that-be. When I arrived at the meeting room, the only person present was Captain Dan. There, already laid out, was a wide assortment of food and plenty of hot coffee to start off the day. While I enjoyed breakfast with Captain Dan, he informed me that he would be starting off the meeting with comments as to the current status of the group, and then would turn the meeting over to me for my input. He let me know that my entire request for training staff has been arranged, with only one exception — that being, unfortunately, that Mr. Imperial could not rearrange his schedule. They had retained the services of a Mr. Kennedy, who was an expert with all the top belts and so forth in judo, karate, and particularly jujitsu.

Colonel Knapp entered the room, followed by a tired-looking Colonel Cole. Cole looked like he was still not awake, and I'd have bet my bottom dollar that our Mr. Cole had enjoyed too many rusty nails in the lounge the previous night. He would most certainly be drinking a lot of black coffee during breakfast, and before Captain Dan started the meeting.

Captain Dan went up to the podium and called our small meeting to order. He started things off as strictly business by saying, "We have been fortunate and quite lucky that the world of our specialized concerns has been surprisingly calm, with no urgent tending required. It seems that most all of the urgent and immediate issues are related to Southeast Asia. We keep our nose out of this area since it is the exclusive territory and dominion of the C.I.A. and the Green Berets as part of the elusive Phoenix Group. This has turned out to be perfect timing for the selection and training of our new group. The fact is that the president has not been proactive in world events outside of Vietnam and Southeast Asia. So this is the committee meeting that will decide all structured and operational issues for the next ten-year period. The new committee members that will be replacing us will arrive tomorrow afternoon. They will be known by code names, per Mr. Benton's recommendation. We will no longer use specific ranks, titles, or designations, but there will be two exceptions that seem to be an ego/image issue.

"Here is the list of new and, as they say in Latin, *sub rosa* personnel:

"Liddy the Ambassador will replace Mr. Dee;

"Mel the Diplomat — for specific purposes related to finances and international banking;

"Mr. Patrick — this code name was changed because Benton was extremely annoyed and upset at our original choice, a personal thing;

"Mr. Lingo — who has an intelligence background and special expertise in world diplomatic affairs;

"Mr. Chrome — quite savvy about the military, with connections;

"Mr. Buck — neutral politically, but politically savvy;

"Mr. Rumble — who is an expert as to international business and economics issues around the world.

"There is one new twist this time around, at Colonel Cole's excellent recommendation. That is, that we have two alternates to replace any committee members who may suffer from an unfortunate illness or death. They will not attend any meetings or be involved in operations, unless some emergency needs require their expertise. They are as follows:

"Mr. Brute — an expert in the field of international relations;

"Mr. Tar-Baby — is an expert in military administration procedures.

"Now, for Mr. Benton's benefit: only the powers above us, and the committee which makes suggestions and requests, have information and details about us. Only these higher powers can evaluate our performance. The higher powers know there is something below us that does not exist, but the 'what' is privy only to us. They do not want to know details about what does not exist. They just know that these nonexistent people are there to accomplish their urgent needs and objectives once requests are made. Only Colonel Knapp, Colonel Cole, and myself will know any details about our new walking Shadows, so the new committee members will know only code names that you may disclose to them, per a particular assignment's need to know. You alone, Mr. Benton, will be the primary intermediary between the new committee and those ghosts you will be directing for our nonexistent missions.

"Now, as for us; we go onto a higher plain of nonexistence with a covert existence somewhere. We will not be lost or buried, but we'll always be able to keep an eye on you. Does this not make you feel warm and secure on your backside? You can trust us, and know that your rear will always be covered. You will be given a very private and secret phone number to call if things do not seem kosher within the clan. You may call the number any time, day or night, for a vis-à-vis tête-à-tête. Now I will be turning the meeting over to you. We will make notes and ask questions after your presentation. It's all yours, Doctor Doom!"

Well, it was now or never to say my piece, and to clear the air as to changes this person expected to see put into place. It had to be shown that I could take charge as a leader for the group, so this person started off with a rather dynamic request.

"First, I want to thank you for putting your faith and trust in me, and granting all my selections of team members. But the first major change that I am requesting is that the terms 'Black Chamber,' 'Illuminate,' 'Fidel la tos,' and 'Immolators' make a quick vanishing act. The terms must just fade away and disappear into the sunset. The point is, gentleman, there is to be no identification or related recognition between the old and the new. As they say, the old is out and only the new is in. We do not want former members and former intermediary personnel connecting code names directly or indirectly with the activities of this new group. So the code names for the new group of trained expediters are to be known only by you, as the higher powers, and never by the members on the new sub-committee. The reason is certainly apparent to you three, since we all had that bad experience once, and we certainly do not want a repeat of a similarly negative incident.

"That is why Kelsey is no longer 'The Artist,' but 'The Kitchen.' Mr. Johnson is no longer 'The Dancer,' but 'The Footloose.' Mr. Vigorritto is no longer 'The Pizza Boy,' but 'The Junkman.' I have also given good Sergeant Turner the code name of 'The Spider,' and we already know Mr. Kennedy's code name is 'Mr. Chop-Chop.' And, for the pièce de résistance, the liaison leader for the clan has a new name. It will no longer be Benton, 'The Music Man,' but just 'Mr. Chahaus.' The name is fitting, and I did not particularly care for 'Doctor Doom.' You will have to talk with some Palestinian from Lebanon who named me, to know what it means.

"Now for the password form of communication that each selected member of the group must memorize, or else vanish if they do not know the code word answers. A bit of poetry must be quoted in the proper order and sequence. It is a follows:

"There was a man who had no eyes;

"He went abroad to see the skies;

"He saw a tree with apples on it;

"Yet he picked no apples, but left no apples on it.

"Now, what is the secret password to stay alive? That, gentleman, neither you nor anyone else will know until after the final sixteen are selected and put under my control and guidance. At that point, they will have the committed and dedicated indoctrination of killing for the common good and benefit of this country, their God, their honor, and their duty to protect the best interests of this land of ours.

"There are some other major/minor issues that would best be discussed while the new committee is mixed in with the old. The 'why' is that the new committee will be the ones who will stand or fall as to their decision-making on certain points and issues, and it will not be your butts next to the flame. The reason is, I would like you to see the new committee members' reactions anew, and make fresh judgments based upon how they react to my comments and statements. I assure you, there will be no surprises and nothing for you to be shocked about, but there must be a mutual understanding between them and me concerning Macbeth, who said,

"'Life's but a walking shadow, a poor player,

"'That struts and frets his hour upon the stage,

"'And then is heard no more.'"

CHAPTER II
Be Careful What You Wish For!

The rest of the meeting during the first day at the Willard Hotel went quite well. This left me a little surprised, for they did not question or challenge any of my recommendations. After a terrific lunch, the old crew talked in general about my comments and what had specifically inspired me to recommend all the changes. They were actually focused more on my integration issues, or lack of integration within the pre-screened and selected candidates, and felt that I should make this a major part of my presentation before the new committee members the next day. Then they wanted me to clarify why Kelsey, Vigorritto, Johnson, and Turner were picked for the training staff.

I started off by telling them, "Please first understand that I have nothing against the other remaining members of our group. All were excellent at their jobs, but they just did not have that aggressive and over-confident, in-your-face attitude needed for this new job. Kelsey is a wheeler-dealer. He just has a natural sixth sense about things, and can talk any woman he wants out of their pants. But outside of these faults, he is a logical thinker, has great organizational skills, and is quite confident in his abilities. So — God forbid — should some unfortunate circumstances occur to myself, Kelsey should be your first choice for my replacement. You would have no regrets on this issue.

"As for Vigorritto, he is cold and deadly, with our needed specialized skills and tactics. He can take a joke, but will not take crap from anyone. He was good enough to shoot beer cans off people's heads at twenty-five meters, and has the confidence, if pushed, to try it at one-hundred meters. A few centuries back, he would have made a great assassin for the de' Medici family. As for Johnson, he is just plain good. If you can get him to stop tap dancing all the time, he will become the resident expert on illusion, deception, and out-of-sight moments. Even if he does come across as a sissy, he is a dangerous sissy, and I would trust him anywhere, any time, any place. As for good Sergeant Turner; I am what I am, and what I am today is because he put me in my place. He gave me the mental and intestinal fortitude to prevail and survive. He, more than anyone else, will refine these young recruits' sniper skills into a fine art. Then he'll kick their asses if they get to cocky, and the rest of us will just look the other way."

Colonel Knapp interrupted at the right point of this discussion. "I would like to interject something of interest around Mr. Benton's comments, for I was the person assigned to interview and recruit your requested training staff. I am not trying to flatter your ego, for I know it is big enough. You would have thought these guys had gotten an invitation from the president. They were elated that you had requested them. They said yes without a second thought or hesitation. The only one that took it as an eye-opening shock was Sergeant Turner. He got this bug-eyed, weird look on his face, and then backed up and sat down as if he couldn't stand any longer. He just sat there, cocking his head and nibbling on his lower lip while staring straight at me. Then he got this big smile that lit up the room, giggled softly, and said, "Yes, where do I sign? And where do I meet my favorite pain in the ass?" At that point,

I knew you had picked the right team. That is all I need to say. I just wanted to mention it as a point of interest before we end today's meeting, so that we can have a nice symposium together after dinner, and Mr. Benton can tickle the ivories."

The dinner was excellent; a nice surf and turf, Caesar salad, and a large piece of apple pie topped with Cheddar cheese for dessert. Then we all drank a little B&B after dinner. Our little group had its own waitress and bartender. The party began to loosen up, with the maestro himself playing the piano and running off at the mouth until midnight. But it was Colonel Cole with his rusty nails, his off-key singing, and his survival training stories that kept the party alive. Then Colonel Knapp thought it was time to close the party down, and told us to forget about tomorrow morning's meeting. He said we would all have a late breakfast and then just sit around and chat about everything that was relevant, or irrelevant. He stated that most of the new committee members would be checking into the hotel by 1330 hours, and that they all knew the first meeting would be starting at 1500 hours. Then Knapp went on to say, "As our survival training specialist Colonel Cole might put it, don't let the bed bugs bite you, stay away from the Panama Canal, and be seeing you in the morning around 0830 hours. Then remember the first rule: Employment is not adoption."

The next day provided an excellent breakfast, a lot of casual conversation, and a fine lunch before we prepared to meet all the new committee members. A nice bit of information was given to me by Captain Dan while we were talking briefly about our former associates; those particular ones who did not survive the Black Chamber experience, and how well their families had been provided for financially from the Purple People Eater's confiscated yacht funds. He provided more clarification with, "We want to assure you that we take care of our own, and your deceased former friends have not been neglected. I should point out that the funds recovered from that yacht — in bearer bonds, cash and stock certificates that were to be secretly transferred to offshore accounts — were worth over eight million dollars. This proves our government's semantics of 'revenue enhancements' and 'depopulation' can be very profitable when transitioning undesirable souls into the great beyond. This confiscation became our off-balance-sheet slush fund to maintain these operations with greater secrecy. Those bonus dollars paid excellent medical and living benefits to get Gary the Chef back on his feet, provided a huge financial payment to each person's parents or wife and, if children were involved, the funds provided large college fund accounts for each child. The same 'take care of' system will apply to any of your new Pookas that may unfortunately end up missing in action. This information is provided to you so that you have a comfort zone in handling this new management leadership role."

Captain Dan and the others knew that I appreciated them sharing this information with me, and trusting me enough to take on this responsibility. The interesting point they made, as to advice for my presentation to the new committee, was not to try and impress them. They told me to simply be myself, with the facts and only the facts. The faith and confidence these older guys had expressed in me helped me become more comfortable and relaxed about the upcoming meeting with the new committee. As proof that time flies when one is having fun, the meeting was about to start in twenty minutes.

When I arrived at the meeting room, the new committee members were already there with Colonel Knapp. Only Colonel Cole and Captain Dan had not yet arrived. As I scanned the room, familiar faces became apparent, for I had seen them before at the Capital Hilton meeting last year. This would make for a much more relaxing conference. This factor made me feel somewhat at ease, and my only wishful thought was for the appearance of Ambassador Dee. My curiosity was becoming real, for I was trying to figure out who Liddy the Ambassador and Mel the Diplomat would be. But all was soon answered. After the social cocktail period ended, everyone placed their little cardboard nameplates on the table in front of themselves when sitting down in their assigned seats.

To my surprise, Colonel Cole went to the podium to start off the meeting, and made all the code name introductions for everyone. Cole reminded everyone in the room about their agreements of secrecy and responsibility, then reminded them of the reality: that they did not even know the other people were in the room, and that everything about everything did not happen, did not exist, had never existed, and would remain nonexistent. He informed them that this was to be a totally new operation, with new code names, passwords and confidential identifications. Cole made it clear that all the Black Chamber terms and rumors they might have heard about were dead and buried; invisible hallucinations of someone's vivid imagination. Then he warned everyone that caution should be taken by anyone planning to dig up the dead.

Wow! Colonel Cole started the meeting off on the right tenor, with a swift-kicking left foot placed at everyone's neck. In a nasty, down and dirty — yet very professional — manner, he made the rules clear. There was now a certainty; one could be absolutely assured there would be no misunderstandings in the room that day. To my surprise, there was no apparent shock or dismay on any of the faces at the conference table. The group must have had a lot of useful pre-indoctrination by the old guys during the past few months, before arriving. This was a clearing of the air between the select members of our little mutual admiration society. He asserted his authority and reassured everyone that there would be no misunderstandings or confusion as time marched on.

Colonel Cole then introduced me to the group, but first told everyone that there would be a little reception at 1830 hours, before dinner, and that the rest of the evening would be for light social discussion. He made it clear this would give everyone enough time to get acquainted, and consider more formal questions and statements at the next morning's meeting. The stage was all mine.

My opening remark was, "Gentlemen, at this point in time, it is like the calm before the storm. We have been lucky so far that there have not been any major disruptions requiring our group's special services. We could not have asked for more during this transition period, while selecting and training new Pookas with a big-stick shillelagh. You can be assured that the final screening program being held at Jug Inn next month will be thorough. We will weed out everyone who is not suitable to be considered as one of the final sixteen Pookas. Yet there are still several points of issue concerning this crop of potential candidates, and they are as follows:

"One: Retract the invitation and remove from the rooster all students trained at the Norwich, Hudson, or other private military academies. Let them grow up to be 'ninety-day wonders (O.C.S. – Officers Candidate School).' for someone else to contend with, not our little group.

"Second: We lack diversification, variety and integration among these selections. By my observation, they do not include blacks, Hispanics, Arabs, Slavic-types, women or Jews. They could well be hidden in this list, but I cannot find them. Think about it! The reasons should be obvious, particularly when all of our operations will be outside the good old U.S. of A. I politely and urgently request that you find some replacement candidates within the next thirty days. Find people who will not stand out like a sore thumb in Africa, India, South and Central America, and definitely in the Middle East. My team does not want to use a lot of dark makeup or create black-faced vaudevillians for a Mummers Parade.

"Third: It would be nice to know that a rejection slip from us does not mean an automatic ticket to Vietnam. Yes, our little sixteen will be risking their lives, but the odds of survival will be in their favor. Now, the other thirty-five may also be risking their lives by being put in harm's way in Vietnam. The fact is, there the odds will be against them and in favor of the prey. You must admit that this thought can be a little discomforting when making hard choices and handing out rejection slips. It reminds me of the German concentration camp selectors, who decided which chosen people went stage left for a chance at survival, and which went stage right for certain fumigation.

"These three points stuck in my craw and needed to be clarified to the group. Now, a few remarks about the world our group will have to play in after their comprehensive training program at Autumn Hills during September. The following is just my opinion as to where we may or may not get entangled in the near future. They are as follows:

"First: Paraguay is not a problem for us because of General Alfred Stroessner, and Bolivia will be no problem because of General Rene Barrientos. Sukarno's state police are making short work of the PKI communists after the attempted coup d'etat last year, and we therefore will have no issues in Indonesia. The Somoza Dynasty does not need our help in Nicaragua, for they have their Sandinista issues in check. Guatemala is in good hands, but I am concerned about Uruguay self-destructing from all their economic problems. Their General Gestido seems to be losing his grip on reality and trying to flush his economy down the urinal. That is the good news, since Southeast Asia and Vietnam are none of our dammed business, and are out of our jurisdictional hands anyway.

"Now, I do have a concern about Argentina and President Arturo Illia. Here the Reds and the Blues may never get their acts together in order to correct things. Yet I have confidence the Peronistas will eventually take care of this flaming liberal, and we should just sit back, with a wait and see attitude.

"The problem uno is and will be Chile, for sooner or later they will require a circumcision at the top. Their new President E.F. Montalva sounds like a bad wine that has turned to vinegar, and therefore should be poured down the drain. This is just my opinion, for it is the higher powers that make these corrective decisions. Next, the higher powers must recognize that the Dominican Republic is still a tick-ticking time bomb, even if the Bosch faction has control. But we are not hold harmless here, because the C.I.A.'s fingerprints are all over these internal problems.

"Best we now move our thoughts to the Middle East and Syria, who will become a bigger and increasingly bigger pain in the ass. Here is where we need to call in a favor from our Arab territory of Iran. We must reward and encourage the Shah's SAVAK terminators to handle the Alawite Ba'thist. This little trick would make the Iranians and the Hebrews of Israel even closer blood brothers, with their common economic interests and Abraham. But there again, do you not think it is strange that we like Nazis in South America but not in the Middle East?

"Anyway, gentlemen, I know what the game is, how the game is played, and how the game is to be played. As the good playbook states in John 15:2, 'We prune the vines to preserve the rest of the fruit.' Therefore, it is quite clear that the meek shall inherit the earth, but not the mineral rights. It is now assumed that all of us in this room recognize the fact that the rest of the world does not play by our rules, or give a crap about the Geneva Convention.

"Lest we forget, one of our close allies and religious blood brothers was connected to the biggest spy rings used against us, and sold our secrets to the communists. They are still involved in subversive activities to obtain our best world order plans and secrets. So remember that old saying, 'Keep a close eye on your enemies and friends, but the closer eye must be kept on your friends.' The fact is, they have never broken up a Persian spy ring stealing our secrets. Therefore, we cannot play by our naive rules if we want to survive, prevail, and maintain some semblance of peace in this world. Captain Dan once said it best by re-phrasing another biblical verse, I Peter 5:8, 'Be vigilant, because your adversary be as a roaming bear or a dragon, walketh about, seeking whom they may devour.'

"So from this point on, one might refer to our little Pooka Brigade, which will be ready to rock and roll into service this October, as the 'Hobbism rabbits' who eat Westphalian carrots."

I then smiled and said, "That's all, folks." I turned the meeting back over to Colonel Cole, but Captain Dan came to the podium to make some housekeeping remarks before we broke for dinner. He wanted to let the new committee know that the meeting scheduled for the next month at the Jug Inn had been reserved as a life insurance conference for top producers receiving advanced training in insurance law. He said the conference was being referred to as the Vice Presidents Seminar. The title was more of a paradoxical joke than they might have thought at that moment. He then reminded them that the night's activities were to be light, sociable, and relaxing; a "getting to know you better" symposium. Then he invited all of us to stay and have a short cocktail hour before we left to freshen up for dinner.

The evening's after-dinner get-together was quite enjoyable. They had good music piped into the room, so I did not have to play a lot of piano, and all of us received the benefit of not having to listen to Colonel Cole singing off-key. Dawn came early and the wake-up call too soon, but headache or not the morning meeting was not to be delayed. I had a light breakfast and a lot of black coffee. Before I realized it, my turn to go on stage had arrived, and I was hardly aware of Colonel Knapp's opening remarks. No question about it, this idiot had consumed too many Black Russians. Oh, what the hell; I would just have to do the best I could under the hangover circumstances.

"Gentlemen, forgive me, because I think I am seeing twenty-four people in this room."

The new Ambassador Liddy quickly interrupted, "Don't worry about it. Fact is, most of us in this room are probably seeing two of you as well! By the way, Mr. Benton, I spent several years in the Middle East babysitting the Pahlavi Dynasty, and 'Chahaus' — for everyone else's information — means a 'real horse's ass.' This only makes me respect you more, after learning from the others last night about your Hilton presentation last year to several members of this group. So no excuses or apologies are necessary."

"Well, thank you, Ambassador Liddy, or whoever you are. Your input is more than appreciated on this particular morning, but I was hoping it would take longer for everyone to learn the meaning about my new identity. But that is life!

Now I had best make a few of my opening remarks before we get into our long day of strategy sessions. First, I want you to have the confidence that my selected trainer spark plugs are in place, and to also accept the fact they are all champion spark plugs. You can take this fact to the bank. The new crew that we will select and provide final training for this September will be many times better at their job than our original crew. This is because we will be providing them with a lot more hands-on practical experience. That experience was learned from our errors and mistakes, for the successful experiences means little or nothing in this real-life game of cat and mouse.

"I do not want you to incorrectly interpret my comments, for I love the human race; I just do not care for some of the people in it. Credit must be given to my Grandmother Jay for her excellent piece of advice: 'Love many, trust few, and learn to paddle your own canoe.' This is why I must issue a disclaimer that is common before all my presentations. That is, never ask me a question if you do not really want to know the answer. A former committee member once said something to me that was a little disquieting. At the time I was not quite sure whether he was serious or being humorous when he said, 'If the Black Chamber is the answer, you really do not want to know what the question is. For everything in this realm of existence is either sell or kill. We either buy them or bury them, and that is the way the covert world turns.' Therefore, the basic rule is that you never forgive, never apologize, never forget, and always get even sooner or later.

"A little bit to spooky, yes? Well, best keep going, for those who do not know me need to understand that I never pull my punches. I will always tell it to you like it is; blunt, direct, and to the point, unless my intentions are to clearly mislead you, misdirect you, and set you up for the fall. Confusing, yes? The point to be learned is to always maintain a barrier or Chinese wall between issues of trust in this covert business of pretext and innuendo. Even in the naive real world, there is nothing better between neighbors, relatives and acquaintances than a fence, a jaundiced eye, and maintaining relationships at arm's length. The issue here is not being negative, cynical or critical about humans in the human race. For after all, the Good Book does say, 'Judge not, that you may be judged.' But I do have the right and necessity of being an observant fruit inspector, since the Good Book also says, 'You shall know them by their fruits.'"

My presentation was finished and I was pooped. All I wanted to do was go to bed for a couple of hours. The rest of the day's meeting were on policies, procedures, rules and regulations, and signing new agreements of understanding that we no see, we no hear, and we no speak, or we could have an epilogue of no breath. The evening's entertainment was again to be simply a social gathering, so I decided to do more piano playing and less drinking, since I would be catching a plane home the next morning. This meeting proved to me that political intrigue and general politics can make for strange bedfellows, for in this room we had a common bond. We were drinking buddies enjoying each other's conversation and my entertaining them on the piano. But the subconscious needs always to remember that employment is not adoption, and terminations can be a terminal sport when deniability needs no evidence in the light of day.

Even with our age differences, it appeared we all could have been friends under a different set of circumstances. Yet the true fact was that looks can be deceiving within a general social and business environment. I doubt if any of them would introduce me to their families. They certainly would not want me dating their daughters, or worse yet moving into their neighborhoods. Yet I would be admired and appreciated enough to kill someone for them on behalf of their shadow government. They would certainly respect my skill as an assassin to do their wishful things for God and country, but they would always prefer that I stay nonexistent, invisible, and politely disappear someday. Once, while expressing to Gary the Chef my thoughts about all their obsequious praise, and all their carte blanche, first-class wine and dine fellowship, I said, "I was born into this world at night, Gary, but not last night."

I really hate flying, and definitely hate waiting at the Pittsburgh airport to change planes. Still, at any cost, it is really nice to be back home again with the wife and kids. There was going to be a lot of work to get done in the next thirty days merely to make a living within my insurance business, not to mention having to take the time to thoroughly analyze all of the dossiers before the Vermont meeting at the Jug Inn. It is better to be too busy and pressed for time than the alternative of not being busy at all. I can understand why the wife would prefer less work and travel on my part. She really does not appreciate my disappearing for a week again in June. Her frustration is that we sold our Mansfield house and are moving to Columbus, Ohio right after the Fourth of July. This has created a nice but touchy situation, since I have not yet told her about how busy this boy will be in September.

The dossiers were more than interesting on closer review, when I had more time to be thorough and discovered certain nuances of interest about these individuals. One guy's hobby was collecting Meerschaum pipes, yet he did not smoke. Another was an accomplished harmonica player and had won amateur shows on television. One person wanted a career in cosmetology, another wants to be a horticulturist, and several considered themselves serious hobbyists as philatelists and/or numismatists. The one person I couldn't wait to meet was considered a semi-professional xylophone player. Another guy would be carefully screened by Johnson, since he wants to be a ballet dancer. It was easy to notice that most were pretty good athletes in one sport or another while in high school, and one was a first-rate Ping-Pong player. This was a wide assortment of individuals. They had successfully finished their basic training and all were top marksmen. They all probably had extensive and secret sniper training on the Q-T with someone as mean and nasty as Sergeant Turner. The thirty-six that were left seemed to be copasetic, and hopefully they would get me nine new replacements before the June meeting at Jug Inn.

It was coming down as a greater responsibility than I had expected or thought about. What an ox-cart burden it can be to decide and plan people's future, or lack thereof. All was easy when the only concern was my own cat and mouse existence, but now I had to pick and choose others for a questionable existence. My enthusiasm — and ego response — to accept this new position and take responsibility for other people's lives might have been a little premature and irresponsible on my part, but I hoped not. As someone once said, "Enthusiasm without knowledge and experience is like running in the dark."

So in all honesty, where was my knowledge and experience in management? How would I prevail in this sink or swim position of responsibility? This might all turn out to be more than I had wished for, and one must always be careful what they wish for, according to someone's philosophy. Any mistakes or oversights in this new management role could, potentially, cost people their lives. The thought had never entered my mind when I accepted the position. I guess this was what people called hindsight, second thoughts, or buyer's remorse. Maybe this could be what real maturity and growing up was all about, and how one slowly gained wisdom and success through many trial and error experiences. This was definitely going to be a position of solid commitment, with no doubts or apprehension allowed. Maybe good old Hickman the Bully, one of my original trainers at the Mount Fuji session, had hit the nail on the head when he humorously said, "This Mr. Benton, the Music Man, is often wrong, but never in doubt. Now this is what we call being very self-assured. This attitude is only allowable when the decision-maker can live with it, learn from it, and correct their mistakes to move on without remorse."

Time sure flies when you're busy, busy, and too busy. The time was here. Only three days before this person would be leaving for Vermont. Thankfully, the powers from above had timely delivered nine new dossiers for my review. The temptation was there for me to call the new private contact number and complain to Captain Dan, Colonel Cole, or Colonel Knapp. I stared at the Circle 6-2150 for some time, before finally deciding not to dial myself into trouble. I buried my thoughts about the issue, and prepared myself for the trip to Hartford, Connecticut, and then on to Jug Inn. Again I had to suffer the misery of Agony Airlines, with a long layover transfer in Pittsburgh. The only good thing was that I'd again be able to get the world's best shoe shine in the terminal concourse.

The big bosses were smart enough to schedule all of the training staff's arrival at the Hartford Airport within a two-hour period. A limo driver was at the gate, with a sign reading Mr. Chahaus. He said they were waiting for one more to arrive, and the rest were at a coffee shop in the terminal. Then the limo driver headed back to another gate. I went to the coffee shop as directed, and felt great joy at seeing Kelsey, Johnson, and Vigorritto. Only Sergeant Turner had not yet arrived.

This was fortunate, for they needed to know ahead of time who Sergeant Turner was. They needed to know that he was black, and that he was my top-notch mentor and trainer. There was no negative reaction, rather a more positive reaction when Kelsey mentioned that it would be nice adding a little color to the group. It was no more than thirty minutes before the limo driver showed up with Sergeant Turner. Sarge had a grin on his face from ear to ear, and he grabbed my hand and nearly took my arm off in his excitement of saying hello. I introduced him to everyone else, and then the limo driver took us out to his limo, which was like a little school bus. We were off for the long drive to Jug Inn. There was very little talking on the trip north to our little resort, the reason being that each had been given their separate copies of all the dossiers, and told to use the time to thoroughly review all of them before we got to Jug Inn.

Jug Inn was a beautiful and secluded spot. The lodge was beautiful, with all these little buildings along a small pond. We were pleased with the excellent treatment we received while checking in and getting our room assignments. After we got our rooms, we agreed to unpack, freshen up, and meet for dinner at 1830 hours in the lobby.

I went down to the lobby a little early and decided to check out the bar. There before my eyes was a nice piano, and they gave me permission to play anytime I wished. Who could resist the offer? My fingers were itchy, and the bartender and his three customers enjoyed my playing "Saint Louis Blues," "Birth of the Blues," "Sentimental Journey," and "The Continental." The rest of the crew arrived in about twenty minutes. From experience, they knew where to find me. We then went to our private, far-off corner table in the dinning room, but only after we had toasted and downed a couple shots of excellent cognac.

The dinner was excellent. After dinner, our little meeting was called to order after making sure we had lots of coffee on the table, and a nice bottle of merlot for each of us to sip on during the rest of the evening, or take to our room. The powers had already informed them of their new code names, the basic purpose of the meeting, and that the big event would be starting the Tuesday after Labor Day in southeastern Ohio.

My opening comment were, "My good friends, we too many times have tempted the Grim Reaper, and several of our friends have met the scythe of his wrath. This is going to be one nice working Ben-Bacchus party for us, before things get serious. Why? The fact is that we already know their weapons skills and their psychological profiles. We also know they are in excellent physical condition, and all about their education and language skills. Now we must learn from them what we do not know, such as how they think and/or understand their beliefs on political and social issues. We also do not know if they can hold their tongues or their liquor. So there will be no training here at Jug Inn. There will just be interviews and observations to see what they do with their free time. Therefore, get them drinking, talking, shooting craps and playing poker, then intimidate and annoy them a little by questioning and challenging their manhood, to see how they will react. Do not abuse them, hurt them, or kill them! We just want to make sure there are no Cross the Preacher types within the group.

"Please write down the names of select individuals that could be of interest, as my pre-screening opinion may be completely in error. Please find the flaw in my thinking, or reinforce my opinion. There will be a simple grading system that all of you will use. You will rank them from bottom to top as being either liberal, liberal conservative, purely moderate, conservative liberal, conservative, or ultra-conservative. No one will be selected to join the new Pooka Brigade unless all five of us are in an agreement. Here is my wild guess list of potential candidates and possible rejections. Possibles: Rex, Vyas, Angelosie, Hickson, Grady, DeMatto, Zeno, St. Amond, Berkich, Papadopoulos, Iff, O'Dell, Arno, Evans, Murder, Toukan, Lawhead, Kamadona, Charvat, and maybe two of the following women: Velda Baird, Delilah Lee, Gerry Godfrey, and Drayleen Gabalac. Possible rejections are Doudera, Secord, Kinchie, Garbutt, Bailey, Law, Layton, Salvo, Pappas, and Handel. I have formed no opinion yet on those few candidates not mentioned; I will probably be wrong on these once we get to know them better. As for the girls, push their buttons to see if they can take a hit, then see if they will fight back by giving you a piece of their mind, or a slap in the kisser."

We decided to close down the evening by first going to the piano bar lounge for a couple nightcaps. My little piano playing totally surprised Sergeant Turner. But first, I told everyone to sleep late, and that there would be a late breakfast at 0900 hours. They were told that the busload of recruits would not be arriving until about 1700 hours. This would allow us plenty of time to recover from any possible hangovers, and give us several hours of free time for more discussions as to our operating procedures for the week. They were told that we would work together on the planning and scheduling of interviewing times, just to make sure we are all on the same page.

But before heading to the lounge, I thought it best to provide some words of wisdom. "We all have to remember that little mistakes you can absorb, but the big mistakes will absorb you. Plus, the reality is that you will never get out of this world alive. So let all of us toast the Grim Reaper on his incompetence, which has not yet gotten us invited to a pinochle game with Azrael."

CHAPTER III
"One Fish, Two Fish, Red Fish, Blue Fish"

There is nothing like a big lunch to make one ready for an afternoon nap. We closed down the piano lounge sometime after midnight, and each of us finished our bottle of merlot to help us relax and sleep better. Should this storyline of the previous night's events makes us feel better, so be it, but we were definitely paying for our sins. Hopefully, by the time the busload of recruits arrived, the fresh air and coffee on top of a nice lunch would sober us up a little more, and clear our heads and bloodshot eyes. Like it or not, it was necessary that we have another short clarification meeting before the bus of candidates arrived in the next few hours. We needed to make sure that our clearinghouse staff would be on the same page. The suggestion was made that we all go into a private lounge area for a short meeting. Once we were comfortably situated in the lounge, my opening comments were short, sweet and simple.

"Fellow comrades of good food and drink, the fellowship and fun stops here and now, until the end of this conference. We now have to put on the face of maturity and seriousness, and an attitude of no bullshit allowed in our space. As I stated last night, we can make little mistakes, but we just do not want to make big mistakes. I had a nightmare about six potential guys like Cross the Preacher among all those dossiers, so put a jaundiced eye on Patterson, Portell, Bushey, Douderea,

Calhoun, and Mahar. Sad part is, that was a hell of a way to lose a good night's sleep. But like you, Kelsey, when that sixth sense hair goes up on the back of my neck, it always seems to give me the right answer.

"Remember that throughout this meeting we keep them in a blind spot as to what we are, what we think, and what we do. We only talk about them, not us. You can use your real last names as before, if you wish, but I am using Benton with a phony residence location of Dade City, Florida. All they need to think and know is that we are very important and authoritative people; the great ones that are making decisions concerning their military careers and future promotions. They will be put on notice that they are to be on their best behavior if they hope to become 'ninth-day wonders,' or get a first-class assignment with diplomatic counsel duty.

"Look, guys! I may be in charge of this new experience, but I am counting on all of you to take charge as a cohesive group. You will have an equal voice with me on the decision-making, even though the final choices on the list will go under my signature and recommendation to the higher powers — for I alone get to sleep well or not so well, based on our decisions.

"Therefore, please get rid of followers, and particularly the team players. Weed out leader types who do not appear to be freelance Daniel Boones that dislike red tape limitations and restrictions. Should any have pride in the fact that they won a second or third place, kill them off, for in this game there is no second place. Now, if they think in terms of a cohesive group of football or baseball players, they are out. We only want outstanding individual performers who live and die on their own performances as wrestlers, swimmers, pole-vaulters, and Ping-Pong players. Find out who is street smart and has down-to-earth wisdom. But do not select the confident intellectuals who think they know more than everyone else, for that is our domain. A couple of good choices may be the found among the farmboys on our list. They tend to be hard workers and social loners who are not group-oriented, except for 4-H clubs. Let's be clear: we cannot afford associates who are educated beyond their intelligence. We only want people whom we might like, since we'll be spending a lot of time with them, and they will probably end up hating us during the hell month of September at Autumn Hills. But that is okay, since we will be teaching them how to stay alive as the stalking cat, survive as the scurrying mouse, and be as dangerous as a porcupine when fleeing for safety.

"Well, enough said. If you have burning questions, please hold them until later tonight, after some deep thought. Now let's go out on the porch to relax, drink a lot more water and coffee, and wait for the troops to arrive. The fresh air will do us good. We can share some good jokes and memories, and tell Sergeant Turner about the Mount Fuji New Grand experience. Then I'll share my thoughts concerning him after he kicked my ass all over Fort Leonard Wood."

Talk about a nice day with nice weather. We all enjoyed relaxing on the porch and throwing the bull around in the nice, light summer breeze. Vigorritto then said, "There is the bus coming up the road with our potential rabbits. We'd better look our best and put on our stern faces. Let's approach the stage, since the curtain is now rising on our one-act play."

We walked down off the porch and stood there like a reception committee. We remained quiet while everyone got off the bus with their luggage. Then Kelsey blurted out, "Aw, shit! You have got to be shitting me. Someone has got to be putting us on. These are just kids. They don't even look like they have graduated from high school yet, and they are expected to become assassins? Who is kidding who? They are all naïve-looking assholes! Oops! Not those couple of good-looking soldiers right over there."

Turner had to comment, "Cool down. Mr. Romero, or Mr. Hotshot, or Mr. whoever you think you are. Put you eyes back into your head and pull up your zipper. Please remember that all of you, ten years ago — including Mr. Benton — looked that young, that naive, and that stupid. You were all nervous and insecure about what might begin happening to you at a similar point in time, and guys like me made you piss your pants back then."

I chimed in with my two cents, "I...uh...I...uh, do not agree with what you said. I just know that I *had* to look and appear older and more mature than this group of kids. They look like nice, innocent teenagers getting off a bus to attend a high school football game. If they were in uniforms, they would look like a high school marching band."

Turner's response was, "Well, my friends, mirrors are deceiving, and back then you only got to see what you wanted to see. And these young people are only seeing what they want to see, and that is five old guys standing in front of them, ready to take charge of their lives."

Finally, the showman Johnson jumped in to bring us back to the reality of the situation, and our responsibilities, by saying, "Don't worry or fret. We'll make our selections and soon convert them from reading Doctor Seuss books to *Mein Kampf.* For they, like us, will learn the principle of killing for the common good in order to maintain the "balance of power" and the "world order" of economics. Like us, they will soon understand the scheme of things, as it relates to our economic interests around the world, and the very warm cold war with the bears and the dragons."

Even in our state of amazement over these young individuals on the playground, we greeted them with open arms and got them checked into their rooms. We told them to show up for dinner at 1850 hours, at the main building where they checked in. After we got all of them checked in, the staff went back to the bar lounge, feeling that we all needed a stiff shot of good whiskey to wake up to the reality of this situation of playing babysitter. But thank God we all had the common sense to order plain black coffee. We gathered our thoughts and sat there, deep in them. Vigorritto laughed and kept reminding us that we had never looked as young as these kids we were in charge of for the next couple of days. The wise old owl, Turner, told us to forget it, grow up, and screw our heads back onto our shoulders. He reminded us to start thinking of where these young people would be next year, and what they might be doing because of our decisions, and whether they would still be alive after next year. Turner's remarks got our attention, brought us back to reality, and made us start thinking business again.

At that point, Turner had set the stage. I told them that the decision had been made as to the handling of all the interviews and analysis concerning the candidates. First, they were not to discuss — in any form — anything about these individuals until the meeting was over and they had all flown the coop. Then, over the next several days, they were to make their own observations, draw their own conclusions, and narrow down their own independent list for the sixteen finalists, without comparing notes. It was made clear to them that we would have our arguments and disagreements as to whom, why, and why not. The disagreements, if any occurred, would be hashed out during the final afternoon — once the candidates, after their final breakfast, left for their duty stations.

I informed my four compatriots that they would be doing all of the interviews, and sending candidates to me only for an additional screening interview. They were told that if they felt a second opinion was necessary, to feel free to interrupt me at any time. The staff knew that I would be spending my time watching, listening, and socializing with all the different personalities of the group in a less threatening and formal environment. If necessity demanded it, I might occasionally select certain individuals at random for a more casual interview session. It was made clear to them again that we would all have to agree on who ended up on the final list. After that, we would turn out the lights, go home, and meet again in September in the Buckeye State.

The interviewing process proceeded just fine, but it took a bit of a toll on the patience of the staff. They seemed to lose their sense of humor, and got worn out by going from nine a.m. to nine p.m. with all the interviews. They were not interested in any after-work partying; just a short, friendly nightcap before going off to their rooms for more work and sleep. The only people having a lot of fun and relaxation were the recruits, by playing basketball and card games, and fishing in the small lake. The nice part was that they even enjoyed my piano playing.

But all good things must come to an end, and all the young people would be boarding a bus the next morning for the trip to the Hartford airport. After lunch, Kelsey, Johnson, Vigorritto, Turner and I would be playing "Knights of the Round Table," to decide who would fill our empty seats within the Black Chamber's Pooka Brigade. After breakfast the following morning, we would ship out and return to our civilian lives.

The time had come where all those old sayings came into play, such as, "put your money where your mouth is" and "shit or get off the pot." And I knew what it was like to be "between a rock and a hard place." The lunch was fine on the last day. We locked the door behind us and got down to business.

I opened the meeting with, "Gentleman, I am sure that each of you has a list ready for your presentation. You will now tell me who the number one person is on your lists, and I will write their names across the top of the blackboard. Then you will each give me your number two choice, and so on, until we have the four columns filled down to the sixteenth runner-up. But first, I would like to have a discussion about the girls. I am hoping at least one made the list, maybe two, but do not disclose this to the group at this time. So, who would like to comment on Delilah Lee? Okay, Mr. Kelsey."

"She is tough, beautiful, and has the instincts to destroy. She is humorously cold with her coy attitude, and she has the brass balls to stand her ground."

"Who would like to comment on Velda Baird? Mr. Johnson."

"She would make a good wife. She is a top marksman who could terminate a cheating boyfriend, and she would be great working at some embassy as security. But she is too sweet, too well built, and has no killer instinct. She couldn't whack a flea."

"Now, who can comment on Drayleen Gabalac? She is all yours, Vigorritto."

"I would not cross this chick, in or out of bed. She would eat you alive in a second. She is as tough as nails and can verbally strip you down skin-first. We have here an excellent mentally and physically conditioned person, terrific skeet shooter, and I would hate to have her looking for me as a targeted prey."

"Well, Sergeant Turner, that leaves you with Gerry Godfrey. How say you?"

"She is a talented marksman, your equal. She was a champion on her high school rifle team. She is good because her father built and owns a gun club, and she loads her own shot with thirty-eight caliber and forty-four magnum loads. She could be one hell of a trainer instructor for guys like you, but she is not a stalker or a predator — no instinct to be more than just a nice pussy cat. That's it, Mr. B."

"This is all nice to know, but do any of you disagree with these remarks? If not, forever hold your peace, and let the chips fall where they may when it comes to the girls on the list. I understand you guys had a private huddle, and agreed to a list of eight questions to alternate between the interviews of the candidates. As I understand it, the questions were quite good. 'What do you think about: Malcolm X? Lester Maddox? Vietnam? The Watts Riots? Che Guevara? Why did you select your branch of the service, rather than go to college? What do you think about the people who skipped to Canada? If you could go back and change history, would you assassinate Stalin, or Hitler?'

"I thought this technique and idea was very good. Wish I had thought up those questions. I am sure the responses helped all of you narrow down the list. So let's get on with the show. I hope that we can soon come to a mutual agreement, without wasting too much time. Now that everyone else is gone, it is our night to party. This little secret Round Table proves that assassins make for the best of friends, and have a pattern of commonality in their thinking process. Let's agree that we have that sixth sense instinct to read people who are good or bad. Let's start down the list!"

My friends had done their home work and their duty in great detail. We had the list completed and had taken a final vote in about three hours, but everyone decided to submit an additional four names to be used as alternates in case some unexpected vacancies occurred within our ranks. These four people were also exceptional, and as equally valuable as the original sixteen on the list. A request would be made and attached to the list, if allowable or practical within this covert system, for consideration to maintain these persons as standby reserves. They wanted to keep Godfrey in reserve, and out of harm's way. The others selected were Mr. McKinley, Mr. Mohr and Mr. Sarr; they would not get code names, special benefits, or attend the Autumn Hills session.

The curtain had come down on the final act at Jug Inn. It was an interesting play, well performed, and we five had one hell of a private backstage party before closing down the theater. The trip to the airport was one deep sleep, and I am sure the sound catnaps repeated themselves all the way home on our flights.

I arrived home at the appropriate time to start getting heavily involved with the packing and housecleaning before the move. A lot of moving preparations had to be completed right after the Fourth of July. This left little free time to organize the schedules and programs for the September meeting, which meant cutting back on my insurance business operations for several months. Therefore, I was lucky that the powers that be were paying and reimbursing me quite well for this desired move to Columbus, Ohio.

Of course, it did not hurt that I had made several large insurance sales in the spring, which exceeded all of last year's income. So the pressure as my family's sole provider was off my back for a while. The wife was tickled to death that we were moving to Columbus. Also, I had promised her that we would all go to Cedar Point and on to Niagara Falls before the September conference. This would give us a couple of nice, relaxing breaks after we get settled in from the move. The children loved the fact that there was a White Castle and a BBF Whirling Satellite restaurant nearby for their favorites: hamburgers, milkshakes and fries.

The summer was wonderful. I had a lot of fun with the family, the trips were great, and the wife just loved the new Eastmoor neighborhood. The move worked out great for me, since Autumn Hills was only be a short drive down Route 33, and not a three-hour drive from Mansfield. Now that everything was close and convenient I could come home for a night once in a while. There would be no need for me to have a room at the Christopher Inn, since I could count on the great training staff to handle and manage things while I was gone during the night. I had talked to Captain Dan once and to Colonel Knapp several times. Both assured me that everything was properly arranged for and in place as to the facilities and the candidates arriving on schedule. Captain Dan had informed me that there was unanimous agreement on the candidate selections. Then he informed me that they had approved the idea of the four alternates, and that they would make special arrangements to keep them in the fold. Captain Dan stated that he and Cole wanted to reiterate an important point for me to remember, and that was "employment is not adoption." He said that during the first day, Ambassador Liddy would talk on subjects similar to those in Ambassador Dee's presentation at Mount Fuji. He said there would be a new staff member, referred to as Mike Lee, who would be teaching rapelling and climbing. Captain Dan stated that Colonel Knapp would be the only old committee member attending the first week of the conference. Dan made it clear that he would return with two new committee members for the last three days, for intelligence briefings, legal paperwork requirements, and graduation. So now all the training particulars were now a go. The entire program's scheduling was approved and completed with all the personnel and participants in place. We just needed to wait for the starting gun.

My wife made a special point of mentioning that I must have liked my new home office in the finished basement. During the last few weeks, I had spent more time with the books than with her and the kids. The point she made was quite clear, so I immediately stopped working for several days, took the family to the Columbus Zoo, made two trips to the White Castle, and took in a movie at the Bexley Theater, consuming lots of popcorn and Milk Duds. After that, it was back to work on my talk for the next week at the Christopher Inn. I needed to make a complete review of all the scheduled activities, and determine who on my staff was assigned to which particular training event. The difficult part, which was more important than most people might think, was matching my sixteen bunny rabbits with appropriate and proper code names.

We had decided to break up these lucky selected souls into two teams, hoping to achieve more realistic and interactive life and death games, and wanted to have the code names reflect the differences. Of course, this complicated things a bit. I had to do a lot of deep thinking, but Elwood P. Dowd accidentally provided me the answer. I did a bit of creative thinking while relaxing and playing the piano late one evening, and after enjoying a couple black Russians with the wife. The point struck me when my wife commented on some goofy things I was saying and doing while at the piano.

"You're no Victor Borge. The best car we ever owned was a Plymouth Valiant, and if I had had longer legs as a dancer, we would never have met at Akron University. But fate meant for us to be a couple. So now we are a family of five, and the only additions will be pets associating with your *Harvey* pooka."

That did the trick. One never knows what sets off a light bulb of creative thought, but this relaxing evening did it. The next morning, all the players had their proper stage names and had been divided into two teams. It would be something the staff might appreciate, and they would live with whether they liked it or not.

Team #1
Kaiser - Mr. Lawhead
Fraser - Mr. Badurina
Studebaker - Mr. Titmas
Packard - Mr. St. Amond
Hudson - Mr. Berkich
Tucker - Mr. Iff
Nash - Mr. Ruffin
Edsel - Miss Gabalac

Team #2
Oscar Levant - Mr. Papadopoulos
Jerry Calona - Mr. Murder
Ed Wynn - Mr. Vyas
Eddie Cantor - Mr. Charvat
Jimmy 'The Schnoz' Durante - Mr. Toukan
Louis Prima - Mr. Jupinko
Danny Kaye - Mr. Rex
Martha Raye - Miss Lee

Not bad, if I do say so myself. I would give this list to Colonel Knapp when he arrived at the meeting, and to the staff once we all got situated at Autumn Hills. There I was, sitting in the basement office, laughing to myself and wondering how the individual candidates would take their assigned code names. The only one that concerned me was Edsel for Miss Gabalac, as the razzing could get a little out of hand. But we would just have to see what happened and handle the situation when and if the humor got out of hand. I'd bet my bottom dollar that our Mr. Kitchen would make the first inappropriate remark about this Ford vehicle. Therefore, I would politely ask him to restrain himself before providing him the list with the code names.

Well, the big day had arrived. I needed to get down to the hotel early enough to have lunch, check out all the arrangements, and make sure there are no hang-ups or problems. This would give me sufficient time to review everything, since no one would be arriving before 1400 hours at the earliest, and I could take a look inside the strange building. I had never seen a tall round hotel before, and doubted if any of the others had seen or stayed in such an odd structure. Putting all these factors together would make for an interesting and exciting meeting of the new creature clan.

Things had all checked out, so I decided it was time to head for the hotel restaurant to have lunch. The timing turned out to be fortunate; who should walk into the restaurant but good old Colonel Knapp, with the new Liddy the Ambassador. They did not immediately see me — they were talking to the hostess about seating — but I got their attention and invited them over to my table. They seemed pleased that I was there, and we talked some business. I told them the schedule of presentations and gave Colonel Knapp the list of sixteen code names. He did not even look at them. He just put the names in his briefcase and asked me about who would be doing what, and when.

The point was made to Liddy the Ambassador that after all the introductions he would have the stage the next morning, starting at nine o'clock, and then again after lunch, until three o'clock in the afternoon. I let him know the timing was based on a similar presentation that had been made ten years before by Ambassador Dee. Dee's talk had thoroughly covered the Diplomatic Corps, the C.I.A., the N.S.A., the F.B.I., and the little Hoover Boys' operations. He smiled and nodded positively, which made me feel awfully good, and then informed Knapp that he would go from 1530 hours to 1730 hours. I added that he could have as much time as he needed, which was a good public relations move on my part, and told them that I would proceed with my remarks after dinner. I let them know that as for the first day, everyone would get checked in and we would have cocktails and dinner starting at 1830 hours. After dinner, there would be social drinking and relaxation until everyone decided to go to bed. I let them know it would be made clear that there would be no formal introductions that evening; everyone would just be socializing with Mr. What's His Face or Mr. Guess Who.

At the end of our little lunch, I told them how I appreciated their trust and confidence, and said, "For me, gentleman, this is a new adventure; a new beginning attached to the end of the last fairy tale adventure with Gary the Chef and the other members of the ancien régime. So that you will understand my thinking, a favorite quote of mine says it all:

'Isn't it strange,
that princes and kings, and clowns
that caper in sawdust rings

And common people like...
You *and* Me, *are builders for eternity?*
Each *is given a bag of tools, a shapeless mass, a book of rules,*
And *each must make 'ere life has flown...*
a Stumbling Block or a STEPPING STONE.'"

CHAPTER IV
Cellophane Talisman

It was quite interesting, sitting in the lobby lounge area and watching the new group of bunny rabbits checking into the hotel, then envisioning in my mind each of them becoming romping and stomping Pookas with a shillelagh. These young people would soon be repositioning souls as members of the Pooka Brigade. They would soon learn what it meant to peel back the onion and expose its yellow sweetness, or the tear-jerking annoyance of its invisible vapors. During the next four weeks, we needed to teach them to see the invisible and to know when to avoid their natural, instinctive reactions. They had to learn to trust that sixth-sense feeling of hair raising up on the back of the neck.

The trainees would need to be told the story about a jet pilot's reactions when he has a flame out and the fighter jet dives toward the ground. The pilot's natural instinct is to pull back on the stick, so the plane goes back up toward the sky. Wrong! He must resist temptation and ignore his instincts. The pilot must push the stick forward and drive toward the ground, to pick up enough air speed to restart the jet engine.

Enough wasted daydreaming for one day in the hotel lobby. It was probably best that I go to my room and take a short nap before dinner.

The social entertainment after dinner was just right. We had a nice little combo of musicians creating a relaxing environment, with everyone reintroducing themselves and enjoying seeing each other again as the select and chosen few. During the evening, everyone got a kick out of my introductions of Colonel Knapp and Ambassador Liddy as, respectively, "Oh, this is Mr. Nobody, and this is Mr. Somebody." At least everyone got the message of anonymity.

Colonel Knapp and I sat down for a while at a corner table, and he stated, "You should know that Cole is retiring from active duty at the end of the year. You will not be seeing or hearing from him again. He asked me to give you his best wishes. You will not be seeing Captain Dan again, unless there is an extreme emergency and you call that very secret and private Sherwood phone number. Good Captain Dan is moving up the ladder of political intrigue as part of the higher powers, the ones who supervise and direct the new committee members, and he will always have an eye focused on your little group. As for me, I will be involved indirectly as the liaison coordinator, assisting the new committee members when necessary for the next eighteen months. After that, they are on their own. Now I am going to share a little secret with you. I was never a major. I was always a flying colonel, and come January it will be a one-star position. So for the next year, you may refer to me as Mr., Mr. Sir."

Colonel Knapp could not keep a straight face during the last remark, and his attempt at being super-serious failed. Laughing, he suggested that we order a few rusty nails from the bar to toast Colonel Cole, and after that a Manhattan for the benefit of Captain Dan. It sounded good to me, and I was happy to see that everyone was having a nice time. A depressing thought passed through my mind briefly — nine of my former good friends and associates had had the joys of their future lives cut short by the Grim Reaper. For a moment there my eyes started to tear up, but that was not allowed for a Senior Master Pooka.

All good times must end. I yelled over the general chit-chat to inform everyone that it was quite late. They were told that their wake-up call would be at 0530 hours, breakfast at 0630 hours, and the meeting would start sharply at 0800 hours. They were told that hangovers were not allowed, and reminded that everyone had to be extremely alert and attentive, or the rest of the crew would be required to take them to the showers for a sobering-up moment. They all laughed for a second, but got the point, and headed to their little rabbit dens for a good night's rest. I decided to call my wife and tell her I'd be staying in a room at the hotel, since the activities started at six-thirty in the morning. She also realized by my conversation that I might have had just a little too much to drink. Needless to say she was not pleased, and I received a minor lecture about maintaining a professional image.

Everyone was bright, cheery and alert the next morning, which was nice and sunny. When it was time to call the meeting to order, I tapped my water glass with a spoon to get their attention, then stood up to start saying my piece. "Ladies and gentleman, I see that you're all bright and alert. We are going to have a long day today and tomorrow before departing for Autumn Hills. The days after we leave this hotel will get even longer and harder, so enjoy and appreciate these two days of learning and relaxation.

"Now for the introductions — but first, open the envelopes being placed in front of you and review your nametag and table placement card. You will see that you are not who you think you are. This will be the final time that your real last name will be used, along with your code name. After today's meeting, only the given code name will be used for all identification purposes. In the future, we will never use your real name again, and you will never again provide your real name to anyone, or anybody, at any time or any place. The only exceptions will be your home, your school, your church, your employment, your regular military unit, and your civilian friends."

Each individual candidate in the room was introduced. With the introduction came a little of their personal background relating to their education, sports, hobbies, and recognized quirks. Then we told them that they could talk about themselves all they wanted, but without mentioning where they were from, where they were going, or who they were going to be with.

My follow-up remarks were, "Ten years ago, there was another new group of high school graduates sitting in the same position you are in today. We went through the same experiences that you will be encountering throughout your training. The advice given to us then is just as relevant today. At the time, a key trainer said, 'Never ever forget that this miserable training is for your good life and longevity, and that you are never considered expendable. We on this training staff are creating a valuable asset, to be preserved and protected, and there will be no suicide missions. We do not believe in depreciation, depletion or replacement of your skills, talents and special abilities. An important factor was learned early on in this game, and that is, it is hard to replace people, but easy to replace things.' They told us that we were magicians for world peace; you know, the guys who make people vanish. Well, enough said at this point. I will now let your new civics teacher, Liddy the Ambassador, take the center stage. They're all yours, Mr. Ambassador."

The Ambassador's presentation went non-stop the whole morning. After lunch, we thought he was going to run past his three o'clock deadline before ending his portion of the program. He did a terrific job. It was equal to, or better than, the presentation by Ambassador Dee ten years before. He definitely pulled no punches as to the N.S.A., C.I.A., and F.B.I., with all its secret little Hoover Boys' operations. He covered all the bases and left no misunderstandings floating in the air. He definitely needed a good strong drink after his marathon presentation.

The Ambassador started off by telling the recruits that on October 23, 1952, Harry S. Truman signed a very secret charter to create the N.S.A. Prior to that charter, a similar operation was referred to as the S.I.S. He told them that the headquarters were located at Fort Mead, Virginia, and that they were the code-making and code-breaking spy ears for the U.S. of A. He said that the charter granted to them and their spy operations complete anonymity, full funding, and little or no government oversight. In other words, it provided them with an out-of-sight existence, and most of their operations were classified as figments of someone's imagination or hallucinations. He said a common term for many of their super-secret operatives around the world was "no such animals."

He was really getting warmed up, and got into the spirit of things with his meat-cleaver coverage of the C.I.A. He made it clear that they have purpose and value, but had become "holier than thou" by firmly and finally starting to believe their own bullshit. He stated that they had gone from truth, justice, and the American way, to Lex Luthor and the Joker trickery that is questionably sinful, un-American, and which many observers think violates the Nuremberg Code. He made it clear that they have and do violate the civil, legal and personal rights of average American citizens, and even subvert our honorable military personnel. He pointed out that they started going bad when they entered into a working relationship with former Nazis, the Mafia, and the unethical international industrial consortium of economic assholes here and abroad. Add into this their stupid adoption of and beliefs in the principles of psycho-political and psycho-scientific warfare, which brought about their "Projects of Evil" such as M.K. Ultra and their De-Patternization Programs. He noted their covert coup d'etats for personal gain and favor, which have the C.I.A.'s fingerprints everywhere around the throats of many politicians, and finger waves up many generals' rear-ends. Liddy the Ambassador went into great detail in explaining these subjects, and he did not stop there.

Liddy said that most of the Farm Boys were administrators and dedicated spies, but many were real Count Draculas — psychotic, criminal, and seriously perverted independent contractors. These weird people were said to create "fog," the fog of information they used to handle disconnected illegal activities, including outright murder, drug dealing, bribery, extortion, blackmail, prostitution, and maybe even killing U.S. citizens abroad. Liddy made a strong point to never, ever trust any C.I.A. personnel, a fact which was being learned the hard way by the Green Berets in Southeast Asia and Vietnam. Their little secret group really loved their joyriding function of de-population. These guys with tiger cages never really cared who they de-populated, so long as they were tagged as communists first. Liddy rightly pointed out that there were good spooks and bad spooks, and those guys were bad spooks. But he ended with humor, saying that their degrees should be in "Fuck-up Capabilities," and that they could easily qualify for Jimmy Olsen's job at *The Daily Planet*.

The Ambassador was on a roll, and he made his feelings quite clear. He was definitely not finished, but when he unloaded on the F.B.I., he wasn't nearly as tough or nasty as Ambassador Dee had been. He pointed out that the F.B.I.'s so-called image was merely good public relations and was deceptive; that what you see was *not* what you get. However, he felt that — unlike the C.I.A. operatives - at least 95 percent of the F.B.I.'s agents and personnel upheld the ideals of truth, justice, and the American way. He clarified that there were real Hoover Boys — those agents who made up the Hoover Agency and were known for collusion, blackmail, illegal wiretaps, and regularly creating false evidence in order to frame people. He pointed out that this was an extremely dangerous secret within the Hoover operation, and in no way could the Hoover Boys' operations be justified as beneficial to our society.

But he stressed again that the majority were innocent, honest, hard-working employees and naive field agents deserving of respect. His issue was directed at Mr. Hoover and his private club of Hoover Boys; this group of insiders would terminate one's existence without question or even giving it a second thought. He said there was no question that Mr. Hoover has his own bundle of dirty laundry, but he was protected because he has well documented everyone else's dirty laundry. With this dirty laundry, everyone becomes a mutual "got you" in a check and balance position over the barrel, and no one wants to be placed in the barrel.

He put a humorous touch on these remarks by stating that sin begets sin begets sin, and it soon appears that the blind are leading the blind. Therefore, there is no one around who can cast the first stone, but if there was, no one would see the arm that threw the stone. He then posed a question to the group.

"Who, and only who, would have the power after President Kennedy died to bar the door and lock Bobby Kennedy out of the Justice Department gym, which is used by the F.B.I.? You guessed it: Mr. J.E. Hoover." Liddy the Ambassador ended by saying, "The bottom line is, as Mr. Benton — or Chahaus — so often quotes, 'Love many, trust few, and always paddle your own canoe.' But maybe I can now sum it up better with my own personal quote: 'Trusting the C.I.A., the N.S.A., or the F.B.I. would be like trusting a samurai to do your vasectomy.' You see? I've always been afraid of politicians and dogs; I don't know why, since I've never been bitten by a dog!"

Thank God for the needed break. Some strong coffee and an urgent rush to the restroom were way overdue. We all got settled down again after the pause that refreshes. Then Mr. Liddy introduced Colonel Knapp to handle all the administrative details concerning everyone's new covert status as peacekeepers. Colonel Knapp started off by informing them that they had equal status and equal pay, and that their new pay grade rank and benefits would be that of Warrant Officer. This created a little excitement in the room. It reminded me when our group was first given the unbelievable news of being a semi half-assed officer and a gentleman. Then he gave them the kicker — that in public and within their units, they would retain and maintain the image of their current rank and pay voucher status. He told them that the balance of their paycheck would be deposited in beneficial trust accounts in Bermuda.

It was made clear that the amount only became fully vested to them upon final discharge from their military status, and they could request necessary funds after release from active duty for school, marriage, buying a home or car, and any general emergencies. He excited them again by telling them that twenty-five thousand dollars had already been put into their accounts to fund the trusts. He pointed out that it was necessary to go over all the mutual agreements of understanding, covenants of confidentiality and restrictions, and contract terms of service. This part was a little boring, but very necessary. It took up most of his time, but he did make it perfectly clear that they were now very, very secret people, officially nonexistent and invisible persons. He finished by letting them know there were several facts they needed to understand, and not forget, that had been clarified earlier in the meeting.

"It is easy to replace things, but hard to replace people. This fact applies to your value for us. It applies as well to targeted terminations and the effect these will have on people we need to influence and for which we need to provide a motivational seminar — with all this being simply to protect and preserve our country's political and economic goals and objectives.

"The second fact is that you will be the very best, to the point of cocky over-confidence. Your eyes will start to turn brown as your internal bodily fluids start going up into your head. So if you want to stay alive, the rule is, believe not thy own bullshit!

"The third fact is that there is such a thing as a shot that cannot be made. You must know when to fold and throw in your hand, or you may crap out in the wrong game. The point is: never, never play in another man's game, or by his ground rules. Make sure you always force others to play your game, on your terms.

"Fact number four is that 'sand happens!' The object of this training is to learn to prevail over your environment, and not just to survive. The key is to follow the rules of experience and learn everything you can learn while here. If you assimilate this learning experience, you will have a 95 percent chance of enjoying long-term immortality. As they say, mortality is 100 percent, but you do not want to play pinochle with Azrael before your dreams are fulfilled. Any of you who have played golf understand what it means when I say 'sand happens!'

"Now, sand happens often at the wrong time. It is often unexpected, and when one is unprepared for issues of family, marriage, and divorce. That is why you can never, never tell the loved ones you trust anything about this life, for all marriages start off with love and happiness. But then all that love and trust sometimes disappears when one files for a divorce. That is why, after leaving active duty, we will always have excellent cover stories for your family, your employer, your school, and anyone or anything else you deem to be necessary. You will always be talking out of the side of your mouth, and the main mouth will have a permanent sipper — or else!"

When Colonel Knapp was finished, everyone was relieved to get a nice break before dinner. Everyone went to their rooms to put away their materials and freshen up for dinner. One thing that so far had pleased me to no end was that there were no apparent cliques forming between any of these individuals. They were all, including the two girls, staying independently friendly and sociable. After the meeting, both Knapp and Liddy complimented me on the group and noted that they were impressed by what they had seen. I quickly informed them that the good words should be given to Kelsey, Vigorritto, Johnson, and Turner. I wanted them to know that those guys had done all the screening and selection, and that I had only provided the rubber stamp. I asked them to excuse me so I could head to my room before my bladder busted right then and there. After a moment of great relief, I called the wife to tell her the meeting was going great, to let her know I was acting very professional, and that I was getting ready to go down to dinner.

After another excellent dinner, the time for me to give my after-dinner talk arrived. When I had finished, everyone would get to party and socialize for a few hours. Again tapping the glass to got their attention, I began, "Well, gentleman and our lady associates, it has been a long day. My remarks will be on the short side so we can have a couple of hours for a 'getting to know you better' party. Before dinner, I decided to take a walk, in order to get a breath of fresh air. I noticed a bulletin board of announcements posted by the church across the street. Its stated religious point was, 'If you're through with sin, come on in; if not, call Circle 6 - 2150!'

"Hey! I appreciate your laughter, but I just gave all of you a very important piece of information involved with your career. The information was provided deceptively by making a humorous remark. Which one of you can tell me what the important information is, in order to get free drinks and snacks after the meeting? The point is, all of you must continually be observant and alert in your new cellophane existence. This is accomplished by recognizing and seeing the invisible, and always trying to know what 'the shadow knows.' It is what you miss hearing, what you miss seeing, and what you refuse or fail to consider that can cause you serious harm in this profession.

"All of you are now entering a new parallel or alternate world of existence. This is where you think you know who you do not work for. But you will never be quite sure who you *do* work for during this new venture, and this will keep all of you in an 'I do not know' posture. That's why; you cannot give anything away, because this silent and secret group operates in a vacuum. Therefore, no one but you can ever hear the bell. You can rest assured that you're not with the C.I.A., not with the F.B.I. or the N.S.A., but attached to a special shadow government unit of 'bill collectors.' The payment is one's existence as a security deposit to maintain world peace. This ends up meaning the preservation of our freedoms and democracy, and maintaining the balance of power as it relates to economic, social, and political issues outside of the U.S. of A.

"As mentioned to you before, as of now, all of you are so secret that you do not know that you even exist. As invisible and nonexistent beings with big sticks, we welcome you into the Pooka Brigade. In closing, I would like to leave you with the words of Shakespeare, who can state things a lot better than I. This story starts with Horatio, who is Hamlet's friend. He informs Hamlet that a ghost resembling his dead father has been seen on the battlement of the castle. Hamlet decides to confront the ghost, but first he says to Horatio, 'There are more things in heaven and earth, Horatio; than are dreamt of in your philosophy.' Now we are finished. Let's have our party, and then all of you can later go to bed and dream about your philosophy."

That night's little shindig was enjoyable and interesting, and lasted into the early morning hours. Everyone was playing the game; Mr. Packard introduced himself to Oscar Levant, Miss Edsel introduced herself to Martha Raye, and Martha Raye introduced herself to Danny Kaye. Everyone really had fun playing the name game, particularly after a few drinks. I had hoped that the party would be an enjoyable final farewell to their past. They had been told that they could let their hair down until whenever, before they entered the dominion of training hell. During the next day's session, I would be telling them that they had had their last night of fun and relaxation for the next four weeks.

After the long night of partying, we had breakfast before it was time to kick off the meeting. The hope was to keep the sessions from becoming too boring, as some of them might be recovering from a hangover. We started by telling them that their walk-up call would be at 0500 hours every day, and the training would continue until 2200 hours every day. We let them know the basic schedule they would be following on a daily basis. First, physical fitness and self-defense, then breakfast followed by lectures, and then extensive weapons training.

"After lunch there will be special assignments and special war games," I said, "like Capture the Flag, Smuggle the Gig, and King of the Hill. You can be assured that they will be more advanced, more dangerous, and far more exciting than spinning the bottle to see who the scurrying mouse becomes. You know those *Tom and Jerry* cartoons? Well, everyone will get a chance to play Tom, then Jerry, and some will, like in *Looney Tunes*, get to be the little yellow bird who says, 'I tawt I taw a puddy tat!' This may sound a little funny, but our cartoons will have life and death scenarios. After playing our games, everyone goes to supper, unless you were unfortunate enough to lose your portion of the game — meaning you were hypothetically terminated, and therefore your needs for food, money and drinks are very small once you've been declared deceased. After supper there will be special assignments and classes until bedtime.

"You already met most of the training staff earlier, at the Jug Inn, but you will have a few new instructors. They will teach rapelling, cliff climbing, canoeing, archery, jujitsu, the handling of the anlace, and the necktie throat snare. Learn your lessons well here, for there may be a time when you will need to become a praying mantis rather than a stalking cat. If that should fail, you'll need to become a porcupine rather than the scurrying mouse, to prevail and survive an assigned mission. By now, all of you have noticed the Chinese drawing or symbol that has been place on the bulletin board. This is the Chinese symbol for the word **CRISIS**. The first half, called an ideograph, refers to **danger**, and the second half is an ideogram referring to **opportunity**. This new adventure will always be filled with potential danger and adrenaline rushes you will never forget. But you will only enjoy them if you draw on all your knowledge and experience to convert the situation into an opportunity. Our staff has only one objective: to make you the best stalking snipers in the world. Remember that when applying your skills in a time of war, you are just an isolated military sniper. But when applying the skills in peacetime, the term used is assassin. Either way, same-old, same-old; your goal is killing for effect, and to provide an unwanted learning experience to other disinterested parties in the world that we wish to influence.

"To provide you with some tension relief during the training schedule, there will be some free time every Saturday starting at 1700 hours that will last until 1400 hours on Sunday. Every Saturday night, we — the staff — will be hosting a Ben-Bacchus party for your relaxation and entertainment. Where we end up will be a surprise, but a word of warning: the group will always remain together. There will be no socializing to any degree outside of the group, regardless of how many interesting and tempting members of the opposite sex there may be in the civilian world. Tonight is again an official party time, and breakfast will at 0830 hours. It is suggested you eat light, for tomorrow we are going to have a late lunch and some beer. We will be going to a quaint German restaurant, Schmidt's, in an area referred to as German Village. Believe me, I have dined there before with an old German friend, and after the meal you will definitely want one of their special giant cream puffs. Let's call it a day. You will not be seeing me at dinner or at the party tonight, so be kind to Colonel Knapp and Liddy the Ambassador."

My evening was happily spent with the wife and kids. I took them to the BBF Whirling Satellite for hamburgers and fries, and each had their favorite milkshake. Then we went grocery shopping at the local Super Dupper store for needed milk and groceries, and returned home to spend a nice evening together. The next morning the family had breakfast together, consisting of eggs in the center of toast, which we call one-eyed jacks. I drank a lot of coffee, got dressed, and kissed the family farewell.

Due to the heavy traffic, I barely got to the hotel on time. Colonel Knapp was going to start the meeting, with or without me. The morning meeting was handled totally by Knapp and Liddy. They talked about diplomatic operations at embassies, aspects around military intelligence, customs agencies, passport and visa operations, and customary procedures for entry and exit of various countries where our services might be required. They again went over the importance of privacy and secrecy. They told everyone again that they were a nonexistent entity, and that they were nonexistent entities to each other, and that everyone knew there were "no such creatures" on this planet.

Knapp said, "Everyone knows that Harvey is only an illusion; the hallucination of Elwood P. Dowd. In our realm of covert invisibility, Doctor Chumley would never get the opportunity to drink beer under a palm tree in Akron, Ohio with a Pooka."

After the meeting at the Christopher Inn was over, the bus to take us to Schmidt's at German Village arrived. Colonel Knapp told everyone to collect their gear and load it on the bus, and that after our luncheon they would be going directly to their training camp. The military bus and driver had been arranged with some bigwig officer, Talley. We were to contact an officer Forrest at the D.C.S.C. depot every time we needed the bus. Of course, bus transportation had already been prearranged for every Saturday night to get us to and from the Ben-Bacchus parties. Our bus driver, a young soldier, was excellent. He had to be, because the streets in German Village were very narrow, and there was nowhere for him to park the bus at Schmidt's. Colonel Cole told the driver to return in two hours, gave him ten dollars, and directed him to find somewhere to enjoy lunch.

Upon entering the restaurant, everyone was stalled for a minute or two looking at the beautiful pastry case. Everyone ordered a mug of German beer, a big Bahama Mama sausage, and a plate of German potato salad. And yes, afterwards they each had a large cream puff with black coffee. The group was really enjoying themselves, but all good things must come to an end. Colonel Knapp stood up to tell everyone how he and Liddy had enjoyed the time spent with them, and he wished them all success in their training over the next four weeks. Then they were told that he and Liddy would be going their separate ways, while we took our long bus ride to Autumn Hills. He indicated that his and Liddy's flights home would be leaving the Columbus airport in a couple of hours. After everyone had said farewell to them, we all boarded the bus and off we went together, down the "yellow brick road" of Route 33.

The trip to Autumn Hills was quiet. Everyone relaxed and enjoyed the scenery. I was the only one to break the silence for several minutes when I said, "How many here grew up with your mother getting your first set of encyclopedias from the grocery store? Well, that encyclopedia was most likely a set of Funk & Wagnalls that you cut your learning teeth on. Right down that little country road is Lithopolis, Ohio, the home of Funk and Wagnalls."

That got the attention of about half the group. It was interesting to see them sit up and look down the empty road at nothing due to a memory. We had about an hour to go, and the bus remained a quiet place for everyone to think and relax. It was a pleasant ride, and before we knew it, we were at the entrance to Autumn Hills. We noticed that the identification sign was covered with a huge notice of closure. The sign stated that the camp was closed for seasonal repairs and maintenance. I noticed a work crew fixing up the entry area; painting the fencing and clearing the drainage ditches alongside the road. There was road resurfacing equipment sitting in the general area. Two of the workmen came over to the bus, talked with the driver, and then opened the double swing gate to let us enter. No question about it; even in civilian work clothes, these were military personnel. Most likely it was the Army Corps of Engineers doing the maintenance work, and the several personnel controlling the restrictions of movement around the area were no doubt military police. The little frame hut up the road, just inside the trees, was probably used for night security personnel. It was quite clear that they planned to keep the area air-tight from outsiders and allow no nosy on-lookers.

We drove up the narrow road about two miles, and then into a clearing with many campsite buildings on the hillside. Standing and waiting for us with serious and stern looks were Vigorritto, Johnson, Kelsey, Turner and two other guys. The two must have been Mr. Chop-Chop Kennedy and Mr. Lee, the mountain climbing and parachuting expert. The bus driver pulled up by the flagpole that was in the middle of an assembly area for retreats. This was a nice area that could be used as a miniature parade ground. Everyone was told to get their duffle bag or suitcase from the back of the bus and quietly go stand in front of the staff. Once there, they were to set their bag down beside them and remain at attention, to show total respect.

Well, well! It appeared that the staff had decided to let
Sergeant Turner play head honcho for this training operation.
Our new Mr. Spider stepped forward to welcome everyone to
the camp. He had a powerful image. He made all of the staff
introductions and then handed out the cabin assignments. He
directed them to stow their gear, make their beds, and relax
or go sightseeing until dinner, which would be in the main
administration lodge at 1830 hours. He announced that I would
be the speaker after dinner, and informed them that there
would be no alcoholic beverages of any type allowed during
the next four weeks. He also made it clear that there would be
no mail or phone service, in order to maintain absolute privacy
and secrecy. He told them to pay strict attention to what he
said and to be sure they clearly understood, then said very
firmly and sternly that there would be absolutely no initiations,
hazing, harassing, or annoying of anyone at the camp, period!
Then he dismissed them.

We staff members went into the main lodge, sat around a
table, and let our hair down. After greetings and handshakes,
Kelsey placed a cooler full of ice-cold beer in the middle of the
table, and Vigorritto made it clear that we were the only ones
allowed to violate the Spider's rules on alcohol.

Now I had to comment, "My friends, it is often our nature
to goof off, clown around, and drink too much, but not here!
Even at our Saturday night Ben-Bacchus parties, we are to be
the high and mighty men of responsibility, and not set a poor
example. Our role is responsible supervision and control over
the group's environment at all times. We are to be the mature
babysitters who will drink and party only in moderation, and
they get to let off steam while under our protection.

"Now, during these next four week we are to be sociable
and friendly, but not friends. You will be very cold, stern, and

completely impersonal. Please try not to shown any form of favoritism, and be a fair and strict disciplinarian. Please control and restrict your humor. When pissed off at them, do not search and destroy. Be merciful, fair and unforgiving. Remember how it was for us? It is also a life and death learning experience for them. We know they are naïve, full of stupidity, and are seeking ego fulfillment. They also have a desire for adrenalin rushes, just like we did ten years ago. By the way, when you're at the mirror tomorrow morning shaving, take a good look at yourself and remember it might be any of them looking back at you. Thank you for this nice cold beer. Let's discuss any issues involving the training schedule, and relax until dinner."

A nice surprise at dinner; the food that the military cooks provided was excellent, and one cook reminded me of Chef Luby at I-Corps in Korea. They set the food out on a serving counter and we helped ourselves, then picked our own drinks and desserts. They had set up two parallel tables that seated twelve people each, with sufficient space in between to move around freely. Once meals were finished, everyone could exit into another room for private meetings. The other military personnel had their own private dining room and recreation area off the other side of the kitchen, which provided them plenty of privacy. We later learned that they had their own makeshift bar, with plenty of alcohol, soft drinks and snacks. They also had a bumper pool table, several nice dartboards, a Ping-Pong table, and two television sets, but all of this was off-limits to our staff and crew.

When the evening meal was over, we all got up and went into the other room. As we shut the door, two young men came into the dining room and sat down at one of the tables, to guarantee that our meeting would not be interrupted. The meeting room had a table across the front with a podium in the middle. There was a large blackboard at the front of the room, and the rest of the room had four large tables set up classroom style. The program was now all mine, so I went up to the podium and started my little conversational talk with the troops.

"The die is cast, and you are all going to become elite Pookas with the Pooka Brigade. By now, all of you have realized from the earlier presentations that the less you know, the less you can unintentionally tell, or be forced to tell under pressure. This factor is extremely important for the benefit and protection of your comrades. The only thing — and most important thing — that you will need to control is your mouth. The imaginary zipper of silence across your mouth that we, by contract, have placed there with an 'or else' is for good reason, so that you can avoid unwanted consequences. This covert game of intrigue, skullduggery, pretext, innuendo and subterfuge requires strict and absolute discipline. But a casual, nonchalant laissez-faire attitude will lead you to experience rigor mortis. The real focus of this training is on your staying alive. The target acquisition is only a 30 percent risk factor, but escaping from and prevailing over your stalking cat is a 70 percent risk factor. Once you make the shot, you are no longer an invisible or unknown entity. As another trainer once said, 'The winner will be the person who comes out of the bear cave alive.'

"We do not care about the leftist or rightist problems in the world. Also, we couldn't care less about who caused the problem, what the problem is, or why it is a problem. Our only care is what it is that the higher powers considered a problem. We are only called on to treat the problems; the causes of the problems in this world are not our concern. The powers above make the decisions as to whether it is easier and cheaper to terminate the problem than to find a difficult solution for the causes of the issues at stake. Therefore, gentleman, we are the spooks that protect the castle's battlement from the outside. Of course, after the drawbridge is back in place you will find yourself on the opposite side of the moat. That places you out there in the open world, all by your lonesome, and you must know how to become an unnoticed, invisible, walking shadow.

"Enough of this serious crap. So, how many of you have solved the puzzle concerning my humorous comment about the vitally important information disclosed on the church's sign? No problem! I did not expect anyone to be prepared to start playing the game, for the secret information you will need to know, and must know, is Circle 6-1250. This information goes along with one of the most important new words in your expanded vocabulary, and that is to know when one is to use the word *apostrophe.* The phone number is the primary contact number that you will always call first when notified of a potential mission, or if you get involved in some difficult situation. Legally, we can contact you for any reason or valid circumstance. The new word will let you know if someone you know, or a stranger you do not know, is claiming to be part of our group. If they do not know how to play our little game, avoid them, vanish, or terminate them with prejudice.

"All of us at Jug Inn were impressed with your mental and physical credentials, and particularly with your diverse language skills. We are quite fortunate in the fact that nine of you speak Spanish, and I hope you keep practicing and improving your skills while here. I see that Vyas and Toukan understand and speak Arabic, since one is from northern India and the other is Palestinian. Of course it might be assumed, and would be expected, that our two ladies studied French in high school. This could be useful in Africa if we disguise them as missionaries. Papadopoulos speaks Greek and a little Turkish, Charvat speaks perfect Italian, and Jupinko speaks excellent Russian, even better than his family speaks Hungarian. Good Badurina is a nice Croatian, even though I preferred Ustasa. Dobra, Cockostay! So that we don't let the rest of you good ol' boy English speakers with American slang and drawls down, we are going to make sure you learn a foreign language. Come Monday, all of you will be given a language course on how to speak the King's English, as they do in Britain.

"We have decided to bring a xylophone into our dining facilities for entertainment, since Mr. Nash appears to be the Scott Joplin or Hubby Blake of the musical sticks. Prior to calling him Ruffin the Nash, we were planning to call him Mr. Red; have you ever seen anyone of his race with red hair? The red hair surprised even good old Sergeant Spider. By now, all of you have realized that we have been using your last names quite freely, even though previously you were told never to use anything but your code names. It will be only these names that show up on you name tags and identification papers. We give you permission — only within our private little group over the next four weeks — to use your last name with your code name. You will never, ever use these in front of or around anyone outside of this group. Only on missions, assignments, or around committee members are you strictly ordered to use only one form of identification for recognition — your given confirmation code name. The only thing ever to be written on documents, forms, name tags, or even signed by you — within or outside of our operations — is your code name. No problem here, for the higher-ups have a unique system to match up your existence with your nonexistence. As with Levant to Papadopoulos, Miss Edsel to Gabalac, Mr. Prima to Jupinko, and Miss Ray to Lee, etc.

"Since everyone here is going to become blood brothers and sisters between only ourselves, we allow variances on rules, so we all have the benefit of getting to know each other better in a more comfortable manner. You can then refer to each other as Mr. Iff the Tucker, Mr. Vyas the Ed Wynn, Mr. Titmas the Studebaker, and Mr. Charvat the Eddie Cantor, and so on. All of the staff members have code names which are different from the code names we had during our previous period with the group. At this session only, you may refer to us by our last names which you already know, even though our name tags say Mr. Chahaus, Mr. Kitchen, Mr. Footloose, Mr. Junkman and Mr. Spider. Mr. Chop-Chop and Mr. Climber will remain anonymous, for there will be no long-term relationship here.

"The staff realizes this is a weekend, but this is not a formal training schedule weekend. Since all of you have had it easy so far, there is no need for rest, relaxation, and Ben-Bacchus entertainment. Starting at 0530 tomorrow morning, you will follow an assigned training schedule of times and places you will be gathering daily throughout the next four weeks. There will be no serious training today. The instructors will just be informing you about your training, what you will be learning, and what will be expected of you at each session. After dinner tomorrow night, you'll get to hear me ramble on again. The purpose will be to provide you inspirational thoughts for dreaming about your future. Now I would like to close with a famous quote from Robert Frost,

"'The woods are lovely dark and deep, I have many promises to keep, and many miles to go before I sleep.'

"Ladies and Gentlemen! We, your training staff, are your consultants as to your new alternative life. They say consultants are people who put a price tag on common sense. This is very true, but your consultants here will point out to you that the price tag now is your life, if you do not use common sense. You are going to get very little sleep during the next four weeks. There will be many miles of learning to go before you sleep, and then you will be able to keep your promises to God, country, duty and honor. So goodnight, Mrs. Calabash, wherever you are. We know where your ass is, and who it now belongs to.

CHAPTER V
"Once a Child of Clay"

We said goodnight to our flock of chicks. The next morning, we would wake up these naïve, innocent teenagers and start transforming them from bunnies into rabbits. Then they will be converted from kittens into preying cats, and from a scurrying mouse into a dangerous porcupine. When we are finished with them, they will certainly no longer be daddy's little girl or mama's big boy who left home to join the military.

For me, looking into the mirror while shaving brings back memories of Memorial Days past; the days when I was president of the Hi-Y, hoping to have a date for the prom, and ending my term as Master Counselor of DeMolay. Joining the military was my way of gaining independence and experience in life. This resulted in my being chosen, screened and selected for training as a displacement specialist. My new status on the following Memorial Day was that of one highly trained master assassin. Now ten years later, during another Memorial Day period, the powers that be have selected me to be the master trainer for new covert terminators and expediters. Thank God I was able to get my hands on the best training staff in the world, for the best was needed in order to mold these boys and girls into the most dangerous people in the world. Once trained, they can play the most dangerous covert game in the world, and for the unrecognized glory and benefit of their mother country, the U.S. of A.

A hypothetical thought: Was the potter with the potter's wheel who molds wet clay into beautiful pottery ever a piece of wet clay himself? At what point in time did someone mold him into a potter? The fact is, I was now the shepherd and not part of the flock. It was far easier being part of the flock, where my only concern was outwitting the fox and hoping not to be neutered or slaughtered by the big bad wolf.

Oh, well. Time to rise and shine. The young people would be doing their training things. I would get to relax while overseeing the daily activities and preparing for my next after-dinner talk. The reality of the little guessing game of responsibility sits hard on one's shoulders, particularly when it is I who must decide who get the opportunity to live a while longer or to become a shadow of death. We will all be hoping that my Pookas are smarter and quicker than the Grim Reaper, and survive. This new burden and the serious challenge of responsibility will definitely help me empathize with the character of Elwood P. Dowd when he said, *"I've wrestled with reality for years, and I'm happy. I finally won out over it."*

We could not have asked for a nicer or more beautiful day. It was a perfect day for the staff to hold their preliminary instruction sessions outside on the lawn area, which had the benefit of picnic tables. With the staff's day's work completed, it was time to gather the flock for an excellent dinner. Everyone appreciated the food, and after dinner everyone gave the kitchen staff and the chef a rousing round of applause for their hard work. My turn for round two of the indoctrination and public relations talks had arrived.

"Before getting started, my good people, please give a round of applause to your training staff for the nice, easy sessions you had today. Starting tomorrow, and every day thereafter, you may not be in such a good mood or want to show your appreciation to the training staff. As you may have guessed by now, I am the good guy overseer of this training program. The rest of the staff has the job of making you or breaking you over the next four weeks. You must listen to everything they say. You will do everything they tell you to do. You will respect the fact that they went through the same nasty program ten years ago, but then it was six weeks of hell. Their job here will be to transform you from whippersnappers into mythical creatures who are not afraid of the dark but cause other people to be afraid of it. During our training days, someone stated the issue in a slightly different way by saying, 'Yea though I walk through the valley of the shadow of death, I will fear no evil, for I am the meanest son-of-a-bitch in the valley!' So all of this should explain, and help you understand your new Jekyll and Hyde existence.

"Since I am the good guy, I present to all of you a little package being passed out at this time. Do not assume this is a Greek bearing gifts. As you open your package, you will see that all of you have been given a chess set. All of you will be expected to become competent chess players before this school is finished. Those of you who play chess will teach the others how to play. These are the first basic rules you must learn to follow:

- Remember that mobility is everything.
- Reduce your pawn moves to a minimum.
- Control the center squares.
- Never move the same pieces over and over, time and time again.
- Play out the Queen early.
- Castling (The Rook) with the King putting it in a safe direction.
- Kill enough Knights and Bishops along the way, and the rest is up to you for prevailing and surviving.

These are strategies for all of your logistics planning as a sniper before you start playing your cat and mouse games. If you follow these rules religiously, you will live well beyond your missions. The training staff can guarantee you that Sergeant Spider will make all of you competent chess players. He will be pounding into your heads the first principle of your new profession: that distance creates safety, along with silence and invisibility. He will train you to be like a submarine; one that runs silent, deep and secretly, and delivers the kill silently as with an on-target torpedo, then disappears into the deep.

The sergeant, though he is not a musician, will be teaching you metronome shooting skills to help you stay calm, focused, and maintain your concentration. You will learn to think with a steady, relaxed beat when focusing on your target. Finally, supplementing this concept will be Mr. Footloose Johnson. He will be teaching you how to be a chameleon by making sure you are using camouflage properly, by blending in with the nature of the terrain within your Gillie suit, and how to always remain incognito enough so that others will think you are just an apparition. If you liked the comics as a youth, Johnson will definitely remind you of Mandrake the Magician. He will always be pounding into your head and talking about creating misdirection, illusion, and out-of-sight moments.

"Our Mr. Junkman Vigorritto is a horse of a different color. He is one of the best at teaching someone how to pounce like a stalking cat and materialize at the perfect moment for the sudden death strike of a praying mantis. He was once referred to as a clandestine expert at chicanery, and you never want to become a central part of his shenanigans. Of all the comics characters we know, he is The Shadow.

"Good Mr. Vig is an expert at close-up kills. He will show you that a number two pencil and a good hat pin are both very dangerous weapons, and he will introduce you to the very secret 'Fletch Gun' and a 'Super Silent 22' caliber pistol. He'll prove to you that both weapons are excellent performers within five meters. These two weapons are considered invisible tools of the trade that are easily concealed. When used, the poor target will never know what hit him, and by then you will have faded into the surrounding environment. For distance shots of one-hundred meters plus or minus, silencers will be a standard item for use, but longer shots will be normal bang-bangs; the reason being that the extended distance provides for more cover and safety.

"The best way to describe the Kitchen Man Kelsey is a knavery, finessing, roguish wheeler-dealer, and never to be underestimated. This dude is quite deadly up close and personal, and at nine-hundred meters. He can leave a mark on someone that they will never forget, so he perfectly fits the comics' character of The Phantom. Good Mr. Kelsey will teach you how to become the undetectable hocus-pocus porcupine, and then how to safely de-rattle the rattlesnake that is blocking you path. These points are extremely important for you as a sniper. Once you convert to the scurrying mouse, the primary issue will be how to finagle yourself out of any problems that may occur.

"I strongly advise you to take good notes and learn everything you can from these proven professionals. In the past, these guys have put their money where their mouths are. Even still, you push them to learn more, more, and more. You will also have sessions presented by two military doctors and survival experts. They will discuss drugs, poisons, killing points on the body, and when ferns and sumac are poisonous and when they are not. They will give you one basic rule never to forget: berries white, death in sight. You will love these sessions. Again, take good notes and memorize everything. One interesting thing I learned during my training session was how to take two flashlight batteries and fine steel wool to start a blazing fire. You will all be mesmerized and want to hear a lot more from these two amazing guys.

"Now take your maps of southeastern Ohio out of the folders. Use your ink pens to mark certain locations that will be mentioned. Once you start playing the war games eight days from now, only your memory and a compass will guide your way to success. There will be no maps allowed for traveling references. Pay special attention to the Wayne National Forest areas and the Hocking Hills State Park. Put special emphasis on Old Man's Cave, Ash Cave, Cantwell Cliffs, Cedar Falls, and in particular Tar Hollow and Burr Oak. Now focus on the little town of Enterprise on the Hocking River, note the Lake Hope area, and see the two little hole-in-the-wall towns of Glouster and Trimble. Your big test will be between Gallipolis and Ironton when you're following Route 141, against tobacco farmers and drug dealers with bows and arrows, spike traps and nasty dogs. You will look like hunters, and you will be carrying a proper weapon. The weapons are not so you will look for problems or that you are hoping to cause problems. They are not to be fired period, unless some surprised drug dealers decide to do you bodily harm. The joke is that many of these drug guys are welfare recipients on the dole as hick hillbillies, but are well off and have nice vacation homes in Florida. They never own these luxury homes; they just rent them as elite, first-class wheeler-dealers. They also have their alter-ego hangouts in Las Vegas and Miami, where they clearly are not bumpkins, hayseeds, or white trash yokels.

"Now, besides learning chess for tactics, you will be required to learn the manual alphabet of hand sign language used by the deaf. This will allow you to communicate silently in dangerous environments. It's possible that you're starting to get the picture, and realizing that you will have less free time and sleep than you had expected. Remember, every hour you are awake means that you are not dead, and that should be a good feeling of relief. Oh, by the way, I just remembered that one of you made a comment about my fancy swagger stick. You should know that it is not a swagger stick. This fancy little thing is just to keep my hand occupied, and is referred to as a quirt. It is carried with pride, since two previous Pooka friends and I confiscated it from four tough Texans in a Laredo bar a couple years ago. Those big tough cowboys thought we were sissy northern city boys, and did they ever misread the situation. There will probably be a time in each of your lives where you will try very hard to be nice, even overly friendly, to avoid trouble, but some people will read this as weakness. They will keep pushing the envelope and never see the real you. The surprise will be that you can terminate their existence in a matter of seconds. That's just life, for the world is full of assholes, and you must learn to ignore and avoid them.

"Well, let's all call it a night. You are going to need all the sleep you can get, since tomorrow officially starts the hell week of advanced basic training every day, and every day after that, for the next four weeks. You may see me around, but you will not be officially hearing from me until next Sunday evening. Oops! I forgot to tell you that all of you will be taking comprehensive tests every Sunday afternoon, between 1400 hours and 1800 hours, on what you have learned during the week. Starting tomorrow morning at 0530 hours, you are officially in the hands of and under the control of the training staff. I wish all of you well, and may you all live through the nights."

The staff knew I would not be around for the next three days, and that I was riding back to Columbus that night with some of the military personnel. They didn't know I was going home to be with the wife and kids. They were probably thinking I would be attending a staff or committee meeting at Fort Hayes, or at the D.C.S.C. depot. Being home with the family was nice, and I devoted my entire time to the wife and children. We had fun, playing a lot of card games and board games, and of course the children wanted me to take them to White Castle for their favorite treat of miniature hamburgers. Only about one hour per day was dedicated to my personal business operations, and only a few minutes used to peruse the week's schedule and activities being staged at Autumn Hills. The wife was told that the faculty instructors at the Ohio University Insurance Conference in Athens were excellent. The point was made that we were fortunate to get the top professors from Ohio University and Rio Grand College to present the academic program, for where else could one get a full year of insurance credited programs in only thirty days? I let her know that Mr. Wiseman had agreed to take charge of the meeting on a daily basis, and better still, that my two main Connecticut insurance companies had agreed to cover the cost, on the condition that they could include forty to fifty of their top producers who needed special training in the estate and business planning areas. Where else could anyone in this business obtain an Estate and Business Underwriting (E.B.U.) degree with certification in merely thirty days? All I had to do was be there four days during the week to give talks and help with the monitoring of testing programs.

When my time at home was over (it was appreciated by the family), I told the wife that the school had arranged, through their R.O.T.C. program, for me to have a vehicle to travel back and forth from Athens. The wife drove me to the D.C.S.C. depot to pick up a military Scout jeep from the motor pool area. This would be a regular means of transportation to get around, without using my personal car; I did not think it would look good for me to be driving my personal car in and out of Autumn Hills, particularly when everyone else was doing all the nasty hard work. The Scout jeep would provide the image of a more active duty status.

I got up on Thursday morning at four o'clock, kissed the wife goodbye, and headed down the road for Autumn Hills. While making the drive, I was thinking that the camp caretaker and his family got a great deal while we were using his facility. He had been sent with his family to a one-week training school at Fort Collins, Colorado, and then to some large camping facility for more practical hands-on training in New Mexico — all expenses paid. After that, he and the family were provided a nice Coleman camper for a vacation throughout the West for two more weeks — again, all expenses paid. This guy and his family had gotten a deal and a real treat, covertly paid for by Uncle Sam. They could never have afforded a vacation like that on their own. And when they returned to the camp, it will have been refreshed, renewed and fixed up with new paint, with the roads resurfaced and all maintenance problems corrected. What a deal!

The security workmen were surprised to see me pulling into the entry gate area so early. But after a very close look, they let me into the restricted area. Everyone was in the process of getting up, so I went into the main building, where the kitchen staff was already hard at work preparing for breakfast. I sat down and poured myself some coffee, and waited until the rest of the crew arrived. The staff was a bit surprised to see me sitting there with coffee in hand. They indicated that things were going smoothly and that they had not been disappointed with any of the recruits so far. This pleased me immensely, and I thanked them for their hard work. Then I informed them to end their afternoon session at 1700 hours so that we could have a short meeting before dinner. Vigorritto made a comment about the Scout parked outside, and stated that he had owned one of the International Harvester Scout four-wheel drive vehicles for the last four years. He mentioned how much he loved the vehicle when going to the beach and sand dunes areas, and when hunting out in the rural countryside. I told the staff that the powers thought the vehicle was needed for getting around to necessary meetings and planning sessions in Columbus.

My day was spent observing the reactions of the recruits, and the attitude and performance of the staff; doing what they say a good spy does — watching, looking, listening, and keeping the mouth shut. I paid special attention to the girls, and thought I should make some special comments at the meeting. The staff showed up sharply at 1700 hours. The recruits were tickled to death at getting a nice long break before dinner, and maybe some extra time to do homework. My first questions to the staff were, "How are the girls holding up? Are they holding their own with the guys?"

The staff provided positive answers, and made it clear that they were all impressed with the girls, so far! I told the staff to be somewhat lenient and forgiving on their physical skills and attributes during the coming weeks, but not on the technical skills and issues. The "why" was simple: they would be more likely to be assigned missions that would require close-up termination in private surroundings, or crowed public areas within five meters of the targeted person. It was made clear that we were to make them the most effective, dangerous, and deadly weapons in our arsenal. Necessity would require us to make sure they are the best at jujitsu, and that we teach them how to flip and use a straight razor. After that, we would show them the trick of putting a razor blade between their fingers and slapping the side of the throat or face of the targeted person, or to down anyone who might interfere with their mission.

The fact of life in the predominantly male culture and thinking of the world is that women are innocent, inferior, and have only sexual attributes. This is what they would capitalize on. Because their sex and looks have a distracting benefit for them, unavailable to us male performers. Most of the time the defending stalkers and searchers will be looking for male assassins, and not searching for noticeable persons other than men after the hit. They seldom expect such shy, inhibited, inferior women to be capable of such manly deeds. It became Mr. Johnson's job to educate them on how to become method actors, and how to use out-of-sight moments and makeup for disguise and deception. We wanted these two girls to be molded into our best elite assassins. This did not mean we favored them and/or neglected the others. We wanted the girls and the others to be the very best at long-shot kills under adverse conditions in both urban and rural areas.

No one disagreed with my thinking, and none of the staff had any complaints or conflicting opinions. Only Kelsey mentioned that everyone had best get through the first week in one piece, so that we could enjoy Mr. Benton's first Ben-Bacchus party that Saturday night. They all wanted to know where the party would be held. I informed them that it was a big secret, and that everyone would know once the bus arrived at the destination. I told them to make sure to tell the troops to clean up well, wear their best casual civvies, and be on their best behavior. Then it was time to see what type of excellent dinner the chef and kitchen staff had prepared for us that night.

Their first Ben-Bacchus party on Saturday night was quite nice, and it gave everyone the relaxing break they needed. They had the benefit of being able to sleep later on Sunday, and having only light classes Sunday afternoon until dinner. That Sunday would be my last major after-dinner talk, thank goodness. The recruits might have wished there were more talks, whether they liked them or not, once they had seen what was in store for them on the other Sunday nights to follow, when there would be no mercy on their souls.

When it was time to talk once more, I got behind the podium to get things moving. "Our little group of centurions: I sincerely hope that you enjoyed the first week of light indoctrination and training. It will become more difficult once you start rapelling off cliffs and rock climbing on similarly dangerous cliffs throughout the Hocking Hills. You must make sure that Mr. Lee the Climber becomes one of your best friends. This will be particularly necessary when he teaches you how to jump out of a perfectly good plane. The powers above tried to convince me to jump out of a plane once, in Egypt. I said no way, and shot the instructor. Just kidding! Instead, they packaged me into a Campbell soup can called a submarine and gave me a claustrophobic drive under the deep blue Mediterranean Sea. Therefore, you must be prepared for anything and have a working knowledge of just about everything.

"I hate to keep bringing up repetitive items, but it is rather amazing — when you're considered to be so secret — that you officially as covert persons do not exist. Those supreme beings above you think that someone may only exist to do nonexistent things. The thing that is even more surprising, once realized, is that those powers that be do not really know what we do or how we do it. They consider us as arrangers to get things done; as soon as possible, and in an efficient and effective manner. The people upstairs know the what-for, and they decide the why, but they do not want to know the how, the when, and the where. They consider us to be some type of secret intermediaries between them and some earthly disease. In a way they are right, since they provide us the nine-millimeter note, and then expect us to deliver it in person.

"So! We have nonexistent people, giving nonexistent orders to nonexistent expediters, for secret nonexistent people to do nonexistent things. Therefore, the accounting standard in this world of politics and economics is zero times zero equals not a real zero, but minus one, minus two, or minus three that will become a nonexistent zero. The political mathematics in this world is not the algebra you learned in school. Maybe it is 'triggernomics' that makes the world go around, and not trigonometry. No wonder the woman holding the scales of justice wears a blindfold; she does not want to see the real truth for achieving the perceived justice in balancing world economics, politics, social issues, and mineral rights. The truth is that justice is not blind. It simply does not want to see how it is carried out in the real world, to protect and preserve our freedoms and our democracy in the world order of things. So the object of all this training is complete invisibility, for your success and safety, so that you leave no footprints in the sand.

"We are now finished for the evening. It is still early, so if anyone wants to sit around and talk a little bit, or discuss anything personal, that is fine with me. I am just going to sit here with my coffee and have another piece of the chef's delicious apple pie."

The first person to speak up was Miss Gabalac the Edsel, and she asked a question that got everyone attention.

"You made some interesting references about things. Without us getting too personal, what is the story about you? The why about you? And the who about you?"

My remarks were simple and direct. "Okay! That is a fair question. My general, impersonal answer would probably be applicable to all the staff members in one degree or another, only our similar experiences that created good and bad memories would vary. First the key people of influence, starting with Sergeant Turner, our Mr. Spider. He once knocked the cockiness out of me, got me to screw my head on straight, and made me a very efficient-thinking sniper. There were several times when his recalled training and advice actually saved my life.

"Next, a person who was undoubtedly the best self-taught and self-trained sniper I've ever known. This guy had produced way over a hundred kills, and he taught me never to get mad and lose control. He always said to just think, thoroughly plan, and then calculate to get even with controlled patience. This man, Joe Kutec, was a top Korean sniper. He deserved many honors for his work during and after the Korean War, but he is probably remembered only by me and Sergeant Turner. I would like to think that a lot of his talent and abilities rubbed off on me during the time I spent with him.

"Why do I appreciate this man? Because during my first real test of a putting the pedal to the metal mission, I temporarily froze up with fear and insecurity until Joe literally kicked me back to my senses. Finally, when all was said and done, I got nauseous, quite sick, and had a painful, pounding headache. Good Joe did not fault me, did not report me, but he did say, 'No fear, no worry, a learning experience.' He then assured me it would not happen again, for my dues were paid by the experience.

"Me? I think like a deist, act like a Freemason, could be called a humanist, and totally disagree to some extent with Voltaire, the philosopher who said, 'I may disagree with what you say, but I will defend unto dead your right to say it.' What an asshole, in his time and ours. The statement is just bad, bad, bad, and wrong. Most certainly this view would not be applicable to Tojo, Hitler, Mussolini, Stalin, or our own Senator Joseph McCarthy. There are some other philosophers that I might give a temporary pass on, based on their writings, if their writings are to be believed and are not in conflict with their actions. My final decisions are always based on the way people walk, not the way they talk. Therefore, I am still contemplating the fate of Mao Zedong and Che Guevara. But it is always best to play it safe by never trusting a philosophical martyr or a religious zealot. The point is, we are not in this business for Jesus, Moses or Muhammad. We're only in this business to protect our freedoms and democracy. This includes protecting our personal economic interests in the world from evil people, evil governments, and evil things. Nothing more than that, period! So all that can be said is, 'Damn it, Janet,' since we can only remove the cause, not the symptoms. Therefore, we are hopefully the good guys, trying to do something right rather than nothing at all. Doing nothing means the wrong guys get their way. Our actions are called preemptive, preventative medicine.

"Well, maybe my comments are a bit too much, and you were told more than you needed to know from Miss Gabalac's question. But that's the me, the why of me. And now I am going to enjoy my pie and coffee before it's too late."

But Mr. Berkich the Hudson spoke up. "I am sure everyone here would agree that we would all like to thank you for the nice party last night. It was appreciated by all of us."

Then everyone came up to tell me how they had enjoyed the party, and that they could hardly wait to see what was in store for the next Saturday.

Undoubtedly, my response to Miss Edsel's question satisfied everyone's curiosity. All the recruits got up, said 'thank you,' and left the room without further questions, to continue their studying before going to bed. The staff and I spent the next hour or so enjoying our evening snack, bullshitting each other about nothing, and relaxing before hitting the sack. The rest of the week would involve a lot of trying and stressful training of the young recruits. But so far they all seemed to be holding up well after their first week's sessions, and it was quite nice to know that they enjoyed the first Ben-Bacchus party on Saturday night.

Before we knew it, the week was over and Ben-Bacchus party number two was enjoyable. The bus arrived on time, the recruits had all cleaned up spic and span, everyone boarded the bus, and off we went, north up Route 33 to Columbus. Everyone was having a talkative and relaxing good time on the bus, and about halfway there I pointed out a restaurant where one of the parties would be held. It was a place referred to as Fred Taylor's restaurant, since the Ohio State basketball coach tended to hang out there a lot. But before that, I showed them the famous tavern owned by Lou "the Toe" Groza. The group needed to be reminded that he was once a famous place-kicker for the Cleveland Browns. They all seemed to enjoy my tour guide comments along the way.

When we started getting close to the party destination, I informed them that we were going to the Jai Lai Restaurant, a favorite hangout of Woody Hayes's (the great Ohio State football coach) for entertaining people. I let them know that they would really enjoy their meal, and that we might be lucky enough to meet and see Coach Hayes. It was obvious that the crew loved the cocktail party, the fabulous meal, the great desserts, and the after-dinner drinking and social hour. Once the party was over, everyone boarded the bus back to Autumn Hills. They were told that if they had enjoyed that evening's activities, the next Saturday's Ben-Bacchus party would drive them nuts, and they would not want to leave its location.

The staff left for their quarters, and I jumped into the Scout and headed home to enjoy the wife and children for another three days. It was nice being home with the family, but my focus was on the much tougher program being provided to the recruits during the next week. I was hoping they would all do well, without any serious injuries. In the coming week, they would be playing modified adult games of Capture the Flag and King of the Hill, and would have twelve security jocks trying to capture a three-man sniper group that had hit their assigned target. The sniper team would have to get back to their retrieval point, unknown to the security jocks, before they were declared killed or captured. The security team would not know where the shot was being made from until the shot hit the target, and the sniper teams would have only a one-hundred-fifty- to a two-hundred-meter lead on the pursuers. Everyone would get their turn on a three-man sniper team until they got it right or were declared hypothetically dead.

After that, they would start playing Kick the Can and Smuggle the Gig. With these games, security would know there will be a hit, and would have set up a protective perimeter of one hundred and fifty meters around the area, to protect the target. Then one sniper would have to get close enough to make the mark, without getting caught, being noticed, or being captured or killed by security. Here, the sniper's decision is to make a risky long shot or chance a risky approach, and then hopefully get back to the retrieval point figuratively alive. During these games, one person plays the potential target, and while the game is in play, they act as a critical observer to critique the event. The intent is for them to come to the same unbiased conclusion, either good or bad, as the evaluations by the staff trainers. The only real concern is that there would not be too many serious cuts and bruises, and that anyone who might be damaged a little would still be able to complete all of their training, without further complications.

Now that my three days with the family were over, I got up again at 0400 hours and headed back to camp to see how well the troops were doing in their second week. Again the security personnel were a little surprised to see me arriving so early in the morning. Once they checked me in, I headed straight for the breakfast area. My need was for some black coffee and something to eat. The coffee was ready, but I had to wait until 0700 hours for breakfast to be ready. While I waited and chatted with the chef and other kitchen personnel, the training staff got there, about thirty minutes before the trainees started to arrive. Turner and Johnson reported that everything was proceeding along perfectly. They stated that outside of a few arguments and temper tantrums, there had been no injuries so far, and the only irritation had been the mosquitoes and a couple of bee stings. They wanted to know where the next Ben-Bacchus party was going to be held that Saturday. I said they would have to wait like everyone else for that good news.

I told them that the recruits would get a double treat that weekend. They would end weapons training at 1130 hours, and tell the troops to quickly freshen up and board the bus at 1215 hours for lunch. Everyone would be back at 1500 hours for a special afternoon session. The decision was made when I noticed that the sessions that day were light, and I had earlier scheduled things this way. This was very thoughtful by me, since the crew had had a really rough week of training. They all agreed that it was a good idea, since the next two weeks would be stressful, physically trying, and somewhat dangerous, and there might be a nervous breakdown or two.

The troops loved the surprise of the Friday afternoon lunch break. They enjoyed relaxing, talking and joking, the great food and drinks, and the nice surroundings of Shaw's Restaurant at the south end of Lancaster, Ohio. It was really nice to see that everyone was acting as equal status companions, and that the girls mixed in as if they were just one of the boys. It was very nice to see their individual togetherness and confidence, but not as structured team players. It was obvious that each recognized and managed their own space, had their own attitude, and their own independence. Wonderful!

Later that day, even I got a little excited when the bus arrived to take all of us to our Saturday night outing. It was clear the staff and troops could not wait to see where they would be going that night. This time I said nothing, just let the bus pull into the parking lot. They looked surprised at seeing the large, upside-down Kon-te-kei boat.

Once we arrived, they were all escorted inside the beautiful Kahiki Restaurant, to the sounds of jungle birds, rainstorms, and Polynesian music. The place was beautiful. There were large tropical fish aquariums all along the walls, and realistic rain and thunderstorms throughout the restaurant. One would think one was on a Polynesian island. We had our own private area that was already prearranged and set up for the event. But the real bonus was the lovely girls in sarongs serving everyone lovely tropical drinks. They first served everyone the famous Smoking Erupting Volcano drink, and then Singapore slings, as ordered. The crew was in paradise. We stayed until they closed, and everyone kept ordering more Smoking Erupting Volcanoes. We just had to make sure that no one ate or drank the hot ice that makes the smoking eruption.

Luckily, we all got back to Autumn Hill without difficulty. I drove the bus back, since I had a chauffeur's license and knew how to double clutch the transmission. We had allowed the bus driver to join the party, and he drank a little too much.

Many slept late and few showed up for breakfast, and many undoubtedly had a nice hangover from those beautifully deceptive fruity drinks. But they needed to be very alert for the afternoon orientation sessions. These sessions would be their preparations for the next week's search and destroy, and the most dangerous game to be played. Our young rabbits would be spending three nights and four days in the wilderness of Wayne National Forest. They would be navigating this wilderness totally on their own and dealing with all of the elements that could do them harm. There was not going to be a talk that Sunday night, but I changed my mind. I thought it best to give them a short presentation, in preparation for the next two weeks of dangerous real-life games. After dinner, I took charge of the program and told them that a few important comments were needed.

"I think all of you enjoyed last night. But your surprise, starting late tonight, is that you will be secretly departing for somewhere unknown, and this is where you will earn your keep. I can still remember sleeping out in the wilderness in my damp clothes under a poncho several times, never being able to build a fire or use any form of light, for fear of getting caught by exposing my position. I'm sure that you know by now, or have heard through the grapevine, that snipers are seldom taken prisoners. When caught, they are usually just shot in the head. Your situations will be a little different, for you are not operating in a wartime environment, where snipers seek out their targets of opportunity, and then it is one man, with one shot, for one kill. But now the game begins. Once it is realized that you have done your job, you will become the hunted prey.

"At that point, never forget the fact that the new hunter may be as good as, or better than you. The key as the hunted is to prevail over your environment and make the stalker play your game. But this will not be your situation. You will know the target or targets, their precise location, their timetables, and all about their security arrangements. Since there is no war, your targets will never, at any moment, be seriously thinking about the dangers of assassination. No one ever thinks about being assassinated before having a nice dinner, a glass of fine wine, a good cigar, or great sex.

"Now that you are beginning to play serious games, I want the peace of mind of knowing that you have learned your manual alphabet and are ready to use that skill for silent movements. I am going to give you six hand language signs, and you will tell me the letter along with message inferred." I then ran them through X for execute, S for stop, L for look, G for go, R for return, and Q for quiet.

"That's good enough, and I am satisfied. I'm sure your instructors have covered everything properly as to your equipment, and the topographical and terrain maps of your assigned area, to locate drug producers and growers. You will all be doing a great public service here, for the game wardens and park rangers don't dare venture into the wilderness park areas for fear of being shot. It is quite sad when families on outings and groups of hikers cannot feel safe within their own state parks. Each of your teams will have three full days to zig and zag throughout the back areas, then find, locate, and destroy the facilities and drug crops.

"You will treat any interference with an appropriate and allowable response. It would be best to silently eliminate the possible interference first. That is why each team will be issued two high-powered dart guns. These are for putting individuals to sleep, if necessary. You will also be given one 700 Remington and a Winchester shotgun, in case a more serious form of self-defense is necessary. With your abilities and talents, you are not to be seen, heard or exposed until you have successfully neutralized any adverse party. Use total surprise and try not to kill anyone, but it may be necessary to injure them badly. After doing bodily harm, chain them to a large enough tree and leave them in the area. The authorities will be notified later of where they can find these culprits.

"Each of you knows your assignments. Team one will be at Tar Hollow, team two at Burr Oak, and team three at Lake Hope. Team four has a special run between Prattsville and Radcliff, which cuts through the drug triangle of MacArthur, Radcliff and Albany. In a way, team four has the toughest assignment. We must hope that all the aerial reconnaissance is valid. Be aware! Many of those whom you may encounter in the wilderness will be college-age students, but ignore this fact. Shame on them. This is only my personal thought: feel free to break a few fingers, remove a few teeth, and break a nose or two. The fact is, good people, we cannot kill them, but we can give them some pain and agony to pay for their sins.

"Now, you should clearly understand that the same rules of engagement will apply next week when you do the wilderness runs through southeast Ohio. Team one will go north to south from Patriot to Greasy Ridge. Team two will go north to south from Northrup to Lecta. Team three will proceed north to south from Thivener to Mercerville to Crown City. Team four will travel south to north from Scottstown to Lecta. Over the next two weeks, instead of dealing with bad dictators, you will be dealing with bad drug dealers. Your training during the next two weeks, with the successful accomplishments in these search and destroy areas, will show and prove beyond any reasonable doubt that all of you will be the best-trained and most efficient and effective snipers in the world. In the field testing, this applies to both distance and close-up target terminations. Rely on your instincts, remember your training, and look forward to the party next Saturday night.

"Oops! Before saying have a nice trip and good hunting, I must tell you: be warned that you are never, never to trust local county sheriff departments or the local sheriff. These areas are famous for poor men getting elected to the office who later retire as rich men. This is achieved by payoffs from the gambling circuits, illegal liquor still operations, and drug-growing crop operations. It is very common, at the county fairgrounds from Gallipolis to Greenfield to Ironton, to have several eighteen-wheeler gambling casinos move in and provide gambling, drinking and prostitution. All this action is accomplished with the so-called air-tight protection provided by the paid-off local sheriff's department.

"This protection backfired once in Gallipolis. A couple of robbers got into the fairgrounds area, robbed all the upscale and high-class local participants, and then made everyone take off all their clothes, down to their birthdays suits. Smart crooks! This show and tell move humorously provided for their safe getaway. The humorless group of nude victims included personnel with the sheriff's department, several local politicians, and several prominent business owners and their lawyers. These hungry nude souls could not depart for Rio

Grande to eat breakfast at Bob Evans. So, if by some strange quirk of circumstance one of these local yokels gets in the way, be nice if possible, or put them to sleep temporally. But please do not forget to chain the idiot to his disabled vehicle. Enough said. Now go close down the 'smoke a rope' Drug Growers of America."

The crew did exceptional well with their third week's adventure, and they really got into their Friday luncheon at the Pine Hills County Club, with lots of ice-cold beer. We booked a private room, as we did not want to interfere with their golfers. I shocked everyone by having Schmidt's deliver fifty giant cream puffs, fifty Bahama Mamas, and lots of German potato salad, and Schmidt's threw in an accordion player for entertainment. What a ball! Saturday night we made a trip to Fred Taylor's (the Ohio State basketball coach) favorite hangout in Carroll, on Route 33. That Sunday night, before their fourth week of rugged challenges, they were let off with no talk or activities after dinner. The grunts took off again late Sunday night for another three days of secret, silent and invisible chores. Their final Ben-Bacchus party would be a total surprise, and quite befitting of them on their last day before graduation. Then they could have a nice long sleep on Sunday before catching flights back to their homes and/or military units on Monday morning.

The four weeks ended with successful accomplishment beyond all of our expectations. The sixteen recruits proved to be first-class honor students. Not enough accolades could be laid at the feet of the training staff, but I would strongly suggest to the committee that they be paid a nice bonus, along with a paid vacation to some nice resort for a week. My first recommendation would be the Rose Hall Resort in Jamaica. If they do not like that, the Homestead Hot Springs Resort in Virginia.

Maybe the best way to express the success of this training school is to base it on the scoreboard information provided to the audience during the days of the Roman Empire. That was, "Lions seventeen, Christians zero!" The final scoring in this event within our coliseum can be stated as, "Pookas seventeen, drug dealers zero!"

CHAPTER VI
New Dogs in the Manger!

Strangely, these young rabbits no longer gave the appearance of being young, naive teenagers. Their movements and actions were no longer like those of college freshmen strutting around campus. Maybe it was the weather, or all their outdoor activities that had given them a more toughened-up look. Their eyes appeared more directed and focused when I talked with them. It was quite clear that these new men and women seemed to know what their personal responsibilities were, and exactly what their new responsibilities in the world would be. No question about it, the wizard team of Kelsey, Johnson, Vigorritto, Turner and the others had converted the bright sunlight into shadows, and created the darkness for shrouding the harvest moon. These sixteen individuals were going to be the best terminators and expediters that duty, honor, God, and country could buy. Every member of the staff made it clear that they would go on a mission with any one of them, at any time, anywhere, and for any reason.

Saturday would be their last Ben-Bacchus party, Sunday would be their farewell graduation dinner, and then they would be going off to somewhere Monday morning. It's like a train and the tunnel; everyone sees the train going into the tunnel, but no one ever sees the train leaving it. The train seems to disappear somewhere within the mountain, just like the people we have finished training as Pookas. They will go from visible humans to invisible spooks, and then will regularly appear and disappear between two alternate lifestyles. So the party would be good for these comrades, who know they may or may not see each other again. They also know that each of their lives may someday be dependent upon the bond of trust they have developed with each other. The party would give them some relaxing relief before they went back to their assigned duty stations. It would allow them to let their hair down, let their guard drop, and have some good plain fun.

It took some real negotiating to arrange the party, for the owner of this country bar out in the middle of nowhere was at first very apprehensive about a request for a closed private party. Finally he agreed to close the bar to everyone else, so that we could have a totally exclusive and private party. The bar owner was told to provide pizza, hamburgers, hot dogs, French fries and ice-cold beer until everyone said, "No more!" We asked him to keep the jukebox going long and loud throughout the night, and that it would also be appreciated if he would personally and privately invite about a dozen local girls. These girls would act as social waitresses and entertainment hostesses, without being too obvious. The bar owner agreed to our proposition once he realized how much money he was going to make on this one Saturday night; this fact, plus my assurance to pay for any damages that occurred to his fancy shack establishment, and that all costs would be covered at 125 percent. He was apprehensive at first because we had told him that these where military people who had just gone through four weeks of hellish war-game maneuvers. We led him to believe that they were preparing for guerrilla activities in Vietnam, and that most might not be alive next fall. This playing up to his hillbilly patriotism got us everything we needed and more. The guy even went out of his way to fix the place up and decorate it nicely for the party, not to mention the twelve lovely county girls he imported from Ohio University — a sneaky move on his part.

When the time arrived, everyone loaded onto the bus, and all were surprised that we turned south and not north, to Columbus. They were quite surprised when we turned up a rural road by Nelsonville and started back into the woodland wilderness, and then over the hills and dales toward the little backwater towns of Glouster and Trimble. They were really shocked when we arrived at our little county road tavern destination. They all started laughing when they read the sign for The Pumpkin Vine, underneath which was a lighted sign that read, "Eats." At that point, they all knew that they were in for a good time, and it was not long before they had let their hair down. The nice part was that they realized the formality of their training was over, and started treating the staff trainers as long-lost buddies.

No question about it, Sergeant Turner may have enjoyed the surrounding atmosphere of friendship more than anyone else. He humorously kept telling everyone what he had thought about them as trainees. The party was a raging success. Miss Delilah the Martha Raye and Drayleen Gabalac the Edsel really got into it, and both proved that they could shoot pool better than most of the guys. The funny part was that the more several of the guys had to drink, the more they fell in love with several of the waitresses, but to no avail.

It was well past midnight when we all boarded the bus for home, and before some decided to get hitched to the lovely college girls. Most everyone slept late the next day. The staff showed up for breakfast with only two of our trainees. Everyone was there for lunch, to talk about the party and their farewell before leaving the next morning at 0630 hours.

The group spent Sunday afternoon cleaning up, packing, and relaxing before dinner. The dinner seemed rather somber, as if the group was wishing the training session had not ended, and that they all could be spending a lot more time together as a cohesive unit. When dinner was over, they all stood and applauded, to thank the chef and kitchen staff. I took charge at the podium, and ended their informal graduation with a few words of congratulations.

Then I raised my hand and said, "Ladies and gentlemen! I do not mean to be crass as I raise my hand to congratulate all of you on your outstanding performance over the past four weeks. You must know that the staff honors and respects all of you. We give you our blessings, we wish you honorable success with all your future endeavors, and we now unceremoniously pronounce you nonexistent persons. You have all gloriously and officially graduated from this nonexistent school, which is now sending you off into your covert nonexistent existence, to do nonexistent things and participate in nonexistent worldly events.

"You know, I had a whole speech prepared about this and that, and other repetitious things. But the hell with it! I'm tearing up my notes, while looking at you men and women sitting there politely, waiting for me to say something important or meaningful. But my thoughts at this moment are on the past, and my prepared words will not work. You already know my cohorts from past adventures on staff here: Vigorritto, Kelsey and Johnson. But I'd give anything if you could have met and known all of those in this elite clan. Your predecessors were great guys, and became my very close friends: Lollich the Crow-Ott, Zimmerman the Hot Rod, Massiah the Carpet Man, Karam the Camel Jockey, Sullivan the Gym Boy, Archer the Swimmer, Bishop the Holy Man, Duckett the Coal Miner,

Spyridon the Walleye, Gardner the Cowboy, Huffless the Guitar Man, and my associates here that I've already mentioned.

"These men would all think and agree that you are outstanding replacements. All would have liked to have downed some boilermakers with you while bullshitting, lying, joking around, and pulling your legs about how good they were when playing in the real world. As good old Atticus Finch stated in *To Kill A Mockingbird*, 'You never know someone until you step inside their skin, and walk around a little.'

"Well, enough of this seriousness. All of you are now curious as to when you may be called into duty. My answer is that I do not know. If there is a mission request, only at that time will I know whom to call, after first analyzing the nature of the mission, and only then will I be able to make the team selections. Currently, with the way things stand, it would be no surprise if zero missions were called during the rest of this year or early on next year. Our president is not proactive in the world, as were Eisenhower and Nixon. He is totally consumed with the problems in Southeast Asia and Vietnam. Therefore, my strong belief is that you will not hear from the higher powers for some time. So you should plan to enjoy Thanksgiving, Christmas and Easter with your loved ones. You may consider Easter as your birthday party time as Pookas.

"So remember this: When you're bore-sighting in for accuracy and focusing in on a target, you do not have the benefit of a 'wind rose.' At the point of your commitment, the only 'windsock' available will be nature's gift of moving leaves on plants and trees, blowing dust, rippling waters and moving clouds. What's left is only your second-nature instinct. Remember you training, remember the metronome, and rely on you individual self-confidence to prevail, for you do not want the Grim Reaper to have you playing pinochle with Azrael.

"My parting thoughts to you come from a book called the *Hagakure*. This book deals with the wisdom of the samurai, and with certain bits of wisdom you should keep near and dear to your heart. 'For the past exists only as memory, and the future only as imagination.' Do not imagine that you are infallible, for your mortality can be 100 percent. Remember, 'It is false thinking to think that all the others we know will die before us, and that we will be the last to go. 'You believe for a fact that death seems to be a long way off, and that you are surely safe. Is this not shallow thinking? It is worthless thinking, and is only a joke within a dream.' You must always fear the Grim Reaper, since this fear, blended with your skills and training, will keep you alive. 'It is not that we don't know that we will die some day, but we grasp at straws.' As the wise samurai understood, 'Whether people be of high or low birth, rich or poor, old or young, enlightened or confused, they are all alike in that they will one day die.' Therefore, you must prevail in making sure the *theys* die first."

Well, that was that. The school was over. Thank you, farewell, and have a nice trip back to wherever. Everyone would soon be reporting back to their military units, or be at home with their families and friends. I decided to do absolutely nothing until the following Monday. The intent was to spend all my time with the wife and kids, and not to report to the higher powers until the next week, unless they happened to call me first. Actually, they did call me first, but not until the following Monday. They directed me again to be at the Willard Hotel in three weeks for a full committee get-together. They stated that they would be sending tickets, and that it would only be a one-day meeting. They made it clear that I would arrive early the first day and leave the following afternoon shortly after lunch, and that they only wanted to have a short meeting was very good news.

Time sure did fly. The week off with the family was enjoyable, and a lot of good personal work was accomplished. Five nice business appointments would be in place when I returned from Washington, D.C. The only frustrating part of the trip would be dealing with Agony Airlines and the Pittsburgh airport once again.

I drove to the airport and left the car in the overnight parking. The early flight did not bother me this time, since I now lived only ten minutes from the airport. Catching a 5:40 a.m. flight created no inconvenience, and there would be no long, boring drive back home after the trip.

The fights were smooth and on time. I arrived at the Willard Hotel without any delays or complications. What a miracle! Once I checked into the hotel and dropped my carrying case in the room, I went to the designated meeting room. All other parties were already in attendance, having deep discussions with Colonel Knapp and — to my great surprise — Captain Dan. After entering the room and getting a few hellos and handshakes, I got a cup of coffee and sat down at the far end of the table.

Their discussion was on our society's new social issues and the conflicts regarding outspoken activism and decreased patriotism by the country's youth. They also were talking about the serious racial problems in our cities. They gave follow-up comments about the president's confusing signals and his lack of a proactive stance on issues in the world besides Vietnam. These guys made no bones about who they liked and disliked. They clearly felt that General Westmoreland should be replaced, that a Mr. Rostow should have an accident, and that McNamara suffered from "analysis paralysis." As they put it, the Big Mac was "the most dangerous man in the world, as a negative thinking expert."

They referred to Clark Clifford as a yo-yo, saying he had completely failed to oversee a Mr. McClone and the C.I.A., as promised. They all agreed that no one really, at any time, gave a shit about George Ball. The current event civics lesson alone was well worth the trip. I just listened with eyes and ears, and kept my mouth shut. I knew that they would be getting to me sooner or later, and would not appreciate the advance notice my speech reading would allow me.

Eventually, Colonel Knapp broke into the conversation, and stated that they would like me to say a few words before lunch, then afterward take the floor for discussion and comments from two o'clock until five-thirty. It was clear that my lip-reading observation time was up, and that my informal rambling should begin.

"Well, gentlemen, it is nice to see everyone here at the Willard again. I must admit at being somewhat surprised to see Captain Dan at this meeting; I thought he had been promoted upstairs to a higher function. Anyway, it is always nice to see you, and I am rather pleased that you have chosen to attend this meeting with the new committee members. But now, down to the basics of what you want to know.

"The school was excellent. The graduates performed with perfection, and the training staff deserves extra fringe benefits and appreciation for a job well done. This I will discuss with you later. I hate to admit it, but these sixteen graduates are far better prepared, efficient and professionally competent than our class of sixteen invisible beings created ten years ago.

"Mr. Kelsey has clearly shown that he would be more than competent as my replacement, if circumstances create that necessity. As for the two females, let's put it this way: You would not want them on your tail or to meet them in a dark alley. I would go on a mission with them anywhere, at any time. My major concern is with Mr. Kelsey. I hope that you can lock him down in some way to remain available for future service to our group. He has been given a very generous offer by a North African Arab country to be classified as an agricultural attaché.

"So, Captain Dan! Curiosity leads me to ask the questions; how and why do they know about his special talents and expertise? Who else from our crew may be getting tempting offers, if any? Do we have a professional 'head hunter' working as an employment agent for international concerns of political and/or economic interest? What if Kelsey should be unavailable? I would change my mind from Mr. Vigorritto to Mr. Johnson as being the most reliable and competent person to fill this position. Well, I see Colonel Knapp is giving me the high sign to close down for lunch, so after our nice lunch, we'll talk some more."

Captain Dan appeared quite annoyed and shaken by my remarks. He did not go to lunch with the rest of us, but instead went straight out the front doors of the hotel, without comment. The luncheon was socially interesting, and most of my time was spent talking with Mr. Lingo. The guy was interested in my Korean and Spanish language skills, and wanted to know what languages my wife spoke. His curiosity forced him to ask how I had learned to speak Korean and Spanish. I told him that my wife spoke a little French from high school courses, and some German and Russian from grandparents and friends in their predominantly immigrant neighborhood, but was very proficient in Croatian since both of her parents were Croats. As for me, I had taken high school Spanish with a Mrs. Pusiterri, and while in Korea, a resident had taught me the language so that I could get around and be more accepted by the locals.

By the time lunch was over, Captain Dan had not yet returned. Colonel Knapp told everyone to get some coffee and get comfortable, and then directed me to continue with my particular remarks and comments on certain issues sent to me earlier, before the conference.

Without hesitation, I stood up and took charge over the meeting. "Gentlemen, during your discussions earlier this morning, you were adequately covering the world situation as it relates politically to our government. In this arena, I have nothing to add that you do not already know about. Therefore, I will comment only briefly on other world topics. The first will be Argentina.

"Argentina is now currently in good hands with the Azule Peronistas, particularly since the socialist liberal Arturo Illia is now out in the cold. We should keep our hands out of their current business transactions. Why? It's obvious, because Argentina is the claimed exclusive playground for the C.I.A. alone. Now, the Dominican Republic seems to have made the right move — with the C.I.A.'s help — by electing Joaquin Balaquer, and as a bonus he got the popular vote, with the strong backing of the military. This should make a lot of American mineral, petroleum, and agricultural interests happy, and therefore, the off-balance-sheet financing for the C.I.A. paid off handsomely.

"The Guatemala concerns have been well taken care by their newly declared El Presidentia, with the sham election of Julio Caesar Mendez Montenegro, and along with the totally suppressive and strong-armed backing of the military. Now, as you have aptly stated before, Southeast Asia and Vietnam are not our concerns, but you made mention of China since it is now a major nuclear power. The Red Guard issue as exhorted by Mao Zedong is a major social revolution. It is an in-house-oriented program for a generational housecleaning. We do not need to be concerned until the turmoil is all over. When things cool down, the Maoist philosophy will take one step backward before taking two steps forward in order to advance his worldly influence. The Chinese have a severe psychological conflict socially by wanting to be something in the world, versus their inhibited, secretive and isolationism of mistrust concerning the outside world. China may be an irritating pain through their puppets around the world, but as a country to itself, the issue is moot.

"Bluntly, gentlemen, I just do not see any urgency anywhere concerning our authorized jurisdiction of operations. The possible exception may be Chile, and their President Frei's announced policies of Chilenization. Outside of a potential problem in this area, there appear to be no drastic corrections that need to be made at this time in history. But who knows what next year will bring? So, gentleman! That is all I have to say for the moment, except to thank you for those ingenious memos you disguised as 'A Guide for Political Science and Current Affairs.' This monthly collegiate newsletter is quite a sneaky way to keep me informed about world events, and where we need to be focusing our attention around the globe."

After that, there was minor back and forth discussion for about an hour or so. These comments were concerns about the school, the students, and my remarks about world affairs. They all listened with interest; but, on the other hand, could care less about what I really thought. The boss men would make up their own minds once a special-K memo arrived from the "Holy Men" above. It was nice that they asked for my opinion and showed a little respect to this much younger whippersnapper on the committee. Colonel Knapp had called for a thirty-minute coffee break when he noticed that Captain Dan had just returned to the meeting. He quickly reminded everyone that dinner later that day would start with a cocktail party at 1830 hours. Captain Dan walked over to me, pulled me aside from the rest of the group, and told me that the Kelsey situation was being looked into. He then told me that any issues around the situation would be taken care of at his level.

After the break, Captain Dan took charge of the meeting. He started off by telling the committee that they had just been given a special-K memo. Dan handed the memo to Liddy the Ambassador and told him that he could present it to the committee. The memo boiled down to the fact that I had to select four Pookas to take a five-week journey next March to the Middle East. It stated that the mission was more for consultation and training of selected Iranian military and SAVAK secret police personnel. The powers that be undoubtedly thought it best to teach the Iranians our skills and covertly use them, along with the Israelis, to keep the balance of power in the Middle East. They suggested sending Ed Wynn and Jimmy Durante, and my immediate response to this suggestion was, "NO WAY! It would be suicide to expose our two best Arab operatives, since they would become a public record before we needed them to perform special covert services in this part of the world. Also, we cannot use two of our best because they are female; this, my friends, would not go over well in a Moslem country. But at least you have given me enough time to make the correct selections, and to get them properly educated and indoctrinated for a mission in this strange part of the world."

What seemed a bit weird, strange, maybe even a little amazing to me was that when our original group finished training, we were immediately put to work around the world, and numerous people were displaced into a nonexistent status. Now, here we appear to be going for months with only advisory duties. This must be the difference between the Eisenhower and Nixon era and the Johnson era. One has to feel a little sorry for L.B.J., since Eisenhower and Kennedy stuck his hand involuntarily into the hole of the honey tree. Now he gets stuck in the honeycombs with tons of swarming bees. Quite sad, since his predecessors and advisors did not give him a beekeeper's net. As the honey bear, he is stuck with being in the wrong place at the wrong time, and in a bottom-line religious holy war caused by a French kiss gone sour. It is clear that this president inherited the box. The problem is that he is in the box, and worse yet the box is in the corner, so it is no wonder that he cannot think outside the box and is not proactive to the wants and needs of the rest of the world. Let's face it; the Eisenhower and Nixon era brought an illusionary peace to millions around the world, with diplomatic gestures and friendly impressions falsely portrayed to the news media, yet the real pressure for peaceful coexistence was created behind the scenes by a professional spot remover (maybe spot removers would be more appropriate) for erasing stains on our humanity.

Well, I had said what I had to say, so let the chips fall where they may. The meeting had ended, and it would soon be time for the cocktail party and dinner. A few new friends might have been made; Mel the Diplomat and I seemed to have hit it off, and I really started to enjoy the guy. It appeared that he had seen a lot of things in the world, and had been to a lot of interesting places — Malaysia, the Philippines, Honduras, and even pre-Castro Cuba. It was a nice social evening, and a pleasure to be mixing with the new committee members rather than playing the piano. The only guys I just could not warm up to were the stuffed shirt Mr. Chrome and Mr. Buck, with his slow, methodical, dragging conversations. Listening to him required extra attention before he got to the point, and it was a good thing no one there asked him what time it was.

The formal Mr. Rumble simply seemed unapproachable. He was friendly, yet not friendly. He came across as the person always in control, with an air of pure authority. Then there was the talkative Mr. Patrick, who seemed to have a very conservative opinion on just about everything in the world. Putting all this in perspective, it was a nice get-together, and allowed everyone to become more comfortable with each other within this covert game.

The next morning's meeting sessions were directed by Captain Dan. The presentation was more like a refresher course on the dos and don'ts in relation to all the secret rules and regulations regarding our nonexistent group. Afterward, they provided us with a nice lunch, we all said our farewells, and then I was off to the D.C. airport and departing for the Pittsburgh airport and Agony Airlines experience.

Home for the holidays was a nice feeling, and the year in business provided a great finale for me. No question about it, the move to Columbus was the right move for my career, and also for the operational convenience of my invisible alternate life. The fact is, strange events and activities go unnoticed a lot more in a major city than in a smaller town like Mansfield. Anonymity is much easier to achieve among a mass of strangers.

When the new year arrived, the team selections for the trip to Iran had to be made, and after that scheduling a two- or three-day conference at the end of February to prepare them for the trip. A lot of time was spent reviewing everyone's file and visualizing in my mind all the contacts that were made with each of them. I finally narrowed down the decision to Louis Prima, Mr. Kaiser, Mr. Tucker, and Jerry Colona. These four seemed to have the personality and attitude to be good instructors. They also had no standout uniqueness that would draw any special attention to them. I worked up my agenda for a meeting at the Christopher Inn in Columbus at the end of February, and made absolutely sure that proper notice was sent to them by the first of February.

The time had come to prepare the four Pookas for their trip to Iran. Two nights were booked at the Christopher Inn for them, which would allow enough time to cover all the necessary ground about Iran in two and half days. Everyone's flights were on schedule and they all showed up at the hotel during the late afternoon. We had a nice dinner, talked about their current activities and duties at their current duty stations, and discussed possible difficulties with personnel at their assigned stations. Then the meeting started, with my laying out the ground rules for the meeting and their trip to Iran.

"You may think, once the mission is explained to you, that this will be a gravy assignment. Please, be not deceived about what may appear to be a simple, yet serious training mission. This could become a very dangerous mission if you get careless, mouthy, cocky, or drink too much. You are to go over there and act reserved, confident, cold, very calm and collected, like mature adults. While in your training posture, act more like Sergeant Turner, Vigorritto, Kelsey, and Johnson. But under no circumstances will you party with and/or get tanked while drinking with these Iranians, for they can drink you under the table. Should this happen, you may awaken with you throat slit, or worse yet, with a desert venereal disease called the Cobra Clap. With this disease, your testicles get huge and filled with puss, and need to be cut off to save you life, not your manhood.

"My point for you to consider is that many of these Iranians have very long memories. These memories go back many years, to when a General Schwarzkopf was the internal security that maintained the Shah's rule for the benefit of Western oil interests. Even then, the C.I.A. was not to be trusted for improving the American image. Their great down-your-throat public relations campaign to benefit only American and British petroleum interests finally backfired in their faces. This all led to the development of the first American-hating Islamic Republic, led and promoted by Shiite Moslem scholars and clerics. The final straw, which really added fuel to the fire, was when we and the British set up and framed Prime Minister Mohammed Mossadegh as a devoted communist. We then used this to justify overthrowing his regime. Of course, we the good guys quickly replaced him with our own little puppet to sit on the throne of the Pahlavi Dynasty."

The next two days were more of the same, within the vein of Iran's history and politics, and their geographical neighbors. It was made clear to them that our hands in this history were not clean, particularly when it came to our petroleum, agricultural, and selfish mineral interests. They were given my variation of an old quote, "The meek shall inherit the earth, but not the mineral rights." My further comments to them were a reminder.

"We grow up and mature in this secret profession when we take the blinders off. By removing the blinders, only then do we realize that we — the U.S. of A. — only support the comptroller of the country. Sorry, I meant the controller of the country. The subject is called 'Geopolitical Economics.' The concept is always based on dollars and cents issues, as to whose ass gets gored in order to protect our economic and democratic freedoms of capitalism. This is why Iran is a favored nation, and why it is an undeclared territory of the United States. It is favored because it severed relations with Egypt to develop economic and commercial ties with Israel.

"At first, Tehran may seem like paradise to you, but do not go outside of your assigned area without a military escort. Do not do any sightseeing, and only stay in and around the upscale areas of Tehran. Know and understand that the Tudeh Communist Party has great influence. They also have a radical scholar that keeps the fundamentalist Shiites dedicated to having the Shah and his foreign supporters removed from Iran. The last time we looked into and studied this issue, you were — and still are — referred to as foreign infidels deviling their land. Believe me!

"Not to be repetitious, but this should be a nice assignment if you just stay sober and always remain aware of and smart about your surroundings. While in Iran, you will not be participating in any preying cat or scurrying mouse games. The only objective is to train these skilled troubleshooters who are loyal to the Shah. You are to make them more proficient, more efficient, more invisible, and completely nonexistent while they do our job for us in the region. The reality check is: it is better them, than us, when playing praying mantis and porcupine in the Middle East. Therefore, what their Israeli business associates don't handle, the new Pooka SAVAKs will take care of privately for money, and not religious reasons. That is called real business for the benefits of more foreign military aid, and recognized as legal by the U.S. and British. My final advice is this: Try to stay out of the middle, and do not allow yourself to get involved with or in anything unrelated to your mission. If there are any nasty riots or assassination attempts on the Shah or anyone else, just look the other way, and have a nice cold beer."

These guys could have passed a college history course on the Middle East. They listened well, asked many interesting questions, and were well prepared for their overseas duties. They did make one interesting request. It did not surprise me. They asked if, on the last night, they could have dinner at the Kahiki Restaurant, and if they might be allowed at least two Erupting Volcano drinks. The request was fine with me; I wanted to go there as much as they did. We had a nice evening of sociable relaxation before they would have to depart and catch their military plane out of the country the next day.

At that point, I thought I was home free and not having to think about anything but the family. This was short-sighted, for the mail delivery a week later had an interesting Political Science newsletter for me to evaluate. I knew from the higher power's newsletter that there would be, in the near future, some top-notch consideration from upstairs, and this would require some type of mission involving Pookas with a club.

The Political Science and Current Affairs newsletter was all about Bolivia and Che Guevara. It was a complete political, social and economic history of Bolivia, and included a dossier with some details about Mr. Che. The newsletter pointed out why the U.S. military, with counter insurgency personnel, might have to become more involved with South America within the next four or five months. The newsletter made it clear that President General Rene' Barrientos Ortuno had unsupportive people within his government, and that his military power player, General Alfredo Ovando Candia, was really a lei den leftist whose loyalty could be considered suspect. The newsletter pointed out that there were several Pro-Castro Marxist Che supporters secretly and privately giving Che aid and comfort. It was made clear that President Barrientos was becoming somewhat uncomfortable with his military's ability to deal with the growing guerrilla forces being organized by Che.

SHADOWS II, SKULLS II & SPOOKS II

Bolivia was some place. It was somewhat isolated from the world, and only had access to the Atlantic and Pacific oceans by five railroads. Its wealth and riches were created from the agricultural sector and the mineral mining industry. The facts were clear: there were lots of thing to catch and eat there, but there are also a lot of things living there that could eat you. The country was a living mountain plateau of rain forest, desert, swampland, and a tropical zoo of everything weird. This zoo sits on a high plateau between two branches of the Andes Mountains. This one little country had toucans, sloths, jaguars, monkeys, ostriches, llamas, lots of nasty insects, and more deadly snakes like anacondas, vipers, and bushmasters than any one place on this earth deserves. If that was not bad enough, they also had nasty lizards and Cayman crocodiles. The powers must have been thinking that they were preconditioning me, and warning me in advance about a mission where my Pookas might have to die. Bullshit! I was already thinking that they should let all those wild things living there take care of Mr. Che. According to the dossier, this Che was quite an intelligent dude, and a ladies' man. It appeared that he was a thinker and put his money where his mouth was — he simply selected the wrong party to join for his views on social justice. Actually, there was really nothing wrong with being anti-imperialism and neocolonialism, and for desiring the basic improvements in life for the poor and downtrodden. The problem was that he joined the communists; where his views were more pro-Chinese than pro-Soviet, and that was the major reason he had left Castro two years before with a "Dear John" letter. The guy was dedicated to a cause, but not to marriage. He had divorced his first wife, a Peruvian named Hilda Gadea, who had one daughter. He then married one of Castro's military personnel, Aleida March, and later deserted her and left her with four children.

When he deserted, he went to (of all the places on this earth) the African Congo. He organized the Patrice Lumumba Battalion; there he felt that he would create social justice among tribal natives who had no concept as to the value of a human life. But he quickly realized that these people were still prehistoric natives, mostly psychopathic jungle-bunnies who liked to kill the people that grew their carrots. He quickly learned that they were still indoctrinated to making people subservient to their will, or slaughtering them — with "them" meaning the whole family of father, mother, and all the children. Good Che figured he screwed up again regarding the good intentions of other world revolutionaries. So while pissed off, he went to China and then to North Vietnam. The problem there was that he did not feel comfortable with Orientals. Therefore, during late 1966 he decided to go back to South American and join his own kind of people.

No question about it, if horny Che had not been so horny and had decided once he left Argentina to be a celibate Jesuit priest, he would have become a bishop in the Catholic church for his writings on helping the suffering poor. It would not have surprised me if, later on in his life, he had become a cardinal. But according to this memo, Che had the willing support of many Catholic priests, particularly those in the rural mining areas. These priests were clearly not interfering with his ideas or his movement to recruit guerrillas in their rural parish areas. These Catholic priests were thinking like the Arabs, with the philosophy of, "The enemy of my enemy, is temporally my friend."

After waiting for some form of orders, the Iran crew had returned successfully from their mission well over three months before. Also, there has been no further mention of issues about Bolivia or Che Guevara since the March newsletter. Even the last several newsletters were just plain gibberish. They presented no relevant information of importance, and only stated what was already known about Sukarno of Indonesia losing his military support. The newsletters did point out that Uruguay was having an economic depression, and poor Androcles and the Lion were still in a helpless position, with the 'Chilean thorn of pain' stuck in the paw of U.S. economic interests. One might have thought the Pooka Brigade would have been given a serious mission in Santiago, Chile by then, and that some of the Chilenization Marxist and Christian Democrats would have been sent to the "sweet bye and bye."

It felt like that weird sensation of the calm before the storm. There had been no hazardous duty to date for anyone, and the summer was there to enjoy, without fear. As a happy family, we went to Cedar Point twice, camping and canoeing at Loudonville several times, and made sure the kids got their favorite large floats from A&W Root Beer at least once a month. Then on the Fourth of July, some not-so-legal fireworks were acquired to excite the kids, and they loved holding the sparklers in the dark. It was a nice summer, and as a family we spent a lot of time at our Eastmoor Swimming Pool. The children were learning how to swim, and I was acting as a diving coach, giving lessons to the young people wanting to learn how to dive. But my big new experience was personally building a twelve-foot by twenty-four-foot enclosed patio addition onto the rear of the house. I was pleased with the fact that I alone laid the concrete slab and footers, did all the framing and roofing, and properly screened in the whole patio. It was beautiful, even if a little uneven, and leaned a hair to the left. But who cared! I had done it. It was a learning experience, and I would never do it again; that decision alone would certainly make my wife a very happy woman.

As they say, one should never speak too soon, or count their blessings before all the blessings have been received. The proof of the pudding was that that summer was the calm before the storm. A couple of weeks before Labor Day, a special-K memo was delivered by special carrier. It was from Liddy the Ambassador, informing me to prepare two base units for delivery to Bolivia. The memo requested that a call be made to Circle 6-2150 within three days after receiving the notice. Again, I thought the assignment would be Chile, but this was not to be. So there was a need to select four more Pookas, since I had already pre-selected four for the next potential mission. But this time the Pookas would get to practice some of their Spanish. They would be advised that it would be more for listening than speaking, and that they will learn more about secret things if others believed they did not speak Spanish.

So, who would get selected to enter the Lion's Den with Eddie Cantor - Mr. Charvat, Danny Kaye - Mr. Rex, Hudson - Mr. Berkich, and Oscar Levant - Mr. Papadopoulos? I would make the picks for the committee, but was going to disagree with them on the teams. There should only be two set three-man teams, or only three set three-man teams, but no two set four-man teams. I would let them know that I also liked the new concept of using only two-man teams, but there was no need to have four men crowded into one team. In the meantime, the additional four requested would be Nash - Mr. Ruffin, Packard - Mr. St. Amond, Fraiser - Mr. Badurina, and the little shuffling Tucker - Mr. Iff.

The time had arrived for making the phone call to Liddy the Ambassador. Liddy answered the phone; he was short and sweet, and told me the teams had to be ready for delivery to Bolivia by September 30. He also informed me that at the pre-orientation meeting to be held at the Christopher Inn prior to their departure, Mr. Chrome, Mr. Rumble and Mel the Diplomat would be attending. He stated that they had allotted three days for the meeting, prior to the group flying to their destination late on September 28. He let me know that the committee members would be there for the first day only, and leave the following afternoon. I quickly interrupted Liddy and stated my concern about the team request. He was receptive to my input, and said it could be discussed with Colonel Knapp, who would be calling me in about a week. I just prepared, sat back and waited, and hoped to get things satisfactorily worked out with Colonel Knapp. My curiosity made me want to ask why he was not attending the conference.

I thought that the Bolivia mission was all he needed to be concerned about, until right after Labor Day, when I got a new monthly Political Science newsletter. This had a lot of innuendo about Honduras, a military attaché being A.W.O.L. or terminally ill, and a secret society of bad boys referred to as "The White Mice." A situation seemed to be presenting itself, that there might be a need to call on the services of Miss Edsel and Miss Martha Raye in the very near future. The situation with the military attaché might require their specialized training at getting up close and personal, for those two sexy creatures would be the best with deception and deceit to deliver a fatal scorpion sting.

As for Honduras: it seemed that certain people, and fruity corporations of influence, had become disillusioned with the banana republic Dictator Osvaldo Lopez Arellano, and the choice would be to either buy him or fry him. The newsletter suggested that he might be doing a little too much over-killing and over-jailing, and this was creating labor problems for some major agricultural interests. Plus, the newsletter suggested that they preferred not to fry him, for they did not foresee a strong, powerful replacement standing in the wings. Like many people often say, "That when trouble comes, it comes in sets of three, and that when the shit hits the fan, it is never distributed equally."

That reminded me of the time when a client, an undertaker, told me that business was good for undertakers every third year, and that it was a matter of record that a lot more people die every three years. Of course, this undertaker's way of proving the fact was that profits go up 30 percent during the third year period.

Well, Colonel Knapp agreed with my Pooka selections, and said the committee had agreed to go with three teams of three Pookas each. He said the committee members would explain everything about the political environment in Bolivia, and the conditions and situations around Mr. Che Guevara. But he surprised me with the information that once the committee members left on the second day of the orientation meeting, he and Captain Dan would be arriving late that evening for an after-dinner presentation, and would do a follow-up presentation the next morning before the teams left for Bolivia. He stressed that the additional information was very secret, and was not even known to any of the new committee members. When closing the phone conversation, he stated, "Remember the North Korean colonel?"

He had made the point loud and clear. The light bulb went on, and I knew the answer. I also knew that this person had to be a part of this turkey shoot, and was planning on allowing his management position to become a little more proactive at the transference of souls.

CHAPTER VII
"Oh, I'd Love to Go to the Party, but I'm Absolutely Dead!"

Anacondas, bushmasters, crocodiles and nasty insects be dammed. I knew what needed to be done, what I was going to do, and the lizards, vipers and jaguars had best stay out of the way. The committee members would learn, without forewarning, who the ninth man would be at the orientation meeting. My family would know that I was being paid to speak at two major conventions, one in Puerto Rico and the other in Bermuda, and also participating in their workshops. It would be obvious to my family that it would be ridiculous for me to fly home one day and right back out the next. So it would now be a good time for my in-laws to come visit with their daughter and the grandkids, and help keep their minds off my travels.

The time had come where the rubber starts to meet the road. I was getting an adrenalin rush just driving down Broad Street to the Christopher Inn. The family thought I had left for the airport to catch a flight, not knowing I would be spending the next three nights downtown at a hotel, and flying out of Lockbourne Air Force Base once the orientation meeting with all the assigned Pookas was over. When I arrived at the hotel, sitting in the lobby bar were the new committee members and Liddy the Ambassador, who had not said that he would be attending the meeting. I walked over to say my hellos, told them everything was in order, and said that the rest of the troops should be arriving over the next few hours. They were provided the agenda showing that Mel the Diplomat would be speaking that night after dinner, Mr. Chrome the next morning, Mr. Rumble during the afternoon, and that I would be giving up my time after dinner for comments from Liddy the Ambassador.

I reminded them, since they were leaving the following morning, that I would hold my remarks until later, with me talking to the troops after dinner the following day. They agreed to the agenda, and we sat around making small talk. They wanted to know about Ohio State's football team, and felt that Navy had a good chance to beat Army that year. When the troops started showing up, the committee members went to their rooms. I stayed around to greet the men and helped then properly check-in and get their room assignments. I invited them to come back down for a drink, since dinner was not scheduled to start until 1900 hours.

I made sure early on, before dinner, to let Mr. Rex the Danny Kaye and Mr. Iff the Tucker know that they were to be the leader of their particular team, and made it clear that they would be the ones to make the primary shot on the target. They were not told at the time there would be three teams of three men each, but were informed that Bolivia was the destination, and Mr. Che Guevara was the target. I had made enough copies of my March Political Science newsletter so they could all read and study about Bolivia and Mr. Che.' But first, I removed the title and source of the newsletter from the material.

The first presentation after dinner was by Mel the Diplomat. He did not cover anything new in his talk, and the men had all the information they needed from my handout.

Mr. Chrome presented a political analysis concerning Bolivia. He stated that if not for a strong right-wing leader, the country would probably become as leftist as Chile. He made it clear that if all the communist parties could stop their infighting and find some common ground, they would be the majority party in Bolivia. The problem was that each wanted the authority of power. He stated that Bolivia had the most diversified communist block of politicians in South America, and he said the French term used to describe the situation was *potpourri,* or "rotten pot." They had Muscovites, Maoists, Trotskyites and Castroites, and Mr. Che thought he could unite them into a common cause peasant revolution. Chrome finished his talk, and then gave all of us in the room a book entitled *Theories and Tactics of Guerrilla Warfare,* written by Mr. Che himself.

After the morning meeting was over, we had a nice lunch, and the afternoon meeting started on schedule. Mr. Rumble was certainly the political economist. He presented all the possible economic risks that could occur to U.S. business interests, and in particular to Gulf Oil's diverse holdings within the region. He made it clear that eliminating Che would be the best way to help General Rene' Barrientos maintain control and the balance of power. He pointed out that the general had more than one Judas in the government and within the military, such as General Candia and General Torres. He said it was fortunate for us that these two leftist generals were different types of communists: one was a Maoist and the other a Castro Muscovite. He informed us that during the summer the U.S. government had sent to Bolivia top specialized military trainers. The trainer's job had been to train six hundred elite Bolivian troops that President Barrientos could trust and count on to maintain military support under the direction of Colonel Suarez.

Mr. Rumble clarified that the special force was necessary, since previous efforts to locate and capture Che had failed. The failures were all due to a group of mole sympathizers within the military who let Che know where *not* to be during military operations. All of us in the room clearly understood that our country had a lot of vital petroleum, mineral and agricultural interests at stake in the region. We also understood that it would be best to nip this Che and his leftist movement in the bud, so it would impress and influence other upstarts in South America. Mr. Rumble took pleasure in the fact that the right-wing military control was the sole basis of stability in Latin America. He pointed out that right-wing military groups had recently overthrown and taken charge of at least thirteen Latin American governments. His point was that these right-wing military leaders had kept a firm anti-communist and anti-guerrilla hand of suppression over troublemakers and disruptive unionists.

Liddy the Ambassador had little new to say. He repeated a lot of what had already been mentioned about the Bolivian infrastructure, and noted that the region of Bolivia we were concerned with was referred to as the Oriente region. He pointed out that it was the largest, the least productive, the most sparsely populated, and the least known area of the country. Therefore, it was a perfect spot for Mr. Che's multiple operational centers to conduct guerrilla warfare activities. The region had four intersecting rivers for private and unnoticed navigation, but river transportation was not popular. This is why successful river transportation had never developed, except for a few small private river vessels. Therefore, this was the perfect spot for Che to move around freely to recruit and mobilize rural peasants. He was in a way operating in the betwixts and betweens of nowhere. Liddy closed with what he thought was humor. "Blessed are the peacemakers, for the peacemakers are those with the big sticks that keep order. You, gentlemen, are the big sticks protecting this country's vital interests around the world, and making sure the meek do not inherit the mineral rights."

Interesting, but boring. These new committee members were too uptight and formal, and would not let their hair down. It was a rather ho-hum two nights for the troops, but at least they had time to think about their homework and to thoroughly review my comprehensive handouts concerning Che and Bolivia. It was nice to know that these new committee guys would be leaving the next morning, and that we would get Colonel Knapp and Captain Dan for the next two evenings. We would then be assured of having a little entertainment while getting the real scoop on this mission. The men made a request that was no surprise to me. They wanted to go back to the Kahiki Restaurant for a nice evening of relaxation. They were happy to know that this was what had been planned for the first evening while Colonel Knapp and Captain Dan were here. All of the really serious portions of the meetings would occur the next day, into the late evening, and early the next morning before we all packed up to leave for Bolivia.

The boss men showed up just in time. We arranged for four cabs and off we went down Broad Street to the Kahiki. We arranged for the cabs to return at ten-thirty to transport us back to the hotel. It was a nice evening with the crew. We partied, ate great food, socialized with beautiful oriental girls in sarongs, and everyone had two or three Erupting Volcano drinks. Even Captain Dan and Colonel Knapp enjoyed the nice Polynesian restaurant with the Erupting Volcanoes, thunder and rain storms, and all the lovely fish and birds. Maybe they were too old to enjoy lovely girls in sarongs.

The next morning, Captain Dan took the podium. He wanted to explain why he and Colonel Knapp had showed up after the new committee members had left for home. He stated that he needed to provide us with additional information that it was so secret, that the new committee members were not privy to it as it related to this mission. Captain Dan then said, "Gentleman, you may or may not know that we here were the old committee that supervised Mr. Benton and his gang. All this was prior to your being trained as the new replacements last summer. Your Mr. Benton, or Mr. Chahaus, is part of the new committee. The higher powers above the committee, and even above our new supervisory position over the committee, have decided that their confidence level for privacy and secrecy is not yet up to the 99 percent level with all of the new committee members. The higher powers know well, plus have full confidence in, Colonel Knapp, Mr. Benton and myself. With all due seriousness, this mission could change global influences and relationships for years to come, so extreme secrecy is of paramount importance, and your role in this operational mission to Bolivia never happened. The fact is there are no Pookas there, they never existed there, no one there ever heard of a Pooka, and we and you do not even know where *there* is.

"During the past two days you were certainly briefed well about Bolivia, as to its political, economic, social, agricultural and zoological environment. Also, great emphasis was placed on Mr. Che Guevara, the target of this operation. Tomorrow evening you will be flown to La Paz, Bolivia. You will have a short meeting at the airport with several trusted Bolivian officials, and will then be flown by a military prop plane to Santa Cruz. You will be accompanied on this flight by Colonel

Hugo Banzer Suarez. This colonel is one of the most trusted confidants to President Rene' Barrientos. Colonel Suarez and Luis Salines are the only two individuals who know key issues concerning the secrecy of this mission. They will be with you for several days of orientation and preparation, and will check out all of your needed equipment. Colonel Suarez will escort you to Vallegrande. At that point, he will direct the activities of his specially trained troops who will act as the hounds to direct the fox into your trap. The problem is, if Che is actually in the area, the Bolivian troops can only hope to keep him and his group from straying outside of his three primary routes. We are acting on very reliable, but still questionable, information. So, gentlemen, we need three traps for one fox.

"Why is there all this confidence in the information concerning Che? For good reason, since it comes straight through reliable Vatican diplomatic channels. They got the basic information, with follow-up information, directly from a Bolivian priest. It appears that Che has three operational centers: at Mizque, Pucara, and Pampa Grande. He is known to move regularly between these three locations, but never stays more than one night at any particular location. One route is from Pucara to Mojocoyo, to Quirogo to Mizque. Another is from Pucara to Moromoro, to Saipins to Misque, and sometimes he skips Saipins and goes through Pasorapa. To complicate issues, he often goes from Pucara to Postrervalle, to Quirusillas to Triga, to Saipins to Mizque. It is apparent that his travels are never on the same route, and we know of only two days when Che and his group will be traveling back to Mizque from Pucara. Therefore, you are going to have to set up your blinds for springing the trap at these different locations, then exist there quietly and secretly for one or two days without being compromised, or killed by Mother Nature.

"Our Colonel Suarez will be dividing his troops into three staging areas. At each area they will be quite noticeable and obvious, and will act as the hounds to send the fox in your direction. You will notice on your maps that the colonel will be placing two hundred troops between Pucara and Mojocoyal, two hundred between Saipina and Pampa Grande, and putting one hundred between Postrervalle and Guadalupa, and another one hundred between Trigal and Quirusillas. This positioning will create the funnel for the fox to run with perceived safety. The fox will not go south to Alto Seco, for he has been told that there are several hundred questionable troops positioned there to capture him by moving north toward Pucara.

"It is really nice to have a double agent that one cannot trust. We made sure that Colonel Cramanas would leak the information to Mr. Che,' and then, to make sure it was relayed on time and with accuracy, the information was also leaked to another Che loyalist, Antonio Arguedas Mendienta. So, gentlemen, this is why we feel that we have all our bases covered. The only negative in the situation — which will certainly irritate Mr. Chahaus, for it also annoys us tremendously — is the fact that we had to cut a deal with the devil. That deal is a very narrow and secret agreement with the C.I.A. The C.I.A. has not been told any details, but they are not stupid. They will sooner or later be able to put two and two together.

"Should there be a nice part to this mission, it is the fact that the so-called winter is over, and the rainy season has not yet arrived. So Che is recklessly trying to make up ground lost due to the winter weather slowdown, and his very serious asthma attack. This Mr. Che guy will be turning forty, and realizes he will not be Jack Benny and staying thirty-nine forever. Che is starting to understand mortality since he got quite ill in Africa with some type of African crud, and now his asthma has gotten to be a real medical problem.

"To top this all off, he has fallen in love again; this time, with a devoted Catholic lady who is much younger than he. She has his same concept of social justice and fairness for the peasants, mine workers, and the downtrodden impoverished of Bolivia and South America. Che's problem is that she is not a communist. She just feels it is her duty as a Catholic to serve the less fortunate, resist the imperialism of foreign business interests taking advantage of her people, and act on behalf of the rest of the people of South America. She can be described as a social Democrat who has a common interest with the Marxists. Our Mr. Guevara has a dilemma regarding middle age, his health, and the joy of a new love. But these are his living problems. Our problem is to shoot him and make him vanish from this earth, thereby relieving him of his living problems.

"The thing working to our advantage is that the new love of his life lives and works for the government near the town of Cochabamba. She often goes to Punata, where Che is hoping to see her in the near future, but not if you can prevent it. Gentlemen, it is now time for a relaxing lunch break, and we will start the afternoon meeting with Colonel Knapp at 1400 hours. There will be a dinner later, at 2000 hours, at Schmidt's restaurant in this town's German Village area."

The lunch was nice. I requested that Mr. Rex and Mr. Tucker sit with me privately, so that I could inform them that I was going on the mission with them as the third team leader. They were told that all of our needed and requested material for the venture would be ready for us at Santa Cruz. We three would be using 700 Remington's with a ten-power scope; the two other team members would be carrying an M-16 A1 and a Winchester pump shotgun. They were also reminded, if they had not noticed, that the area in which we would be operating was hilly and mountainous terrain, and the foliage was mostly evergreen trees and brush in the east, with deciduous trees and vegetation in the west. I pointed out that during this time of the year, the evergreens would provide the best cover. In the deciduous areas, one could not make their cover obvious, and had to be more particular in their use of camouflage.

They were told that I also had ordered specific and strange survival items, since this area of the world was full of Mother Nature's nasty insects, reptiles and animals. They were told that we would discuss these items at Santa Cruz. I let them know that I had not yet informed the bosses who the third shooter would be. The bosses might have already surmised this, since I had performed a similar delicate mission for them about ten years before, and possibly why Colonel Knapp had dropped a heavy clue on me earlier that would practically assure my desire to participate in this mission as the voice of experience — with a taste for revenge.

The lunch went a little too fast for me, as there was more to talk about with Rex and Iff, but soon it was time for Colonel Knapp's afternoon presentation. Colonel Knapp went up to the podium and got straight to the points of the mission, without pulling any punches. He started off with, "This mission is all black and white. We know the good guys and the bad guys. We know who the target is, and where he is most likely to be. We know to terminate anyone who interferes or gets in your way while you are completing a successful mission. Remember, anyone and everyone around Mr. Che is expendable after your primary shot is made. Also, absolutely no one must be able to assist him or help him escape. Again! Anyone near him, that tries to touch him, or even looks like they will be trying to aid him, gets terminated with efficient dispatch.

"This is just my opinion, based on my experiences in this covert life of subterfuge and skullduggery. In this environment of political intrigue, I would trust no one, for it could still be a major ruse. All this information is not from Che's lips to my ears. It is questionable third-party information from a priest. Since I am not Catholic, I prefer not to trust either source with your lives. So for your peace of mind and safety, please assume that anyone and everyone might stab you in the back. If there is any doubt or apprehension about anyone, just cancel their ticket and terminate their role in this performance. We will handle any repercussions later, but you will be safe and alive. The other U.S. military or government personnel you may see or come in contact with will not have the slightest idea who you are, or why you are there. Avoid them whenever and wherever possible, and you'll avoid possible complications.

"A lot of very secret work has gone into this project during the past few months, and for the most part, the left hand does not know what the right hand is doing, or why. The big secret of this mission is to be known only by you men, myself, Captain Dan, and a few select powers above us. Of course, we can rely on good Colonel Suarez for one hundred thousand dollars, and his life on the line.

"The major secret is that Mr. Che Guevara is not to die; he is simply to vanish and disappear forever into never-never land. Mr. Benton has performed this type of a mission before — one of deceptive reality, performing an assassination in order to deceive other parties. That mission paid off politically and handsomely as to the world order in the Far East. This man Che is key to all the information about Castro, about Castro's plans and objectives for the region, and about key Castro operatives around the world. He is also aware of the involvement of China's thinking as to Southeast Asia, and has verification of key western military advisors training the North Vietnamese in U.S. military tactics. Prior to coming to Bolivia, Che spent time in China and Vietnam as an observer and consultant. He has now been operating in Bolivia for about a year, and has been in constant contact with other communist revolutionaries throughout Central and South America who are cooperating with his old boss, Fidel Castro.

"All information that we will be able to obtain from Che will be vital to our country's major interests around the world. It well help the U.S. and its allies put a checkmate on the plans of potential troublemakers, and Fidel Castro. The reasons why some people suddenly change in life, have conversions and awakenings, are often as strange as strange can be. Our duty here is not to question why, but to do or die, and to successfully complete the mission. Mr. Benton will cover all the particular details with you at Santa Cruz regarding how the shot will be made and the participation of the special medical unit to be established at Vallegrande. If we pull this off, you will all be unsung, unknown, and unrecognized heroes. You will have nothing to show for it except for a nice nonexistent adventure in South America with nonexistent people. Well, gentleman, let's end this day, take a good thirty-minute break, have a relaxing social hour or so on me, and then leave for Schmidt's so that I may enjoy one of their famous cream puffs."

Everyone enjoyed their Bahama Mama sausages with German potato salad. They loved the good German beer, and really enjoyed the cream puffs and strong black coffee. Since we had a private table off in the corner, Colonel Knapp stood up and said, "Captain Dan should have mentioned that, back in 1958, we loved the man who was the topic of our main discussion today. But now he is considered a varmint. Like most famous artists, he will probably enjoy the paradox of death —known slightly when alive, only becoming world famous after death. In this case, with his actions and writings, he will most likely become a real martyr to the world. But it is doubtful that his ex-wives and children will agree with history."

The next morning's meeting was more for the clarification of issues and of the three team's assignments, then to address any concerns someone might have about the mission. Team one was to consist of Eddie Cantor, Danny Kaye and Mr. Hudson; team two would be Mr. Packard, Fraiser and Tucker; and team three would be Oscar Levant, Nash and myself. After a review of the maps and target locations of the Bolivian mission, the meeting was finished by lunchtime, and we all had lunch together. We said our farewells to Colonel Knapp and Captain Dan, and later that afternoon a military bus picked us up at the hotel and drove us directly to Lockbourne Airbase, to catch our flight on a military transport jet. As soon as we got on board, we made sure everything we needed was also on board. The pilots took off, and we were headed for Homestead, Florida, then to San Paulo, Brazil, and on to La Paz, Bolivia to start the new adventure.

We had a three-hour layover at Homestead due to some weather issues, so we had someone take us to the Air Force P.X. for some food and drinks. Afterward, we boarded the plane again for the long flight to San Paulo. Everyone was taking the trip seriously; all were reading Che's *Theories and Tactics of Guerrilla Warfare.* When not reading or sleeping, we played poker with torn-up paper as chips. During the trip there was no discussion about our mission. The trip was like our group was traveling on a getaway tour vacation. We just enjoyed ourselves and relaxed, with nothing on our minds but idle thoughts. All our conversations were about meaningless trivia, but underneath this facade was a lot of nervous tension.

The plane stopped in San Paulo only for refueling, and then we were off for La Paz, Bolivia. That leg of the flight was more rest and poker. It was a pleasure to finally land at La Paz, get off the plane and into the open, and breathe fresh air. The plane taxied off the runway to a building about a hundred yards away from the little terminal. We were escorted inside the building, and there were armed guards all around the place. There was a big table with food and drinks in the middle of the building, and we were greeted in a very friendly fashion by Colonel Suarez and Luis Salines. They indicated we would all eat, drink, relax and talk a little before catching our antique prop plane to Santa Cruz. Colonel Suarez stated that General Rene Barrientos would like to have attended the meeting, but did not think it wise, due to all the unwanted attention it would draw to this get-together. Colonel Suarez went overboard reassuring us that everything was ready on his end, and that his highly trained and top-notch troops would be moving into positions near Vallegrande on the sixth. He then indicated that the special medical team with their mobile unit was already positioned in Santa Cruz, and that all of our needed and requested equipment and supplies were stored at his small military compound. The colonel was a nice guy, even if he was a strutting peacock of confidence. His associate Salines was a friendly guy who didn't talk very much, and showed no expression — pro or con — about the mission.

Colonel Suarez told us the plane was ready and that we could depart at any time. We went to board the plane while the colonel walked Mr. Salines to a waiting automobile. I ask the Spanish-speaking members of our crew if they had said anything of interest during our brief meeting, and several started to laugh.

"The Salines guy said to the colonel, 'Are these young kids they sent us the ones who are to take on Che and his guerrilla band of revolutionaries?' The colonel told him, 'Be not misled or deceived. They are highly trained assassins, never to be underestimated. You should know they will kill anything or anybody that I point to while here in Bolivia.'"

This undoubtedly put good Salines in a somber mood. It made the point clear to him that as a group we were not kids, and this must have made Colonel Suarez feel a little powerful at that moment. The colonel climbed into the plane and off we flew in this bouncy and shaky prop plane. The plane had regular passenger-type seating, but when you entered the back door it was like climbing up a hill to get to your seat. I would bet anything that a lot of the plane was held together with temporary wire fixes. To our relief, we arrived safely at the Santa Cruz airport, and immediately got into an old-type school bus for a trip to the colonel's military compound. I thought we were going to a mountainous area, but it looked like prairie lands. We noticed lots of cattle, sugar cane, and even rice paddies all along the roads. Once at the compound, we were taken to the building where all our supplies were located, and where we would be staying for several days. The colonel pointed out a target range about hundred yards away, and stated that it was for our exclusive use, with no local observers.

There was a large topographical layout of our assigned area on a table in one corner of the room. There were also blown-up maps on the wall around the area, and blown-up photos of nine people on one section of the wall. One was Che Guevara, and the others were Cuban and Bolivian personnel. There was one photo separated from the rest, with a purple line drawn around it, which looked like Che Guevara. Later, Colonel Suarez informed us that it was, as he put it, a duplicate look-alike. With a big laugh, the colonel said, "We are keeping this man on ice until the mission is completed, and then the duplicate will no longer be a standby actor."

The next day, after checking over all of our equipment, we thoroughly checked out our assigned weapons and went out to the firing range for the entire afternoon. We fired every weapon many, many times, and then went back to clean them so that they would be ready for use on our mission. But the fun started when we opened a couple of boxes of my requested survival supplies. The men wanted to know why there were wildcat piss bottles and several bags of a sticky tar wax type grease. I explained to them that I had been trained by one of the top survival colonels in the business when first recruited into the program, and he always made the point that it is better to be safe than sorry when in strange lands and hostile environments.

"My good men," I said, "you may, and can, call me eccentric, paranoid, nuts or extremely cautious. But I do not want, intend on, or plan for the creatures of Mother Nature to get the best of us while we are trying to complete our mission. Because we certainly do not want Mr. Che laughing all the way to the bank about how Mother Nature saved his life, and how some stupid Americans bit the dust. Remember, my brave young heroes, we are going to be living as invaders in this strange, hostile and unfriendly environment for two nights and days. There are things we can eat out there, but remember my write-up about the things that can eat you.

"We are going to be out there in a stationary camouflaged blind, in the dark, with no heat source except our own bodies. We will be eating cold rations while everything else is looking for a warm food source. Of course, taking a crap and pissing on the ground will help spotlight our position for Mother

Nature's creatures. Like it or not, sometimes the food chain pecking order works in reverse. Therefore, these idiot items are to prevent this from happening to you or to me. So laugh all you want, but give me no shit. The fact is, I don't want to be bitten to pieces by insects, stalked by a creature, or nailed by a viper. And for God's sake, don't go near the water, or drink it.

"Let's take the deet item. You will want this all over your clothes and your body for insect protection. The wildcat piss is to scare away some animals who fear meeting their predator. The bags of sticky waxy tar grease are to rub around the base of any tree, and for placing a good coating about five feet up the trunk of the tree near you. This to make sure the tree creatures prefer to stay in the tree, and do not come further down the tree to feed on you. The hundred feet of heavy fiber rope is to be laid on the ground around your blind to irate crawling things. In these ten-pounds bags are sharp, multiple-angle tacks, to be spread on the ground just inside the rope's loop. Pity the thing that comes down on the sharp tacks. The pepper is to be dropped sparingly on the trail behind us as we near our blind position. This is to cover our trail from scent detection, and be assured that the sniffing stops there. Believe me, scent is an amazing thing. It can be helpful or dangerous. My uncles hunted deer with bows and arrows, and before going into the woods they always rubbed deer piss on themselves. Good for them, but bad for the deer."

The crew was told to relax for the rest of the day, and that we were going to have a nice dinner on the colonel. He was going to take us out to some restaurant with a lot of Bolivian-type of entertainment. I told them that the next morning they would be spending all their time memorizing the maps and topography layout, the proposed locations for each team's position in the wilderness, and the faces of those pictured on the wall. They were reminded not to drink too much on this outing, not to speak Spanish, and never to leave the group by one's self, even if there was a need to go to the restroom. Everyone got the point. They all clearly let me know that they understood what I was making reference to concerning our safety.

The colonel gave us one hell of an evening out on the town. We thoroughly enjoyed the food, the drinks, and the musical entertainment. The group was asked if they noticed anything about the patrons in the restaurant, all of whom were undercover members of the colonel's elite military group. Those other guests were there to guarantee our privacy and safety, and everyone followed the rules.

The next day we all started off the morning bright and cheery, for we knew it was the day for the survival rules and regulations of the hunt. I used a big pointer stick to point out key areas and locations over and over again on the topography layout, then selected different team members to find the exact on-the-spot locations with the maps. The point was to make it clear that they were to see and visualize these maps in the dark, in their sleep, and in their subconscious mind, for instinctive reactions as to movements and directions in the wilderness. They were forcefully reminded that this was not the U.S. of A., and that from this point on, our travels would be on poorly maintained dirt roads and narrow paths. They were also reminded that we would find lots of obstacles to make their movements at night or in the daylight more difficult.

Each team was given their assigned location for establishing their blind, being sure that they had flexibility for covering a broad area of target visibility. Team one would cover Che's known route by Saipina, for he might be at Pampa Grande and not Pucaro. Yet he could get lucky and slip by team three, which would be set up just south of Moromoro. Team two would be the Pasorapa checkmate if he got by team three. But he might not go north to Saipina, and take his other route from Moromoro to Pasorapa for getting safely to Mizque. The troops of Colonel Suarez would stay in their assigned positions on the seventh, then early on the eighth would start closing the funnel to create a narrower corridor. He would also have a small Piper Cub observation plane flying over the area.

All this activity should make Che the fox run the gauntlet toward us sometime on the eighth, but we would be in place on the seventh just in case he decided to head back to his beloved a little earlier. Therefore, in the early morning of the eighth, the troops north of Alto Seco would start moving toward Pucara. The two hundred troops in the west straddling the Grande River would stay put. The four hundred troops by Vallegrande would move west toward Moromoro and the Ichito River. I told them that since it had been a long day, we needed to relax our brains, and that the colonel had arranged for lots of food to be brought to our facility. He also personally guaranteed that we would have plenty of ice-cold beer of some type. Someone suggested we turn on the radio for some good music and relax while playing cards, and that this time we play hearts rather than poker. We were also hoping the evening's meal would be as good as the previous night's.

The next day after we finished organizing, double-checking, and packing all of our gear, it was suggested that we go back to the gun range, since we had nothing better to do at the moment, and practice firing our weapons some more. It would be best that we double-checked our bore-sighting at two hundred meters, and made sure the M-16s would not jam due to bad powder and cheap parts. We would all have been much happier if our men had had AR-15s. We practiced firing the weapons off and on for about two hours. When we were satisfied that everything was in working order, we decided to go back to our building and give the weapons a thorough cleaning before taking them into the wild. Shortly after we returned to our quarters, one of the colonel's aides entered the area. He informed us that we would be going the next morning to meet the doctors with the portable medical unit, and that they would brief us on their duties and responsibilities in coordination with our field operation.

Again the evening meal was brought into our facility; no beer this time, just several bottles of wine. After dinner, we played topography layout and map games for a couple of hours. By then, all of us could get around that area of Bolivia blindfolded. Everyone knew what to do survival-wise with Mother Nature's pests. Our gear was packed and the weapons were in perfect working order. That night we all slept like babies.

After a good breakfast, we walked about three hundred yards down the road to the building where the mobile medical unit and doctors were located. Colonel Suarez was already there with his aide, explaining to the doctors where they were going to be located at Vallegrande. These doctors had been attached to the special military unit that was giving special training to the six hundred Bolivian soldiers during August and September; now they were connected to our mission.

The bird colonel doctor started the presentation with comments I did not particularly care for, and I told him that the meeting would end right then, without discussion. I made it clear that he did not give orders, did not get directly involved in our mission, and did not tell us how to do our job or who we do the job with. This nut colonel wanted each team to take a medical doctor along for the ride, the reason being that they could be immediately available to treat and care for any wounded guerrillas captured on this mission. My response was, "Stop! No way, no how; no, no, period!"

The asshole bird colonel responded, "Sit down, soldier! Do you know who you are talking to? I can have you arrested for insubordination right now."

Now I was really pissed, and spoke up loudly and rudely back to him. "Listen closely to me, Colonel Bird Shit. I can declare you dead, and your kiss-ass associates will have no one to give them orders. Now if you don't like my ground rules, tough shit. You will now start listening to me, or we are out of here."

At that point, Colonel Suarez quickly walked over to the bird colonel. He pulled him aside and walked about twenty feet away from us, and had a serious conversation with him for five or six minutes. The colonel doctor came back with a new humble attitude. There were no apologies, but the colonel — without expression — asked what suggestions might be made for the mission to run smoothly and efficiently. At that point, my associates were in shock. They thought my ass was going to be grass, but they learned a good lesson as to how much authority and influence Pookas have when on a mission.

I turned to them, and quietly said, "My fellow comrades, the lesson here is that when you're on a mission, you kiss no one's ass, and you do not play second fiddle to anyone. Should he have continued to be nasty and forceful by putting us in a box on this issue, the doctors would have vanished and disappeared once we were out of camp and in the wilderness. But good Colonel Suarez politely informed him that his welfare was expendable, and that our authority came from a power higher up the ladder, which supersedes his authority."

The colonel got the point, and understood that the number one responsibility there was my men's health and welfare, being the top priority of any mission. Our concern was not the health and welfare of Mr. Che Guevara. We informed the colonel that we would properly do our job, and his concern should be that his doctors do their job. It was made clear to the colonel that we knew how to make a chronically ill shot as well as a terminally ill shot. I made it clear that it would be up to his medical team to get there on time, once they received our radio communication that the job was completed. We reassured him that no one would successfully come to Che's aid, no one would be able to help him escape, and anyone's efforts would mean their terminal illness. The colonel just wanted to be sure that we knew where to make the best shot so as not to kill him, and stressed that it be made away from the head and the center of the body.

The meeting was shorter than the colonel had expected, but it was quite clear to him that everyone was ready. He merely had to be sure that his team was up to par. The colonel informed us that his unit would be set up just outside Vallegrande, at an abandoned airfield. He told us they would have a helicopter on station and it would be used — if necessary, based upon the distance to the scene of recovery — or to carry the wounded party out of the Vallegrande area.

When the meeting was over, I went to the colonel and his doctors to say that we were not trying to be difficult, but his suggestion would have been a burden on a very secret operation. I let him know that the assigned team doctor would have been a white elephant to the rest of the team, which would have put everyone's lives at risk, and that the at-risk part would require his team to become collateral damage. My final comment was, "Gentleman, the fact of life is that your doctors are not trained how to kill. They do not know how to efficiently handle a weapon, and we just would not have the time to defend and protect their bodies, should things go awry."

These military medical doctors showed little reaction to my gesture of reconciliation, so I turned and walked away without further comment. We all left the facility and walked back to our quarters for a couple of cold beers. That evening, the good Colonel Suarez had a nice meal catered into our quarters again, but he and his aide did not stay around. He let me know that he and I were the only ones going to meet right after breakfast.

The colonel was right on time. Just as breakfast ended, he arrived in his jeep and we were off to town for me to see an important item of interest. We stopped in front of an old-style jailhouse facility, got out of the jeep, and walked into the building. The colonel took me to a side room and told me to say nothing; just stand by to observe and listen. We went into a very secluded section of the jail with several cells. They were all empty, except the one in the rear left corner. Wow! Standing before me was Che Guevara. The colonel smiled and put his finger over his lips to remind me to be silent. He asked the prisoner if there was anything he needed or wanted. The prisoner's cell looked better than the rest, with a clean bed, a table full of food, and a large bottle of wine. He appeared well taken care of in his state of isolation. The colonel then motioned for us to leave. We left the jail without comment, jumped into the jeep, and started down the road. Suddenly, the colonel pulled over to a Bolivian tavern, for us to break bread and share some wine.

We sat at a nice table near the window and ordered a couple of beers. The colonel informed me it was the "carbon copy" at the jail, and that the double had been held there for the past two months. He stated that the double had been found at some wilderness outpost called Cobija, where he had committed a crime and the local authorities thought they had captured Che Guevara, based on the photos at the police facility. The colonel said that when they realized what they had, the prisoner was transferred to La Paz. General Barrientos and the U.S. diplomats realized his value, as the U.S. was talking with the Vatican diplomats about the issues in Bolivia. The colonel commented that it was a great coincidence for us, and a better prison situation for the carbon copy. Rather than being in a hellhole at Cobiji, he now lived in the lap of luxury at Santa Cruz. The prisoner had been cleaned up, had great dental work completed, and nice clean fingerprints taken. He was, without his knowledge, waiting to become a stale Ginger Bread Cookie.

Colonel Suarez was not only well educated, but was a strict right-wing military type. Yet he had a very strange sense of humor while giving me this information. The colonel told me that we would be leaving for Vallegrande the next afternoon. He stated that it would take several hours, since Vallegrande was about a hundred and thirty to forty kilometers away, and that the road was not in the best condition. He informed me that two hundred of his special troops had already left from Sucre to get into position on the west side of the Grande River and the Ichito River. He asked what we planned to use as a code when we broke radio silence once Che and his band were spotted. I told him that we had worked out the code with the group the day before. Team one, located at Saipina, would say, "*La papgaya es verde.*" Team two, located east of Pasorapa, would say, "*De que color es el coche.*" Team three, just south of Moromoro, would say, "*La grabadora es grande.*" If the colonel's staff heard and received the message, they would say, "*La cerveza!*"

Now the colonel wanted to know if we would mind having him and his aide join us for dinner that night. I let him know he was more than welcome to sit at our table any time. He told me that he liked my style, and how I had put the U.S. colonel in his place. He made it clear that he also thought the U.S. colonel was a sophisticated pain in the ass, who looked down on the Bolivians as inferiors. His following comment made the point.

"So if you need to shoot him, I will swear it was an apparent suicide due to a nervous breakdown."

This statement let me know that the colonel and I had an understanding, that I could rely on him, and that we could trust each other completely throughout the course of this mission. We finally left the nice little tavern after a few too many drinks. He dropped me off back at my quarters, and said he and his aide would be seeing us in a couple of hours for dinner.

The dinner was a nice surprise. The food was great, there was a lot to drink, and he brought in a Bolivian band and dancers for the private entertainment of our small group. The colonel stated that he wanted to give us a party to remember, just in case something went wrong and some of the group might not get to have good times again in this lifetime. We were all starting to like this Colonel Suarez more and more. The guy was one of those leaders who cared for his troops, and maintained their loyalty by his example and constant honors and recognition. It was one hell of a party.

The next morning we had to pack up our individual gear and get it loaded on the trucks. The colonel was right; it was a long, boring trip to Vallegrande, particularly when sitting in the back of deuce and a half trucks on poorly kept roads. At least the weather was nice. When we arrived at Vallegrande, we did not stop for any sightseeing, and drove directly out to a very private and remote airstrip not far from Vallegrande. Most of the colonel's people were already set up, and the mobile medical unit with the doctors was in place. It was obvious that those guys had gotten up very early that morning, in order to have all their equipment ready and in place. The colonel said he would be driving teams one and two up near Saipina and Pasorapa, and that they would have plenty of time to get into position. Laughing, he told me and team three to have a nice walk.

The little hike with equipment would be about eight or nine miles, after they dropped us off about five miles down a rough dirt road. The rest of the trip down the road would be mostly in off the road terrain, and again, we were lucky it was spring and not the rainy season. At least we would be spending the night at the airfield, and would get a little more rest and sleep before trudging off into the wildness the next day. It was very doubtful that any of us would get much sleep while spending two nights in our wildness blind, due to the fact that while in the blind, we would be surrounded by the company of Mother Nature's beasts and all the nasty insects of prey. We would all have to remember the old saying that, "It is never nice to try and fool Mother Nature."

CHAPTER VIII
"Any Dead Fish Can Swim Downstream!"

The good colonel assured us that once the radio message was received, he and his troops would move in rapidly, and whatever group made the call needed to know that they would be on their own until reinforcements arrived. He stated that his troops would close the box on the spotted position, but the troops west of the Grande and Ichito Rivers would remain in place so that there would be no escape to the west. The colonel explained that they hoped to capture — or terminate — the whole herd, should they decide to fight to the death by devoting their souls to Karl Marx. The colonel had his aide drive us out to our drop-off point. He gave us long, colorful woolen ponchos to wear over our clothes and gear, and nice knitted caps with earflaps to help disguise us. The hope was that in this wilderness we would not be as noticeable as complete outsiders. No question about it, the Orienta Region was pure backcountry wilderness, a subtropical area which during the summer was probably murder with all the rain and humidity.

For me, the walk into the area was pure hell. I was no longer in the active military, no longer nineteen, and no longer in top military fitness. It was a good thing that I went to the European Health Spa regularly, three or four days a week. At least the health spa helped me to maintain some level of physical conditioning; otherwise, I would be dying of exhaustion. I was already breathing twice as hard as my associates. For the first time, I was having second thoughts as to what the hell I had gotten myself into by committing to this physical endurance suicide — and we were not yet one-third of the way to our destination. At least we looked proper in the Bolivian clothing, and any causal observer would probably think we were farmers carrying a lot of corn or other crops to the market. A good close-up look would have given us away, since we were wearing leather combat boots, and farmers in that area go barefoot or wear sandals. But no reason for concern, since that part of the country seemed deserted, with little population, which was why Mr. Che could move around so freely in the Orienta region.

I finally told the team to take a short break. I did not have their endurance and needed to catch my second wind. Papadopoulos and Ruffin both laughed, then quickly sat down on the ground and jokingly told me that this was the trouble with going on a mission with an old man.

I responded, with a smile, "Old man my ass. You may be able to out-walk me, but this senior Pooka can out-shoot both of you at any time, day or night, and still get the best-looking girl on the dance floor."

The short break was nice, and appreciated. We were back on our way, and I felt it strange that we saw nothing except birds, and that the only noise we heard was from the various types of birds. Yet this was a good sign, for if there had been a lot of activity in the area, the birds would probably do less singing and squawking, and that might mean we had unwanted company somewhere. In the case of a wildness adventure, silence is not golden; it might also indicate that we were the prey.

Finally, we got to our approximate location and had to decide where best to set up the blind. It needed to provide us with great visibility, but assure us of excellent invisibility among the areas evergreens. A better spot which we found could not have been available anywhere else. It was a small ridge that ran east to west through the river valley area, from the higher hills down toward the river. It appeared that several trails merged about four or five hundred yards south of our position. The merger of trails was undoubtedly to go around the ridge near the river without the necessity of climbing over higher ground. Then I noticed there was another, similar high ridge farther to the south. The merger of trails in the area was probably created by people traveling from Guadalupe up to Moromoro. This gave us a perfect field of vision between the river and the higher hills, and we agreed that Che would intentionally stay closer to the river for an easier escape to the west, should a trap occur.

As we set up the blind and laid down all of our Mother Nature security measures, I told the guys to find comfort in the fact that we were not in the worst areas of the country; that here, the most we might encounter would be wild pigs, nasty mosquitoes and flies, and the possibility of a snake, but that the ants and termites would leave us alone.

Well, we were all set up in our little home away from home. Each of us took our turn keeping watch over the area, for two hours on and four hours off. As night was falling, we ate some rations and made light conversation about the military units they were attached to. Then we discussed their future plans once they were out of the military; college, or as professional tradesmen, such as a tool and die man. The first night proved to be moon-bright, calm and peaceful. There were a few animal sounds in the wilderness to provide a little excitement, but when we finally went to sleep on the ground, we slept well.

The next day we saw several groups of peasants and farmers walking on the trail. It was apparent that none of them were guerrillas or point men for Mr. Che. At one point when Papadopoulos and Ruffin were on watch, they were playing chess with the little chess set given to them during their training program. I noticed that when they messed up they kept their mouths shut, but slammed their fists into the ground. My team was very good; they made no sound, allowed for no light reflections, and although excitingly bored, made no complaints. They asked me why I was so quiet. I told them I was having flashbacks to the men I had trained with, and the missions we were on together throughout the world. That answer satisfied their curiosity, and they knew not to ask many other questions. The day was long, but we got to see a few llamas being led by farmers, several goats up on the hills, and several huge interesting birds gliding in the skies over our area.

Another night was upon us, after absolutely no activity that day. If the informant's information was correct, the coming day would be the grand event that everyone claimed would help change history. It was another quiet night. We heard some rustling sounds and animal noises throughout the area, but there were no people movement noises and, thank goodness, Mother Nature left us alone to play another day.

Suddenly, a kick on the leg startled me out of my little dream of taking a pink jeep over the mountain on Saint Thomas. Papadopoulos motioned for me to be quiet. He pointed down through the valley, and gave me the binoculars for a verification look at the activities of moving personnel. Groups of people were appearing at quite a distance down the river valley. The guys did not appear to be peasants or farmers, nor were they military troops of Colonel Suarez, and they clearly had a point squad walking out in front of the main group. Thank God we had spotted them early. I told Ruffin to get the radio ready, and to make the call as soon as they got closer and we could verify that it was Che's group. Then I told them that I was going to hold off on the shot for as long as possible, to achieve better accuracy and not have too much weather deviation. They were instructed not to waste their shots if the group started moving toward us. They were reminded that I would do all the firing to eliminate attackers until they got close to the hundred-yard marker we had placed in the area. Only then would Papadopoulos make selected shots with his M-16. Ruffin was instructed to stay with the radio and to only use the shotgun for covering our backs, or if they started getting too close for comfort near our position.

I was certainly wishing that I had a sixteen-power scope, rather than a ten-power scope. With a sixteen-power scope it would be possible to make absolute verification of Mr. Che a bit earlier on. We got lucky: they stopped temporally after hearing one of the observation planes, and then rushed for cover until the plane had passed over the area. During those few seconds without movement, Mr. Che was spotted and in my sights. Mr. Ruffin was instructed to make the call and say, *"La grabadora es grande."* He received an immediate response of, *"La cerveza."*

Now all we had to do was wait until they left their cover and started moving up the valley closer to us. The low-flying plane must have spooked them; they remained under cover for about fifteen minutes, waiting to see if the plane circled back and around to spot people in the area. One thing was for certain: they could not see us, and there was no light reflection from the morning sun on our position or equipment. My boys were getting a little fidgety and nervous, since they had never shot anyone before, or been put into a real-life combat situation that might get them killed.

My comment to them was brief. "Just look at this mission as similar to your successful drug dealer sweeps back in Ohio, where you successfully applied what you had learned and prevailed over the situation in that strange southern Ohio wilderness. If you're nervous, just breathe deep, focus your mind only on them, and think of absolutely nothing else. Remember, gentlemen, we have the advantage here of surprise and expertise, and they really do not stand a chance against our talents."

It appeared that they felt it was safe to start moving again. The point men were about three hundred meters from our position, off to the right and toward the river. The main group with Che was back about another hundred meters. I told the team not to talk to me or make a sound, and to let me stay totally focused on Mr. Che until the shot is made. The wait for Che to get closer seemed like forever. The weather was perfect, with very little breeze, and he was getting clearer and clearer in the view of the scope. While concentrating on making the shot, I suddenly thought to myself that this shot was for Bishop and Spyridon, with my desire and hope being that Mr. Che would get to feel their pain without dying. A little difficulty presented itself for this no-kill shot, since Mr. Che was not coming straight at me, as preferred. I knew it would not be a center chest hit, but I did not want to cut his spinal cord in half, or something worse, with this side-angle shot to his midsection. Finally, I thought to myself, so be it; it will be the medical doctor's problem once I made the shot to punch his clock.

Good Mr. Che was now in range. I could clearly see the front and right side of his face, and he looked determined to get wherever he was going. I was determined to make sure that he did not get there on time. I lowered the scope slowly down to his navel and kept the crosshairs just at the edge of his stomach. A humorous thought entered my mind, that I might get to give this Argentinean doctor a free appendectomy. Wow! Did I ever need to get my mind back to the job at hand.

I took a deep, deep breath, and then shook my head to clear out the cobwebs. Taking another deep breath and letting the air out slowly, I focused right on Mr. Big. The shot appeared to be a successful, on-target shot. Everyone in his group scattered and hit the ground. One loyalist started crawling over to Che, but my dead-on aim focused on him, and his crawl was to dig his own grave. In the meantime, the point men realized where the shot had come from. They started running up the little hill toward us, but had some quick second thoughts once Papadopoulos dropped three of them to the ground as stilled corpses.

Another loyalist was foolish enough to try and get to Che. His dedication, loyalty and devotion made me feel that I could not just kill him, so I shot him through the hips. I noticed Mr. Che was trying to get up, so I took it upon myself to decide that he needed a booster shot. To my surprise, he was barely standing, holding his stomach area and trying to drag himself to cover. My only choice was to make a nice clean shot through his left leg, to stop his nonsense. The shot left me hoping that I had not severed an artery in his leg. That could have meant he would bleed to death, and I would be in deep shit with everyone.

But lo and behold, here came Colonel Suarez and his troops, from all directions. There was some resistance by Che's guerrillas, but most were killed. Several others surrendered, a wise move on their parts. A little shock was in store for me and Papadopoulos. For the first time, we noticed that Ruffin had been shot in the right shoulder and was leaking a lot of blood.

The guy was unbelievable. He had kept his mouth shut, not wanting to distract us, and had just sat there quietly, trying to take care of himself. It was no wonder he wanted to be a doctor.

We gathered up Ruffin and his gear, and started down the hill to get him help. A banana helicopter came over the trees and landed in a nearby clearing, just short of where all the action had occurred. Several doctors and medics jumped out and started looking for Che Guevara. When they found him, they provided him treatment immediately for about twenty minutes. They bandaged him up, plugged him full of tubes running fluid into both arms, and loaded him onto the helicopter for a trip back to the mobile medical center. The helicopter took off, but left a doctor and two medics behind, who found time to take care of Ruffin. The doctor said Ruffin was lucky, since the bullet had gone clean through his shoulder without damaging any main bones or primary blood vessels. The medics did a temporary bandaging job on Ruffin and gave him a big shot of morphine. It would have been nice if we could have gotten our boy on the chopper, but they were not thinking about our welfare. So poor Ruffin would have to endure a rough jeep ride back to the airfield. At least he would be feeling no pain, due to that heavy shot of morphine.

We got to ride back to the base with the soldiers. The several prisoners that were captured were in the group, and the medical team left behind was able to keep an eye on Ruffin. The bodies left behind were to be buried on the spot, without honor or marked graves. This would be a new potter's field in the Orienta region, to fertilize the soil. We finally arrived back at the airfield and were glad the rough trip was over. We noticed a large prop plane that had just taxied to the end of the runway. It just sat there, and no one got out of it. We saw the colonel doctor go to the plane and talk with the pilots, but no one got out of it, and the doctor headed back to the medical facility.

We took Ruffin to the medical facility for treatment. While there, we could not observe anything because most of the doctors were working behind a screened area. There were about seven of the colonel's military elite guarding the perimeter and not allowing anyone to go near the area. Our assigned doctor cleaned Ruffin's wounds, stitched and bandaged him up, gave him a shot of penicillin, and topped off his services by giving him another shot of morphine. Then we were asked to leave, and they requested that we go back to our temporary quarters and wait until Colonel Suarez and bird colonel doctor came to talk with us. Again, this Colonel Suarez was some guy; he had a table set up with plenty of food and wine for us to enjoy. But neither colonel showed up that night. The other two teams arrived in time to enjoy the fine food and wine.

We all slept soundly through the night, until awakened early the next morning by the loud sound of the prop plane revving up it engines and preparing to take off. The only person not to wake up was Ruffin. The morphine must have done it job, and it was good that he was able to sleep without discomfort. The rest of us went outside to watch the plane, which had already been loaded up with its cargo. It taxied around a bit, revved it engines some more, and took off down the runway, barely missing some trees as it lifted off. I turned to the rest of the crew and let them know that the prize package was on its way to never-never land. I suggested that we get some coffee and search for breakfast, wherever we could find it.

Someone said to locate the medical team and the other officers, and there we would find our breakfast. The fact was, they would not have the nerve to ask us to leave their facility.

We all walked over to the medical facility, and there before our eyes a first-class breakfast was being served. We walked up and placed our orders with the cooks. It was quite noticeable that the officers were a little displeased by our boldness. The bird colonel doctor stood up to approach our little group. At that point, I pointed to him with my left hand and kept a serious look on my face, put out my right hand, shook it back and forth as if to say no, then stopped the movement and pulled tight my trigger finger. Colonel Bird Shit got the message. He stopped dead in his tracks and returned to his table, anger all over his face. Clearly, he had not forgotten the wise words of Colonel Suarez.

We sat down and enjoyed our breakfast without officer interference. I then decided to give the troops some good news, telling them that when we got back to Homestead Air Force Base, they would have the choice of going home on leave for seven days, or going on a carte blanche, seven-day R&R (Rest and Recuperation) vacation to Bermuda — the choice was theirs. This really gave them the surprise lift they needed. They were grinning ear to ear, and I definitely knew which choice they would all be making once we got back to the States. They asked if I would be going to Bermuda with them, but I said that would not be possible, as there was a powers' committee meeting in Washington, D.C. for a vital debriefing session on the mission.

After breakfast, we all went outside for some fresh air, without the officers. We noticed a group of soldiers escorting all the prisoners down to the far end of the runway. We got the shock of the day when they lined them up quickly, then shot them all. Strangely, they picked up one of the bodies and dragged it back up the runway to the medical facility. It was the Che look-alike, and he was as dead as a doornail. We moved out of their way as they came up to enter the medical facility, and several soldiers blocked the entrance. Meanwhile, the other soldiers were digging graves down at the far end of the runway. Curious, we decided to hang around, just to be nosy. It was no more than twenty minutes before the doors opened wide and they dragged the carbon copy back down the runway. All of us were a little shocked to see that the body now had no hands. Both hands had been cut off just above the wrist. Our group had now seen everything we wanted to see about Bolivia. Here was an example of where enough was enough. They took the body down to the end of the runway, to bury it in another unmarked gravesite.

We now started to change our opinion about good Colonel Suarez, having witnessed the Bolivian justice system firsthand. I told the men to stay put or go back to their quarters, and said I was going into the medical facility for some answers. When I entered the facility, the good colonel greeted me. I immediately asked why they had cut the hands off the dead guy. He just smiled and said, "It is a pre-holiday gift for Fidel Castro."

He took me to the medical unit to show me the hands, which had two black playing cards tied to them with string. The right hand had the three of spades, with the left hand having the three of clubs. The colonel's only comment was, "The cards are to let Fidel know that he has played out his last and wrong card hand in this region. This is to show him that he is now down two hundred points. We just want to make sure that Fidel gets the message loud and clear."

Now I fully realized and understood about the powers above making a deal with the devil, as to the fingerprinting and the great dental work on a nobody prisoner from Cobija. The world would think Che Guevara was dead. We few would know a documented Che Guevara of record was deceased, but the truth was: what you see is not what you get.

Our time was up in that country, thank God, and according to Colonel Suarez we would be flying out the next day. My thoughts were again on Shakespeare, for his *Pericles* may have summed it up best with, *"One sin, I know, another doth provoke; 'Murder is near to lust as flame to smoke."*

The next day, in came an old World War II prop plane for paratroopers. It was supposed to be our plane back to La Paz. One look at the plane had most of us feeling that we would be safer walking back to La Paz, and that this might be a plot for our coffin of silence.

Reason finally prevailed, for it would take several weeks to walk back to La Paz. The better choice would be to risk our lives in this antique and get home in a couple of days. We made it safely back to La Paz, with some relief, and caught our flight back to Florida through Brazil, and soon landed at Homestead Air Force Base in Florida. The troops were reminded to let me know, before we landed, whether it would be leave at home or R&R in Bermuda for seven days. They knew I had to make a call to the committee, for arranging all the flights out of Miami the next day. There was no surprise — they all wanted to go to Bermuda. I told them that we would all be celebrating the success of our mission the first night back in Florida by going to Joe's Stone Crab in South Beach.

The guys were quite happy to be back in the good old U.S. of A. I made the call for the group to have their R&R in Bermuda. Mr. Lingo gave me my flight schedule to Washington, D.C., and we all checked into our overnight accommodations. When it was time to take off for Joe's Stone Crab, the military provided us the transportation. The restaurant gave us a nice secluded corner for our little celebration. The guys loved the restaurant, an old building with rickety floors at the end of South Beach. They enjoyed the first-class service with waiters in tuxedos. They loved the stone crabs. Not one of them had ever eaten stone crabs before, and they enjoyed everything else that went with the meal, even the Key lime pie.

After dinner I proposed a toast to Nash the Ruffin, who had been nosy enough to stand up to see what was happening, and so became the first Pooka shot or injured on a mission. Everyone stood up and gave a toast to Mr. Nash. He enjoyed the honor, even though he was still having a little pain and discomfort.

I stood up and told the group that it had been a pleasure and an honor to have participated with them on the mission, that each member should be proud of their self-discipline and their professional actions and performance while on the weird errand. I directed them to enjoy Bermuda and to make it a great vacation. They were told that no one would have the slightest idea when they might be called upon again for another mission. They were reminded that the things they had seen, heard, and done on the mission were to be forgotten, but they were to retain what they had learned about trust, foreign justice, the power of authority, and how to deal with assholes one might encounter. Before we went our separate ways, I wanted to leave them with some words of wisdom, based on my knowledge and experience.

"First: when you are out there alone, where your life, and the success of the mission, depends on you alone, never shake hands with a C.I.A. agent. Never let a C.I.A. agent touch you, and always bank on the fact that they will not be working for your best interests. Second: trust and work with the F.B.I. at arm's length, but totally avoid the Hoover Boys. The F.B.I. is one thing; the Hoover Boys are another type of creature altogether. The C.I.A. contractors and rogue agents from the funny farm are always considered to be creeps to avoid, and the Hoover Boys are just weird enough to give one the creeps. These type of people would make Colonel Suarez look like a liberal left-winger, or as they might say in Washington, a libertarian. Colonel Suarez just had a man's hands cut off, but the C.I.A. and the Hoover Boys will cut off your balls.

"Should any of you be on a mission outside the country, where any of these guys create interference or risk compromising your mission, it is safer to terminate them and ask questions later. Always remember this saying: 'It is better to be tried by twelve than carried by six.' The only guys I cannot say anything bad about are A.T.F. agents. They tend to play it straight, since they are not as political as the F.B.I. or the C.I.A. Even they quite often consider the F.B.I. and the C.I.A. as a negative hindrance to their men and covert operations. Well, enough talk. Let's have another drink of two before going back to the base.

"Oh! Lest I forget; should you have some free time while enjoying Bermuda, please search out and say hello from me to Cummings Zuell, Neil Halliday, and Bill Maycock. They are nice people; you will like them and find them interesting. One runs with the bulls in Pamplona, Spain and is a great sailor. One has climbed Kilimanjaro in Africa a couple of times, and the other is a political and financial guru and a loyal Freemason. It is up to you to decide who is whom. So cheers, and I wish you all farewell, with a great trip tomorrow."

The next day we all had breakfast together, said our goodbyes, and caught our separate planes for Bermuda and Washington, D.C. I checked into the Willard Hotel at about 1600 hours and went directly to my room. In the room was a nice basket of fruit, with a bottle of wine and a note requesting my presence to meet parties of interest in the lobby at 1830 hours. It was about that time, so I went down to the lobby.

Only Colonel Knapp and Captain Dan were there waiting for me. They said they had a private room set up for dinner, and that after a good meal and a few drinks we would have a nice private meeting for my ears only.

After dinner, Captain Dan made it clear that he was not really there, and that we were not actually having this early meeting together. He stated that the full committee meeting would start at noon the next day, with Colonel Knapp, and that after lunch I was to make my debriefing presentation. After that I was free to go, and would catch my scheduled six-fifty p.m. flight home. He gave me the party line for dispensing information to the committee by saying, "Tomorrow, you will inform the committee that Che Guevara is deceased, dead and buried. Tell them he was too seriously wounded to survive; after extensive surgery and unproductive medical care, the doctors decided to put him out of his misery. We are certain that the Secretariat for Non-Believers and the Vatican diplomats will be disappointed, but they must understand that accidents happen, and that things just don't always go as planned. So when the committee questions you about who made the shot, just say one of the selected team members. Tell them that the shot was perfect, but when the guerrillas resisted the Bolivian troops, Mr. Guevara was seriously wounded by their weapons' fire and a tossed grenade."

I jumped into the conversation with, "Okay! Mr. Che is dead. I understand that. But between you, me, and the fence post, how is he recovering? Is he cooperating where possible, so far? And what hole will you make him disappear into someday?"

Colonel Knapp said, "Our prize is at a top medical military facility under a new identity. He is being treated by the best doctors that money can buy, but he has not recovered well enough for any debriefing or friendly interrogations. In time, he will be buried deeply into a witness protection type of a program. At this point, arrangements are being secretly made for where he can live out his life; this life being with his new love in Hibbing, Minnesota, or somewhere else similarly isolated, and a friendly Don Scott's airfield just in case someone needs to shoot him again."

Captain Dan now commented, "An interesting point was made by one of the higher powers; that you adopted or naturalized Croatians seem to be involved or related, directly or indirectly, with all of our successful operations around the planet over the past eleven or twelve years. Your original group had Lollich the Crow-Ott who preformed well on several missions. This group has Badurina the Frazier. Plus, the key intermediary priest between the Bolivian priest and the Vatican Diplomat was a Croatian priest in Paraguay, and this priest had been an underling of a former Croatian, Cardinal Alojze Stepinac.

"Then our government had this Croatian, Tony Pivac, who helped coordinate all the parties involved, and even went down to Paraguay to verify all questionable issues for us. This guy knew and learned just whom to safely contact concerning Che Guevara. Therefore, this Tony Pivac can be credited for some of the success in helping to formulate the mission. What all this proves is that not all Social Democrat priests in South America are liberals in political unity with the communists, and that many understand the necessity for right-wing authoritarianism to maintain order."

Colonel Knapp jumped in again by saying, "Oh, by the way, not meaning to take over you job, but while you were gone on your mission, we found it necessary to select four of your crew for another mission. This group will be returning sometime next week. This selection darn near went awry, with potentially bad results for Mr. Chrome and Mel the Diplomat. The mission problem was about the issues mentioned earlier concerning the death of a ranking military attaché and the 'White Mice' situation in Honduras. We had to act on this situation immediately, for the necessity to act was a blessed and urgent opportunity we could not pass up. But the crew we selected played a frightening game on Mr. Chrome and Mel the Diplomat. They started off by saying, 'Water, water everywhere, and not a drop to drink.' Our committee members stood there dumbfounded, and your people just seriously stood there staring at them. Then Miss Edsel took charge and told the committee to excuse them, and that they would all be leaving. A big mistake was made by Mr. Chrome when he yelled at them and said they could not leave. Miss Edsel told them that they would have to excuse them, or it would be deemed necessary to terminate them on the spot.

"There is no question that you trained your people well. Suddenly, Mel the Diplomat got his brain in gear and said, 'There was a man who had no eyes.' This saved the day, as everyone remembered the code word at the end of the limerick. The team of Miss Edsel, Miss Martha Raye, Mr. Studebaker, and Mr. Ed Wynn was ready to play the game. The men only went along as out of sight, backup security for both the girls. Who would suspect a guy from India around their area to be connected with them, or a freckle-faced, young-looking kid with a soccer ball that fits Titmas to a tee? We gave them plenty of pre-training and time to set up their targets, and told them not to rush the circumstances. We provided them the best cover stories possible for Honduras. It seems that only the Middle East, and Central and South America, will be the places concerning our little peacekeeping operations. It is clear the president's men have little time for anything else, outside of Southeast Asia and the problems here on the home front."

Well, my instructions were quite clear, and we had a nice evening together that did not exist. When it got late, Colonel Knapp said that he would see me at lunch the next day with the other committee members. Captain Dan informed me our moment of farewell had come, and it would most likely be the last time we saw each other. He made it clear that he would be staying out of any future proposed missions. After our good nights, I went to bed and got a good night's sleep.

I got up early to have a nice breakfast, and then walked down to the Mall area to look at the government buildings and monuments. I returned to the Willard just in time for lunch and went directly to the meeting room. Everyone had already sat down and lunch was being served. After the greetings we chatted about football, and the lunchtime was short and sweet. Liddy the Ambassador requested that we start the meeting promptly, so that I would not miss my plane. He only stated, "The floor is all yours, Mr. Chahaus."

My report was off the cuff. You might call it shooting from the hip. I just told it like it was, and showed remorse and regret that Mr. Che Guevara had been accidentally killed. I told them that the Bolivians had cut off both his hands and were sending them special delivery to Fidel Castro. I thanked them for making the arrangements for my teams to vacation in Bermuda for R&R, and told them that Colonel Knapp had already informed me of the urgent priority mission ordered while I was gone. I decided to bullshit them a little with fairy tales about our time in Bolivia. I talked about seeing big snakes in the trees and crawling on the ground near our positions, how one team had a brief encounter with a couple of jaguars, how another team had to shoot a wild pig, and how a large lizard crawled into our blind the first night out. I let them know that was not the worst of it: the food was terrible; the mosquitoes, flies and fleas wanted to eat us alive; and how the weird jungle sounds in that dark, humid wilderness had made it hard to fall asleep. Colonel Knapp was the only one who knew that I had them eating out of my hands and was leading them down the primrose path to somewhere. They liked my presentation, even though it was a lot of bullshit and deception, and Colonel Knapp kept quiet the whole time.

When I had finished, Mr. Lingo thanked me for the presentation, and stated that it was very unlikely that there would be any more assignments for the rest of the year, unless something strange or unknown suddenly appeared on the horizon. Then he asked if I regretted not being able to go to Bermuda with the rest of the gang. My response was short. "No way. I prefer to be home with the wife and kids, and I also appreciate the good news that I'll be able to enjoy all the holidays with the family, without interruption."

Ambassador Liddy stood up and said, "Thank you for a dangerous job well done. We appreciate your teams' efforts. We regret that Mr. Nash was wounded, and that your group had to endure such intolerable conditions on this mission. Thank you again, and you're dismissed to go home to the wife and kids."

They did not have to tell my twice. I was out of there in a flash, caught a cab, and headed for the airport. The negative again meant going home while passing through the Pittsburgh airport with Agony Airlines, and a long layover between planes. I got something to eat at the airport. The shoeshine stand was closed, but at least the connecting flights were on time. I was able to get home in time to kiss my loving wife and watch *The Tonight Show* with Johnny Carson. I needed a little humor to relax before falling asleep. I figured it would be best to tell the wife about my successful convention talks and workshops the next morning, after breakfast with her and the kids. As I was going to bed with the wife, I got this funny Elwood P. Dowd thought, where he said in the play *Harvey*,

"You, in this world must be Oh-so clever, or Oh-so pleasant. For years I was clever. I recommend pleasant."

CHAPTER IX
Another Day, Another Dollar; Maybe or Perhaps?

Last year had been busier than expected. The committee was right about no more assignments before the end of the year. The holidays were wonderful, no one on the Pooka team got killed, and the time devoted to home and family was fabulous. One nice thing was that none of us were asked to get involved with the Arab-Israeli War, since the Golan Heights were not our concern, and I did not want any of our guys going to Syria or Egypt. We were also fortunate not to have been asked to assist the new Third Reich Somoza Dynasty in any manner. Most likely, people thought that they'd have liked to dig up Luis Somoza for some form of reincarnation to the throne, while hoping that someone would make Anastasio vanish. Anastasio was proving to be a real dangerous showboater. That was good for his family and friends, but bad for the peasants, the unionists, and the F.S.L.N. (Sandinistas). At least someone in the world had a good heart during the holidays, arranging for some guy in South Africa to get a new, functioning heart as a Christmas present. That was a first.

As a wise man once said, "Just when one feels the safest, someone is going to kick you in the ass." Poor L.B.J. just could not seem to get a break. The Chinese New Year came, full of excitement and allowing the president and General Westmoreland a chance to bend over and kiss their butts goodbye. Good old Abe Lincoln had to be turning over in his grave on Valentine's Day; there might not be many people with forgiving hearts available in today's society. The North Vietnamese showed the general to be the idiot that he was, being too egotistic in thinking that might makes right, and allowing himself to be educated beyond his intelligence. The general's mistake was underestimating a man who was street smart and had gained wisdom from the former land of the French. This little Viet Minh general did not think like a West Point general, but more like a down and dirty street fighter. Oh, hell; even George Patton might have gotten his ass kicked in Vietnam.

Oops! The Navy's Pueblo incident with North Korea was just a Chinese New Year appetizer; the main entree was the Tet Offensive. No question about it, the oriental mindset of patience, deception and distraction had sucked us into the web of being the main freak show in the world. It looked like more action and trouble was headed toward our little group and was just waiting around the corner. I needed to start doing my homework assignments and deciding whom to call into service once those special-K memos started showing up. The fact was, they would not get us involved anywhere in Southeast Asia, but North Korea was a different story. Our group would probably get orders to teach them as few lessons by making some of their diplomats around the world disappear. It would be the perfect situation to prove that our calculated long shots could make a solid impression. Good shots would be letting them know that they should not be screwing around with our spy ships. Since they had done this without permission, we needed to teach them poetry with, "I shot an arrow into the air, and where it landed I do not care," just so long as the fletch separated the body from the soul. Oh, hell! No calls, no word, no special-K memos, and everything seemed to be falling apart in the election year. Many negative events were making sure the president looked bad. Those events would guarantee that no Democrat got elected, and that Big Stick Nixon again got a chance to be president. It seemed clear that all the turmoil had blocked everyone's thinking about us, since all those negative events were not playing in our ballgame or the arena within our sphere of influence. The year seemed to be going to the dogs. It sucked, and our hands were tied, with the shocking events freezing us in place with inaction. First, Martin Luther King got whacked. Then the Soviets invaded little old Czechoslovakia to prove their might. Now Robert F. Kennedy got whacked (which had the fingerprints of programmed De-Patternization all over it). Even Lee Harvey Oswald himself could not have provided a better example of programs and organizations gone awry. To top off the turmoil, college students — our country's future — were striking, getting involved in protest rioting, becoming draft dodgers, and threatening to destabilize our society, along with all the integration problems combined with the Black Power movement.

The year was not even over yet, and it was a little unnerving to try and raise a family of three kids in this unsettling social environment. One hated for their kids to see the news, or even walk to school alone. The entire social, political, and anti-war negativism with civil insurrection was making me appreciate the Paraguayan President General Alfredo Stroessner and his aide, Ramon Duarte, even more than before. It appeared as if I would need to change political parties, and register as a Republican in order to get a new perspective with Nixon and Agnew. It certainly did not appear that they could make anything worse than it was. But it would not surprise me, should Nixon win the upcoming election, that our little group would start getting assignments again, for Nixon understood the Eisenhower Doctrine of spot removal.

Poor L.B.J. was just in the wrong place at the wrong time. McNamara had not done him any favors when he was there by his side, and had done him even less of a favor by resigning and sticking him with an 'Et tu Brute' of Clifford the Dove as a born again Hawk. It was quite obvious that our group would not be called into action that fall when the military took over the governments in Panama and Peru, for the military controlled about everything in Central and South America. It was very unlikely that any of them would need our help in the near future. There was some concern about the Philippines' political stability, with the student riots, the rural farmers revolting, and the intensifying conflict between the Christians and the Moslems. But they undoubtedly had some strong-handed military officers who could take care of things, like maybe Ramos Enrille.

It also appeared as if our group would become even less involved with covert terminations and transitioning of souls, since the U.S. government had formally recognized and established a sniper training program under executive orders, and with the approval of Congress. This meant that we would soon be getting some relief workers who would be working on regular military pay. Those grunts would be doing the miniscule killing of ticks, mosquitoes, fleas and flies, and leaving the elephants, lions and tigers to the Pooka Brigade. The first sniper school was scheduled to graduate in December, and my curiosity was killing me as to how many of our turn-downs and rejects were part of the program. The real curiosity was whether they would publicly recognize our covert sniper group on a more legalistic and legitimate basis, or replace us with the new, low-cost shooters. The bottom line was that they were probably planning to graduate new lambs for the slaughter in Laos, Cambodia and Vietnam. Of course, this all could explain why there had been no assignments, no contact from committee members, and no special-K memos for our group's consideration. But either way, for whatever reason, the Pookas had it one hell of a lot better duty-wise than our original group of Black Chamber Immolators working for Azrael.

They had the nerve to put out a public relations film about the Green Berets, glorifying them with movie star icon John Wayne, who must have been wearing blinders at the time. If the Duke really knew or suspected the truth about the Green Berets and the C.I.A., with their Phoenix Group operations, he would not have gotten near that film with a ten-foot pole. His role in the film could come back to bite him in the ass, and embarrass his good American image. Speaking of embarrassing a good American image, nothing could have completed that process better than the Chicago Democratic Convention at the end of August, with the Chicago police acting like Swastika Nazis, and thousands of National Guardsmen running around with guns like banana republic right-wingers. That showed a worldly sight of turmoil facing American politics, with anti-war and draft-card-burning demonstrations all coinciding with the integration issues and social conflicts causing further urban instability. Those social rebellious acts focused a jaundiced eye on our country, and have made a lot of regular everyday American citizens feel nervous and insecure.

No question about it, 1968 was certainly not a year to be proud of, or considering bragging about. Yet the family and I had a nice holiday season at the end the year. This helped us celebrate the 1969 New Year with hopes and wishes for a better year of peace and quiet in this country. Wrong! Guess I was speaking too soon. But we did receive some nice news — we were invited to the Inauguration Ceremony and Ball for the newly elected president. A few weeks later, just before leaving for Washington, D.C., the news stated that two Black Panthers had been assassinated on the U.C.L.A. campus in California. What a way to start off the New Year. But my wife and I were determined to have a nice time in Washington, D.C., regardless of all the negative news in the press. The end result was that we did have a wonderful time.

The inaugural speech was interesting. It was not the Nixon style I remembered. Despite the biting cold weather, I paid particularly attention to his wording, for this would provide a lot of insight for the Pooka Brigade. Thank God I had my black cashmere topcoat and Swiss-style felt hat to keep me warm. The people around us probably thought it was weird that I was making notes during the speech. The new president said some interesting things, such as:

"As nations, we must open lines of communications, and we must not live in angry isolation."

"We invite adversaries to peaceful competition, and must lift up the poor and the hungry."

"Time's are on the side of peace." (Here Nixon is referring to the international and domestic scenes of conflict and division of thought between people and nations.)

Then his questions to the nation:

"What kind of a nation will we be? What kind of a world will we live in? The future will be determined by our actions and choices."

Nixon kept stressing certain words and phrases: peace, trust, spirit of America, and the American spirit. Nixon was clearly saying the right things, and making it plain to everyone that he intended to do the right things for peace and security within our society and throughout the world. The speech certainly made me feel good, and provided some confidence in me as to him becoming an effective president.

The ball at the Pension Building was an extravaganza. We were some of the youngest people there, and I quickly noticed several former and new committee members. No formal or personal recognition was shown, only a distant look, a wink, and a smile. My curiosity begged to know which had arranged for an invitation to be provided to a political nobody. Regardless, I appreciated it as an off the cuff honor, and my wife loved the little square bracelet trinket souvenir with the Presidential Seal that read, "Forward Together." I was like a kid in a candy store, collecting everything from matches to napkins, and even plastic champagne glasses with the presidential seal on them. These would all make nice little gifts for my friends and associates back home. The event was nice and we loved touring Washington. Before we knew it, the fun was over and we soon found ourselves getting needed extra sleep back home, in our own bed. It is always nice to be home in one's own bed.

The winter was uneventful, and spring was just around the corner when I finally received a "We-Un" (Western Union telegram) from the powers that be. The communication did not call for me to contact anyone. They simply requested my attendance at two days of meetings at the Willard Hotel in Washington, D.C. at the end of April. My transportation had been pre-arranged. Maybe that meant our group would start getting some action, since the new president was not frozen in place like the former president. The new president could make his mark without the handicap of former commitments and advisors. At least the powers had given me sufficient time to get through tax season, and not shock the family with a sudden departure for another training conference.

So there I was again, sitting in the Pittsburgh airport. It was becoming a monotonous part of my life; waiting for a connecting flight on Agony Airlines and letting my imagination run wild about what the committee meeting at the Willard would be about. They had given me no real clues or indication of possible missions in the Political Science newsletters, for those were only informative facts about Central and South America. Only slight special notice had been given to Panama, the Philippines, and the complicated issues around Vietnam.

I arrived at the Willard Hotel in time to check in before going to the arranged cocktail party and dinner with the committee members. They were there in full attendance, but I was a little apprehensive without having Colonel Knapp or Captain Dan there. It would certainly have been nicer for Ambassador Dee to have been in control of the meeting, rather than Liddy the Ambassador. Maybe I was just full of crap, but I had never become completely at ease with any of these new committee members. Even though they were quite friendly, they seemed too sophisticated, too intelligent, and too political, from what I overheard (or over-read, with my speech reading talents) of their social commentary. What was overheard was not the issue, but what my eyes over-read had caused me some concern while at this meeting of the committee.

The meeting was not very exciting. The interesting fact was that we Pookas, under the current situation, would have few assignments. Therefore, less subterfuge and fewer covert displacement activities, unless there was a radical change in the temporary policies of passive actions put into place by the higher powers. The president and his advisors seemed to have made it clear that they would first emphasize and stress negotiations, rather than confrontations. The president had made it very clear, in his speeches and through his advisors' communications, by stating over and over again, "Must have trust between men. Trust between leaders. It's best to have relationships of trust, rather than not trust."

The president, according to Liddy the Ambassador, had made it clear that he was going to first reach out with the right hand of friendship and understanding. Then he planned to travel the world, to find and develop cooperation among world leaders to settle troubling issues. Should this diplomacy fail, then he would use the left hand of covert subterfuge, with big stick Pookas as a last resort. This little committee gathering had provided our group some good-bad news, and some bad-good news, meaning that we would not get to use our skills, and that we would get paid for doing little or nothing. Apparently, no one for the time being would be putting their lives at risk, and some real assholes in the world would get to live a bit longer while the president tried kissing their asses for peace, trust and harmony.

The only thing they seemed to be concerned about was the president's wishy-washy attitude of no commitment one way or the other toward Israel, and the problematic issues in the Middle East. I decided to give them my two cents.

"Gentlemen, since we apparently are going passive and dormant, I strongly suggest that you do not put us in cold storage without further recognition or input. Nearly all of our team members have been discharged from active duty. They are now in reserve status, and developing their careers and family life. Also, I have not had any contact with them since sixty-seven. They are probably sitting around feeling insecure and paranoid about their secret lives, for I have been there, and know all about the feeling of not being wanted or of being ignored by the higher powers. Therefore, I make the suggestion that we have an informative training conference for all the members of the Pooka Brigade. This conference would be to get them all fired up and refreshed out of their boredom. The perfect place to hold the conference would be the Homestead at Hot Springs, Virginia. There are some good wildness areas; skeet, trap and gun ranges in the area; and the place provides first-class, upscale privacy for them to feel wanted and appreciated. Plus, they all need to know and understand the situation as you have explained it to me."

There were no real comments by anyone on the committee. Mr. Rumble said that the committee would consider the suggestion, and the silence made me feel like the idea had gone over like a lead balloon. There was no letting one's hair down at those cocktail parties and dinners. They were all business or social nonsense conversations about baseball and the past basketball season. Everyone left early, right after dinner, to go home or go to bed at the hotel. I spent two nice evenings in the bar. One evening got weird when Mel the Diplomat came into the bar. He sat down beside me for what appeared to be a holy conversion type of conversation. He told me about his assignments in the Philippines when acting as a bag man for Marcos. He talked about his time in Honduras, and his distasteful duty in Vietnam (where he had no respect for the Green Berets), and his total dislike of the C.I.A. He then told me stories about those guys that would curl one's hair. One was about the infamous Tiger Cages to hold Vietnamese prisoners, how they murdered people, and how they were into smuggling and extortion. He pointed out that when the lid blew off their wrongdoings, a lot of heads would roll. He said, "This was only one of the reasons everyone is cooling it; there is a case where our troops desiring body count success and promotion massacred a whole village, Song My, and this included hundreds of innocent people."

The good Mel was undoubtedly indulging himself with a little too much brandy, and started telling me things that I was probably not to know. He then surprised me when he turned and asked, "When deciding who dies, are you not playing God? Then someday, when you must stand before God, what are you going to be able to say for yourself? You have killed people for reasons you do not know; not in the self-defense of combat, but by outright assassination. Would it not be logical that God will cast you down into Hell for your violation of 'thou shalt not kill'?"

I turned to and looked him straight in the eye, and said, "Look, boss! I do, did, and have done right for God, duty, honor and country. Why? Because this country stands up against evils, and against communism, to defend our freedoms with some truth and justice, along with the representative image of the American way of life. Maybe economics is a part of it. Remember, Jesus even raised a wealthy man from the dead just to collect money he owed him, and that is bottom-line economics. You had better go back to the Bible and see that Samson used the jaw bone of an ass to kill thousands for God. David killed a big shot with a sling shot for the prize of sex with a beautiful princess. Then Moses got pissed off and drowned many, many Egyptians; this event being after the example of Noah, with God's orders, allowing everyone else in the world to die by drowning. God also does not like people not following orders, when providing real first-class terminations with Sodom and Gomorrah, and then turning a guy's wife into a pillar of salt to make a meaningful example for humanity.

"Of course, I do not want to leave out all the plagues upon the land. And I'm sure he did not appreciate Herod's killing of all the baby boys, or John the Baptist having his head cut off. But what else was he to do? For after all, Mel, he is only God. You and I, Mel, are in Caesar's world, and our group is doing God's work with honor in this world. So if we do not play God with our sling shots, who will play God, to stop the future or potential Hitlers, Tojos, Stalins and Mussolinis? You need to do more deep thinking, Mr. Mel, before you get further confused and bewildered in your religious conversion. You may want to review your biblical studies some more, and remember what Jesus did to the money changers in the temple."

The actual fact was that this weird conversation with Mel the Diplomat provided me with an entertaining evening and some emotional relief, while at the same time I got some excitement between the smoothness of my black Russians and knowing that this graduate from the funny farm on the Charles River was an idiot. The guy was likeable, friendly and nice, but he was still an idiot. God knows how he had gotten to be a successful diplomat, but it was quite obvious that he must have committed a lot of sins while in Columbia, Philippines and Malaysia.

The rest of the meetings were nothing new, nothing in particular, but there were a couple of things for me to be concerned about, and it looked like this person might need to make a secret call to Sherwood 5-0501. The meeting ended in an unspectacular manner. I made my annoying flight home through Pittsburgh, and enjoyed getting back to be with the family.

Several negative thoughts were lingering in my mind concerning Mr. Chrome and Mel the Diplomat, but I decided not to make the call to Captain Dan. This was not the time to make any waves that could hinder a decision by the committee concerning a possible Homestead conference.

By the middle of June there had been no word from the committee as to the proposed Pooka conference, so I decided to call each member of the team to inform them about the status quo situation of no missions. I wanted to let them know the whys for the dormant period of passive negotiations rather than confrontations, and to remind them that they were not forgotten, only on stand-by. They were all pleased to know that I was trying to get the committee to approve a one-week conference at a nice resort. They were told that the conference would have some light refresher training, and some political and economic analysis of world events. I told them that it was too late to plan such a meeting that year, but hopefully a conference could be held the next spring. I let them know that they would not be hearing from me again unless there were changes as to mission necessities. It was nice talking with all of the crew, especially with Miss Gabalac the Edsel. She let me know, in no uncertain terms, that their mission had been a little hairy, but that everyone had been efficient, cooperative, and overly protective of each other. Regardless of a few close calls, and some nasty bumps and bruises from close contact defense methods, the mission was 100 percent successful. Edsel was one tough cookie. I had to feel sorry for the person she brought the hammer down on, who was either dead or completely disabled.

About the only thing that appeared in the news was a story concerning New York cops viciously beating up and brutalizing a bunch of gays at some Stonewall Inn, a gay bar and nightclub in Greenwich Village. What a sad commentary on the police department. It saddened me, since several of my friends were gay, and I clearly remembered what had been done to one discovered in my basic training unit. Most of those guys were no weirder or stranger than several screwy heterosexuals

I have had contact with during my career — like Cross the Preacher, a couple of college professors, a pro football player, and several covert operatives in the game of skullduggery. July proved to be quite interesting. While camping over Fourth of July holiday weekend, our family got caught in a flood at Loudonville. We lost our camp trailer to the river, as did hundreds of other people. We had to run for safety in the middle of the night, as heavy rains broke two dams around the Ashland area. The river's water level in the area of Loudonville rose twenty feet or more in a very short period of time. We were all soaking wet in the middle of the night, wearing only our night clothes. At least we each had a blanket. The next morning we sat in a Laundromat wrapped in the blankets while drying our pajamas in a dryer. The only thing we saved was the car, which was parked up by the lodge near the road. We lived in the car until the floodwaters lowered, and when the roads were dry and clear we left for home. It was one memorable Fourth of July. We knew that Allstate Insurance would be getting us a new camper, and after that we would just have to hope that things would be better on Labor Day.

The newspaper during that time showed that there was a war in Central America between El Salvador and Honduras. I would put my money on Honduras. Then on July 20, a Buckeye from Ohio walked on the moon. That evening, we watched the televised moon landing at a friend's while playing a card game called Authors and downing a few beers. He had to be a friend, since he was a former Farm Boy who served with the C.I.A., but he knew nothing about me except that I sold insurance. No question about it, those events made July an interesting month.

During July and August, the President started traveling around the world to build relationships. He spoke to the troops in Vietnam, and went on to India, Romania, Indonesia, Thailand and Great Britain. Upon returning home from his trip, he received some bad news as a present, one which undoubtedly gave him a bad case of indigestion. That was when the news broke about the murders and improper criminal activities of the C.I.A. and the Green Berets. The news did not surprise me; my thought was, So, what else is new?

It looked like Mel the Diplomat was right on target about their bad behavior and the exposed negative effects of the free fire zone concept for open killing to increase body count statistics. Orders to kill anything that moves, regardless, is bad, for it creates the psychological freedom that allows the brutal contempt for human life by military personnel. The Westmoreland concept of overwhelming mass people performance seemed to suggest that the generals directing the war felt that our people were expendable, since they had free access to never-ending drafted resources. All this pent-up anger and knowledge was probably what gave Mel religion. But now that it was out in the open, what religious effect would it have on the American public, and how would they react? Clearly, this was the type of wave-making that Nixon did not want. His quoting Thomas Paine might blow up in his face, with the words, "not a place on earth might be so happy as America." The president's big mistake was having General Earle Wheeler as the Chairman of the Joint Chiefs of Staff. The guy could be a philosophical twin to Clifford Clark, with his idiotic concept of creating a fighting stalemate in Vietnam and then switching to hawk, without the wisdom and common sense of being street smart.

By now, I was becoming a little annoyed. The committee had not had the courtesy to contact me about rejecting my idea, and the more I thought about Mr. Chrome's over-read comments, the more pissed off I became. I also felt that I should mention Mr. Buck's overly inquisitive nature, about unwanted probing questions concerning past operations, the people involved, and how we had operated. Buck had been giving me the feeling that he was doing a comprehensive report for someone, or gathering information to write a book. Add Mel into the mix, and there was sufficient reason to call the private number for Captain Dan. Maybe he could give me a little more insight into the mood of the political environment.

I made the phone call. Captain Dan only informed me that he would have to call me back in about three days, which he did, right on the button. He let me know that he would fly into Columbus to see me during the second week of November. He did not ask any questions, he made no comments, and he simply said that he would be staying at the Christopher Inn for only one full day. That was good enough for me. It gave me sufficient time to organize my thoughts and questions for him, and to hope that he would realize that I had not wasted his time.

When the day came, I waited until I thought Captain Dan would have checked into the Christopher Inn. I had told him that I would meet him for dinner at the hotel around 1830 hours. When I arrived at the hotel, I had the desk clerk call his room and let him know I was in the lobby. Dan showed up in less than ten minutes. I asked him if he wanted to eat there, or go to a nice place, the Wine Cellar. He liked the idea of going somewhere else to eat. The evening at the Wine Cellar was excellent. Dan and I talked about the Nixon inauguration, about Woody Hayes and Big Ten football, and about my successful business career, but not a single word was spoken about the reason for his trip to Columbus. Captain Dan made it clear early on that our business would start after breakfast the next morning, so we just had a nice evening together. The only near-business talk was about our former associates and how they were doing in life.

The next morning we met for breakfast at eight-thirty. Still the conversation was light chit-chat, so I decided to wait until he indicated that he wanted to start talking shop. When breakfast was over, he suggested we go up to his suite, where there was lots of privacy and room to work, and he would order in coffee and morning snacks.

Once in the room, with the door shut, we sat down at a table and Captain Dan said, "Okay, let's have it. Who do we need to put the quedas on, for one reason or another, and why?"

Captain Dan certainly had gotten to the point quickly, and wasted no time in wanting to get to the meat of the issue, so I started off with, "There are three committee members who bother me one hell a lot. They have created some serious concerns in my psyche, maybe due to all this talk about being dormant, with no assignments, and that the president wants negotiation rather than confrontation. Confusing, yes? We all matured with, and remember, the Eisenhower and Nixon era, with their big-stick philosophy of maintaining order in the world. This was when our group's very high period of activities helped maintain the balance of power. But I'm sure you will have an answer for me; one that I can rely on to tell my team members before they get too soft, comfortable, or lazy. That is why I asked the committee members last spring to set up a training conference, so we can keep them excited and help them maintain their effectiveness and efficiency. These people are no longer on active duty status, and we just cannot forget or neglect them. You will need sharp Pookas if they are called on for a mission, and these people are entitled to a refresher course to maintain their abilities and capabilities.

"The powers above and you have a lot invested in this crew, so their talents need rehearsal for them to stay professional and valuable. We are now going on two years where none of them have been used to any degree, one way or another. Everyone can get rusty, particularly since they are no longer on active duty. This whole group should have a minimum of one week — even better, two weeks — of comprehensive training and first-class relaxation. My suggestion to the committee was that it be held this year at the Homestead in Hot Springs, Virginia. They did not say no; they just did not respond, and let it die on the vine."

We discussed Mel the Diplomat in great detail; his religious conversion; his loose tongue regarding his diplomatic service as a bag man for Marcos, and exposing the issues concerning the C.I.A. and Green Berets in Southeast Asia that had not yet been known at the time. All my biblical responses to Mel the Diplomat were clarified for Captain Dan. This information seemed to have given Captain Dan a little surprise and discomfort.

Next, I unloaded on Mr. Chrome. "This man, in my opinion, is way out in left field. Maybe I should have said way out in the wrong right field. This guy could clearly qualify as a Grand Wizard for the K.K.K., and run for governor of Alabama. I seldom read lips anymore, yet my rusty speech reading tells me this is a dangerous man to be an insider with our group. I sincerely believe he thinks and feels that blacks, Jews and people like me should be sent on a suicide mission, to guarantee an accident. His conversations I did not hear, but what I over-read reminded me of people that the Chef and I encountered before, in 1963.

"He talked about some black — or brown — judge in Memphis, Tennessee who was asking too many questions and exposing too many unwanted points, and he said that maybe this judge should be put in his place, alongside Mr. M.L.K. Now, if this is not enough, you check him out through Mr. Buck in a casual way, and you will learn that Mr. Chrome has no love for our National Security Advisor. He thinks he is as dangerous as the Rosenbergs were with our atomic secrets. I now will be very blunt, good Captain Dan. If you do not replace Mel the Diplomat and Mr. Chrome, I will need to consider quitting my position with the group. I'm hoping this will not be the case. Look! You can always replace them by telling them that the group is being disbanded. Say it is due to the president's tactics of good public relations, appeasement, negotiations, the cultivating spirit of trust with more trust, and trust between world leaders."

I let Captain Dan know it was time to discuss Mr. Buck. Not necessarily to replace him, but for the higher powers to keep an eye on him, for he was just a little to nosy and inquisitive. I clarified in detail all our former conversations and the specific questions he had asked. I asked why he thought Mr. Buck had not brought up the subject of Mr. Chrome's political and social leanings to the higher-ups, or at least to Liddy the Ambassador. The rest of the day we talked about politics, some interesting issues around the world, and about the president's extensive travels around the world. Dan gave me two surprises: first by really liking my idea for a training conference and saying that he would start working on it immediately, and then by stating that he would take me out that night for a fun evening at the Kahiki Restaurant.

We had a ball at the Kahiki. They let me play the piano in the small lounge next to the entryway of the restaurant's seating area. I spoke Korean to the little Korean waitress; she loved waiting on us, and enjoyed my piano playing. Our Smoking

Volcano drinks were on the house, but not the fabulous meal. After dinner, I dropped Dan off at the hotel and we said our farewells, for his flight would leave the next morning at 0755 hours. It appeared that my little vis-à-vis tête-à-tête with Captain Dan was well worth it, and of real value for the best interests of our secret covert Pooka Brigade.

The year end was uneventful for our little group, but not for the president. Along with the C.I.A and Green Berets issue, the president got an embarrassing slap in the face by the poorly thought-out blunder of sending Nelson Rockefeller on a political tour of Latin America. The guy was seen as representing all the negative economic and capitalistic interests of our foreign businesses in Latin America. The president did not remember, or forgot about, his little trip to Venezuela. He could have asked anyone associated with our group, and he would have learned why there would be violent anti-American demonstrations. After all, it was — and still is — the American consortium of economic and business interests in full partnership with the right-wing military dictators that for years absconded with all the wealth, and left the majority of the people poor. To top off these embarrassments, some idiot authorized an amateur assassination attempt on President Omar Torrijos Herrera of Panama, and two of somebody's farm agents get killed in a failed attempt at an improper assassination. These were just two guys dancing on the head of a pin. They were out of their class for the situation, and were probably a couple of naive young guys who had graduated from the last sniper school, or new young enthusiastic Farm Boys who could speak Spanish. Whoever put the assassination attempt together should have been hung up by their balls with barbed wire, and their bosses sent to a real pig farm.

The New Year was showing me that the president was no longer green at his job; that he had gotten his feet put to the fire and received stabs in the back. It appeared — by his statements, along with his advisors' comments — that the vagueness was no longer there. He was no longer wishy-washy, and might well become a dangerous hawk. One could safely assume that Venezuela, Peru, and particularly Chile, might be getting some special attention in the near future, with a little covert subterfuge and 'anlace skullduggery.' But who knew? The president still had the major inherited problems of Southeast Asia, with Laos, Cambodia and Vietnam. They could not pay me enough to be president. But who cared? I made more money than him anyway, but I did not have his room and board, along with a multi-million-dollar expense account. Now that would make a big difference!

The New Year seemed to be going in the right direction. As a family, we had a wonderful holiday season. I dressed up and played Santa Clause for the children. We had our new Coleman camper parked out back, in the rear of the house by the garage, and my homemade patio had withstood the winter. I volunteered to be a Cub Scout leader and the wife volunteered as Girl Scout leader at our children's grade school. This had proved to be a lot of fun for the family. Since I was in such a positive mood, I changed all the insurance companies I had been doing business with, and by doing so I got a far better general agents compensation contracts and better recognition trips for successful performance.

Then I got what I was hoping for, a call from Captain Dan, who apologized for not calling sooner. Dan said it had taken a little arm-twisting, with some added pressure from above, but that I would be getting a phone call from Liddy the Ambassador telling me that the training conference has been approved. Then he stated, "I hope you do not note some hostility in his voice, since all of this was done over his objections. He felt it would be wasting money, and that it was just not necessary to coddle some locked-in contract employees. But do not get annoyed, for a power above me put him in his place. That power made it clear to him, beyond all reasonable doubt, that you guys were a more valuable asset than his committee. This higher power bluntly informed the Ambassador that two members of his committee have been replaced and reassigned, and that a new Captain Green would be the sole replacement for Mel the Diplomat and Mr. Chrome."

Captain Dan then decided to be humorous. He told me that he had good news and bad, and said, "I need to apologize. I could not get two weeks for your training program. I was unable to convince them on even one week; therefore, you will just have to accept ten days at the Homestead. Also, as requested, Sergeant Turner will be there to help with the training, and again you made him an extremely happy man. He was tickled to death at reminding me that he was the man who kicked your ass once, when you were a young, cocky and naive asshole trying to be a man."

I told Captain Dan that there was only one minor, additional request that I had forgotten to mention previously. It was for him to arrange for Johnson the Dancer to attend the training conference. I made it very clear that I would appreciate him getting this arranged and approved, for Johnson's expertise would be invaluable at this retraining and refresher conference.

Captain Dan interrupted me and said, "By the way, I forgot the most important item: the approved and arranged dates will be May 18 to 28. Also, a new committee member will be attending the conference. Do you have any suggestions as to which other committee members might be welcome to participate in the training sessions?" I informed him that the only other committee member I'd like to see there would be Mr. Lingo, no one else. With that, the phone called ended.

That left me a little over three months of planning time to start putting together a solid program of activities for the training session. Liddy the Ambassador called several days later, to inform me that the committee had approved my idea, and that a special training secession had been approved at the Homestead for May 18 to 28. I acted pleasantly surprised, and was overly obsequious in thanking him for his hard work and dedication on behalf of our group. His call was short and sweet. He stated that his staff had already made the hotel arrangements for a businessmen's conference, and that his staff would notify all the team members about the training session and their scheduled flights. This took a load off my mind, since Liddy's staff would be doing all the trivial work, and I would not have any minor pressures or interferences when preparing for the program.

Wrong! I had gotten comfortable a little too soon. Two special-K memos were received, for activation of two teams of Pookas that had to be at their assigned destinations by the middle of March. I was to select the teams and have their pre-orientation meeting at Columbus, and then they would be transported directly to their assignments. I immediately called Liddy the Ambassador. He informed me that we would not know the destination for our mission until three days before the orientation meeting, and that each team could be on-site for up to two weeks. This was an unwanted, yet interesting, predicament. But I started making calls to each team member, and giving them the option of a two-week working vacation to somewhere as yet unknown. My own curiosity had me wondering where we might be sending the Pookas. Most certainly, if some wild guesses were made based on all the news accounts, it could be Iraq. The socialist Ba'athist were currently in the mood of executing many of their opposition; the lucky ones merely got arrested, put in prison, and tortured. Maybe we were needed to help the opposition break the strong bonds of love between Iraq, France and Russia. We could not piss off Iraq any more than they already were, with their anti-U.S. attitude and their considering us as the major Zionism center of the world.

Then again, it might be Chile. President Frei seemed to be having some serious problems of the type that could have a very negative effect on a lot of U.S. economic interests. It was a fact that we would not want Chile to go completely Marxist as a Russian satellite. But I hoped and prayed it was not going to be the Congo's People's Republic or the Congo's Democratic Republic, for that would be like participating in another Vietnam French screw-up. I decided it would be best to stop my wild thinking about where, and get hopping as to who would be the invisible rabbits with the big sticks. The best way to get started was to sit down and start making the phone calls, hoping to find everybody at home and that the ones preferred did not have conflicting schedules.

The two teams were selected, and would be coming to Columbus for a stay at the Christopher Inn for two nights. Team one, going to who knows where, would consist of Miss Gabalac the Edsel, Oscar Levant the Mr. Papadopoulos, and Jerry Colona the Mr. Murder. Team two would consist of Mr. Lawhead the Kaiser, Louis Prima the Mr. Jupinko, and Martha Raye the Miss Lee. The choices were based on my second-guessing that both missions would be in Latin America, and each of them could speak a little Spanish.

These were the right selections. The two teams were checked in at the Christopher Inn by dinner time, so I went to have dinner with them and give them the meeting schedule for the next day. At dinner, the only business comments I made related to their destinations. They were informed that they could, between themselves, decide where they would go, or that I would make the decision. Or better yet, at the start of the meeting the next morning, there would be a coin flip to decide who would go where. They were told that their decision was between Guatemala and the Dominican Republic, and that both missions were classified as open-ended missions. The targets were as yet unnamed persons, and subject to covert embassy selections at the last minute to benefit the individuals in power. We all had a few drinks and shot the bull after dinner. I said good night, and told them I'd see them after breakfast the next morning, around 0900 hours.

The next morning everyone agreed to a coin toss. The results were that team one would go to Guatemala and team two to the Dominican Republic. Each team was given a packet of complete information on their destination, with maps, information on specific U.S. personnel, and key cooperative political and military personnel in their assigned country.

"Good people!" I began. "Let's first talk about Guatemala. Here the FAR (Rebel Armed Forces), with additional left-wing guerillas, are doing their best with kidnapping, terror, violence and murder to destabilize the government. They want to intimidate the newly-elected President Carlos Osorio so that he will not take office come July. The problem is they are taking out this political vendetta on foreign diplomatic officials serving in the country, and on their own key residents of influence. My own personal assumption is that one of your key targets will be a former army officer and guerrilla leader, Antonio Yon Sosa.

This guy is unlovingly referred to as El Chino, and you will be the invisible shadows in the jungle to ring his bell. In this jungle, you will move silently and slowly, in Gillie suits, and then will sit and wait patiently for all targets of opportunity. Remember, the rule is one bullet for one kill.

"We know the area El Chino operates out of, and you will move secretly into the area. No one — I mean no one — on our side is to know how, when, and where you are going. You are to take no unnecessary risks. You are only to make long shots, so that your distance provides safety. Two of your team members are excellent marksmen at six hundred to nine hundred meters. The third team member will carry an M-16, all will carry a side arm, and all will carry extra ammunition. Now, to make it clear one more time, there will be no shots at less than two hundred meters. The exception is only if pure necessity dictates such action for immediate self-protection; and if necessary, kill anyone who gets in the way, with or without prejudice."

The morning was taken up with Guatemala. It was good that the other team was absorbing all of the target logistics and tactics. They were told we were breaking for lunch, and I'd be taking them to another nice restaurant out by the Kahiki. I let them know that the Red Ox Restaurant was one of the best luncheon places in Columbus. It had excellent club sandwiches, and the owner was a nice Greek guy named Strangess. This would give Papadopoulos a chance to order our lunch in Greek. Pete, the owner, took great care of us at the Red Ox, and everyone enjoyed the meal. But as we passed the Kahiki, everyone requested that we have dinner there that night. They did not have to ask me twice, for I was already pre-sold on the idea. We made it back to the hotel a little after two o'clock, and the meeting started.

"Listen up!" I said. "Now we will talk about the Dominican Republic. This will probably be a different type of mission, yet the circumstances of the country are similar — murder, terror, kidnapping of the wrong people this time, violence, and one hell of a lot of apparent suicides. We are not really there as pro-Balaquer. We are there more for the protection of our economic interests and to maintain order and stability, since our side is anti-Bosch. Again, I am making assumptions that Boschites are to disappear, with the former President Godoy having an accident or being an apparent suicide. Our real primary target will be a well-kept secret, an underground Bolivian operating in the Dominican Republic.

"This guy is Pro-Bosch, and he has been a secret coordinator of subversive activities against Balaquer. This Bolivian would like to cause trouble between Haiti and the Dominican Republic, and he thinks of himself as the new Mr. Che Guevara. When he left Bolivia at the end of 1967, he vanished and skipped into the Dominican Republic. He secretly got a completely new identity, look, and background. When this Colonel Cramanas left Bolivia, he took enough assets to live well for the rest of his life. So now, through some old secret arrangements and communications, President Juan Torres would like to have him returned covertly to Bolivia with some of his followers, to keep influential right-wing politicians and military personnel in check."

The rest of the afternoon was all about Bolivia, and I reminded several of the team that we had a beneficial interest in Bolivia, as to Colonel Suarez. Then I gave them my closing lecture.

"Remember! Each of you are the boss of your operations once in your assigned country. This is where you have jurisdictional authority over all aspects of your mission. You are the boss as to when, how, why and where. So if anyone tries to exert an adverse or negative form of interference, tell them bluntly to fuck off, and if that is not enough to deter them, terminate them. You must remember, as strange as it may sound, that you cannot be court-martialed. You cannot be prosecuted for anything, and you're allowed to be 100 percent insubordinate. But for God's sake, don't abuse the privilege, and use common sense. Remember: the first rule is others die first, and you live first."

They were told that both the missions were unusual and strange, and informed that both teams were alike in that they were only on call for emergency situations that might, or might not, pop up. The call to action might be on a spur of the moment decision by someone with the diplomatic service that they did not know, and that they were not to trust. The orientation meeting was declared at an end, but I wanted to leave them with one lasting thought.

"Please, my good people, just a reminder: If you wound a king, and do not kill him, you're in big trouble." I reminded them that they would be leaving early in the morning for their flight, and at the Homestead Air Base they would be catching separate flights to their destinations. Then they were reminded to take it slow on the Erupting Volcano drinks at the restaurant.

As soon as we walked into the Kahiki Restaurant, the little Korean cocktail waitress remembered me when I started speaking Korean to her. She went right to the manager to seek approval for me to play the piano. First, we all sat down in the piano bar, ordered hors d'oeuvres and Erupting Volcanoes for everyone, and I played the piano for about an hour before we were seated for dinner. It was another great evening. I told them that a military bus would be at the hotel to pick them up at 0845 hours for the ride to the airport, and after that night we would not be seeing each other again until the May training conference. I seriously reminded them that their first official contact concerning the mission must quote to them, "There was a man who had no eyes," and so on.

My job with that mission was finished, and the group was on their way. I had to start concentrating on my work, and on completing the arrangements for the May conference. But first, I had a Cub Scout Pinewood Derby to run at the school. After that, I needed to work with the P.T.A. to put together a committee for constructing a spooky funhouse for the school's annual fund-raising festival in the fall. One must admit, it was sort of strange that I had suddenly switched directions — from doing community service for the country that stops people from aging, to doing community service for the community and school to help young people come of age. Oops! Guess it was time for another Jekyll and Hyde show.

CHAPTER X
Embarrassing Shadow of Shame

Crap! May fourth! As if things couldn't have gotten any worse. There would be a real damper on the special training conference starting in a couple of weeks. I was so angry that I was thinking we should have been given a special-K memo to whack shit-head Americans who were killing Americans. Our team of Pookas who risked their lives for this country's political and economic interests around the world would now be in the dumps. They would feel betrayed by the idiot politicians and military personnel in this country who must have the I.Q. of a tulip. What idiot could even imagine giving live ammo to draft-dodging weekend warriors who have insufficient training, and who have no spine to start with? They definitely must have been mentally impaired. Whoever they were, what they had done was criminally negligent, and everyone involved should be charged, prosecuted, and maybe even sued for all their personal assets, their personal asses, and their first-born children.

There was no excuse, valid or invalid, PERIOD, for killing six students and wounding others on the campus of Kent State University. There was no reason in the world for live ammo to be in those weapons in order to maintain crowd control of students. The incident made me embarrassed and ashamed to be a Buckeye. I might have to change my voting registration from Republican back to Democrat. Sadly, the head idiot involved in the tragedy was the Republican governor of Ohio, and I had voted for the guy. The National Guard general and other officers involved in the incident should have been court-martialed, dishonorably discharged, and drummed out of the service. Those draft dodgers had already made the year turn out to be the worst year yet, even worse than the miserable year of 1968.

Those weekend warriors and right-wing conservative politicians were very fortunate not to have been dysfunctional Latin American leaders; had they, for instance, killed six American exchange students and wounded more on one of their campuses, one could have been assured that our teams of Pookas — with committee approval — would have proven to them that mortality is 100 percent. Maybe we could have gotten the Iranian SAVAK or General Stroessner's Pookas to do us a favor in reverse. How, as the leader, was I to put a positive face and attitude forward to the younger rabbits I would soon be supervising at the Homestead? They would be looking to me for answers to this ridiculous event. One thing was certain: Sergeant Turner and Johnson would really be pissed. I also would have bet that Captain Dan, along with all the powers above and that be, were in a state of confused turmoil as to their oath of duty to country and honor for protecting our democratic freedoms, and to a system of justice that had just been radically abused.

Our President Nixon was not the one at fault, yet he was now responsible for seeking justice for this violation of his words, "Spirit of America, The American Spirit for trust and cooperation to re-build America, and that 'Times are on the side of peace." Maybe so, but not here at home! The President might have just gotten an answer to the question he presented to America: "Now what kind of a nation will we be?" It looked like the president would need to put his money where his mouth is, after his statement of, "The future will be determined by our actions and choices." Okay then, Mr. President, use your words to find justice for those young people at Kent State, for there is no statute of limitations on murder, whether intentional or criminally negligent. It was time for the good president to destroy all the people around that disgraceful incident. One good idea would have been to deport Governor Rhodes and his National Guard officers to Argentina and let the Peronistas decide their fate.

It was a very sad day for America — in view of the "Spirit of America" and "the American Spirit" — as if the fact that young people were dying in Vietnam was not sad enough, we had added to the death toll at home by killing our own young people on the campus of a college dedicated to higher learning. Just imagine, think, and realize that the C.I.A. and the Green Berets had nothing to do with these student killings. So maybe we should have then nominate Lieutenant William Calley as head of the Ohio National Guard, or run the R.O.T.C. program at Kent State University.

The committee provided me a little relief at that point by having Mr. Buck and Mr. Rumble debrief the two teams that had been sent to Honduras and the Dominican Republic, but that certainly did not relieve the real pressure on me for the upcoming training conference. I had already talked to Turner and Johnson on the phone and told them what I expected them to do at the session, and they had assured me that they would be fully prepared. The true test for a successful meeting was at hand. Everything had been prepared and I was ready to leave for the required T.E.C. (Technical Executive Conference) Group meeting at the Homestead. The hope was that the group had mellowed out a little over the issue of the Kent State shootings;

when I talked with them on the phone, both Turner and Johnson had been quite disturbed about the shootings. I practically had to beg them not to show any negativity concerning the Kent State incident while at the conference.

I arrived at the Homestead the night before the conference was to start, just to make sure everything was in order. The registration people were curious about the nationality of my last name, Chahaus. I pulled their legs by telling them it was a mixture of ancient Egyptian and Roman which had migrated to Scotland with the Roman Empire, and now it was a Scottish name within the Campbell clan. My explanation held their interest, especially that of one young clerk who was studying western culture and tradition in college.

The first evening and the next morning were spent looking over the agenda. The first people arrived at the hotel at 1330 hours, and I made sure to be the first on the scene to greet them. Each person was told to check in and return to the lounge bar area by three o'clock for the welcoming reception, and that dinner would start at seven o'clock.

The first shock of the meeting occurred when I saw someone from my past checking into the hotel. I just watched, then went up to the registration desk and asked who the guy was. The clerk stated that he was Captain Green and was with our group. I darn near crapped in my pants; I knew the guy — we had gone to grade school and high school together. He was a genius and had received a Congressional nomination to attend the U.S. Naval Academy. We were never in any activities together, only a couple of classes, but we had lived in the same neighborhood. Whoa! Something had to be done immediately, for it was too close to home for comfort. I made an call to Sherwood 5-0501 and said it was very urgent that Captain

Dan call the hotel immediately, before he went to the john or did anything else.

Captain Dan called me back from somewhere, and the return call was made in less than fifteen minutes. I told him all about Captain Green and suggested an easy solution: contact him at the hotel, say there was an emergency in Washington, D.C. that required his special naval intelligence knowledge, and tell him it was at the request of Admiral Grant Sharp, or someone else of importance.

I sat in a corner of the lounge, watching the reception desk and hoping something would happen before we accidentally ran into each other. Nothing about this was mentioned to Turner or Johnson after they sat down at the table to enjoy a drink and snacks. In about an hour and a half, Captain Green was seen checking out of the hotel, which meant that the first challenging issue had been solved by Captain Dan.

At dinner the first night, the conversation was light and general chit-chat, but after dinner a few remarks were necessary to cover the agenda for the ten-day program.

"Well, well, well! You're no longer naive kids or amateur soldiers. All of you have become true mature magicians for world peace. Both the guys and the girls here have graduated at the head of their class as professionals who know how to make people vanish. This is not really a training course; more like a relaxing refresher course to keep your skills sharp. I know that many of you thought, 'Oh, shit' when you saw Turner the Spider here. You were thinking that this would be a hell week. So the joke is on you, since you are all completely wrong. He is here just to coordinate your shooting competition and to be reassured that you have not lost your skill. If you have looked at your schedule of events for the next ten days, you have noted that there is plenty of free time for golf, tennis, and croquet.

"Turner, Johnson and I have agreed that we can no longer treat you like kids. Why? Because all of you have passed the test of Azrael, and several of you have a few scare-marks from the experience. Breakfast will be at 0700 hours every day. Classes will be from 0830 hours to 1230 hours daily, with competitive events at the skeet and trap ranges. Competition at the local rifle range will occur from 1500 hours to 1800 hours on the days specified on the agenda. The open afternoons are for your entertainment of choice. Each day, dinner will be at 1900 hours. The social cocktail party, not a cocktail hour, will be after dinner, and it will last until whenever. The objective is that when this meeting is over, your favorite phrase will be 'La vita e bella,' even with the confusion of a dual lifestyle and a secret alternate existence.

"Per a quote from one of the committee members, you have all qualified as very efficient and proficient 'do-did' and 'did-do' Immolators. So I now present all of you with your formal Pooka Brigade patch, which can be worn proudly without explanation. A friend of mine named Harold Toppie designed the patches and had them made for us. The symbol on the patch is a large rabbit with red eyes carrying a shillelagh over his shoulder. You will note a small skull and crossbones patch on the rabbit's shoulder. This was the symbol of the original group that Johnson and I belonged to, in the early days of our unofficial shadow operations within a nonexistent shadow government. So let's have no questions, and no business discussions of any type, on the first evening of this important symposium held in your honor. You may consider the rest of the evening as a carte blanche Ben-Bacchus party."

The next morning everyone was ready for their first session, being run by yours truly. The first announcement made was that there would be two committee members arriving in the afternoon. The group was told that it would be Mr. Lingo and Mr. Patrick, and that they were to discuss nothing about missions, or anything else with them, unless they felt the committee members knew about the particular subject matter. The less said the better. They were informed that this was for the protection of their privacy and confidentiality. Otherwise, they could be completely sociable and friendly to these higher powers.

"Now, many of your morning classes will be conducted by Mr. Footloose Johnson. He will be covering vanishing acts in great detail, and testing all of you on illusion, makeup, out-of-sight moments, deception, distraction and camouflage. Johnson will also be making some of you up to be unnoticeable or invisible. Your assignment will be to locate the disguised person, or persons, hanging around this resort. Turner's little competitive program will find out who the best skeet and trap shooters are, and who will be the champion on the rifle range with the M-16. Before I start my session, does anyone have any questions?"

Mr. Badurina the Frasier stood up to speak. "With all due respect, Mr. Chahaus, I have a serious question because of my background. My grandfather and father were in one of the columns of the Bleiburg death marches in Yugoslavia conducted by Tito after World War Two. They were fortunate; thanks to some British tank crews, to be able to escape from the column. They eventually ended up in this country to live free, without fear. The Kent State killings, and the assassination of past leaders, lead me to think that there are issues we should be fearful of concerning our government. You probably have some opinion and/or answer for us. We here have all been discussing the issue since arriving at the hotel, and feel confused about who and what we are to be loyal to in this situation."

The question was of no surprise. I had known the issue would come up sooner or later. My comments were, "Mr. Badurina, I have no pat answers. I know it is not the fault of our president. It is the fault of a state governor with his National Guard officers, who had uncontrolled wild hairs up their asses, and who were stupid enough to allow live ammo in the weapons held by poorly trained weekend warriors. We cannot condemn the whole country for a single state's idiotic leaders. I'm sure every other state governor, along with federal officials and regular military personnel are very embarrassed about the Kent State incident. I personally feel doubly bad, since I voted for that governor. I live in the same state as that governor, and worse yet, I live in the same town. No one ever said the United States was perfect, and that we do no harm. We certainly have our number of bugaboos to lower our heads in shame about, and clearly have too many leaders with bats in their belfries. But I have been all over this world, and I still have not found a better place than this place which I call home. I've found many places that were a lot worse.

"I hope that in some small way I provided all of you an answer, for it is the best I can do. There is no simple explanation for the incident, before or after the fact, but enough is enough. We must get on with this morning's session. And I want you to have a pleasant and enjoyable nine days, without considering which blithering idiots in this world need to be vanquished. You know, the not-so-humorous part is that most people do not realize how strange this world is, or can be, when the people in power do not get their way. You, in this covert life, have a strange advantage over most people, and this will help you tremendously in your future careers. You have learned that seeing the invisible is the trick, since what you see in social politics and social economics is not what you get, and the most you will encounter is illusion for political expediency and necessity. Those of you who are going to college are learning the basics, with the foundation of whatever, but I am sure you have already realized that most of it is not practical on the street and in the real world. As time goes on, all of you will understand the saying, 'Those that can, do; those that can't, teach.' This is not necessarily a bad thing, for someone has to teach the basics, require rehearsals, and grade everyone on their development. But most professors and teachers are only observers of, and not participants in, the real world. They would not comprehend your schooling, where there was nothing below an A, and no second place.

"Your advantage is that you are all participants, but first you must still learn everything the observers can teach you. Once learned, you can make practical use of it on the street. Without knowing it, you have already realized that there are more dimensions to this world than ordinary people or scientists think about. There is always one more dimension, referred to as the creative image of invisibility; the one that is classified as nonexistent. It never happened, and we do not have the slightest idea what you're talking about. So within your profession there are no known details, but only the devil to pay. It is not what you see, but what you cannot see, that decides your fate. It is not what you find, but what you cannot find, see, or touch, that gives you that sixth sense and makes the hair on the back of your neck raise up. This learned instinct will give you an advantage over your competitors in this world. Well, enough philosophy for this morning — once I get wound up, I just cannot shut up. Let's start talking about and testing your marksmanship skills.

"In the envelope placed before you is a test comprised of sixty questions. Those who cannot pass the test will have to go to bed early, without enjoying the social hour. Those who miss more than three questions must buy everyone else's drinks, and anyone who misses only one question will not be allowed to have any drinks. But first, you need to be given a brief review concerning your judgment calls every time you focus in on a target, regarding distance and how your effectiveness can be affected by wind, temperature and humidity. We will not be talking about the 700 Remington or the special made Custom Mauser Waffen Sporters. For this test, your thinking will be based on the M-16 A-1, with an assumed bore-sighting at one hundred, two hundred, and three hundred meters. All questions will be multiple choice, except the last three. These last three questions are rather impractical in reality, but practical in theory if you unfortunately find yourself in an adverse situation with no other options.

"The simple answer to the last three questions would be to have a more powerful weapon. But we want to know the negative effects and adjustments necessary for a successful shot, taking into account distance, wind and temperature. We all know that none of us would even want to make a shot with an M-16 beyond one hundred and fifty meters, but that's life, and this is only a test. We know that rain is not a factor, the target is assumed to be stationary, and humidity will not be a factor at these stated distances. We've provided you with three temperature assumptions of thirty-two degrees, eighty degrees, and one hundred and five degrees. The test is all yours. Now I'm going to leave the room to get some coffee. Please do not share your answers, for the person who does not know the answer may cost you your life on a future mission."

When they finished the test, it was time for lunch. I felt it necessary to make a few closing remarks.

"This afternoon, I'll be grading your tests, but I will not disclose the results until after dinner tomorrow night. We do not want to deny you an enjoyable evening with the guest committee members. You will all like Mr. Lingo. He loves people who speak foreign languages, so — just for fun — never greet him or start a conversation in English. Use the language other than English that you're most familiar with. He will get a real kick out of our little game. I blew his mind once by greeting him in Croatian and then speaking Korean and some Spanish. The other gentleman, whom you'll also enjoy, is Mr. Patrick. He is quite interesting politically, very opinionated and on the conservative side. He will probably explain the whole Nixon doctrine of negotiation rather than confrontation to you, and Nixon's desire to develop trusting relationships among all the world's leaders via his extensive travel plans. But please! Do not allow any conversations to develop about Kent State University, the C.I.A., the Green Berets, or the Vietnam incident at the village of Song My. Also, you hopefully do not need to be reminded that there is to be no discussion of or comments about past missions, period! This order will assure that we can all relax and have a good time. Let's hope that you learn more from them than they think they might learn from you."

They were then told to have a nice afternoon with Turner the Spider, and a good time at the next morning's session with Footloose Johnson. I told them I'd be seeing them at dinner. After a nice lunch with the gang, I went to my room, called the wife, and took a nice long nap. I did not even get up to meet the committee members when they checked into the hotel. They knew how to find their rooms and read the program schedule, and we would be seeing each other at dinner.

Dinner that night was excellent. Everyone enjoyed conversing at the table with Mr. Lingo and Mr. Patrick. After dinner, both committee members were asked to say a few words to the Pooka Brigade. Mr. Lingo went first.

"Ladies and gentlemen, it is an honor to be here with you at this symposium, and I cannot wait to participate in one of your Ben-Bacchus parties. But first, you need to know that there are people out there who appreciate what you are doing, even though it is unnoticed and unrecognized, and they would like to thank you. The difficulty is that they do not know whom to thank. They do not know who you are, or even that you really exist. Beyond a dozen or so people in this political game of intrigue, you are all just a figment of someone's imagination, and the game being played is one of 'truth or consequences.'

"Please remember that you are the preventative medicine arm of a shadow government operation. Your primary function is to protect and preserve American's rights, privileges, and freedoms in an unsympathetic and conniving world. You can all be assured that your preemptive actions taken have been justified and valid, for we only receive mission orders to prevent a greater wrong, or a greater injustice, that may occur from a passive attitude, a passive response, or complete inaction. We deal with problems only in the abstract, but you have to deal with them in the concrete. I envy you for your talents and professionalism, but I do not envy your job responsibilities. It is nice to meet all of you, our group of special centurions, face to face."

Wow! Mr. Lingo said the right things in a short and sweet manner, and he held everyone's attention. I hoped that Mr. Patrick would be able to top this off for a nice evening, as he stood up and began his remarks.

"Honored centurions, I would like to start off with a statement about life and about people made by Winston Churchill. It will require a little philosophical thought, but with your experience, I'm quite sure all of you will get the point of the story. Mr. Churchill said, 'Dogs look up to you, cats look down on you, and pigs look you straight in the eye as an equal.' The idea here is that pigs do not sniff or scratch your ass; they just provide you with nice juicy pork chops. Besides that, they know how to enjoy and survive in the mud because they have the developed hide of a rhinoceros. I cannot imagine the toughness of your hides, and the strong mental discipline you must need to live this covert and unglorified dual life and existence. It would be extremely hard for me to imagine what your friends, relatives, teachers, employers and pastors would think, or how they would react, if they knew the real facts of your lives. I should wish, hope and pray that if your secret lives are ever exposed, you are recognized as heroes rather than treated like lepers, and appreciated rather than feared."

Mr. Patrick went on to tell the group briefly about Nixon's diplomatic trips and those he planned to take during the next few years; trips designed to create harmony, trust and cooperation between nations and peaceful relationships between world leaders. The group enjoyed hearing all the comments, which made them feel a lot better about the current circumstances in the world and here at home. But the crew was beginning to get a little impatient for their Ben-Bacchus party to begin. They, like anyone else, realized that too much seriousness can kill the goose, and put a damper on a good night's entertainment.

The committee members enjoyed their four days with the group. They even entered into some of the fun and games with Johnson's shadows and deception training, and they shot some skeet and trap with the guys. We all played a round of golf with them the last day. Needless to say, they must have played a lot more golf than we had, for my ninety-two did not even come close to Lingo's and Patrick's scores, which were in the low eighties.

The Pookas all had perfect test scores on their sniper shooting skills. They had fun playing Footloose Johnson's games of illusion, distraction, and out-of-sight moments. Everyone got into the competition with Sergeant Turner at the skeet and trap ranges, big time. The real surprise was that those who knew how to play golf did so, while those who had not learned how to play golf took regular lessons with the club's staff and pro. They had their own private tournament the last couple of days of the conference. But the biggest surprise was that two of the beginners took to it like ducks to water. They played in the tournament as though golf was second nature for them. The ten days went very fast, and everyone enjoyed the entire program.

The time came for our farewell dinner, with recognition and awards for the different events, and the final Ben-Bacchus party. I took over as the master of ceremonies after dinner. First, I asked the group to give Johnson and Turner a round of applause for their fine programs. The group responded with a loud, boisterous show of appreciation, and this made Turner and Johnson very happy campers. Then it was time for me to announce the winners of the various competitions.

"Ladies and Gentlemen, the first winner to be announced is a real surprise to me, for none of this staff knows where she learned to shoot skeet like an Olympian. The best of the best skeet award goes to Miss Gabalac the Edsel. Okay, you can now sit down, Miss Edsel, and quit showing off with all you wiggling and giggling. As for the rest of you guys, you can stop all the oohing and aahing; you all saw how good of a dancer she was, and how good of a dancer Miss Delilah Lee was, at the parties.

"The next person gets two recognition awards for being the best on the trap range, and for having the best points score on the rifle range. He won by the skin of his teeth over everyone else's excellent scores, but someone had to win. This honor goes to Danny Kaye the Mr. Rex. Okay, you can stop your bowing and finger-pointing at all those who just lost money to you. But do not forget that I get 20 percent of your winnings on both competitions.

"Actually, Mr. Footloose Johnson should get the next award, for helping the two individuals win in the categories of out-of-sight moments and complete deception. The sad part here is that most of you playing the game knew the deception was going on, but if you were the targets, most of you would now be dead and the terminator long gone. The two being recognized for this honor are Mr. Ruffin the Nash and Mr. Jupinko the Louis Prima.

"There is one more award for having a sharp eye. This observant person stayed alive to play the game another day. The 'on the ball' award goes to Mr. Iff the Tucker.

"Our champion scratch golfer, with a thirty-six and a thirty-nine, is Mr. Lawhead the Kaiser. The handicap winner with the lowest score is our own Martha Raye the Miss Lee. Now, guess who won on the coquette green by destroying everyone with pure skill and tactical play? The winner is none other than our own Mr. Footloose Johnson. The only real competition he encountered was from Ed Wynn the Mr. Vyas. This I do not understand, as this is not really an American sport. Who knows? Maybe this is a big game out there in the never-never land of Hollywood. We Midwesterners just cannot get past football and baseball."

With the recognition completed, it was time for the Ben-Bacchus farewell party. They were informed that the music, snacks and booze would be available for as long as they wanted to remain awake and party. They were told that their transportation from the hotel to the airport would not be leaving until 1145 hours, and that none of their flights left until after 1700 hours. They all knew that the farewell breakfast would be at 0845 hours, and that it would be best if they were already packed to depart. We all had a lot of fun and fellowship, and when we boarded the big bus to leave there was a sense of let-down. Still, we all needed to get home to our careers, schooling or whatever.

There was not one single assignment given, or a committee meeting held, during the rest of 1970, but I had a feeling a couple of times that there might be a "We-Un" for action. Our president was pressed to keep his word by going to Mexico in August, then during September and October going to Italy, Spain, Ireland and Great Britain. The real shock was his going to Yugoslavia to visit with Mr. Tito. One had to give the president credit, for he gave one hell of a terrific talk to the United Nations at the end of October. Meanwhile, we had gotten lucky in Lebanon when they elected Suleiman Franjieh as president. He was just the tough guy the Lebanese people needed to maintain order, suppress the troublemakers, and preserve and protect the Paris of the Mediterranean. But the shit hit the fan when the Popular Front of Liberation (PLO) of Palestine and their Black September group hijacked four passenger planes and took more than three hundred hostages. I figured we might get called up for immediate action, since no one was going to allow expert Jewish snipers into the desert near Amman, Jordan. But I changed my mind when I remembered that we had many recently-trained military snipers in the region.

I was quite certain the group would be activated when the Chileans elected Salvador Allende Gossens to office as a Marxist Socialist. This guy vowed to make radical social reforms and create Chilean nationalization of foreign industry and commerce. If so, his days were numbered, for his goals were in complete conflict with many other financial, political and economic interests around the world. I figured that I would need to start thinking about who might be best for an extended vacation in Santiago, Chile. The question was: how many teams might be involved? At least my homework would be out of the way once a special-K memo arrived, and all the necessary research packages would be prepared for immediate use on short notice when called by the committee. It was doubtful that anyone really gave a crap about the Congo being the first African province to declare itself a communist state. But maybe we should be more concerned about General Marcelo Levingston becoming the new power leader in Argentina, after certain of our pro-interest parties took care of President Arambura. But nevertheless, the New Year came and went, with us collecting our high unemployment checks. And sadly, there were the deaths of Jimmie Hendrix, Janice Joplin, and the six unfortunate students at Kent State University; a few lost souls whose voices would not be heard again.

It looked like most of the covert hard work put into Central and South America by major U.S. corporations to protect and preserve their petroleum, agriculture, mineral and banking interests had faded away into the Socialist and Marxist camps. The new rhythm of the meringue was the beat of the anti-American imperialist rhetoric being sounded by Peru, Chile, Uruguay, and our friend Bolivia. Plus, there were clear echoes of negative social change heard in Ecuador and Columbia. Apparently, the two ringleaders encouraging everyone in the region were President Torres of Bolivia and President Allende of Chile. So where was our good Colonel Suarez when we needed him? But again, I seemed to have been thinking and speaking too soon. The news reports stated that Colonel Suarez had ousted President Torres of Bolivia with a military coup, and that General Lanusse had overthrown and replaced General Levingston in Argentina. Both of those guys were smart, for they knew it was always best to put the opposition into a cell, or plant them in a cemetery. Also, they appreciated the temporary use of a cell for necessary interviews before the occupant committed an apparent suicide.

Amazement was not the word for this inactivity. The long dormant state with no missions was beginning to seem ridiculous, but the president and his men must not have wanted to screw up the stew with too many elements playing in the game of world politics. Yet no one told the C.I.A. to stop screwing around, and they were radically screwing up things in Argentina. Now that they controlled the theater, they were clearly mismanaging the stage in their efforts to mislead, misdirect and deceive the people of Argentina, along with those of the U.S. of A. Maybe spies were allowed free reign to roam as they might and do as they pleased, regardless of whom they hurt, and never having to be accountable for their collateral damage. I just could not believe the White House had sponsored that play in Argentina. Even worse, they allowed the first act of the play to continue, with all the deceptive promotion and encouragement of riots, bombings, arson and shootings, which could well turn out to tarnish the C.I.A.'s and our country's image worse than Vietnam had. It was a disgrace; all the bribery, extortion, blackmail, and false rumors and stories that were the same old standard C.I.A. blueprints for operations. The blood on the fingerprints of atrocities everywhere in Argentina belonged only to the C.I.A. for their encouragement. They, along with their cohorts in Argentina, needed to be held accountable and pay for their sins.

There was the president, saying he wanted peace, trust and tranquility, but with the C.I.A. screw-ups first in Vietnam and then Argentina, one could only wonder when the other shoe would drop, and fall on the bald eagle's head. The Pandora's Box of troubles couldn't be playing out well with the president's tactics of offering the open hand of friendship for trust and cooperation, and negotiation rather than confrontation. I'd have bet good money that China and the Soviet Union were looking with a real jaundiced eye at the White House's policies, and that wise old Castro was probably laughing all the way to his party rally against U.S. imperialism. After all, it was the C.I.A. screw-ups, not the Kennedys, that gave him his established place in history.

Yet Nixon announced in July that he was going to China the next February, and his key advisors said that he had plans to go to the Soviet Union that next summer. There should have been some serious discussion at those meeting about U.S. actions and intentions around the world. But the Olympics in Munich got all the attention that summer, with the attack by Palestinians on the Olympic village. The P.L.O. killed two Israeli coaches and took an additional nine hostages, which were killed later. As they say, what goes around comes around; everyone wanted to forget who the terrorist were that blew up a hotel and killed all those British officers and other hotel guests. And who had told the Palestinians to pack up and leave Israel immediately with only what they could carry? It all showed that short, selective memories create interesting history, and a lot of those closeted memories would someday come back to haunt even the U.S. of A.

Well, well! Surprises never seem to end, for what should appear but a special "We-Un" from the committee. They were requesting me to appear in Washington, D.C. during the last week of September. There must have been something going seriously astray, since it was doubtful that they wanted me there for my personality and friendship. They certainly could have found a better piano player than me for a lot less money. Since command performances must be honored, I started doing some comprehensive homework — extensive reading of newspapers and magazines, and paying more attention to the radio and television news. The question that occasionally crossed my mind was: is this committee just periodically testing me, or might they really be relying on my input and insight? Regardless of what I thought, they would be expecting me to make a comprehensive report on what I saw happening around the world. Then they would give me their take on things. But this time, I was bluntly going to ask them why our group was still dormant and held in an inactive reserve status, and why they were letting our special talents go to waste. The situation we were in did not seem right, especially when there were obvious opportunities for the necessary displacement of the evils in the world.

I hoped it was not going to be another do-nothing meeting. I was tired of going through the Pittsburgh airport for connecting flights, and getting another shoeshine that was not needed just to kill time. A change of hotels would not be a bad idea either, for the Willard had to be the political intrigue center of Washington. The hotel always seemed to be full of stuffed shirts and people like those on the committee.

There I was, sitting at the hotel bar, bored, before the meeting even started the next morning. I wasn't even excited about making a presentation to the group. Maybe I was just getting older. I was asking more questions, but the answers no longer seemed to make sense and they bothered me more than usual. Maybe as one gets older, all the formal game-playing bullshit wears off and becomes less impressive. And too, I had come to enjoy in life a good beer, a night of bowling, and a visit to the Villa Nova in Worthington for a great hamburger. It seemed like the more formal people got, the more phony they became. This was probably due to the fact that they never had to come down to earth and assassinated someone relevant.

As events would have it, my boredom was subsiding because of something that piqued my interest. I noticed Mr. Buck and two other distinguished gentlemen sitting at a corner table, off to the side of the bar. The two men had their backs to me. Mr. Buck must have checked into the hotel earlier, since he apparently had a meeting with these guys prior to our scheduled meeting. The guys looked like politicians, due to their serious and formal appearance of being all business. My over-reading of Mr. Buck's one-sided conversation led me to think they were probably senators or congressmen.

The visual nosiness was not good. I decided to close my eyes and enjoy my black Russian and peanuts. But my curiosity got the best of me, even though my speech reading skills had diminished somewhat from lack of use. The guy was easy to read, with his slow and deliberate mouth movements and very specific gestures. I quickly got the uncomfortable feeling that my speech reading should never have occurred, and if it was noticed, my physical being could be put at risk. I finished my drink, quietly left the bar without being obvious, and made sure to stay unnoticed when other people walked between me and their table. I did not gather all the points of the conversation, but I got enough to know my loose lips could put me in the hot seat. I would have to play it cool at the meeting the next day, before considering making another Sherwood call to Captain Dan. Weird events like this were beginning to make me think that I was starting to become too old and paranoid for the arena of covert politics and skullduggery. At least at that point, I was getting paid for doing nothing hazardous or dangerous to myself or my fellow Pookas.

A good breakfast is the way to start a good day. They had an excellent buffet breakfast set up in the meeting room, and I felt fresh and relaxed after a good night's sleep, thanks to several black Russians. The meeting room started to fill up with the committee members. I noticed three new faces among the group, but none were the men who had been with Mr. Buck the previous night, thank God! After breakfast, Liddy the Ambassador stood up to take charge of the meeting. He introduced the three new members of the committee by their code names of Mr. Brute, Mr. Bowler and Mr. J-Ark, and then introduced me to them. They apparently already knew each other from previous get-togethers. Liddy asked me to make my presentation first.

I stood up sharply and said, "My comments, gentlemen, will be short and sweet. I have more questions than answers. I would prefer to reserve any additional comments and input until later on in the meeting, after I have heard other comments. I do not intend to make any comments about issues within the United States, since that is not under the auspices of this committee. Our only concern is dealing with foreign obstacles that interfere with our multiple international interests. Therefore, the only major problems noted in this hemisphere are Chile and its President Allende, along with Uruguay and its leader, General Seregni. The rest of the region seems to be in a semi-stable position.

"Now for my concerns as to the Far East, excluding Vietnam, Laos and Cambodia: there is, from what I see and hear, a real problem developing with Indonesia. This problem is with their President Golka, who is directing the country to become a communist satellite of either Russia or China. But his choice of alliances will be conditioned upon which one provides the most military and economic aid. It should be noted that some military officers might step in and solve the problem for us in Indonesia, but the Philippines could become a little unruly with their demands that we vacate their country as soon as possible. Remember, gentlemen, stable anarchies have been known to disintegrate, even if the power structure is made up of seven or eight controlling families. But here, rebellious people and the youth of the country being aligned with communist help could change the picture.

"Everyone thought it was a good thing that Hafez Al-Assad threw out the Ba'athist leadership of Al-Attassi and Al-Jadid, and then executed most of the right-wing Ba'athist who wanted to totally destroy Israel. They also thought Al-Assad was less radical, and would be more moderate politically, for favorable relations with Israel. Wrong! He only wanted to replace Egypt as Russia's favorite Arab, and he will soon turn his lion's teeth and claws in the direction of Israel, once he gets enough Chinese and Russian military and economic aid. Syria, my good friends, will be a permanent boil on everyone's ass or, as they say, 'A pimple on the ass of progress.' So it would not surprise me at all if it was learned that the C.I.A. helped Hafez Al-Assad dispose of Al-Jadid. Now, as for Iran and Iraq: we should be content as long as they are bickering among themselves, for if things should get out of hand, our SAVAK-trained Pookas will maintain order and stability within the region along with Jordan, who is probably our best and most loyal ally in the area.

"I end my commentary by being a little inquisitive and curious about the passive reserve status of our group. No one is complaining, since it is not our Pookas getting killed as sacrificial lambs or participating in these slaughterhouse screw-ups by other government officials and agencies. As a matter of fact, it is greatly appreciated that the Pooka Brigade is not being misused, and better yet, being paid to stay alive. But being totally dormant while all this crap is going on in the world does not compute, particularly since the C.I.A. and others have free reign to screw up everywhere. All these screw-ups are completely contrary to the president's published pronouncements made to the world about openness, trust, cooperation and respect. So it seems clear that you on the committee know something that I do not know, or that I'm not privy to at this point in time. Therefore, my presentation is over, and I'd be very interested to know your thinking on the subjects mentioned after our little coffee break."

After the morning coffee break, Mr. Liddy stood up and stated that Mr. Lingo would start off by answering my concerns. Mr. Lingo began his comments with, "There is some unknown reason that befuddles all of us on this committee, and even some of the powers above us. Currently, the C.I.A. has the inside track and the ears of the president's staff. One must remember what happened to the murder charges against the Green Berets; the ones who were in cahoots with the C.I.A. up to their eyebrows. The C.I.A. basically told the White House to shove it, by refusing to cooperate and testify in the case, so the White House ordered the case be dropped. Then we have the case of the young 'harkened' congressional staffer who discovered the issues of murder, abuse and torture of Vietnamese prisoners in the Tiger Cages in Vietnam. With this incident, the government, military, and C.I.A. officials threatened to destroy the staffer; similar to the helicopter pilot who tried to stop, and then exposed, the Song My mass murder incident. These same guys are turned loose without restrictions in Laos and Cambodia, and no one even wants to talk about blunders in Panama, Argentina and Chile. When it comes to the C.I.A., one can only say, 'What else is new?'

"By now you must realize that there are over three hundred, maybe even four hundred, highly trained snipers that have graduated from the recently established U.S. military sniper program. These snipers are used for all the basic, standard, and primary-type terminations, and for special combat assignments. This makes our little group rather insignificant to the general order of things, even if all these individuals have been trained primarily as combat snipers. These snipers have already been used extensively for minor terminations around the world, and many have lost their lives due to their inexperience regarding worldly assignments. The higher-ups have now realized that even the best-trained combat snipers, with the best talents and abilities, cannot easily be converted to high-priority work that requires a lot more than mere shooting skills. So the President is between a rock and a hard place, and his own words about covert deeds have him boxed into a diplomatic corner around the world. You and your team have an assigned mission coming your way, but I will let Mr. J-Ark tell you about it, since he is an expert on the subject."

Liddy the Ambassador interrupted to say, "Before J-Ark begins, I would like to mention a few details about Chile. This was an embarrassing screw-up by White House staffers, and by one of my ambassador friends shooting off his big mouth. A year ago, Project Fulbelt was created and put into effect — over the objections of myself and others — and the C.I.A. deceptively rolled forward with the project. It failed, and a lot of people got killed. The State Department felt the plan would be successful because the C.I.A. had General Roberto Viaux in their hip pocket, and felt they could control and influence three other generals: Tirado, Canales and Valenzuela. Sadly, one general turned out to be a traitor to the group, and this gave full credibility to Ambassador Korry's loose lips. Now his loose lips have created another embarrassing event, with a direct slap in the face to China and the Soviet Union. Well, enough said. I just had to get this issue off my chest to the group. Now I will let Mr. J-Ark tell you about you mission, but after lunch."

The lunch was friendlier than expected. Three of the new committee members were sitting around me, and there was a lot of general conversation about my remarks and the bases for my opinions. I took particular care to avoid Mr. Buck, for I did not want to get involved in one of his probing conversations. The guy was just too much of a snoop for his own good.

When lunch was over, Mr. J-Ark took center stage to inform me about the upcoming mission.

"The proposed mission for your group will involve the use of two teams. One will be your best at long-distance effectiveness, and the other the best at getting up close and personal. You will be given everything we know about the targets, but your group will have to play it by ear and improvise on the spot when and where necessary to accomplish the objectives. There are three targets; One is primary and the other two are secondary, but it is preferred that they be part of the completed package. The two secondary targets are generals on the take who make the illegal operations work successfully. The key target is the world's leading heroin smuggler. This target was so-called arrested in this country, with a lot of U.S.

pressure, but there are several political and military leaders refusing to grant or allow extradition. The joke is, even though the target is under a so-called arrest status, he is still living in the lap of luxury, and he and his in-pocket generals are still controlling his worldwide drug operations.

"The only reason the guy is safe in this country is that he was a Nazi collaborator in France during World War Two. Perhaps the president of his country envies and respects right-wing, fascist-type people, particularly ex-Nazis with money and influence. But our State Department claims this president is a valuable ally in the region. Why? He is a solid block against the communists, strong against the liberal influences of the Christian Democrats, and he hates the socialist leaders in the rest of South America. So if our good friend and ally, General Alfredo Stroessner, and his Chief of Police, Ramon Duarte, refuse to cooperate and do not allow for extradition, we will expedite extradition to Purgatory and/or Hell for Mr. Monsieur Andres (otherwise known as Auguste Joseph Ricord).

"So far, his money is speaking louder than words, with huge drug money payoffs hindering cooperation for extradition, but his arrest does severely restrict and limit his activities. The government restrictions limit his business and social activities to within one hundred miles of Asuncion. He is not allowed to cross the border of Paraguay into Argentina, or he'll be put under sever open-door plantation arrest. Therefore, the call-up of your teams will be on very short notice, and it will not happen until sometime after the first of the year. The president first wants to continue all forms of friendly pressured negotiation, but this farce has already been going on since April. You will be given packets of complete information concerning the subjects involved, and you may schedule an orientation with your teams in January."

The rest of the afternoon was a rehashing of issues and speculating on the future effects of current political and economic events. But afterward there was a nice cocktail party and an excellent dinner. A piano had been placed in the room for me to play. Relaxing and socializing while playing the piano helped me become more comfortable with the committee members, but not with Mr. Buck.

The next morning after breakfast, I headed for the airport to catch my flight home. All the flights were on time, with no difficulties in Pittsburgh. Once home, I thought it best to sit down and think through the Mr. Buck issues before calling Captain Dan. My input worked once, but it might be quite a different story this time, based on the information I'd be providing to Captain Dan. I did not want to end up in a pickle with the powers above, for as the old saying goes, "Once a pickle, never a cucumber again."

When my mind was made up, I made the call to Captain Dan. My fingers dialed the Sherwood number. I was put on hold for about ten minutes, and then a stranger's voice came on the line. The stranger said, "Captain Dan is no longer here. He has a new assignment, and I have replaced him in handling these particular duties and special assignments. I am to be considered your new intermediary, and you can make any necessary reports to me in the future. You may refer to me as Mr. Felt. From now on, I will be handling your information. So, what is the information concerning your operation at this time?"

This I did not like. I did not know this shit-head from Adam, and there was no way in hell I would open up to a stranger. So I said, "Okay! There was a man who had no eyes. . ."

I fell silent. Finally, Mr. Felt asked me what I was saying, and what the point of the call was. I gave him a blunt answer. "Well, what I am saying is, get me someone I know who is not an interloper, and who would have completed my statement. Your mistake; this is just one emergency communication you screwed up on. You will just have to live with that until I get to speak to someone I know personally. Goodbye!"

This brief conversation and hang-up had to have pissed off this Felt guy royally. But there was no way I would make the same mistake as I had in 1963, even if it meant cutting off my nose to spite my face. I would just wait and see what happened, and let the chips fall where they may. There is always the exception, but it only takes one that is misplaced to screw up everything and everyone' when that one exception gets people injured, abused, or killed in our Twilight Zone existence.

CHAPTER XI
White Elephants, Black Sheep, and Wart-making Toads

It looked like someone might be upset about my incident with Mr. Felt. There must be some turmoil above since I refused to talk with the guy. A good ten days had passed, with no communication from anyone, and then came an unexpected phone call from Colonel Knapp. This meant that Mr. Felt had searched high and low for someone to make contact with me. I was ready to communicate with someone I trusted and knew.

My first words to him were, "Just for my peace of mind and to be sure that you are really Colonel Knapp, please answer two questions. First: is this your real military rank? Second: what is the final password to our little limerick game?"

Colonel Knapp's response was, "You are aware of my new rank, and what you want is apostrophe, period!"

My reply was, "Okay, you are who you are, but that Mr. Felt was not who he is. I do not talk to nobodies or strangers. So rather than you flying to Columbus, or me flying to wherever you are, let us both fly into the Pittsburgh airport. We can have our meeting for a few hours and then fly back to our homes the same day. If that idea is fine with you, let's pick a date now and book our tickets."

We agreed on a date, the timing, and where to meet. The meeting was on for the next week. I assured Colonel Knapp that he would not be wasting his time and that I did not think I was overreacting. I told him that this had the strangeness of a past negative event that we were both familiar with.

The phone call was out of the way, but the matter would not be put to bed until the next week. I knew that I had better organize my thoughts well, and make an accurate presentation regarding what I had observed and over-read during Mr. Buck's get-together.

My early flight was on time, and when I arrived at the restaurant we had selected, there was Colonel Knapp, having some toast and coffee. I said that I hoped this did not mean we could not have lunch together, or that we would not get to socialize a little during our business get-together. Colonel Knapp said that we had plenty of time, since both our return flights did not leave until after 1800 hours, and that he had already scheduled a limousine to take us to a restaurant called the Le Mont for lunch. He said the limo would wait and return us to the airport after lunch. Colonel Knapp had our meeting well-structured and organized, time-wise. The Le Mont restaurant was unbelievable and had excellent food. It provided a fabulous view of the joining rivers and downtown Pittsburgh.

At the start of our business discussion, my first comment was, "What I am telling you is not 100 percent accurate. I have made some assumptions, due to the fact that I could not read or hear what the other two parties may have been saying, but by their reactions there was a lot of agreement. You need to know that I cannot speech read as well as I could ten years ago, but Mr. Buck's lips would be easy to read even for a beginner because of his very slow and precise diction. Mr. Buck and his guests were never aware that I was in the area. The lighting in the bar was not great, but it was quite sufficient to see his lips moving. The best way to start this off is to say that this guy is totally anti-Nixon and against his pending trips to China and Moscow.

"He made it clear that we should not be appeasing Russia and China; that we should isolate them, and that someone should be having the president's plane deliver a bomb along with him. This statement was made in a joking manner, and they all seemed to enjoy the joke. Buck wanted their cooperation for an insider conservative movement to dump Nixon as the president. Then he suggested to them that the C.I.A. was the only agency on the proper course and doing the right things in the world. He made a strange comment; that he and Hoover had talked about handling or taking care of several liberal dissident congressmen, with Hoover making it clear that these particular congressmen would not be a problem for anyone prior to the election. That was when I assumed these other two guys were probably conservative senators. He told them that Hoover would have a well-designed plan to provide a perfect year to reduce liberal thinking in the Halls of Congress.

"There is no question that this Mr. Buck is a right-wing conservative, to the far-far hawkish right. Guys like this fit in well for us in Central and South America, but not here at home. I had mentioned some of my concerns about Mr. Buck earlier, when Captain Dan had Mr. Chrome and Mel the Diplomat replaced. Back then, I had set aside all the issues and reasons for concern at the time. Now I would like you to replace him. Tell him that new executive orders have directed our covert group to be disbanded, and thank him for his dedicated service. After that, how you and the others handle what you now know is completely up to you, and I wish to be kept totally out of the loop."

I made it completely clear that I might have been reading things into a one-way conversation that were invalid or might not exist, but I felt that it was my responsibility to the powers above to report the issue. Clearly this information did not make Colonel Knapp's day. He was subtle at showing his concern while trying hard to stay composed and make polite conversation around the issue. The only direct and serious comment he made was about Hoover and the Hoover Boys, where he likened Hoover to a clown that puts on a clean-cut image for the kids at the circus. Knapp made it clear that under the clown's makeup was a person who could be vicious, vindictive and dangerous to those politicians he did not like.

Knapp further elaborated on his thinking by stating, "Hoover in his day was one thing, but power and turf control changed him into ruler, king and dictator. He not only went way out into right field, but completely out of the ball park over these last fifteen or twenty years. He got all his power during the forties, with a free hand at counter-espionage and anti-sabotage activities. He was given full unlimited and unrestricted authority to curb subversive activities in the federal government, private industries, and social institutions. He started off on the right foot, but ended up with two right feet. During the fifties, he started abusing his power and exceeding his jurisdiction with secret covert ops at abusing the rights of American citizens. These guys, his boy toys, were referred to as the Hoover Boys, not the F.B.I."

He admitted that Hoover was a good disciple, then stated that he was, and knew how to be, a Judas, a Brutus, and a Benedict Arnold — while all the time praising the glory of motherhood, apple pie, and the American flag. Well, Colonel Knapp could not have made plainer how he felt toward Hoover and his secret little group of Hoover Boys. And I definitely got the opinion he did not care for Mr. Felt when he said, "This Mr. Felt is a power player. He is on the president's team, but he is not particularly liked by the president and most of his staff. You really pissed him off when you shut him down. It is a good thing that he is a new kid on the block and does not have the slightest idea who you are. This Mr. Felt is like the odd man out of the president's in crowd, yet he remains inside because of his connections and influence, which are mostly through his wife's connections. He is a cold, ruthless, blunt and calculating politician whom one should never turn one's back on, unless one is a major political campaign donor working with the Marriott's.

"You should also know that the next year could be quite dull, with few covert political actions. Direct orders from the Capitol state that we are not to create covert waves or incidences while the president is trying to negotiate and moderate issues with China in February and with Moscow in May. The stand-down orders sent to everyone and every agency are quite firm. This is, therefore, not a time to be pissing off anyone. It is an interesting time in Washington. I have been in this game a long time, and have never seen so many people who are so paranoid about everything and everyone. The Admiralty House, White House, and the Executive Office Building have become Rod Serling's *The Twilight Zone* around the president's inner circle."

The meeting was a little frustrating for both of us, but overall it went great. The limo got us back to the airport on time and we went our separate ways. But I did get an interesting smile and comments out of Colonel Knapp when asking several questions about him and others.

"This may be none of my business and you do not even need to answer me. We have known and have trusted each other a long time. So, is your name really Knapp? Are you now a general, as previously stated?"

Knapp's answer was, "No, and yes."

"Is Captain Dan really a Captain Dan?"

His answer this time was, "No, and no."

"Are we Immolators and Pookas really a deeply buried, covert secret? Do we really have the benefit of a truly invisible nonexistence, as we have been led to believe?"

His answer was, "Yes, and yes! Plus, the new Mr. Felt has no clue who you are or what your group does. You can rest assured that the Black Chamber is just a figment of someone's overactive imagination. One of the original guiding hands who started this whole secret operation is still the guiding hand — and he, them, or they will never tell."

These were comforting words and answers. I was able to relax on the plane back to Columbus.

It was nice to be back home, enjoy the family during the holidays, and try to finish out my business year with some successful insurance marketing. As I looked back on the year, it was really no weirder or stranger than any other. Jim Morrison died of a drug overdose. Some guy named D.B. Cooper skyjacked a Northwest passenger plane, then did a high-altitude bailout with two hundred thousand dollars, tax free. This Cooper was either very good, or very nuts, but he certainly had the guts to play a dangerous game. One bit of good news was that they convicted Army Lieutenant William Calley for the Mai Lai Massacre. A few deserving prisoners got terminated during the Attica prison riots, but sadly, as always, there was collateral damage to some innocent and undeserving hostages. Over the past several years, it had begun to seem like everyone in the world wanted to kill everyone else, and justify it as trying to find justice or stopping evil. Then if that justification did not work, claiming to be insane and unable to help themselves. Surely there was an oxymoron relationship in there somewhere.

Thank goodness the year was over and done with. The New Year's celebration with the family was nice; we all went to a great party at the Croatian Club. The kids loved all the foreign dances and the authentic food and desserts. But by the middle of January, there had been no word from the committee or Colonel Knapp. I decided that I had better call Liddy the Ambassador's private number, Circle 6-2150, and seek approval to go ahead with the Paraguay orientation meeting if the project was still on. Liddy said there was no immediate urgency since both governments were still in heavy and nasty negotiations, but that it might be good to hold the orientation meeting the week after Valentine's Day. He informed me that Mr. J-Ark and Mr. Brute would attend the meeting, and said to let him know as soon as possible the place, time, and number of days needed to cover the program. I gave him an immediate answer of two full days and three nights at the Christopher Inn, and he could arrange for whatever days he wanted to schedule during that week. I said that I would call back in two days with the members of the two teams, and he could make the arrangements for everyone to be there. I let him know that I would immediately call those selected, to forewarn them of their future travel plans.

Team one consisted of Miss Gabalac the Edsel, Mr. Toukan the Jimmy Durante, and Mr. Charvat the Eddie Cantor. Team two would be comprised of Miss Lee the Martha Raye, Mr. Berkich the Hudson, and Mr. Jupinko the Louis Prima. These Pookas would be the best for an operation in Paraguay, and be less conspicuous when getting within the operational space of the targets. The team members names had been sent to Liddy the Ambassador, and everything would be ready when they arrived at the Christopher Inn. I spent two days getting in touch with each of them, to inform them of the dates, times and place, plus let them know it would be only a preliminary orientation, and that the potential mission would not occur for another sixty to ninety days. They were all okay with the dates, and were quite pleased that they did not have to fly out the day after the orientation session. I was not surprised when all but one asked about going to the Kahiki. Yeah, these were the people to take care of Mr. Auguste Ricord and his operational generals on the take. It might even be possible that General Stroessner would really appreciate us for getting him off the hot seat. With our actions, he would not appear to be a traitor to all the paid-off military and politicians involved in the international heroin consortium, business conglomerate, or so-called agriculture enterprise.

What is really nice: the president is in China, the Pookas in Columbus, and we are all having meetings to make the world a better place. The meetings with the Pookas went well. Mr. J-Ark and Mr. Lingo made excellent presentations about the nearly isolated country of Paraguay; its government structure, agricultural economy, and transportation system. The Alto Parana River is the commercial highway to the outside world from the Port of Asuncion. When those guys, finished the Pookas knew more about Paraguay than they did about the United States. The speakers made Paraguay seem exciting, interesting and a beautiful place to visit. Berkich made an interesting note about all the pictures they were showing us. He pointed out that the area looked more like a nice European city because of the buildings' architecture, huge walkways and tree-lined streets, and the town squares with grass and central fountains. Both of the speakers agreed with his observation.

Within its cultural environment, our little group would not seem to be out of place.

The night of orientation day one, we went to the Kahiki. Once there, Mr. Lingo and Mr. J-Ark seemed to enjoy the outing more than anyone else. This was only reasonable, since it was their first time at the restaurant. The next night, the entire group went out to a new place, Max and Irma's, for a magnificent hamburger or whatever sandwich they wanted. Each table had its own telephone so that patrons in the restaurant could call each other. The atmosphere was nice and relaxing, and we had an enjoyable evening and a lot of fun. Miss Gabalac and Miss Lee received many phone calls from admiring males in other sections of the restaurant.

The news that both teams liked to hear best was when Mr. Lingo showed them the new infrared night scopes. He said these would be available on the mission, and the crew realized the significance of such an item in their arsenal. It meant they could operate around the clock, all twenty-four hours of day and night, with even better camouflage in the darkness and safely getting a lot closer to the target. Mr. Lingo really floored them when he produced a new type of flash protection silencer to be mounted on the M-16. This meant that nighttime shooting became a thousand times more practical for efficient kills, and everyone would have additional safety while being the escaping mouse of prey. He also informed them that all the new gear would be waiting for them in Paraguay, and that all other missions would be equipped with the same type of equipment. I started thinking that several of our original team members might still be alive, had equipment like this been available ten or twelve years before.

When the orientation meeting was over, everyone went back home to do their thing, and to sit around and wait to see what might happen. I received an interesting letter from Colonel Knapp. It stated that the policy of my client, Mr. Buck, has lapsed. The premium had not been paid within the grace period, and my renewal vesting commissions would immediately stop. This was good news. I could completely relax and get back to my own personal business. It was going to be one busy spring, with all the things the wife had us doing with the Cub Scouts and Girl Scouts, and the many P.T.A. activities. Thank God I was now a coordinator, and no longer an on-call shooter.

As we prepared for the Memorial Day weekend, there had been no calls to action, but there had been one hell of a lot of interesting news. My peace of mind was often haunted by what I had over-read in the Buck conversation about taking care of and handling dissident liberal Congressmen. But talk is just talk. Then I remembered my original training with Mr. Imperial and Hickman the Bully. These trainers had made it perfectly clear that 90 percent of all successful assassinations are perfect accidents, apparent suicides, even appear to have been by natural causes, and the negative case cannot be proved or disproved. The 10 percent of obvious assassinations that can be proved had best be protected with the C.Y.A. of distance, camouflage, illusion, and out-of-sight moments. They often reminded us, in very subtle terms, that, "In this business you're either good, or dead. So talk is cheap, and small change rides the bus."

The difficulty was that I now looked at every event with a paranoid and jaundiced eye, and just couldn't help it. All this was due to the nature of my training, noting that everything has the potential of being a perfectly arranged termination. How could anyone in this business not feel that way, with the existing U.S. government projects like M.K. Ultra and De-

Patternization? With the approved cooperation, research, and testing of psychedelic and hallucinogenic drugs on American citizens by the C.I.A.? The government's actions, along with the research of the Battelle circus and the C.I.A., would probably be classified as illegal criminal activities. Most certainly these secret activities violated the Nuremberg Code by the use of "mind chemicals" with control-inducing properties to generate cerebral responses that affected the brain and nervous system for an involuntarily controlled, predictable response. Combine controlled hallucination-inducing properties with electroshock therapy, and one gets normal-looking zombies who commit involuntary assassinations on call. All of this was not so strange or hard to believe, particularly when syphilis and the Tuskegee Institute experiments were in the news, and we had learned that nuclear isotopes and radiation chemicals had been secretly fed to U.S. schoolchildren in New England, to see what mental and physical damage these might do to them. No question about it, a lot of government agents and scientists would never be able to scrub their hands clean of these toxic sins.

As for the rest of the world, it was a good thing for President Caldera of Venezuela that executive orders were given to cool it. Too bad; the guy was another Allende with the Caldera leftist formation of "The New Force," but he might have enough problems with Colombia to stay out of our hair for a while. Both countries were doing a big military buildup by acquiring French Mirage jets and German-built submarines. But good President Borrero of Columbia knew how to handle the Marxist National Liberation Army, and the rest of his problem population. He could simply export them to Venezuela, and give Venezuela his many social immigration problems. Maybe Venezuela would pay a little less attention to causing trouble over oil rights in international waters.

One had to feel compassion for the new President Bordaberry of Uruguay. The guy had his hands full with the first-class Tupamaro guerrilla movement. It had excellent leadership and had already started assassinating government officials selected as part of his new leadership. At any other time we would have gotten special-K orders to help him solve this problem, but Nixon going to China and Moscow proved to be quite fortunate for a lot of the troublemakers in the world. Had there not been those key diplomatic trips, that year would have been bad for Allende of Chile and Caldera of Venezuela. They got a diplomacy pass for a free ride through another year.

In El Salvador, the no-holds-barred Colonel Molina, who might well be a right-wing crook, knew how to keep troublemakers in line and exile his competition. The guy would stay in power for a while, as it takes a lot of nerve to arrest and exile the people's newly-elected president and vice president. The liberal university professors and college students quickly got the point of his self-reelection speech; the one which pointed out that everyone is expendable.

As for Argentina, it looked like the Peronistas would soon be back in charge. Then they could start to work on correcting the C.I.A.'s mistakes, and put the strikers, students and terrorist back into their proper places as good citizens, good ocean swimmers, or as good hole-fillers. The only other country in the region that might need some help for a good right-wing coup d'etat would be Honduras. Their leadership was liberal — too liberal — and too friendly with Castro. Yet we were considering interfering in Paraguay, when Honduras was the real problem as the major smuggling point into the U.S. from China and India.

Maybe, as mentioned before, I had heard too much, been told too much, and seen too much. And then our country's conservative F.B.I. nemesis to politicians had died, and the good ol' boy conservative from Alabama had been shot. A good mathematician might assume that the scoreboard now showed liberals two and conservatives four in the covert handling and taking care of liberal dissidents. It had been one hell of a six-month period for apparent accidents, suicides, and unfortunate events with good timing in an important election year. Weird; it used to be fascism versus democracy that got people killed, then it became communism versus democracy that got people killed — or, in the past, religious differences with the Inquisitions. With these days of deviant discontent, it was liberals versus conservatives that was apparently getting people terminated. The winter of 1971 and spring of 1972 created a lot of curiosity that suggested to me that cat-killing questions would be best ignored. My only concern during that strange period of time was to raise my family, continue my education and get a law degree, and progress successfully forward in my business career. All the while, I was trying very hard not to think or even care about the rest of the world. When that occurred, my peace of mind always seemed to get jolted back to reality. It never failed. The committee made contact by sending a special-K memo just before what I had expected to be a pleasant Memorial Day weekend. The notice stated that Paraguay was a "go."

Calls were immediately made to all the team members. They would meet in Miami on June first, depart for Paraguay the next day, and could be in Paraguay for up to ten days. It was made very clear to them not to push the clock or make time a factor, and to take all the time they needed to do the job right. Then I informed them to take semi-warm clothing, since the cold weather was beginning in that part of the world, and that they were not expected to have time to go skiing.

They were jokingly informed that there were no mountain ski resorts in Paraguay, and that they were not to take any side trips to Argentina, Bolivia or Chile for a tobogganing adventure. Any serious discussions with them were avoided, for they already knew the risk and seriousness of the mission from the orientation conference. The point was to let them know to play it cautious, take their time, take no shit from anyone, and use the light of the winter moon.

Well, the president got to be wined and dined in the Kremlin. Then he visited our puppet in Iran, saw beautiful Austria, and went to Poland to see why they make all those jokes about Poles. In the meantime, our people were probably freezing their asses off at Asuncion Central, and trying to get things organized to efficiently bring the target to their selected opportunity. Then came a very surprising phone call from Liddy the Ambassador. He stated that the U.S. and Paraguay had come to some tentative agreement, and that they must immediately cancel the assignment. He wanted to know what code words the teams were given, to use on this mission for information validity and verification. This was logical, as the embassy did not want any of their people getting whacked or having a difficult time. I asked him if they had already terminated any of the parties. He impatiently said that he did not know; he simply needed the code password, pronto. I gave him the answer by saying, "Okay, okay! Since this is a Catholic country, you had best write this down carefully. There are two words in play here, 'Transubstantiation' and 'Eucharist.' They must be given in this exact order — my crew does not like variations on a theme."

Liddy was sure in a hurry. He just thanked me, said goodbye, and hung up. That had been a close call, and maybe a bit too late for someone's good health. Hopefully, they could stop things in time and get our teams home safe and sound. If all went well, at least the Pookas had an interesting experience and a little learning vacation while seeing a different part of the world.

The rest of the year saw no activity on the part of our group. I was not even contacted by any committee members, and the only contact I received in December was another interesting invitation to the Inauguration and Inaugural Ball on January 20. From the president's victory speech, the theme of the inauguration would remain the same as before, with him stating that it was his responsibility to build peace in the world so that in the future people would say 'God Bless America.' The president's forward thinking theme of 'The Spirit of '76' might run into some difficulties and roadblocks from what was being seen and heard on the horizon. It appeared that it was all Republican conspirators who had broken into the Democratic headquarters at the Watergate the previous June. This all appeared to be some weird story that someone had dreamed up out of left field; it was doubtful that anything good would come of that political blunder.

Of course, what had been very embarrassing to the United States the previous year was the beautiful actress, Jane Fonda, going to North Vietnam and picking up the nickname of Hanoi Jane. Overall, the last year had been very mild in terms of negative events in the United States and around the world. The White House undoubtedly meant what it said about cooling down outright covert skullduggery. Therefore, everything was just thought processing, and not processing the covert actions of people's thoughts.

The Nixon doctrine seemed to be working, with his intention to find "peace with honor, not peace with surrender." Then there were his comments in Peking that "Nations should talk about differences rather than fight about differences." There were even more wise words in Russia, "We shall sometimes be competitors, but we need never be enemies." It was obvious that when it came to international relations, this president put into practice what he had been putting into words. So far he was making me feel good about voting for him and Spiro Agnew.

Mr. Agnew would definitely be my man for the Spirit of '76.' That was why, when Agnew and his wife entered the ballroom at the Pension Building, we all started chanting, "Agnew! Agnew! Agnew in seventy-six!" He really got the message that the crowd loved him. Nixon had made a lot of great remarks showing his support for Agnew, particularly at the convention, but Agnew had made some remarks that struck my soul when he expressed how he felt about being the vice president: "...being as under flickering strobe lights that alternately illuminate or shadow one's unwritten duties."

That was something any one of the invisible Pookas could be thinking, and something that had crossed my mind many times over the past several years. The sad part was that some of my secret friends, who lost their lives as Immolators, would remain unknown soldiers, with their deeds never illuminated, and always buried in the shadows.

The inaugural was really cold; it had to be colder than the last one. Some of my excitement came from driving on icy roads in cold and snowy weather, just to get to Washington, D.C. on time. To complicate the issue, there was a nasty accident on Interstate 70 right at the beginning of our trip. There was very little traffic and we were moving at a nice clip when a car about fifty yards in front of me started sliding. It flipped over and slid upside-down off the road, over a little embankment and into a ditch. I pulled over to help, but there was no one else around to have seen the accident. I told the wife to stay in the car, and then started running toward the other car. I suddenly stopped, frozen in place, wondering what I was going to see under that flattened, upside-down car. I heard children crying for help from under the car. I ran over and tried to pry open the bent door, to help the people out of the wreck. Thank God none were seriously injured. They had only small cuts, bruises, and some minor broken bones. Finally some help — an approaching big-rig truck driver — noticed the accident. He called for help, put out some flares, and helped me with the injured people. Once the state police and emergency services got there I gave them my name, and we were once again on our way to Washington D.C.

Regardless of the weather, the unexpected accident, and any inconveniences of lodging and expenses, the trip to the inauguration and ball was worth it. It was a nice, memorable experience, most likely because I had gained a new respect for the president when he said in one of his speeches:

"My approach in the second term is that of a Disraeli conservative with a strong foreign policy, adherence to basic values, conserving and not be destructive of basic values, and have reforms that work, not reforms that destroy."

Nixon kept stressing responsibility, a better need for trust and cooperation, and developing a new feeling of self-discipline with our social and political actions in the world and at home. I liked what he had said, and what he had been saying; it had kept the Pookas of the Pooka Brigade sassy, happy and alive. The president had proved a lot of his naysayers wrong when it came to his foreign policy. The president's diplomacy with China and Russia provided just the right amount of influence and pressure needed for North Vietnam to sit, talk, listen, and agree to a cease-fire to end the Vietnam War.

What a nice way to start off the spring: move our clocks forward and hope for a little peace now that our last troops were out of Vietnam. Now all we had to do was get our butts out of Cambodia and stop all the bombing and the C.I.A. interference there. Perhaps things would calm down for the rest of Southeast Asia. Regardless of a few leftover diplomatic issues, all this proved that Nixon's strategy was on the right track.

Now he had better start paying more attention to things at home. The new Congressional Investigative Committee and the Watergate issue was creating some embarrassment for the White House and the Republican Party. After all, this Liddy person was a very active Republican lawyer, a former F.B.I. agent, a special assistant to the Secretary of the Treasury, and he worked directly under the President's Chief of Staff. The named creepy burglar Liddy, along with his fellow creeps, were making the president eat some of the words he said at an October speech last year: "We must battle all forms of crime in America. We must stay on the offensive against crime until all crime is put on a downward trend."

Nice words, but how were we to classify this in our society? "This" pertaining to the crimes mentioned by the media concerning the activities of these political hobgoblins. Who else would come under the little black cloud of practicing right-wing, fascist spying activities? This amateur screw-up by a so-called professional was probably making old man Hoover turn over in his grave, and had the C.I.A. director looking for cover.

What a shock! All these misfits around Liddy that no one had ever heard of were former F.B.I. Hoover Boys and C.I.A. operatives. The intermediary money man managing this political game of covert intrigue had to be extremely good at his job with money-laundering payoffs. These guys, with whomever else, were the Republican Party's hobgoblins of screw-ups. They were making Nixon eat his words from the inaugural speech, "Now a chance to restore respect for law in this country." Boy, talk about bad timing, and being in the wrong place at the wrong time.

The rest of the world kept operating, with or without our interference. Maybe when left alone for a while, they would take care of their own problems. Uruguay did not need us, since the military leaders were kicking the Tupamaro guerrillas' butts. Good President Bordaberry was following the military's orders and directions, and had created a benevolent dictatorship form of law and order. He was benevolent to all his people, except for the left-wing socialists, the communists, and the over-educated liberal democrats. All those people would need to seek political asylum in exile, or be terminated as a matter of public policy for the public good. This Bordaberry sure knew what side his bread was buttered on; otherwise, the military would have made him toast. One thing was for sure: anyone would have hated to be on the wrong side of the military generals who formed the National Security Council and their new Council of State. A single blackball vote in that assembly did not get one replaced; it led one to have an apparent suicide. Wouldn't it be just the thing to solve a lot of our problems if the Watergate hobgoblins had some apparent accidents and suicides?

At least the Peronistas of Argentina were back in charge again, with Hector Campora. It would not have surprised me if Peron did not return to become a permanent resident again, and end his exile status. There again, one had to feel sorry for anyone who crossed either the Azul or Rojo Peronistas; their Azul blood would soon run Rojo if they were not good ocean swimmers.

Thankfully, the president ended the Vietnam War. All the young men and women returned home, and all the killing was put to rest. Perhaps there would be a lot of happy picnickers on the coming Fourth of July. I knew that I was feeling good. I had already out-performed my stated business goals and objectives for the year. As a family, we went camping at Salt Fork State Park, set up the Coleman camper, enjoyed the campfire, and laughed all weekend while watching stupid boaters launching their cars and trucks into the water with their boats. There is nothing like new boaters who do not know how to handle slanted concrete ramps to provide entertainment for the onlookers who need a good laugh.

All this Forth of July harmony and peace of mind came to a quick end. There was an urgent phone call from Ambassador Liddy, requesting my presence in Washington, D.C. in only three days. He said that the tickets would be waiting for me at the airport and clarified that it would be a one-day meeting. I'd fly in for one evening and leave the next day after lunch. I asked him what I needed to prepare as a presentation, and what the meeting would be about. He stated that he had no comment, and all would be secretly and privately discussed behind closed doors at the committee meeting. This really got my curiosity up, as it had to be something very serious with such short notice. I immediately went out and bought all the news magazines and newspapers I could get my hands on, and then started watching television news as a break from reading while doing my political homework.

The trip on Agony Airlines was not so bad. The layover to switch planes was short, and I got to Washington, D.C. on time. When arriving at the hotel to check in, I did not see anyone I knew. I got my key and checked into my room immediately, but decided to stay out of the lounge that night, so as not to risk another experience of over-reading someone's personal conversation. There was a note in my room stating that all meals and social activities would be in our assigned conference room, and at 2030 hours there would be a private, non-business social cocktail hour. I thought that was nice; it would keep me out of the bar, and I could still have a couple of drinks with someone familiar to me.

When I arrived at the room, everyone on the committee was there. It seemed like they had all been meeting earlier that day, but there was no business or mission talk with me that evening. All the conversations were about the uneasiness in Washington concerning the Watergate situation, stopping the bombing in Cambodia, and that the president was considering moving Kissinger up to Secretary of State. Still, it was somewhat strange; not once did I hear anyone talking about sports, and they all went out of their way to be particularly nice and friendly to me.

The only guy who seemed totally uptight was Mr. Rumble, who remained a little aloof and formal. By his demeanor and dress, he had to be the richest person in the room. That guy, along with Mr. Lingo and Mr. Brute, was pure business. They were not the beating around the bush type of politicians. Anyone would have thought Brute, Bowler, and J-Ark were my bosom buddies. It was an enjoyable evening, but my mind was on the next morning, and just what time bomb they would be placing in my hands. It is always a bit dangerous when people are being too nice and overly friendly to you; it's like they are getting you ready for the kill.

The next morning after breakfast, Liddy the Ambassador took charge of the meeting. He got right to the point by saying, "You are here, Mr. Chahaus, because certain agencies in our government have screwed up terribly in South America for a second time. There is now an urgent need to correct the situation one way or another. You would normally not have been contacted by the committee, but through assorted diplomatic channels there was a strange request — that no one understood — for a Mr. Chahaus through one of our South American consuls. Fortunately, someone within our operation knew certain factors relating to this name, and contacted the higher powers with authority to take action on the request. Because of this request, and recent related events and activities that have gone south, so to speak, you will be taking a long trip to Asuncion, Paraguay. On your return home, you will have an orientation meeting with your Pooka Brigade for several days at the Fort Hayes facility in Columbus, Ohio.

"This meeting in Paraguay, which you have been requested to attend, is a completely covert and secret meeting of top priority. We on the committee do not have the slightest idea who made the request or whom you will be meeting with, but we do know what the concerns are relating to the issues of this little get-together. For your edification, the issue is Chile. On June 29 another attempted C.I.A. coup failed to oust President Allende. Again the head of his secret police, Rodriguez, was effective and efficient. The coup was quickly put down by General Bachelet, Defense Minister Gonzales, and General Gonzales. Chief Rodriguez knew the exact time and place for the little rebellion to start. They had another loyal insider spouse who voted for President Allende's government in March, and her husband was one of the conservative supporters of the people who tried the attempted coup. So it looks like this Vina del Mar socialite may not have to ask the Catholic Church for a divorce, as she may well be a widow before their Independence Day. Now President Salvador Allende Gossens is feeling fat and sassy, overconfident, and comfortable with his military's support and improved legislative power.

"Once your conference in Paraguay is over, you will be flying back to Washington, D.C. before going home. You will give us a full briefing on the meeting, and any potential strategies for handling the Chile situation. Then you will tell us exactly how many days you will need for the orientation meeting, who you want as speakers, and what equipment you will need for planning the logistics of an operation. As of now, the special-K orders have a yellow caution light. Other agencies just got their lights punched out and endured a little humiliation. So this meeting in Paraguay will decide if there will be a green light to go, or a red light to cease and desist."

The rest of the meeting was taken up by the committee members giving me their opinions and knowledge about Paraguay and Chile, and advising me on diplomatic protocol and procedures. They all wanted to know if I had any idea of how and why my code name was mentioned, and why someone would think that I might have some special importance in attending this secret conference. All I could say was that I did not have a clue, and they would all know once I returned from my little covert vacation. When the meeting was over and there was nothing else to discuss, we had a nice cocktail party with great hors d'oeuvres. The dinner was excellent; lobster and steak. After dinner, it was just political social talk, wishing me well on my trip, and general farewells until our next meeting in several weeks.

My thinking process was at full speed on the trip home; not about the mission, but the cover story for the family. While in the Pittsburgh airport I noticed a group of Boy Scouts with their leaders, and this gave me the perfect answer for my predicament. The next day I made a call to Liddy the Ambassador, asking him to send me a telegram immediately, and to state that due to several last-minute cancellations there were two openings at that summer's scheduled Woodbadge training course at the Philmonte Scout Reservation. The wife knew my interest in this Woodbadge training, and she would certainly not mind me taking advantage of this special training opportunity.

The cover story worked. The wife was excited for my great new scouting opportunity, but was not happy that it was in New Mexico.

When the time arrived for me to go on my unknown adventure, the wife helped me pack for the trip and drove me to the airport. I reminded her that she'd be seeing me in about ten days. I told her that when I got back, we would all go to Schmidt's in German Village to have Bahama Mama sausages and their wonderful giant cream puffs.

This unexpected opening of a secret trap door let me know what Dorothy might have been thinking and feeling while on her little adventure down the Yellow Brick Road, to seek the Wizard of Oz. Maybe this was just one of Captain Dan's little adventures, where he always said, "The winner will be the one that comes out of the bear cave alive."

CHAPTER XII
Chile Con Carne and Paella

I got one heck of a lot of unwanted flying time: Columbus to Atlanta, Atlanta to Miami, Miami to Brazil, Brazil to Asuncion. The Asuncion International Airport was much nicer than I had expected. When I departed from the plane, two men with a sign reading "Senor Chahaus" were waiting for me. They picked up my luggage and escorted me to a limo. The surprise was that these two guys did not look Spanish, but more European. By their walk, talk, and gestures, I knew they were plainclothes military or secret police. They both spoke pretty good English. They told me that they were first going to stop by the hotel to get me checked in, and would leave my luggage in the room.

The trip from the airport was nice. They acted like tour guides, and the place seemed like a quaint European city. Finally, we arrived at a beautiful place on the river that they referred to as the Legislative Palace. It looked French or Romanist by it architecture. This was a real city, not a village. But I was a little disappointed at not seeing massive snow-capped mountains, but they did point out Argentina to me. The interesting thing seen on the drive was a group of Mennonites walking down the sidewalk. I suddenly realized that this was not Mexico or Central America.

After the escorts stopped the vehicle, they escorted me into a side entrance. I got an uneasy feeling, with a strange thought about Daniel entering the lion's den. I did not have a clue about who I was going to meet in the building. Inside, the door and the stairway area were solid security. We went up three flights of stairs on a beautiful formal staircase. The building was beautiful, pure European. We entered a beautiful meeting room, which looked like it was for royalty only. There were about a dozen people standing around having coffee. At that point, no one looked familiar to me. At the top of the stairs, outside the meeting room, were a lot of security people in civilian clothing. There were no military uniforms in sight. A person at the other end of the room, by a large conference table, turned around. I recognized him, and my chin nearly hit the floor. The immediate question was: why was he here at this secret meeting in Paraguay?

It also explained why someone knew about making a request for Mr. Chahaus. The big question was how he got the request processed through the system without making any unnecessary waves, which would have created unnecessary snooping by other government agencies. That would be one of the first questions asked of good Colonel Suarez. The colonel had just realized that I had entered the room and was staring right at him. He got a big smile on his face and walked toward me with his welcoming hands up in the air. He said something quickly and loudly in Spanish that got everyone's attention. Everyone in the room turned toward me to give their greetings, and a gentleman who looked like Bob Hope spoke up and gestured for everyone to sit down at the table.

By the looks of things, I was a nobody there, mixed in with big-time players. That clearly explained all the first-class security suits. The speaker stated that he would first like to introduce all participants at the conference, and said, "This is

Senor Rega' and Senor Videla from Argentina. On this side of the table are Senor Leigh, Senor Meriano, and Senor Bonilla from Chile. The four young men with them are Senors Larach, Bergeses, Sauer, and Ugarte. Sitting beside our guest, Mr. Chahaus, is Senor Suarez from Bolivia. For Mr. Chahaus's benefit, I am the El Presidentia of this country. While at this meeting, there will be no rank, privileges or political positioning, for we are all here with one stated cause and purpose. We in this room during the conference will have equal say and status.

"Only we in this room know that we are here, except for General Augusto Pinochet, and he is not going to mention it to anyone else outside this room. The stated purpose of this gathering is the removal of Marxism in Chile. Even though Doctor Salvador Allende was democratically elected, he is an embarrassment and hindrance to our country's objectives. Our intent is to give this medical doctor a dose of his own medicine. Strange as it may seem, medical doctors have given Chile and Argentina a bad name. Doctor Allende must go the way of Doctor Che. Now Senor Leigh has something to say."

This Leigh guy stood up and addressed the group. "We are here because we want to get rid of the red tint on the white star of our flag, plus exterminate Marxism in our society, which broadly includes the socialist, communist, and liberal Catholic leftist. The June incident was a mistake. It was instigated by your C.I.A. with some rebellious hotheads. But the time is still right, because the reformists and revolutionaries are bickering between themselves. And even the people are protesting in support of the miners and truckers who are on strike. Even the working-class farmers and workers who had supported Allende have become disenchanted and discontent over economic issues. We may have further comments, but currently we wish to see what others of this group have to say."

Mr. Suarez spoke up, and stated that he had several comments that needed to be made before the group. "As all of you know, our special guest here is Mr. Chahaus. Senor Chahaus, you should know that it has been made perfectly clear to the group that you do not exist, and that you also have a negative view of the C.I.A. and the U.S. State Department, and that you have little confidence in the ability of U.S. diplomats to keep their mouths shut. Those from Chile at this meeting certainly understand this point, due to the 'loose lips sink ships' loudmouthed U.S. ambassador who passed on the phony promises of support by the C.I.A. and the backstabbing U.S. National Security Advisor. Live and learn. An Hasidic friend of mine once said, 'never trust a Jew.' I thought it was a Yiddish joke; I should have listened."

"The fact is, Argentineans and Chileans do not trust the integrity or the competence of the C.I.A. So I have injected into our common cause that there may be another option. I informed this group that I had met and worked with this other option six years ago, but I did not to any degree disclose the circumstances of our past association. The group was informed that you were American, and that you were a very secret operative. I let the group know you had great insight, common sense, a good talent for operational logistics, and that you could be trusted completely. Outside of your secret work in the past for our government, I have two other verification references as to your ability. They also have assured me that you have no connection with the C.I.A. or with U.S. military intelligence. You are only a someone or a somebody who is sometimes there when needed somewhere in the world, to make adjustments on wannabes.

"We all realize the C.I.A. is here, that they are involved in all of our country's affairs, and that they are politically and economically involved by orders — both good and bad — from your government. This is something we all have to live with. We do not particularly like it, but we have open minds here to hear your input and comments on our ideas of how to handle our delicate situation. At the moment — as a compliment to you — you, and only you, are the one U.S. person they are willing to trust and have confidence in for a new solution to the Allende problem. Then too, maybe the gentlemen from Argentina might have a few questions for you, since I mentioned earlier to them that you could be a dedicated Peronist."

My stomach was starting to make noise from hunger, but these guys were not having a social hour until nine. Dinner was not until ten o'clock; I was used to eating at about six. They say the people here like to have dinner late at night. It is no wonder everyone in Central and South America drinks a lot of dark coffee and takes an afternoon nap. Many of the good restaurants do not open up for dinner until after nine o'clock. It looked like I was going to have to get used to late eating while in South America. That definitely meant I would not be sleeping so well at night.

The meeting finally ended. The Spanish hors d'oeuvres during the social hour were different, but very good. It gave me some private time to talk for a minute with Colonel Suarez. Once off in the corner, I asked him about the two other references, and how in the world he had been able to make contact with me through the diplomatic system. I also asked how things were going for him as a new President.

He said, "I could certainly use some of your people at this time in Bolivia. Should it happen that your group comes this time, they will have permission to shoot to kill. This is why some former associates of yours say hello. While talking with them once about a special Pooka group that did some work in my country when I was a colonel, they provided me with the details of how to get a message through the system. Your former associates suddenly started laughing, and one stated that he knew all about the group. They told me that they had both been on missions with you in earlier days, and that I should say their code names to you — the Artist and the Carpet Man — and you would then realize that nothing was rotten in Denmark.

"Your friends are my agriculture, mining and railroad consultants for the Guaqui-La Paz Railroad. They are retained to handle my domestic and personal political problems. They are about the only people I can trust at the moment, for my loyal commander of the Rangers, Colonel Selich Chop, that your government trained in sixty-seven, plotted a right-wing coup against me. His attempted coup nearly succeeded. At the same time, the communist, liberal leftist, and union leaders have tried to terminate my presidency. So I am regrettably forced to cut the fascist right-wings off my team, and at the same time cut the Maoist and Marxist left-wings off my political condors. I have disloyal traitors on both sides all around me, so I had no choice but to fire General Zenteno as Commander of the Armed Forces. Now I am President and the Commander of the Armed Forces. After this issue with Chile is handled, I am going to crack down hard on my leftist liberal politicians and union leaders, with the assistance of your amigos.

"Mr. Artist, but not Mr. Carpet Man, knew about what he called the Pooka Brigade, and then he put two and two together. He told me to tell our little group here that there was a way to contact your operation, but it had to be through a particular Norwegian diplomat by asking about 'Black Chamber Pooka Rabbits.' Apparently, the message system worked without causing any harm to anyone, and you are here to see if your advice and input may help or hinder the situation. By the way, how do you feel about your former associates? Do I need to have any concerns?"

My comment was short and simple. "Colonel, you can trust him and him, whoever they are, for I did not hear this conversation. But you should know that assassins make for the very best of friends. If I'm right, you were having an illusion about talking with a guy who looked like the old movie star Tyrone Power, and his associate was an Arab on a flying carpet. I hate to say this to you, Colonel, but you have been watching too many movies."

The colonel started laughing, and then said that we should join the rest of the group for dinner. And what a dinner it was. All was very upscale and first class. After dinner, we were all reminded that the meeting the next day would be at the hotel, since we were all staying at the same hotel, and that the meeting the following day would be at a different location. It was made clear that we would never be meeting twice at the same location, and dinner each night would be at a different place. The point was clear that security and secrecy was the priority of this get-together, and each of us had two security personnel assigned to us for escort transportation and security.

Since my two guys were not Spanish, I felt a little more secure. I took a gamble, as they were driving me back to the hotel, by speaking a little German, and then a little Croatian. What a surprise when one started talking to me in Croatian! I let him know that I did not know enough to hold a conversation; that my wife was Croatian, and that her father had immigrated to the U.S. after World War II. He said his parents had come to Paraguay after World War II to escape Tito, and that his associate's family came from Prague, Czechoslovakia. I was then completely at ease with these two guys. They gave me a sense of security. I knew that if anyone tried to get near me, they would quickly be taken care of, and I would be going safely home to my Croatian wife once the meeting was over.

During the next two days of the meetings, everyone else did all the talking; I just asked a few questions for clarification of the subjects and issues presented. These guys knew the subject matter and were quite thorough. They had photos of key Marxists, and of all the key locations throughout Santiago, Concepcion, Valparaiso and Vina del Mar, with all types of angle shots of the giant Presidential Palace that took up a whole city block. They had many photos of the University of Chile and of particular professors and student leaders. There were also photos of some key industrial buildings in Concepcion, along with photos of a few dozen union leaders. They pointed out the National Stadium on a map and showed many photos of it. They stated that it would be used as a collection or gathering point with certain aspects of the operation.

Then this guy Bonilla said, "Our National Security Chief, in coordination with Army General Escobar, will start making assigned arrests in the middle of the night on the date chosen for the operation to begin. There are about three hundred individuals on the first strike list of names. The second list for arrests includes about nine hundred names. The third follow-up list, once the primary arrests are made, includes about three thousand other politically active individuals. The first group is mainly politicians, military officers, and some police officers, along with a couple of priests. But the primary first strike will be to focus on President Salvador Allende, General Alberto Bachelet, General Carlos Gonzales, and Defense Minister Jose Gonzales, plus Allende's personal bodyguards."

The guy did not say it, but I could tell that this crew's offer for token surrenders — if the coup was successful — would not be fruitful or beneficial to those who surrendered or were eventually captured. It was quite interesting to see that the two assumed generals from Argentina were giving firsthand advice on how to handle those that surrendered or were captured. The point was to make sure that there would not be a counter-action by the rebels against the successful takeover later on. The key was to put the Allendeites in a cell or a cemetery as quickly as possible. They sincerely meant, with incarceration, to provide the unfortunate and sorrowful with the pitiful acts of apparent suicides. This would show that these Marxists did not have the courage of their convictions to stand trail, defend their beliefs, or try to become martyrs. They made their point by laughingly stating that, "You see! There is always a simple solution to every problem."

Colonel Suarez pointed out that transportation logistics would be no problem. He clarified that all necessary ground operatives and equipment would travel by train from La Paz to Arica, Chile; from La Paz to Antofagasta, Chile; by aircraft from La Paz to Pudahuel airport at Santiago, Chile; and by the main highway from Mendoaz, Argentina to Santiago. He stated that truckers would be used to move assets from Arica to Santiago, since the highway was better and quicker than the antiquated railroad system in those areas. He pointed out that all of the parties involved would first gather at Asuncion, Paraguay for any updated informational changes, and then meet each team's individual escort for guiding them to their assigned locations. He told us that the designated escorts would remain with them until their assignment was completed, and make sure they departed Chile in a safe manner. The Colonel finally suggested that my teams might need at least two days at Asuncion for familiarization with the other personnel, and for any necessary updates and review. His closing statement informed us that all would be flown to La Paz, and each team would be dispatched separately throughout Chile, with the assistance and direction of their designated escort. This provided me with one hell of a lot of information to absorb, and a suitcase of material for use at my orientation meeting back home.

On the morning of the third day, we all met at a government military building. The whole group was sitting around a large table, waiting for me to start giving them my opinions. It was a little inhibiting, with all the South American big-shots sitting and sipping their coffee, and staring at me like a room full of opossums. I was beginning to feel like a dartboard. As I began my lecture, I did not bother to stand up. I did not want to look like the only tree in the dog pond while making my presentation.

"Gentleman, all your points were well made. I completely understand your reasoning, and have had similar concerns about Chile over the past several years. I must also tell you that these similar concerns about Levingston in Argentina and Torres in Bolivia had bothered me, but some very astute people took care of those two issues. Before coming to this meeting, I did my homework on the history of Chile. The history showed me that the Chilean motto fits this planned action by General Augusto Pinochet Ugarte. The motto states, 'By right, or by might.' This is very appropriated for the times. The red on the flag of your selected coup day will not symbolize heroes, but show a flood of red blood for its new Independence Day on September eighteenth. But first, reality checks of your individual egos. Remember, if you are winners, you will be heroes that prove the theory of 'might makes right.' But should you lose, you will be traitors put on trial and executed. Think carefully about the old saying, 'Should you wound a king and not kill him, you're in big trouble.'

"I do not want to ruin your day, only to remind you that in your excitement and enthusiasm, the Grim Reaper will be watching over you as well as your Marxists, Unionists, and Social Democrats. Therefore, relating to my group, there will be only two code words used in this operation. These two code words, 'Pyramid' and 'Ziggurat,' are only to be known by those of you in this room. Any misuse, improper disclosure, or forgetfulness with big mouths will automatically get people killed. The intention is not to put a damper on your thought processes, but to remind all of you that this is more than just a serious intention. It is a very dangerous operation. Your plan is excellent. The decision to act quickly after the June twenty-ninth failure is quite ingenious, for the Allende crowds are most likely overconfident enough to not consider a follow-up response at this point. They have let their hair down a bit too far for their own good, and are unknowingly processing their own death warrants.

"Therefore, all of you in this room are betting on their overconfidence and negligence, and your quick response to be an unexpected surprise. So let's be good gamblers, and go with seven or eleven as the dates for operation Ziggurat. This, gentleman, is your delicate decision to make. These dates will give you plenty of time to clean things up before the Chilean Independence Day on the eighteenth. Rest assured that our personnel will be ready on whatever date you choose, to attempt the coup on President Allende. Now, there is one major request for secrecy. This last important request is that no one else in your governments is to know that we exist, and that you definitely do not ever mention it to anyone within our government, or any other government. There is no intention to be rude or obnoxious with the following remark. I can assure you that you do not ever want us to lose our faith, trust and confidence in your ability to keep a secret, and to maintain our friendly and cordial relationship. The point is that we do not exist. We are non- existent, and I'm the invisible person attending this meeting, which never occurred anywhere on plant Earth."

It appeared that my point had been made, and they all had gotten it. They sat there in dead silence, with deeply serious and thoughtful expressions on their faces. Luckily, Colonel Suarez broke the tension in the room by saying, "Hell! You only go around once. You only live once. So let's take a good long break for a couple of good drinks. The bar is now open, and the drinks are on General Pinochet."

Thank God it was the last day of the meeting. Everyone had covered a lot of ground to pull off this conference. It would be nice to catch my plane out of there the next day. But according to Colonel Suarez, only he, myself, and our security guards would be going out that evening for an extravaganza of entertainment, good food, and excellent drinks. Colonel Suarez proved to be a man of his word; the nightspot restaurant was very nice. But we all ended up getting a real surprise — and for me, it was a shock. The evening presented me something in common with my old accomplice Gary the Chef, who had been the liaison leader for the original group of Black Chamber Immolators. The evening was going great. The orchestra was entertaining everyone with Spanish music. Suddenly, the Spanish music stopped, and they started playing German music — more like the oon-pah-pah music one would hear in Munich. We noticed a large group of European men entering the main restaurant area. Among them were five younger blond men who definitely looked German. They were all catering to one rather distinguished-looking gentleman with black hair and a strong face. He had a nice leather topcoat over his shoulders. Everyone in the restaurant immediately noticed him; he was obviously an important person. But the shocking part was that several other patrons in the restaurant stood up and saluted him with the raised right arm of a Nazi salute.

This was unbelievable. I had seen this type of thing in the newsreels as a kid, where all the fascist Nazis at giant Bonn meetings stood up to salute Hitler. I turned to the other people at the table and asked, "What the hell is this? What just happened here? Who in heaven's name is that person, to get such attention?"

With commanding authority, my security guard escort told me not to speak — to remain quiet and not to draw any attention to our table. He informed me who the man was, and said I was the only one who did not know him. He was a very protected and respected person in Paraguay, and you did not want anyone in the restaurant to think you might be a Jew.

Colonel Suarez added to the conversation by stating, "He was a very well-known German officer. In Paraguay, he is a very well-known medical doctor and is widely respected by many here and in parts of Argentina. The world does not know that he is here. Everyone says they do not know where he is located, and everyone agrees that he cannot be found. Now you know a very big secret, one that only a few thousand people in this area know, and you are part of the collective group who knows a secret that the Jews of the world would like to know. Mr. Chahaus, behold the very famous, and infamous, medical doctor from Germany, Doctor Joseph Mengeles. He is one medical doctor you are not allowed to shoot."

What a way to end my trip. I would have loved to know where Gary the Chef was, or how to contact him. I'd have let him know about this incident, and have him realize that we now had a hell of a lot more in common. The man's image would stay in my mind forever, but my lips would be sealed forever concerning the incident.

Before I left, I gave my farewell to the colonel and the escorts, then completely shut my mind down, boarded the plane, and enjoyed the long, long flights to get home. One thing learned from the whole situation was that *Gulliver's Travels* was right on the mark: the talking horses of humanity were 100 percent right about the human Yahoos.

Finally! The plane landed at Washington, D.C. and I went to get my luggage. Standing there was a limo driver with a sign reading "Mr. Chahaus." He assisted me out of the terminal, loaded my luggage into the trunk of the car, and drove me directly to the Willard Hotel. While checking into the hotel, I was hoping that the committee would be having a nice dinner that night — one of good old, and not too spicy, American food. When I got to my suite, there was a nice basket of crackers, wine and cheese, and a note informing me that everyone would be gathering for dinner at 1930 hours. That gave me time to freshen up with a shower and a shave, and to take a well-deserved nap. I was worn out from all the traveling, because I just can't sleep on planes.

The full committee had not yet arrived, but the long-time-no-see Captain Dan was there. I knew then that this was a top-priority mission of importance to the White House. The key portion of the meeting would start the next day. During the evening, it was all light talk about the trip, the scenery, how I liked the city of Asuncion, and general nothing details about other interesting people at the conference. I did not mention the Doctor Joseph Mengeles incident. Doing so might well have gotten me tied up in a lot of political and diplomatic bullshit that I did not care to get involved in at that time, or any other. The last thing I wanted to do was get involved in issues of Israel, for I had no burning desire to meet Isser Harel or Golda Meir.

The next morning after breakfast they gave me the podium, and the dancing to stage left and stage right began. "Good members of the committee, plus our special guest, Captain Dan, I do not wish to antagonize any of you or piss you off, but I do not plan on telling you anything in particular about my trip, or the details concerning the mission. Why? Simple! When dealing with this country, there is a history of two previous failures that got people killed. They were killed due to the incompetence of one ambassadorial diplomat on site, along with questionable C.I.A. agents. I want to be assured that our people live to tell the story, by not trusting anyone connected to our government."

Liddy the Ambassador quickly interrupted by stating, "Excuse me, Mr. Benton. We are your supervisory committee. We are under the direct authority and orders to supervise all aspects of this mission, per our special-K memo from the higher powers. We are not here to waste our time, and we expect complete and thorough responses to our inquiries. Do you understand me?"

I looked at Captain Dan, to try and read a response in his expression, but he was calm and stone-faced. I started again.

"I understand you. I understand the committee's concern. Now you need to understand that the complete operational plan for the mission is in place. All is set as to the kick-off date, the timing of actions to be taken, the assignments and responsibilities of the parties involved, and all passwords and codes to be used. To be clear, everything is currently in motion for making the coup happen at President Allende's expense. We even know who will be arrested, when and where, and who will hopefully be made extinct. If all goes as planned — without a spouse traitor or a mouthy ambassador — it should all be over in a matter of a few days.

"Everyone at the conference certainly realized that the State Department and the C.I.A. have their role to play in this, but they will be involved on a need-to-know basis at the last possible moment. The dedicated people involved in ousting Allende and Marxism from Chile are very apprehensive of the former National Security Advisor, they have little confidence in the C.I.A., and they do not want to be arrested for summary executions before they overthrow the communist elements in Chile.

"Look, gentleman! This is serious business. A lot of people are going to die once this coup goes operational, and the objective is that we do not lose too many of our Pookas in this venture. Again, gentleman, it is not you going to Chile, it is not you pulling the trigger on another human being, and it is not you who have to get your asses out of there alive. That is why I am also requesting that no members of the committee attend the Pooka orientation meeting at Fort Hayes in August. The reason and the key are to maintain complete secrecy and avoid any potential security breaches. With all due respect, there will be no more information provided to you, Mr. Liddy, or to the committee. If the completion of my presentation is not enough, so be it."

The formal stuffed shirt, Mr. Rumble, stood up to threaten, "Let me make something clear to you, young man. You work for all of us at our discretion, and you will provide us the answers we request of you. Like it or not, you are just an errand boy to accomplish that which needs to be done, as ordered by higher government authorities that you work for. You will start cooperating with this committee now, or else."

Captain Dan still said nothing as this guy crossed swords with me. So I sat down quietly, looked at all the committee members, and said nothing. After sitting there for a minute and looking at them, I said, "Or else! Well, now! I would like to ask all of you a few questions, which you do not have to answer. But please, just sit there and think about what your response might be. Just how many people in this room have every assassinated anyone? Just how many people in this room have seen death up close and personal? How many people in this room were ever considered dead by their friends, and had the pleasure of interrupting their own wake? How many of you in this room have ever given a direct order for others to risk their lives, and to die at your orders and directions? I have done them all, so your 'or else' does not mean shit to me. I do appreciate and enjoy the association with all of you in this room, but this mission is going to be my way, and under my rules, unless you have the balls to go out there in the world and put your life on the line. So, pardon my French, but fuck off with your subtle threats."

That got the room's attention. Several people were taken aback, and one could have cut the tension with a dull knife. Finally, Captain Dan stood up and said that everyone was to take a break, and that the committee was to stay in the room during the coffee break. He suggested that I take my break with a brisk walk around the block. By the look of things, everyone's lunch that day had just been ruined by me, and I had not yet told them that I would not be there for dinner. They did not know that I had changed my tickets at the airport to fly out later that night. Captain Dan's suggestion was taken seriously, so I left the hotel and walked around a block or two. I found a nice little place to have coffee, and spent my time having coffee and reading a local paper. When my time was up, I walked back to the hotel and entered the meeting room. To my surprise, no one was there but Captain Dan and Mr. Lingo.

Captain Dan said, "Your point was made. You won the argument; the meeting will be officially over after lunch. But one definite compromise is requested by the committee: that Mr. Lingo will be allowed to attend the Fort Hayes conference. Since the meeting will be ending early, you may change your flight home to an earlier flight today."

It was agreed that Mr. Lingo would attend the orientation meeting at Fort Hayes. Then Captain Dan asked Mr. Lingo to leave the room, and stated he would be seeing him at lunch. He turned to me and said that he had never seen me so uptight, but he completely understood where I was coming from. He said that he had considered speaking up earlier, but decided to wait and see how I would handle the situation, and how much crap I would take from the committee. He told me that he had politely put the two committee members in their place, and had informed them that I had a greater operational value to the shadow operation than they. He said they all got the point. Dan apologized for them being a little uptight, and said that everyone in Washington was uptight those days because of Watergate. The Watergate issue had everyone paranoid, and had made everyone suspicious of everyone else. Plus, there were sneaky reporters trying to find a story anywhere, and by any means, to create a headline. He pointed out that a lot of people's asses were on the line over Watergate, and that Senator Sam Irvin was going to hold everyone's hand to the fire until he roasted the weenies of those involved.

After lunch I headed right to the airport, and was able to get an even earlier flight home. It was nice to be leaving Washington D.C. after the fiasco of a meeting with a committee that now had a long memory. Once home, I called all of the

Pookas, to tell them that the original orientation meeting date was wrong. It had been changed to the last three days in August, and they would be receiving an informational packet with some details, accompanied by flight tickets to Columbus. I let them know that the committee would be establishing and arranging for all cover stories to their families, school or work, and that they would be on an extended vacation or seminar trip for up to twenty-one days.

The next several weeks were spent reviewing all the material, preparing the presentation for the orientation meeting by making numerous overhead projector slides, and spending the rest of my time with the family. I was having a strong desire to figure out how to go on the mission with the Brigade, but I had to accept my responsibility, and not start becoming an irresponsible leader.

When the time came, I was more than ready to meet the crew. I knew their accommodations would be adequate, since I had spent some time at Fort Hayes earlier in my covert career. Mr. Lingo arrived a day early. He made sure everything was adequate and in order — the meeting rooms, meals, and sleeping facilities. It was time for the rubber to meet the road. All the team members would be checking in that afternoon, and our first get-together would be at 1830 hours, for dinner.

Everyone arrived on time and without difficulty. They all showed up for dinner on time. There was a lot of glad-handing and light social talk, and everyone enjoyed themselves throughout the dinner. The strange thing I noticed was that no one questioned or complained about being gone for up to twenty-one days. It appeared as if they all wanted, and were craving, a vacation with some action. Then I remembered how it had felt when I had gone through long periods of inaction, had heard no word from anyone about missions, and had felt that I was being neglected or punished for something I might have done wrong. Of course, the insecurity was just a figment of one's imagination, but it had felt like wanting a date for the prom, and no one wanted to go with you. Not a strange thought, for I had no date to the prom, and with the guidance of my insecurities I enlisted in the army. And look what that had led to.

After dinner, I welcomed them formally to Fort Hayes, introduced them to Mr. Lingo, and told them to enjoy the evening with drinks, relaxation, and conversation. They were told that after breakfast the next day, things would get complicated and serious. They were informed that no one would be leaving the base until they departed to catch their transportation to Paraguay, and that there would be no Kahiki, Schmidt's, or outside wining or dining. Then we told them, in order to make them feel good, that Schmidt's would be delivering Bahama Mamas and cream puffs to us after our sessions the next day. This made everyone feel a lot better, and the rest of the evening was like a class reunion to remember.

After breakfast on the first day, we got strictly down to business, and pulled no punches about the dangers and pitfalls of the mission. We gave them maps of Chile; city maps of Concepcion, Valparaiso, Santiago and Vina del Mar; and numerous photographs of their assigned areas. They were provided different angle photos of the huge Presidential Palace in Santiago. There were also nine blown-up photos of the key targets to be eliminated, should they appear in the scope. All had a subtitle underneath, stating that a similar event would occur to any related or associated personnel with the primary targets in the target area. On another wall were eight large photos showing two angles each of all four corners of the Presidential Palace. These would allow the assigned shooters to be familiar with what they would be looking at, once stationed in position. On another wall were photos of the National Stadiums in Santiago and Valparaiso, and many photos of the University of Chile. One of the group thought the Santiago Stadium looked like the Rubber Bowl in Akron, Ohio. Another rabbit mentioned that Santiago looked like an oversized Las Vegas; in a desert valley surrounded by snow-capped mountains on one side and plain mountains on the other.

They were informed that some would meet an old acquaintance during the travel stage of the operation, after they left Asuncion, Paraguay, and upon arriving at La Paz, Bolivia — that being the El Presidentia of Bolivia, who was our one-time host, Colonel Suarez. I let them know that they would be spending a couple of days at Asuncion with their four assigned guides and escorts. Those people would go over every detail of their travel plans and their assigned target locations, and would show them photos of individuals to avoid and/or pay special attention to, should they appear in their vicinity. It was also made clear to all that if anyone looked cross-eyed at them, started giving them any special notice, or made them feel insecure and uncomfortable that they should — just be on the safe side — terminate them.

I assigned the teams to their escorts and target areas. "Lawhead, Ruffin, Murder and Titmas will be going to Concepcion with Mr. Bergeses. St. Amond, Iff, Rex and Jupinko will be going to Valparaiso, with the guidance of Mr. Ugarte. Gabalac, Vyas, Papadopoulos and Berkich will be traveling with Mr. Larach to Santiago. Miss Lee, Toukan, Badurina and Charvat will follow the orders of Mr. Sauer on the way to Santiago."

They were told that I had met all of these guys, that their families had paid a severe price under the Allende government, and that they were dedicated anti-Marxists. Again, I reminded them to trust no one, and that disloyalty came in many shapes and forms. Therefore, they had permission to terminate, if necessary, any suspect person. I let them know the odds of completing this mission without casualties were quite good, as these guys had already learned from two previous mistakes and were now better organized and prepared. They had better and tighter security in place, and had the benefit of an unexpected surprise. The crew was given the passwords of Pyramid and Ziggurat, along with the date of September 11 and the coup's starting time of two o'clock in the morning. They were reminded again to never repeat this information to anyone, at any time. This I told them, in a very firm and stern manner, when Mr. Lingo had left the room for an apparent bathroom break. I explained that we did not want any of this particular information getting back to the committee, or leaking to the loose-lipped mouths of the diplomatic community.

The big surprise everyone got during that session was when we brought in a clothing consultant. His job was to be sure that they were all dressed properly as liberal, hippy-yippy graduate students, or professors doing research while on sabbatical. He even made sure that all of their new luggage and bags would look the part, with some peace signs and psychedelic art. The teams soon got the point that they were not to look like neat and clean professionals. The consultant also told the men not to shave their faces, the girls not to shave their legs, and all to let their hair look somewhat unkempt. They should wear only sandals, or shoes without socks. The strange little guy was good; a little light in the loafers, but he did his job well. He had gone to secondhand clothing stores, Goodwill, and The Salvation Army to buy used luggage and clothing for everyone. He was quite funny, and told them how good they looked in things that did not fit, or had suffered a little too much wear and tear. The girls did not really mind the loosey-goosey grandmother dresses. The entire session was humorous, like watching people backstage getting ready for a theater production of *Li'l Abner*.

The three days went by fast. Everyone was ready, and they were confident that all would survive the mission if everything went well in the first twenty-four hours. They understood the mission was the job, that the priority was their safety, and that they were not to risk dying foolishly or irresponsibly for someone else's country — or for the mineral and petroleum rights of some greedy industrial persons living in this country. They were told that when the mission was over they would go directly home, and there would be no debriefing sessions. After they had relaxed for a week or two, I would be calling each of them for a simple and short report on the mission.

On the last day, once the meeting had ended, I said to them, "I expect to be talking with all of you in a few months or so. While in Chile, all of you must rely on your natural instincts and your sixth sense, when the hair goes up on the back of your necks. Please remember that distance makes for safety. This is why your target weapons will be special-made Custom Mauser Waffen Sporters with two changeable scopes. You'll have one scope for daytime and one infrared scope for early morning hours. Once your shots are made, leave the weapons for some Chilean collector, and get your asses out of there as dumb and naive students. As they say, 'now hear this.' I do not want you to consider trying any shots under a hundred and fifty meters, give or take, and better yet, three hundred meters — unless it is an emergency situation or absolutely necessary. This distance will provide you a greater surprise on your designated targets, and less chance that the target's personal security will be aware of your position.

"If any of you should get caught up in some unexpected or unfortunate sweep arrest carried out on the general population, just keep your cool, and first be sure they are not pro-Allende. Should the group arresting people be clearly pro-Pinochet, request an English-speaking officer of senior rank and quietly say to them, 'Bonilla, Leigh, Merino, and Escobar Ziggurat.' You will not have to do this if your escort is still with you and alive, but one never knows what a situation may develop into, and all of you must be prepared for unanticipated changes that may occur on this mission. So, my companions, I wish you well. You do not need luck, for all of you have been trained to be the very best. Therefore, have good flights tomorrow, enjoy Asuncion and La Paz, and give my regards to Colonel Suarez."

The bunnies were off, hippity-hopping around South America, while I could only sit around and wait, say a few prayers for them, and try to keep my nightmares to a minimum. The waiting was nerve-wracking, since I had to wait until the eleventh to start watching the international news. When the eleventh had come and gone, the news was both good and bad. Apparently, Pinochet and his forces had won the day, but the news reports stated that two Americans had been killed. The Marxists were out and the Chileans had a new Independence Day from communism — on the eighteenth, over thousands of dead bodies. But the knowledge that some Americans had been killed was driving me nuts. As strange as it might seem, I got a little relief from the pressure from the entertainment of watching tennis matches gone wild and Billie Jean King tromping on little Bobby Riggs at a grand exhibition. The little cocky fart did not stand a chance. She made him eat his words, and then put his foot right in his mouth. It was great entertainment and took my mind off the Pooka Brigade for a while.

Eventually, the time came for me to make my calls to the troops. The great thing about the calls was learning that all the Pookas had done their jobs and had made it out of Chile in one piece. Everything had gone as planned, except for all the brutality, with no-mercy summary executions by the Pinochet forces that they witnessed. They explained that the two American killed were probably C.I.A. agents, and that they were not killed by the Allende resistance which lasted for several days, but by Pinochet's secret police. As for Allende, they disclosed that he was wounded while trying to escape from the Palace. Several of his security personnel were terminated. When some of Pinochet's military officers arrived on the scene, they noticed that Allende was only slightly wounded. They immediately shot him several times, to be sure he was dead, and dragged him back into the Palace. One point the team made quite clear: there was no mercy shown to Marxists, Unionists, or identified troublemaker students and professors. It was just bang-bang, you're dead, with no hearings, no trials, and no rights.

It was certainly going to be some report that would soon be provided to the committee. The report would be stated as clearly as the team had presented their information to me. I hoped some of the powers that be upstairs would lose a little sleep at night over the atrocities their Mr. Pinochet was delivering on his people. It looked more and more like the president and his secretary of state had made a deal with the devil, and that they were more comfortable with the devil and his forces than with the communists. After all, many of us knew that what was bad for U.S. corporations was bad for Allende, and what was good for U.S. corporations was great for the devil.

This successful mission, which seemed to have backfired as far as the White House's expected results, had been put to bed as far as I was concerned. But as a Republican, my bubble started to burst over Vice President Spiro T. Agnew's resignation. The words of the president's convention speech had come back to haunt him. His statement that he had 100 percent faith and confidence in Vice President Agnew, and my (now regrettable) words of support for Agnew in seventy-six seemed a little ridiculous. Adding all this to the Watergate paranoia left me wondering what would be next? What other shoe was going to drop that would embarrass the president? Who else in the world was going to piss us off enough to get dispatched into never-never land? It certainly did not take me long to learn the answer to those questions. We suddenly had an all-out war in the Middle East, with Syria and Egypt attacking Israel, while all the other Arab countries blamed us in one way or another. Engaging in discourse with the Moslems did not work, so they decided to cut off our vital oil supplies as punishment. It looked like our Pookas might get called up again to protect our vital security interests, and for the benefit of our "petrodollar economic" concerns.

That last year had turned out to be a crazy one. Consider the fact that we just about had another American Indian war on our hands, all over the seventy-one-day siege at Pine Ridge Oglala Indian Reservation led by Russell Means and Dennis Banks of the American Indian Movement. I thought I'd seen it all, until they awarded a Nobel Prize to the wrong person. When I first heard the news, I thought it was a prank by some newsperson. It was a disgrace. The scorecard for honors was unbalanced, and there was a cacophony of arguments and rebuttals for that embarrassing mistake. The person being so honored lived with blunders that had caused thousands of apparent accidents and suicides, along with tons of collateral damage. Now a single handshake with a smile made him, what? This also explained why two members of the Nobel committee resigned in protest. Meanwhile, as embarrassing as it might be, the only man of honor who refused to accept the award was Le Duc Tho of North Vietnam. The award was apparently only for our guy's public persona of sorts, and not for all his accountable lost souls. The award could not go to the president, since his image was being tarnished over Watergate; particularly since the Saturday Night Massacre, where the U.S. Attorney General's Special Prosecutor, Archibald Cox, was fired unceremoniously, and the president had his favorite nemesis, Sam Irvin, hanging around his neck. That phony from the funny farm on the Charles River never deserved an award of such caliber and prestige. His private life of skullduggery and subterfuge had led to many deaths by covert screw-ups from political and economic intrigue around the world. The guy got two B's and one C only for Nixon on Peking, Moscow, and the Vietnam cease-fire. He got massive F's for fuck-ups in Chile, Argentina, Guatemala, Africa, Panama, the Philippines and Indonesia. As one of the former committee members once so aptly stated: not an award for covering up crimes, protecting government criminals, and abusing the decent C.I.A. people who only wanted to do the right things for their country.

The guy had an obligation to get the pigs out of the farmhouse and off the farm. Instead, he expanded his pig and hog operation at the expense of all the other beneficial farm animals. The committee members knew him better than anyone else, and said that he perjured himself before Congress and the Foreign Relations Committee many, many times by lying though his teeth. As Colonel Knapp once said, "He is the chief deceiver in our government, and the mysterious man of deception and betrayal, along with being the real master spy. It would have been best if everyone had feared this man more than J. Edgar and the special Hoover sweeper men."

Oh, what can one say? Life is just one big law, and we'll call it the Law of Probable Dispersement. That is, "When the shit hits the fan, it is never distributed equally." Yet there had been stranger things I had noticed over time. Like who had the connections, and the political contacts of influence, to help a former Harvard College professor easily escape from prison unnoticed? Who then helped him, together with his wife, easily skip the country unnoticed, only to show up later, safe and sound in Algeria, with a lot of money? Maybe no one at the time had a Mandala puzzle to figure out this complicated arrangement for putting two and two together by simple historical associations. Let's see; what word associations might there be? Okay, we'll start with Hobbism, psycho-political, psycho-scientific, T. Leary, West Point, Battelle, Harvard, Nietzsche, Haig, Califano, Verboten, G. Gordon, D.L.R. and Ford.

But the stranger thing at that time in our history was that people were losing their cars by having them stolen or burning up their cars for the insurance money, just because the price of a gallon of gasoline had gone from $0.229 and $0.259 to the unbelievably high prices of $0.499 and $0.529. Everyone was beginning to think and act like the world was coming to an end; that only decent people drove diesel cars, while they watched the stock market go to hell in a basket. Apparently, it seemed like all that any good communist had to do was come out of the closet and say boo! since the Arabs, with the Russians, had our oil cans in their squeezing little hands.

Oh, what the hell! Time marches on, and what goes up sooner or later goes down. Then what goes down soon or later usually goes back up, and for every action there is a reaction that the Arabs might not soon forget. Those Arabs did not want to misinterpret the Nobel Peace Prize being given to some American for making the peace. The award really was not for peacemaking, but for peacekeeping efforts, and for his personal disturbing of the peace to protect influential U.S. economic interests around the world. The last time I looked at the map, all those oil-rich Arab countries were assumed to be part of this world. Oops! Part of whose world, that might be viewed through rose-colored glasses? It might have been a good time for remembering that the "past is prologue" — by reading in the good book Deuteronomy, chapter 25, and keying in on verses 17, 18, and 19. One should note, "lest thee not forget Amalek, for Amalek is here today, and Amalek will be here in all our future tomorrows."

CHAPTER XIII
"Triskaidekaphobia"

Being negative is not my thing, but there was this lingering premonition that it was going to be a year when things just went wrong. Black cats might interfere with opportunities while creating bad luck, and a lot of people were going to suffer from some misfortunes they had not planned on. What could one expect, with O.P.E.C. tightening the energy screws on us? How could we stop Watergate from tearing our system of government apart? What about those so-called trusted, honorable men who turned out to be crooks, burglars, thieves, and just plain dishonest people? It was clear that the stock market did not like what it saw, and people were losing money left and right in their mutual funds. Their real estate investments were suffering, and the high rates of inflation were hitting their wallets. One thing was a fact: that no government "plumbers" in the administration would be fixing the leaking pipes of the economy.

Meanwhile, Peron was definitely handling things in Argentina by whacking his anti-government factions. Mr. Pinochet in Chile was not taking crap from anyone; the captured key Allende leadership apparently had committed suicide while in jail, and before going to trial. Very convenient! It looked like it could be very possible that the Pooka Brigade would be called into service again in the very near future, to make corrective changes in Venezuela. Why? Venezuela now had an identical Allende-style government in place with its new Marxist President, Carlos Andres Perez. Looking on the bright side, Anastasia Somoza was maintaining his Somoza Dynasty with an iron glove, and United Fruits was making damn sure their puppet Garcio stayed in power. Not that anyone should be distrustful, but it just might have been possible that Anaconda Copper, U.S. Steel, Gulf Oil, Texaco, Standard Oil, United Fruits, Gulf and Western, and all those other American petroleum interests really did own and control the world.

No matter. Who was holding all the potential winning cards in the political and economic game of poker? It looked like it would take all the running that we in America could do simply to stay in the same place, as far as our standard of living was concerned. Yet in all of this economic frustration and bullshit, there appeared to be an opportunity for a new kid on the block to start moving out in front of the crowd. While everyone was being down in the mouth, I was thinking that it was the right time to change the direction of my career, and to capitalize on the opportunities created by panic, fear and despair. There had never been a better time, in my memory, for making such a move. Let's face it, most all of the current and former experts were becoming has-beens. The new tax laws were changing the competitive situation within the advisor and consultant community. The real gift for a special opportunity was the passage of a new tax law that everyone referred to as E.R.I.S.A., which industry professionals jokingly said meant, "Every Ridiculous Idea Since Adam."

Yet some people do get honored in this world for their loyal services. As when General Pinochet went to Asuncion, Paraguay, and pronounced President Stroessner an honorary general in the Chilean Army. Then just when one thought that couldn't be topped, Argentinean President Peron stepped up and made President Stroessner an honorary general in the Argentine Army. Maybe all this special attention would send Stroessner in the right direction, to coordinate a coup against President Perez in Venezuela. Then the new right-wing dictator could make Stroessner an honorary general in the Venezuelan Army. It was clear that someone had to do it, for our government was in turmoil, and I was quite sure that the people in power had other things on their minds. A drowning president and his fellow Republicans couldn't have cared less about President Perez, Golda Meir, or Mabutu Sese Seko.

With all the crazy things going on in Washington, it was no wonder that the Pookas were an afterthought, and probably had been forgotten about by the powers above. There had been no word from anyone on the committee since I filed my final report on the Chilean mission. Everyone must have been lying low, and not wanting to make any noticeable waves in and/or around Washington. But I was not sitting on my duff. I had terminated all of my current business relationships — to the displeasure of my wife — and was negotiating and interviewing with companies to establish a new direction for my career. My intent was to proceed forward on an independent career path. It might have seemed like a rough row to hoe, but the hard work would be worth the risk. One cannot move forward without risk or taking chances in this world. Who wanted to be a landlocked employee, without the freedom to fail?

But suddenly, my only comment was "Oh, shit." Just as I jumped off one solid horse of financial security to try and mount a new horse of opportunity, there came an unwanted special-K memo. This might mean that everything in my life would have to be put on hold at the wrong moment. When I made the call to Circle 6-2150, Mr. Brute came on the line and informed me that there would be a major business conference with the entire Pooka Brigade the last week of that month. He said that all the registrations and records would declare the group to be marketing people for the Integrated Marketing Group. Everyone would be flown into Washington, D.C. After spending one night at the Willard Hotel, we would board a train the next morning bound for the Greenbrier facility in West Virginia. He said to contact all the troops with the information, and to let them know that they would be receiving their tickets and information packets via special delivery.

He then told me that only one current committee member would be attending this private, confidential and secret conference, and that would be Mr. Lingo. He further stated that Captain Dan would be there, with a very invisible and nonexistent guest. He said that even the committee did not know about the guest, and that this nonexistent person would be, in his vernacular, from the higher powers above the higher powers over Captain Dan.

I had to guess that this was going to be one big mission. Who knew? It might entail terminating numerous Maoists, Fascists, Marxists, or just plain evil people. Based on what was in the news, and on my observations and knowledge concerning things around the world, I would have first put my money on Perez of Venezuela. He and his people would have been a lot easier to knock off than a bunch of Arabs. There was no way we would go to Africa to help any tribal idiots who simply liked to kill and enslave each other. Egypt was a different story. It could, perhaps, be a mission to Syria, or a few other Arab countries, but that would not have been favored by me. That mission would only happen if the president's recent trips to the Middle East were a bust. The president was trying. He had gone to Egypt and Syria, to Saudi Arabia to see King Faisal, had visited Jordan's King Hussein, and then had gone to Israel, where he got a cold reception with a slap in the face. I was banking that Israel's negative response to the president, versus the Arabs' neutral yet cordial response, had put the knock-neds lower on the hit list. After all, our guys would stand out like sore thumbs in the Middle East, and would not fit into the cultural environment. The only people who might assimilate without special notice to any degree would possibly be Vyas, Toukan, Ruffin, Badurina and Jupinko. The rest would be completely obvious, with an American target on their backs. Of course, now that I thought about it, the president had not gone to Libya to talk with Colonel Kaddafi, and he had been a thorn in our side. Who knew? He could be a target of opportunity.

Well I had done my homework. The wife wanted me to learn everything that was beneficial at the upcoming conference, without too much partying. She told me that she had a little surprise vacation planned for us, with the Coleman camper, once I got home from the conference. It was refreshing to know that I had the confidence and support of my wife during this stressful and unnerving period of career transition. She strongly believed that if we all got away for a while, I would settle down, relax, and do better with my negotiations and interviews. The thought of a vacation made me feel good while I was on my way to Washington, as bored as ever, sitting there in the good old Pittsburgh airport with an hour-plus layover between flights.

Because of the recent newspaper headlines, I had started to feel sorry for the old country relatives of Papadopoulos and Spyridon. The Greeks had simply picked a fight with the wrong people over Cyprus. I liked the Greeks. I liked their baklava; I liked those hamburgers wrapped in grape leaves; and I had enjoyed my week's vacation on Cyprus with several of my associates. I hated to think it, but the Turks were going to kick their asses. When I was in Korea, the Turks were the toughest of the tough, and just plain mean.

The connecting flight was on time, its arrival at Washington, D.C. was on time, and my arrival at the Willard Hotel was right on schedule. Once I had checked in, I turned to head for the elevators to go up to my room. I got the shock of a lifetime from what was standing about twenty feet away, smiling happily at me. This was unbelievable, not possible, no way. Standing there were several of the original Black Chamber Immolators. What a sight for sore eyes! Before me were my old friends Gardner the Cowboy, Sullivan the Gym Boy, Lollich the Crow-Ott, and Archer the Swimmer. The only ones missing were Kelsey the Artist, Massiha the Carpet Man, and Johnson the Dancer. I did not think Kelsey and Massiha would still be operating in Bolivia. The meeting would be a real treat for the Pookas of the Pooka Brigade. But this created some wild thinking as to who would be the team leaders? Who would comprise the separate teams needed for this super mission? It certainly had to be serious, big-time action to bring back the members of the old Black Chamber crew.

We all shook hands and hugged each other, then the quiet man, Gardner, said that we should all go into the bar and wait for the others to arrive. It was Gardner, of all people, who suggested that since we only had to catch a train the next day, we should celebrate our reunion that night with a wild little party, for old time's sake. He said that he had already checked out our meeting room, where the social hour and dinner would be held, and that there was a piano in the room for me to play while Johnson danced all night. The gathering of our surviving and prevailing members was great. I could not have asked for anything more important and inspirational at that point in my life. I immediately realized and was confident that my risky career move was the right thing to do at the right time. I informed the guys that, whether or not they realized it, they would be meeting all the people who had replaced them as Immolators, and that those young people had performed with excellence on many difficult missions. I told them if they had thought we were good, these people were really top-notch; talented and skilled professionals at any distance, or at being very up close and personal.

I then noticed one of our Pookas in the lobby, and mentioned this to the guys. They all turned to look, and several stated that they did not see anyone I might have been referring to in the lobby. My comment was, "You guys must be blind, or you have been retired too long."

Sullivan the Gym Boy said, "I am not blind. There is only hotel staff and some businessmen or politicians standing out there in the lobby area. There are no terminating Immolators."

It was a joy for me to point out that which was not obvious.

"Wrong and wrong! You could all have been facing death from your rusty observation skills. That good-looking young lady is not hotel staff or someone's secretary; she is a first-rate assassin. You will be meeting Miss Gabalac tonight, so mind your manners, or your tongue could end up being stuck to the roof of your mouth."

The group was taken aback a little to know that we had women in our secret little group, but most agreed that in today's world it was probably a good idea. We all had a few drinks, then I excused myself in order to check into my room and freshen up a bit. I let them know I'd be seeing them all at dinner. Once in the room, I found an unexpected note on the desk. It stated that I would be in charge of that night's gathering, and to make sure everyone got to the train on time. Captain Dan and Mr. Lingo were handling all preparations at the Greenbrier. That was logical and practical, since nothing of importance was to occur at the hotel. They had stuck me with the responsibility of making sure our group did not party too hard that night.

Since the powers had given me the yoke of responsibility, I got to the meeting room early and instructed the bartenders on the rules of the game. The first rule was to make weak drinks. The second was that no one in the room was to be served more than two drinks before dinner or more than three weak drinks after dinner. I then told the bartenders if anyone should, by chance, notice or complain, they were to point the person in my direction, and let them know that they should talk the matter over with me. The bartenders got the message.

No one got too high, or even a little drunk, and the entire evening went well. There was a lot of nice, social chit-chat, and then humorous entertainment by yours truly on the piano and by Johnson the Dancer. Kelsey and Massiha showed up just in time for dinner. We gave each other friendly hellos and said how good it was to see each other. However, during the rest of the evening they seemed a little withdrawn, and apprehensive about being around me. It was possible that they were concerned with my personal reaction to the Bolivia situation with Colonel Suarez, or that they both had become high-priced mercenaries. I decided that I would put their uneasiness to rest while we were on the train the next day. I would let them relax by telling them that I couldn't care less about what they were doing, and that I was tickled to death at hearing from them through Colonel Suarez. I would then let them know that my only hope was that they stayed well, and continued to be paid well.

After breakfast the next morning, our whole group gathered in the lobby. They were instructed about boarding the bus that would soon be at the hotel, and what we would do about luggage and seating once at the train station. Apparently, the news media in Washington was curious about everything and everybody — new or old — staying at the hotels in the area. A man walked up to me with his assistant, told me that they were reporters, and said they would like to ask me some questions. They wanted to know why we were staying at this hotel. I told them we were not staying at the hotel per se; that ours had been a one-night stay for our company agents who had flown in from around the country. I said our one night at the hotel had been for gathering together the top producer agents for our annual Honor Table convention. I let them know that we were waiting for a bus to take us to the train station, where we would continue on to our convention site in West Virginia.

The guy was getting too nosy and curious. He wanted to know where I was from, and why that hotel had been selected for the start of our convention. I told him that most of us were from the Midwest, some were from the West Coast, and a couple were from Atlanta. As to why the company had selected that hotel for our one-night stay, their guess was as good as mine. The reporter wanted to ask more questions, but I cut him off by yelling out to everyone that our bus had arrived and we should get moving. I told the reporter it had been nice meeting him, that Washington looked like a nice city, and that it was time for us to leave. The reporters were definitely looking for something. I remembered having seen them in the hotel the day before, but at the time hadn't known they were inquisitive reporters.

The train station was closer than expected. The buses drove all around the Mall for a sightseeing trip of the monuments, past the Library of Congress, and to the train station. We all boarded this nice old train. Our group had two cars to ourselves. We had another nice sightseeing trip for the several hours it took to get to the Greenbrier Resort. Once we arrived at the Greenbrier train station, a shuttle bus picked us up and delivered us directly to the Greenbrier for our registration and check-in. The check-in went quickly and smoothly, since Captain Dan and Mr. Lingo had pre-registered all of us at the hotel. All we had to do was pick up our keys and head to our rooms.

The hotel was one big mother of a building, out there in the wilderness. It was a mixture of Greek and German architecture, and the old-fashioned rooms were of a pre-World War II design, not like the Willard. That must have been the way politicians wanted it; the hotel was only a set decoration, sitting on top of a super-secret government bunker used for protecting politicians and the Washington elite. Someone must have still liked us, since in each room there was a large basket of fruit, cheese and crackers, and a nice bottle of white wine. Included was a formal, handwritten invitation to dinner and a beautiful chrome cigarette lighter with an American flag and a bald eagle decoration on the side. All the first-class, upper-crust treatment had my suspicious nature making me a little eerie about what the mission might entail, and if the risk was going to be much greater than any of us desired. But it was time for cocktails and hors d'oeuvres, and a great dinner would probably be the order of the day. After dinner we would see what the powers had to say concerning our life expectancy.

Everyone enjoyed the evening. The food was excellent, and the string quartet for entertainments was exceptional. We were all waiting for someone to take the podium and tell us why we were there. It was not surprising that Captain Dan was the one to start things off. He welcomed everyone to the conference, then went around the room giving code name introductions, and occasionally threw in a humorous remark concerning one the Immolators or Pookas.

Then he got serious and said, "It is nice to see all of the surviving members of these groups, the old and the new, sitting here tonight around these tables and enjoying each others' company. We should all take a moment or two during this meeting to remember those who did not make it to this conference due to unfortunate circumstances beyond their control. You Pookas are quite fortunate that none of your group has met with misfortune. There have been several serious injuries, but you all survived. With the original group of Immolators, eleven received serious injuries on missions, and seven did not survive. You can be assured that this country did not forsake or forget them, and that none of their friends in this room will ever forget them. Everyone's service, dedication and loyalty to this country of yours was and is highly appreciated. But unfortunately, you get no medals, no honors, and no recognition; you simply do not exist, and you never were.

"This shadow operation was the brainchild of the Eisenhower administration. It clearly pushed the envelope of great covert secrecy. The purpose was to operate without unnecessary red tape and get the necessary and primary things done. First, protect this country's principles of freedom and democracy, and then protect America's political and economic interests around the world, hopefully avoiding unnecessary red-tape complications. The main benefit of the shadow operation was for use under only the most drastic emergency situations affecting this country's system of government. But then it was decided that there needed to be a secret, sub-level, preventative medicine operation. This sub-group was to develop a structured organization for creating a covert specialty of terminators and expediters. The purpose was to carry out preemptive actions in order to avoid future difficulties and complications of serious consequence on the world stage.

"The shadow system for government security proved to be the proper and correct decision by the Eisenhower administration. They understood the reality of the frailties of our system of democracy, versus the fundamentalist and authoritarian systems of other governments elsewhere around the world. The president was more worried about the powerful and influential people in the world, rather than the wealthy people in the world, for he understood the problems and conflicts of socialization throughout the world. That is why he warned America about issues which the average person in this country did not comprehend. He warned about the rise and influence of the military-industrial complex. He clarified that the word 'Industrial' was a general, broad-based, brushstroke term to include the C.I.A., the F.B.I., and the N.S.A., along with other government defense agencies. The point was made many years ago by a former committee member we knew as Ambassador Dee, when he told the following interesting story.

"After the fiasco of the McCarthy Era, the firing of General MacArthur for thumbing his nose at the President of the United States, and after the negotiated truce to end the Korean War; the main government spy and police agencies were put to a field test for testing their competence and ability. The test was to be for each agency. There was a fox within this isolated and enclosed wooded area of Virginia, and the C.I.A. was first given the job to go into the woods and find the fox. After many, many hours, they failed to find the fox. They ended their test by stating that there was no fox, there never had been a fox, and that foxes do not exist in this area of Virginia.

"Then it was the turn for the F.B.I. to try and find the fox. They entered the woods, and became frustrated after many, many hours of looking for the fox. They set fire to the woods, and suddenly a black bear whose fur was on fire came out of the woods yelling, 'I'm a fox! I'm a fox!'

"Next to be tested was the N. S. A. Yet even they, after many hours, became frustrated when searching for the fox. They came to the conclusion that there was no fox, but informed the president that they had heard something in the woods. They said it could have been a wolf, or maybe a coyote, but more likely it was just a large rat.

"These actions so disappointed the powers that be, that they felt they needed a more effective and efficient form of problem-solvers. The result was the covert shadows of the Black Chamber who were immediately recruited and organized. They were led to understand that the fox was a rat. The key was to terminate the fox before it ruined the woods with its rabid mouth of ideas, while all the time hiding behind the bear.

"Therefore, this being so, the thou's of the you's were then created. That's when the lights were turned off, our creations went out into the night, and the shadows disappeared. This all brings me to the point of the current mission, which will be covered in great detail by Mr. Lingo tomorrow. The mission requires that you put zippers on your lips, keep your eyes and ears open, and always keep your mouths shut. Why? As of Labor Day, your call to duty is finished. You are all released from your commitments and obligations. The groups are kaput. Once you leave here, you may all go your separate ways, and do all your separate things, without future interruption. So party for the rest of the evening, and we will see you in the morning.

"But first, one last comment. True, the Pooka group's confidential contracts and service agreements state that your obligations run through nineteen-seventy-five. But we see no foreseeable circumstances that might require your future service. Besides, the political environment is too hot, Congress has a burr under its saddle against covert anything, and it does not take long to look at a hot horseshoe when held in one's hand."

The group was in shock. We did not know whether to laugh, cry, sit still in silence, or yell out a big "Yahoo!" Then, joy broke out through the room. Everyone glad-handed each other, and Johnson the Dancer started singing "You Are My Sunshine." Why that song? Who knew? Everyone started singing it too, and then we all headed for the bar to celebrate. Actually, the song only had meaning to those of us whose original training was at the Mount Fuji New Grand in Japan. At that time and place, it was rather common to sing that song with the Japanese. Party that night we did, and it was nice to see that the group did not segregate itself into the old and the new.

It was extremely interesting, and humorous, to hear the members of the original group outright lie and exaggerate to the new Pookas about difficult missions where they had to climb mountains, rappel off tall buildings, and swim through raging rapids to escape capture. There was no problem with this; the Pookas knew those old guys were full of shit, and everyone enjoyed the exaggerated storytelling about fictitious adventures. It was really nice to know that Gabalac and Lee fit in perfectly with the total group. They clearly showed that they could handle themselves, by holding their ground and maintaining their turf.

The next morning came a little too soon, since no one had hit the sack before two o'clock, and all of us had clearly had too much to drink. But a good breakfast and a lot of strong coffee got us on the ball, and the meeting started with Mr. Lingo saying, "I see everyone survived the night, that Mr. Benton was still able to play the piano at midnight, and that you are all here, bright and ready to learn about your complete nonexistence and becoming extinct. Very soon, the Black Chamber will be only fodder for the paper shredder. The historic events and activities of the Chamber will be turned into volumes of shredded documents. That which might happen to accidentally or unintentionally remain somewhere in the Library of Congress will have all references to the shadow operation completely blacked out, even while in its thirty-year lock box."

To my surprise, Mr. Jupinko the Louis Prima spoke up, and asked why all this was ending prematurely during such difficult times in the world. Mr. Lingo looked at Captain Dan, to see if he wanted to answer the question after statements had already been made, or if Captain Dan would take the question for discussion. Captain Dan gestured to Mr. Lingo that it was his ballgame, so Mr. Lingo started off by saying, "Well, well, well! Let me see how to put it in very short and blunt terms. The reality is, everyone and everybody is getting too inquisitive about the nature of things around Washington. Events have everyone looking and searching under every rock. Why? It is all due to the new Watergate terminology and the word 'Plumbers.' Officially, the Plumbers were known as a Secret Special Investigation Unit (S.S.I.U.). Now, the related problems for Congress, the Supreme Court, the Diplomatic Corps, and the American public, is that the persons involved were all trained and trusted F.B.I. and C.I.A. agents. Here is an example where the cream became sour milk, for these guys forgot that this is America. These Plumbers were not concerned with the fact that political loyalties do not outweigh or overrule honesty, integrity, and loyalty to the American citizenry as a whole.

"However, these so-called good and loyal Americans — the terms being used loosely — were burglars, robbers, extortionists and blackmailers. It would not surprise me if making arrangements for what looked like apparent suicide was not one of their best covert credentials as Hoover Boys, or contracted C.I.A. agents. Again, the good people with the F.B.I. and the C.I.A. suffered another black eye. The resumes of their employment history were a disgrace being exposed, and a clear reflection and embarrassment to their former agencies, friends and families.

"Now with all this Watergate and Plumber exposure placing a stain on the American flag and the Pledge of Allegiance, it has a Wild West Senator and some of his colleagues and staff up in arms, and they want blood. The Wild West Senator leading the charge is ordering everyone to look under every rock, turn over every stone, and cast a wide net with a jaundiced eye on every investigative government agency, from the C.I.A. to the N.S.A. and the F.B.I., all with a particular focus on the past Hoover Boys. We do not want to be viewed under this microscope. We do not want researchers asking about what they think they may be seeing, and we do not want to become a target of curiosity. Therefore, it has been decided that the group has served its purpose, and in today's political environment has outlived its usefulness, and original intent.

"I hope I have properly answered your question and addressed the concerns of the group to your satisfaction. This is your last formal day of business sessions. The rest of your days here at the resort will be your time: to relax, play golf, party, or request any general or private discussions with us as to issues you may not comprehend and need clarification on.

"But now, let's cover the issues for this meeting which must be a major concern to all of you, and that will provide all of you with peace of mind. First off, all of your Bermuda Trust accounts have been released. All your personal records at the Naval Base have been destroyed. So now there are no records of any trust accounts or deposit transactions. This means you can go there at any time for your funds, or have your funds transferred to anywhere else in the world.

"The next item of importance is that there are no passport or visa records relating to any of your travels. The only records are of those personal vacations or business conference trips in conjunction with your personal lives. Only those will show up on the U.S. Customs' records. Also, all records of meetings at any military facility, or transportation on any military aircraft, have been expunged. Even if not expunged, all that might be shown would be only untraceable code names. In fact, no one outside of the two of us and Mr. Benton in this room knows who you really are. After Labor Day, this information will be held only in someone's fond memories. All paper references of addresses, phone numbers, and so forth have been, or will be, shredded and/or burned. This is how the lights go out and the shadows disappear."

The rest of the meeting time that day was spent clarifying covenants and restrictions, and giving everyone a chance to ask questions of interest or address concerns. We then had another nice evening, with a pleasant social hour and an excellent dinner.

After dinner, Captain Dan took the podium. He stated that there were some recognition awards to present, but first he wanted to make a few remarks. He pointed out that, since the very beginning, he was closely related to both groups. He went on to say, "This has always been an interesting group. You have learned from experiences and associations that only a few in this world are aware of, and this form of association — both positive and negative — has changed who you might have been. It certainly will affect what you will become, and who you really are. I have for some time, due to my experiences in this job, considered myself an amateur expert at history. I have analyzed the principles of socialization's effects on history, from a simple structured existence with traditional thinking and fundamentalism in thought, to the complex and diversified socialization of this modern-day society.

"Socialization is the lasting thing you have within your group that has set the pathways of your futures. This, along with the socialization you may have with your family, your community, and your religion, as it may affect your politics and economic positioning in our society. So within your new singular life arena, the one you will now be returning to as a molded individual, there will be people whose lives you have influenced, and people who have influenced your life. Many of these people may never have heard of you, do not know you, or do not even realize that you may exist.

"All these people are referred to as 'significant others.' Why? They have unknowingly affected your maturity and direction in this life. So how many people in your life, whom you know, do not know you? Some may or may not even remember who you are, but have influenced the direction of your life. Certainly the Black Chamber or Pooka Brigade is, and will always be, a 'Significant Other' within your personal life. Why? Because the experience has changed your view of people in the world, and your view of political, social, and economic politics in the world as to your understanding of economic realities. As Mr. Benton so aptly put it once: in the field of marketing, when it comes to being a participant rather than an observer, the successful principle is 'sell or kill.' Well, I've given my two-cents-worth of philosophy for this night. And now, to present the awards."

There was a stack of frames and plaques on the table beside Captain Dan. He picked up a nice wooden plaque with a brass plate attached, and announced that he would like me, Mr. Benton, to come forward to the front of the room. He told everyone that he wanted to present this plaque to me for my years of service and dedication to the group, and to show the appreciation of a grateful nation. Everyone in the room stood up and applauded.

Captain Dan turned to give me the nice plaque. To everyone's amazement, the brass plate was blank.

Mr. Lingo spoke up, saying that was the best they could do, since they did not exist, that we did not exist, and therefore it was an invisible recognition that only my mind could see on the brass plate. The shiny brass plate would always, and only, reflect my image. Mr. Lingo and Captain Dan passed out similar awards to everyone else in the room. The very small words etched at the bottom of the frame only read 'Certificate of Appreciation.' Captain Dan ended by saying that all of us in the group had learned a lot, that we had also matured a lot more than most human beings at this stage in their lives, and that he wanted to leave us with a philosophical thought before we started partying.

"Some German philosopher once said that a person is not who they are by the last actions or conversations you had with them. They are who they are by only including all their past relationships and conversations. Maybe another way, or a simpler way, to make the point might be to point out that a leopard never changes it spots. The leopard's state of passive calmness is a false image, since the leopard is just waiting for an opportunity to pounce and take advantage of another unaware situation. So the converted pussycat will, by instinct and past actions, always revert back to being the leopard. Also, beware of strangers and Greeks bearing gifts of opportunity."

The awards ceremony was over. Captain Dan ended the meeting, and the partying started again. This time, our leaders had arranged for a little combo of musicians to entertain us for the rest of the night. We had good music, an open bar, and drinking among friends — what could be better? Now that all the formal business was over, most had already arranged to play a lot of golf, and several had arranged for a river-rafting trip somewhere in the mountains. I mostly played golf and tried to spread my time around, in order to spend some semi-private time in conversation with each of the Pookas. I certainly did not neglect my old buddies; we had our philosophical and psychological conversations between boilermakers. The boilermakers proved that we were not as young and sturdy as we once had been, and that our stomachs no longer had a cast-iron lining. After the second episode, we all thought it wiser to quit that routine, and return to something milder — like milk or cream.

The conversations revealed a lot of generally interesting information about these happily released troops regarding their education, careers and family life.

Archer the Swimmer became an officer and graduated from the Naval Academy.

Johnson the Dancer was still a professional in showbiz, and was involved with some show called *Hello, Dolly!*

Gardner the Cowboy was now a general surgeon, trying to save people rather than terminating them.

Massiah the Carpet Man was a mercenary, but still helped in the family's Oriental rug business.

Kelsey the Artist became a true high-paid mercenary. He kept gibing me about an easier way to get rich. The guy was strictly "have gun, will travel," and he loved being referred to as an agricultural attaché. He kept telling me that at the moment, he could open a dozen high-priced doors for me around the world; I could easily make two hundred thousand or more per year, with all expenses covered, first class. Boy, this type of conversation could get one's ego thinking about career changes. But with my great wife and kids, I reasoned that it might be better to be poor, healthy and wise — while still alive.

Sullivan the Gym Boy was the shocker; he became an embassy diplomat. He was assigned service in a Central American country, where years earlier he had terminated several key people. Maybe the experience had made him really qualified, with an insider's perspective on how diplomacy really works in the world — and always knowing how to cover his ass.

Lollich the Crow-Ott was the owner of a struggling and developing restaurant and catering business. As he put it, he was making it, and success was just around the corner. He stated that he had catered for some well-known groups, like the Duquesne University Tamburitzan dancers when they came to his town for shows. But he made it clear that all the Croatian weddings and picnics throughout the area were what had kept him surviving in the business.

DONALD JAY DENTON

Good old Vigorritto the Pizza Boy did not like or enjoy his family's salvage and trash business, so he had decided to get a law degree. He had become a lawyer and was on his way up the ladder of success.

Me? I was the only other survivor left from the original group. I had successfully gotten my law degree, and was now struggling to become a qualified business and estate analyst with my E.B.U. I, II and III certifications. I was not complaining; I was just paying the price to become successful without killing people. Face it! It was a far better fate than that of my former friends and associates: Huffless the Guitar Man, Bishop the Holy Man, Duckett the Coal Miner, Karam the Camel Jockey, Zimmerman the Hot Rod, Spyridon the Walleye, and the other guy I do not want to mention, or even think about.

Most of the new breeds were still in school or developing their careers.

Mr. Jupinko the Louis Prima was learning to be a master tool and die maker.

Mr. Lawhead the Kaiser was taking over his family's dairy farm and local dairy business, with distribution to stores in his area.

Mr. Badurina the Frasier was starting his own construction company.

Miss Gabalac the Edsel was taking advanced courses at a university to become an actuary, with a degree in statistical economics.

Miss Lee the Martha Raye was going to law school, teaching dancing at and Arthur Murray Dance Studio to help pay her way. Plus she intended to find a well-heeled older gentleman. She had a point. Why fool around with struggling young men with potential when she might find a rich, established older man who was divorced, a widower, or whatever it took, to enjoy the comforts of the good life?

Mr. Rex the Danny Kaye was studying at becoming a Foreign Service diplomat, for which he would be well qualified.

Mr. Iff the Tucker was working as a professional with a national non-profit organization, raising money and managing the operations in his area.

Mr. Titmas the Studebaker was studying to get an advanced degree in aeronautical engineering. Man, had he ever taken on tough studies! He was hoping to get into some military academy.

Mr. Berkich the Hudson Hornet was going to medical school, with the hope of becoming a general surgeon and specializing in neurosurgery. Wow! What ambition.

Mr. Ruffin the Nash was going to medical school to be a general physician.

Mr. Papadopoulos the Oscar Levant was going to dental school and wanted to be an orthodontist.

Mr. Murder the Jerry Calona was training to become a store manager for a national grocery store chain, and was currently an assistant manager.

Mr. St. Amond the Packard was going to college with the hope of becoming a radio and television announcer. He was selling air time and advertising for a local station in his home town.

Mr. Vyas the Ed Wynn was studying to become an Osteopath, and wanted to specialize in children's orthopedics.

Mr. Toukan the Jimmy Durante was going to college to learn the restaurant, convention and travel business. For his present income, he was working as an area manager, supervising several franchise restaurant operations in the central area of his state.

Mr. Charvat the Eddie Cantor may have had one of the nicer jobs — he was learning to be a master brewer for a major brewing company.

Knowing all this about these people made me feel good. Just knowing that everyone was working hard, trying to get their education and become successful, or were already successful —even if some were mercenaries — was enlightening. The interesting thing about our old group being together was that we seldom mentioned anything about our missions. Our time was spent talking and laughing about our Mount Fuji training experience, and reminiscing about our special group trip to Interlaken, Switzerland — the trip when we were hired to protect some big muckety-mucky Build-A-Better-Burger conference for the rich and secret elite, and the politically powerful.

The conference was at it end. Everyone had had a nice experience during our final time together. The last supper for our secret little crew was about to begin. The traitor of our original group had been hung out to dry years ago. I was curious about who would give us some parting words of wisdom on the last night, but that would be revealed shortly after dinner.

We had all finished dinner were sitting around, chatting and sipping on our after-dinner drinks, when Mr. Lingo asked us to remain seated at our places. Suddenly, the double doors to the meeting room opened, and three formal guys in suits entered the room. They stood there, looking at everything and giving everyone the once-over. Then, in walked the special guest. Everyone was in shock — amazed by what they were seeing. Everyone to a person stood up and applauded. I was flabbergasted. All I could say to myself was, "I'll be dammed; if it isn't the Man himself."

The special guest stated that he could not stay long; that he had watched over us from the beginning, and that he wanted to give his personal thanks to all of us for our duty and service to the country. He personally shook everyone's hand, wished us well in our future endeavors, then turned and left the room as quickly as he had arrived. This unbelievable experience was short and sweet. I sat down in amazement, and said to Archer and Gabalac, who were sitting next to me, "Did what just happened, happen? Was I seeing things? Has my imagination gone wild?" No question about it, everyone else in the room was feeling the same way, and did not know what to do or say about it at the moment.

Captain Dan spoke up. "Ladies and gentleman, what just occurred in this room for your benefit did not happen. You heard nothing, you saw nothing, and we have yet to celebrate the end of our covert trip together with baked Alaska, black coffee, and B&B. So let us all enjoy this last night together and say our farewells to each other, for after breakfast tomorrow, the buses will depart for the Washington, D.C. airport at 1045 hours."

It was nice to be back home, knowing I could get on with my career; a career without further interruptions coming out of left field as to special alternative lifestyle activities dealing with humanity's hemorrhoids. For me personally, the rest of the year was great. But the rest of the country was having a year of embarrassments, disgrace, and unwanted turmoil in our economy. Our form of government was being tested and having an incredibly bad year. That year would definitely go down in history as a terrible year. Luck and good fortune were not around to benefit many people, and our president resigned in disgrace. The new President Ford just seemed to be in the right place at the right time, to gain wanted or unwanted power and fame through someone else's misfortunes.

DONALD JAY DENTON

My big question of the year was: what was this Symbionese Liberation Army that had kidnapped the Hearst heiress? What the hell was this Army crap all about? I thought those radical Black Panther types had eliminated themselves with the handling of John Huggins, Al Carter, Ron Karenga, and the nut-cake Angela Davis. I would not have been surprised; maybe I would even have expected it from the Palestinian Black September group, but not from some misguided Black Power Army. Maybe the Black September group was too busy in Lebanon, with the ridiculous war between the urban Christians and the rural Moslems. The Christians in that war did not stand a chance in the long run. Their reasoning, based on so-called Christian ethics, would allow the Moslem fundamentalist to win hands down, for they did not care to understand the Geneva Convention.

The next big disgrace after the president's departure was an army captain and medical doctor named Levy being prosecuted for telling the truth. He exposed the Green Berets and the C.I.A. for what they really were. The prosecution of this doctor was a joke on humanity. It could be talked about in law school as one of the great injustices; for it showed that the military and politics controlled the Supreme Court. It was amazing that the government did not prosecute him for insulting John Wayne's phony movie image as a Green Beret. The doctor should not have called them liars and thieves; he would have been better off saying they were killers and murders. That claim could have been easily proved and supported by their track record and the historical events of the C.I.A. There are very few people I've ever felt sorry for, but I did for this man. The army ruined an honest and innocent man. One could say that it was a bad year all the way around.

But it was not too bad for me. I received my E.B.U. I, II and III certifications with perfect scores, and officially could call myself a business and estate analyst. Yet I ended that year pissed off, since a person I respected and looked up to apparently had dirty feet of clay. That left me very frustrated and confused about politics. The sad part was that this religious Quaker I had trusted was only a mover and shaker; not a true Quaker, but a pickpocket Quaker gypsy. The result was, we had a new unelected president that no one knew about for sure. It was doubtful that he could handle OPEC, since the Arabs had complete distrust for him. When he was a congressman, he was strongly pro-Israel, and that did not sit well with the Middle East.

The only really curious part about this transitional presidency was not the pardon; it was that the out man who was the former president's director for the Office of Economic Opportunity was now heading up the new president's transition team. There seems to be some very curious relationships here with related strange circumstances? How so, did these certain people benefit so well from the bloodless coup? It makes one wonder what other great rewards that person or persons would be receiving from the newly unelected president for public and/or covert services rendered. One thing about my little covert life was that I had learned to suspect everyone, suspect everything, and only trust people at arm's length, or not at all. Therefore, there were a lot of things about the situation that did not smell right. Besides Watergate and Plumbers, there was something else rotten in Denmark. Of course, if I could have put my finger on it, the good Senator Sam Irvin would have had me on his staff. But my deep throat was not big enough to swallow all the designer bullshit, or cough up disloyalties while hiding my face in the shadows for lack of integrity.

This referred-to deep throat was a well-designed plan, and a well-coordinated specific spark of intent and purpose. As several detective friends once told me, when starting to solve a crime or mystery, first search out and identify who would gain or benefit the most from the crime. They clarified that the beneficiaries of any crime, except crimes of passion, commit the crime for the benefits of freedom, financial gain, power and influence, or to get even for a perceived wrong done to them. These political events made me think and ask: Why are those who were the fade-outs suddenly becoming the insider movers and shakers? Again, what would a good solver of a Madala puzzle with the key clues surprisingly discover?

Well, the new president was now the new president. We all needed to give him our support and wish him well. But the unelected president would never get elected, for he carried with him too much Republican baggage of others, and of his own making. Yet I've learned it is best to let bygones be bygones, to forgive and forget, to quit living in the past, and to set my sights forward. With hard work and study, one can achieve success. The principle was to stay focused on only my issues, and to try to ignore the outside distractions of the world's economic problems and its politics.

Being released from the shadow government's Black Chamber was like removing a ton of bricks off my back. It made me appreciate the feeling that cows and other farm animals must have when they are released from the barn into the warm spring air after a long freezing winter. The new single life obligation was wonderful, compared to the past dual life existence. So now, my attitude in life should be, who cares? I was going to proceed full speed ahead, concentrating on my career, and let the worldly issues of evil and man's inhumanity to man stay in the dark to be ignored. I had paid my dues, so the world was now someone else's problem. As long as the adverse evils stayed off my property and out of my personal life, I couldn't have cared less what happened in the world, or in other parts of the country. Just stay off my turf and out of my way.

Not so surprising, my wishful thinking at the wrong time in my life. Our family vacation was a trip to Mackinac Island, to spend a relaxing time over the Fourth of July at the upper peninsula of Michigan. What a nice vacation it was. At the same time, my professional career could not have been better. Who could have wished for more? Maybe I did not wish hard enough.

On July 21, after nearly a year of peace and quiet, an unexpected occurrence happened that would have had one quit playing blackjack. How could it be that on July 31, I with four recalled Pookas of my selection, were sitting on a government transport plane at thirty thousand feet over the Gulf of Mexico? And sitting across from me, between four guarding Pookas, was the "Man in the Iron Mask." This anonymous avatar must have been of great significance and value to good old Uncle Sam. Who could have known what the July 21 "We-Un" from the powers above would lead to? This mission was more than strange; it is downright eerie.

I should have earlier said to myself, while basking in my success and contentment, "Be not so quick in letting the guard down, and always remember that fame is fleeting, and one's perceived freedom and peace of mind may also be fleeting." There I was, thinking that being put out to pasture with a retirement watch meant all was finished and kaput, with no more Pooka games. Wrong!

Why now a "We-Un"? The final play, with its last act, had its closing curtain call the previous year. What was this epilogue all about? Who was demanding a command performance? Why had the theater not closed it doors? It appeared that I had wrongly believed that the game had ended and the final whistle had been blown. But it seemed that the time clock still had a few second left on it; time had not run out. Apparently, the powers above that giveth can also taketh away. Given the circumstances, the powers must have suddenly identified a most dangerous game that needed what only the so-called retired Pookas could provide.

So on the same day, July 21, a call to the powers above was made. I was not really surprised that the Circle 6-2150 number was still working. The surprise was that Mr. Lingo answered the phone. He immediately got to the point by saying, "We are asking for a special favor, and hope you will freely volunteer to meet our special request. Yes, you were formally released earlier than expected, but 'nota bene,' as per your service agreement, the official commitment to duty does not really expire until December thirty-first. This mission will require time and sacrifice, but you and your four-member team will be given nice financial rewards. Mr. Knapp and I will be flying into Columbus tomorrow morning, and we have already reserved our rooms. We will see you at the Christopher Inn for lunch, and at that time you will provide us with the names of your team members."

The call ended with a short and sweet goodbye. My assumption was that they did not want to inconvenience this drafted volunteer, so they were flying into Columbus. But they want this recalled person to be willing to risk his neck, for what? No question, this out-of-left-field "We-Un" was annoying, and meant some urgent C.Y.A. planning on my part for the benefit of the wife. I told her that two top executives with a major New York firm were flying in to see me, and wanted to retain my services to call on eight or nine of their marketing offices. Their intent was for me to be a trainer to the office's top producers for advance marketing techniques of business and estate analysis. I let the wife know that I would make no decisions while meeting with them, and when I returned home after the meeting, we would discuss the offer and make the decision together.

The time flew faster than expected. A good night's sleep was not really expected; my mind kept up a racetrack of active thought, and I had a real déjà vu feeling while sitting there having breakfast with the wife and kids. She reminded me to control my mouth, make no commitments, and that we would decide on the potential opportunity that night after I got home. Well, at least I had her thinking in the right direction, and receptive to a possibly rewarding experience and financial opportunity. I was prepared for the meeting, and it was time to head down the road to the Christopher Inn. But first I kissed the wife goodbye, and told her that I would probably be home about eight o'clock, since they had invited me to have dinner with them.

Once at the hotel, Lingo and Knapp escorted me to their private meeting room and stated that lunch would be catered in. They immediately asked for my team member recommendations, so I handed them my list. It included Miss Lee the Martha Raye, Mr. St. Amond the Packard, Miss Gabalac the Edsel, Mr. Rex the Danny Kaye, and the addition of one back-up name, Mr. Lawhead the Kaiser. Knapp immediately took the list, asked me to get some coffee and rolls, and went directly to the phone to call the names into someone, located somewhere. Then he got his coffee and rolls, came back to the table, and said, "Let's talk." He then asked if I had any questions.

"I most certainly do. Why?"

Mr. Lingo decided to answer my unasked simple question. "You and your team are an uninvolved, unknown, neutral entity without any relationship — directly or indirectly — to the persons or issues involved in this mission. The fact is that other federal and state agencies were not considered reliable or safe. We got the message that the powers could not risk a possible mole or informant within other agencies who could sell out the package. The powers wanted to reduce all the risk factors possible, and so our group — being the best-kept secret of secrets — is now paying off big time for Uncle Sam's needs. This very secret mission does not require dispatching, displacing, or terminating hemorrhoids of humanity. The mission is only for the protection and preservation of a valuable U.S. hemorrhoidal asset. Now, Mr. Knapp has a few remarks."

Knapp sat there for a minute, smiling at me, and then said, "Doctor Doom will not be providing any kisses of death on this mission. Again, by a weird series of circumstance, your code name was requested by unknown third parties to act as an intermediary between two unrelated and unknown parties. It appears that you have valid credibility between and with one of the primary parties to this never-happened and secret transaction.

"Originally this situation was unknown to the powers, but then events and circumstances, which you're not privy to, required certain people within the government to ask that we have special services provided by the Black Chamber once again before we all disappear into nonexistence. As for this mission, your team will come together here in Columbus on July thirtieth for the orientation, and the adventure will commence during the early morning hours on July thirty-first.

"Yes, you will soon understand why this is a strange mission. It may even seem comical, but I assure you that it is deadly serious; so serious that mistakes or leaks of information could get people killed. Why strange? You, with your team, will be acting only as a transfer agent between parties involved with this secret agreement. The party of the first part has no knowledge of or participation in the actions required and expected of you and the party of the second part. Only select members of our shadow government group know the whole scenario, as secretly directed by executive orders for mine and your ears only. Mr. Lingo will go over the details and particulars of your adventure."

Mr. Lingo wanted to lighten up things a little. First, he asked me how I was doing in three different languages: Spanish, Croatian and Korean. After my simple response in plain old English, he started his little lecture.

"The party of the first part will deliver a product to you late on July thirtieth, more likely during the early morning hours of July thirty-first. That anonymous party's participation will end, and they will not have the slightest idea of who you are. This is why your team is a vital part in handing over the subject to the party of the second part of this diplomatic snooker game. At that point, the party of the second part only wants to see and deal with you personally, to verify the validity of this secret international diplomatic agreement. It was made very clear, with firmness, that the second party will only take receipt of and the exchanged responsibility for the package if you make the delivery. This is what has frustrated a lot of people upstairs, and has created a lot of curiosity as to who this Mr. Chahaus is. But have no fear; your secret is safe with us, and soon will be dead and buried in the archives of nonexistence.

"A career diplomat will come to you at the plane while refueling at Homestead, Florida. There will be no conversation. He will be giving you a package, and you are not to open the package until the plane takes off. At your next destination, which will be San Pablo, Brazil, another career diplomat will be meeting you at the plane, and directing all your activities during this period of your intermediate layover. You will remain in San Pablo approximately ten to twelve days before proceeding to your final drop-off destination.

"I think you're beginning to understand the gravity of this mission. The U.S. government owes this person a major favor. It has guaranteed him a vanishing act and promised him that he'll leave no footprints in the sand. So the package bypasses Hell and Purgatory, and gets a free pass into Paradise with a hell of a lot of money. I'll now let Mr. Knapp provide the goodies."

Knapp started off by saying, "Good pay, yes, but note the not-so-good part: you and your team will possibly be gone for up to twenty-one days. Yet who knows? Maybe they will enjoy a fully paid summer vacation in a winter wonderland. They may like getting away from their current actives and commitments for a while. Oh, yes! The best part is that you and the team members will have deposits made to the O.S.T. accounts; five hundred dollars per each day of service rendered, plus your account will receive an additional deposit of five thousand dollars. Of course, all of the expenses from start to finish will be covered.

"A final point needs to be made. Everyone will need to be very professional. If anyone refuses to follow directions, tries to communicate with or get near your package, you are to perform your services on them — with or without prejudice.

This package's life would not, if discovered, be squat at any time in the U.S., or elsewhere in the world. Once your team completes the transaction, you return home, and all knowledge of the events will be erased. It never happened. Then all of your group, and you, may finally retire in peace, never to be cellophane people again. Now, let's have a relaxing evening and dinner at the Japanese steak house you mentioned. Afterward, you bring us back to the hotel and we go our separate ways, for our flight leaves very early in the morning."

We had a nice dinner at the Japanese steak house, and the manager — whom I knew personally — provided us with free drinks from his private stash of bootleg white lighting. If you could get the stuff past your nose, it was the smoothest and best-tasting stuff ever. Knapp made it clear that this was our true farewell dinner. We would no longer know each other, and would never meet again. At the end of the evening, I dropped them at the hotel and went home to sell my wife on this terrific, money-making career opportunity.

Undoubtedly, I was successful at convincing the wife about this rare opportunity. She became receptive to the idea when she realized the additional money could be used to help with the down payment on a new house in Worthington. She wants more than anything for our three kids to get into a better school system. So she sent me off with her blessings, as long as I kept calling her regularly over the next couple of weeks.

I waited at the Christopher Inn for my team members to arrive. The orientation meeting was short, sweet, and to the point. Then Gabalac the Edsel suggested we all depart early, with an interim stop at Schmidt's in German Village for a Bahama Mama, hot potato salad, and black coffee with their great cream puffs. This was a great idea. I then said that we would still have a little time left for a beer or two before departing for Lockbourne Air Base. The time at Schmidt's was spent in general conversation, telling humorous stories about the occasional conflicts that had occurred with their dual lives. They made it clear how happy they were about being picked for this assignment.

We waited on the tarmac with the plane for over seven hours, and it was going on two o'clock in the morning. Suddenly, coming out onto the tarmac were three big, black International Harvester Travelall station wagons. They stopped right beside the plane. Three armed guys got out of the front vehicle, and three others out of the back vehicle. They stood there and looked around for a minute, then directed someone to exit the middle vehicle. It was one strange sight. It had to be our package, as weird-looking as it was. The person was wearing a pilot's jumpsuit with combat boots, and wore a well-designed and close-fitting nylon mesh mask over the face. The look was topped off by a very expensive straw Stetson hat. All I could think of was the song "Strangers in the Night," and St. Amond the Packard commented that we were secretly taking delivery of "The Man in the Iron Mask."

There was no discussion or other form of communication between the parties of the first part and us. The party of the first part watched us enter the plane with the package, and they remained on the tarmac watching us until the plane finishing taxiing to take off. Eerie! There we were with this chameleon, and all parties were to remain silent and have no communication with it, unless it related to food, drink, or going to the john. The flight was awkward, to say the least, with this Halloween spook in our presence, but several of the team were able to take a nice nap.

We arrived at Homestead Air Base for a refueling stop. Within minutes, a diplomatic carrier arrived at the plane's doorway and asked for Mr. Chahaus. I responded, and he handed me a sealed envelope, then retreated back into the darkness of the airstrip. We took off in about an hour. Once our plane was well over the Gulf of Mexico, I opened the sealed envelope, studied the contents, and then communicated the information to the team. The directions were quite simple. We were to go to San Pablo; upon landing, a diplomat would meet us at the plane and escort us, with our package, to an exclusive private medical clinic.

A medical clinic? No way! This was a first-class resort for those with lots of money. We had a private section, along with the package, that was first-class accommodations, with the medical facility right down the hall. Once we turned the package over to their medical staff, he stayed secluded within his medical area and living quarters. We took alternating eight-hour shifts with two-person teams to keep track of the package, and constantly monitored the area to avoid outside interference. The package was going to have some major plastic surgery, and the plastic surgeon informed us that he would be kept exclusively within the medical unit for the first three or four days. The surgeon then showed us a viewing area, where we could visually observe the package while in recovery. View we did, and it was quite strange. While in recovery, the package looked like Medusa, with snakes as hair on the head. The package had all these blood-draining tubes coming out of all parts of the head, and at the end of each tube was a little vial to collect the blood. It was disgusting, unpleasant to look at, and the venture convinced all of us that plastic surgery was never to be part of our lives.

Otherwise, we spent twelve fabulous days at this very exclusive medical center. The male members of the team could hardly keep their eyes off the beautiful Brazilian female staff members, and the Brazilian male staff members could hardly resist the images of Miss Lee and Miss Gabalac. When the package was ready to be moved, the same diplomat showed up to deliver us to a waiting plane at the airport. Once we were on the plane, he handed me another sealed package, said to have a nice trip, and exited the plane. The package seemed to be doing well, and had as a disguise a light gauze wrapping all around the neck and head, with openings only for the eyes, nose and mouth.

After we were airborne, the sealed envelope was opened, and we discovered that our destination was Asuncion, Paraguay. It stated that we were not to get off the plane, that we would be meet by someone I personally knew, and that we were to remain on the plane after delivery for the return trip back to the U.S. The team was a little disappointed that we would not get to stay awhile in Asuncion, since I had told them what a great place it was for sightseeing, entertainment, and fine food.

But we were in for a surprise. Upon landing, two people approached the plane to take delivery of the package. One was their Chief of Police, the Mr. Schnoz Duarte; the other was a long-time-no-see from the old days, Ambassador Dee, or whoever he was. We had a brief moment of reunion, then away they went, and off we flew. The game of foreign intrigue involving a persona non grata person from the U.S. of A. was now completed, finished, over, and buried in the past. What a nice ending to a successful career as a visitant specter.

As for the rest of my life: the results of the past year had ended up producing a good personal business year for me. The industry had granted me lots of recognition and an invitation to the Honor Table group. I had been recognized as a member of the Centurion Club, an exclusive list of only the top ten producers, and had provided the wife some nice trips to Jamaica and Marco Island. But for some people it was not a very good year. In fact, it had been rather a bad year for Squeaky Fromme, Jimmy Hoffa, the U.S. Embassy in Saigon, and the C.I.A. The Wild West Senator, Frank Church, sure put the wieners of the C.I.A. into the flames. I would bet good old Muammar Kaddafi could just kiss President Ford's and Senator Church's butts, as his ass was now off the meat hook.

Then unwise President Ford pre-pardoned all the dangerous and evil people in the world by signing Executive Order #11905, which was to become effective on March 1, 1976. It was a bit of dimwit thinking on religious, economic and political conflicts that our country would come to regret over the years. Section 5 (g) regarding restrictions and prohibitions on displacements and terminations to preemptively control the evils in the world was something we would be required to follow, but not the rest of humanity's hemorrhoids in the dog and cat pissing world.

So finally, what had I learned about humans and human nature over the past years while playing in the shadow government arena of intrigue, skullduggery, innuendo and pretext?

First: Specific goals with time-frame-limited objectives are wrong. It can inhibit and restrict one's real potential with disappointments stuck on time limitations. The point should only be one of having the goal, and working earnestly toward the goal, regardless of how long it takes.

Second: That people never really have long-term objectives. When the shit hits the fan, they quickly revert back to the short-term "now and now," while setting aside the "sweet bye and bye." This is simply because most people cannot tolerate or successfully struggle with the thick and thin of paying the price to be successful.

Third: Humans, with their human nature, have only selective and short-term memories, particularly when not wanting to admit to their own incompetence and shortcomings due to their own action or inaction. Why? They never understood the farmer's sage advice of, "One cannot fertilize the field by farting through the fence."

Fourth: In life, learn how to get to the point, make the point, and cut to the chase. In the business world, one must learn how to identify window shoppers, and then get rid of them with the principle of successful marketing referred to as "sell or kill."

Fifth: Always keep your word, even if it hurts, and follow the basic rule of success: "Serve First."

Sixth: Know that there is no such thing as a free meal. If you and the world want peace, one cannot kiss or kibbitz with troublemakers. One can only kill troublemakers in order to maintain and preserve security and peace of mind.

Seventh: There is no such thing as gravity. The world sucks. Therefore, "It is never nice to try and fool Mother Nature."

The Immolators and Pookas were the "crème de la crème" of young Americans dedicated to duty, God, honor and country. It is just so sad to know that some are now playing pinochle with Azrael, and that the Grim Reaper did not allow then to enjoy a full life, with a wife, children, and the benefits of wonderful grandchildren.

So God bless! This may not be the end of it, and Executive Order #11905 may, out of necessity, be short-lived. If not, our peace and security may be short-lived with "Another OP'nin,

Another Show," and the world will need to remember that "a bee with honey in its mouth has a stinger in its tail."

The End? Not so quick! For there are lots of tomorrows left for intrigue and skullduggery.

307118

Made in the USA